THE LAST CHAMBER

A SEAN WYATT ADVENTURE

ERNEST DEMPSEY

138 PUBLISHING

JOIN THE ADVENTURE

Visit ernestdempsey.net to get a free copy of the not-sold-in-stores short story, RED GOLD.

You'll also get access to exclusive content not available anywhere else.

To the English teachers who asked me if I was still writing, years after I'd even seen them. Penny Kennedy (Ms. Kilgore), Sam James, Jodi Ruf, and Debbie Higgens, thanks for kicking my butt. I wouldn't have kept writing without you.

PROLOGUE

MOSCOW - 1944

The tension in the room could have been cut with a spoon. Stale cigarette smoke hung like a thick, bluish haze in the musty air. A single light bulb hanging from the ceiling did little to illuminate the dark, cinder block room.

"Where was this picture taken?" A barrel-chested, middle-aged officer demanded in a gruff voice. The man's head was rimmed with graying brown hair, his portly face red from stress and vodka.

The young Soviet pilot looked up at him from a chair at a small wooden table. The airman was in his low to mid-twenties. His skin was still smooth and healthy. He sported the short haircut of the military, piercing blue eyes, and a strong jaw line with a little dimple in the center of his chin. Sincere confusion filled his face.

"I don't know, sir," he said in mumbled Russian. He was clearly afraid of the higher-ranking officer.

"How can you not know?" the large man raged, pounding his fist on the table. The action caused the pilot to jump in his seat.

"We have taken thousands of pictures, comrade," he explained. "It is our job to bring them back for analysis. It is nearly impossible for us to remember the exact location of every photograph." His lips trembled as he finished the sentence.

Two other men stood in opposite corners of the room, watching the exchange silently. They both wore black suits and ties. One was a slender man with a black flat top. The other one was blonde with the same haircut. A stout physique and broad shoulders made him seem slightly more imposing than his partner.

"I'm sorry, comrade," the young man continued. "I do not know what else to tell you. We were flying over the area at the Turkish and Armenian border. That picture had to be taken somewhere in the mountains nearby, but where exactly, I cannot be sure."

A bead of sweat rolled down the high forehead of the Russian officer. His eyes narrowed above fleshy cheeks. When he spoke, his voice was low but intense. "Our analysts have searched through seven hundred pictures of this area. We sent more planes to the region you speak of and took more photographs. Yet, when they returned, none of them produced an image of this location." He slammed the thick piece of photo paper down on the table.

The pilot looked down at it, desperately trying to remember where it had been taken. The image portrayed two ridgelines on opposing mountains. In between them was a narrow valley. The span, though, was oddly shaped, unlike anything he'd ever seen. It appeared as though a long, rectangular box had been placed there centuries before, and the valley itself had eroded around it, taking on the same shape.

"It was somewhere near the town of Ararat in Armenia. That is all I know," the pilot said finally.

The officer looked over at the two agents standing near the door. The blonde one nodded his head once and blinked slowly.

"Well, comrade. We have scoured that particular area and found nothing. Ten different planes have photographed the region you describe, and none have brought back this image. So, you are either lying, or this image is distorted."

"I'm sorry, sir," the pilot spoke up. "But what is so important about this region? Why are we taking so many photographs there?"

The officer's face flushed red. Before he could speak, though, the blonde man in the suit stepped forward and raised a hand. "Allow me, comrade." His tone was even and deep.

The roiled officer moved off to the side as the agent took his place in front of the terrified pilot. He reached into a jacket pocket and pulled out a pack of cigarettes, offering one to the trembling young man, who accepted. After lighting the cigarette for him, the agent put the pack back in his pocket and let out a deep sigh.

After a few seconds, he finally spoke again. "We have reason to believe that somewhere in the area of this photograph, there is a large weapons cache. Our concern is that there could be something there that would present an imminent threat to Mother Russian. We must neutralize that threat as soon as possible."

The pilot took a hesitant drag off the cigarette and released a slow puff of smoke out of his mouth. "Is the threat nuclear?"

A quick raise of the eyebrows and a cock of the head told the young man it might be. "We are not certain," the agent replied. "But we cannot take any chances. That region needs to be pacified immediately, but we also have to know what we are dealing with."

The young man nodded, understanding. "Sir, I think I might be able to find the area again where that picture was taken. If you would allow, I could do another fly over and see." His voice sounded hopeful.

"Are you certain?"

"I do not know exactly where it is, but I believe I can find it if you just give me the chance. I only want to help Mother Russia." His mid-ranged voice sounded desperate.

"Good. That is all I needed to know," the blonde man smiled and stepped aside.

A second later, a muffled pop interrupted the silence. The other agent held a pistol at arm's length behind the head of the man in the chair. A thin trail of smoke drifted up from the sound suppressor's barrel. The young pilot slumped forward onto the blood-splattered table with a thud.

"It is a shame we had to kill him," the officer commented. "He was one of our better reconnaissance pilots." His gravelly voice held a hint of regret.

"We cannot be too careful with these sorts of things, comrade," the blonde agent commented. The man with the gun looked over at them casually. "Too many people with information create too many leaks. Wouldn't you agree?"

The hefty commander looked down at the floor, then back up into the icy blue eyes. "Yes, you are correct. And we must take every precaution to protect the best interests of our country."

"Exactly," the blonde said with an emphatic point of the finger. "Now, I wonder who else knows about this photograph."

"Only three other people have seen it. We have a small group assigned to the analysis of the pictures that come from that region of the world," the officer shrugged.

"Would their names be in that file over there?" he pointed to a stool near the door and a manila folder that rested on top.

The man in the uniform nodded. "Yes. They should be listed inside."

"Good," the blonde agent patted him on the shoulder. "And of course, you know about the photograph as well."

Fear crept onto the man's chubby face. "Now wait a minute," he scowled and raised a finger. "I am a high-ranking officer in the Soviet military. You do not have the right to accuse me of anything, no matter what your KGB bosses say."

"We aren't accusing you of anything, comrade," the blonde retorted. "We are only fixing leaks."

Another pop echoed off the block walls again. The officer wavered for a moment before collapsing to the floor. The look of shock still filled his lifeless eyes. A small hole on his sweaty forehead leaked a thin trickle of blood.

The agent with the gun shoved it back inside his jacket. "I'll have the cleaning team come in here right away."

The blonde nodded. "Have them put him in one of the military jeeps and set it on fire. Accidents happen all the time, after all."

"What about the three analysts?"

"They shouldn't be any problem. Once they're out of the way, we will be the only ones that know about the picture. We have to make sure it stays that way." The blonde agent walked over to the table and picked up the photograph. He gazed at it for a moment, absorbing the image with a kind of wonder. "This must not fall into the wrong hands. If the United States or Great Britain were to get their hands on it, we would be doomed."

"Are you certain we will find what we are looking for?" The dark-haired man grabbed the file near the door.

"Certain?" the blonde raised an eyebrow. "Nothing is certain in this life, comrade. Let's just say it puts us one step ahead of the others."

"So you believe the other countries are looking for the same thing?" The man's flat forehead wrinkled slightly.

"I believe that if the stories are true, whoever uncovers this secret first will be able to rule the world."

1

CAIRO, EGYPT

The first thing Sean Wyatt noticed when he regained consciousness was the intense ringing in his right ear. He couldn't remember what happened, but his eyes were closed. The dark haze began to give way to blurry light as he slowly opened them. The high-pitched whine in his ear was accompanied by a throbbing in the back of his head, like a jackhammer pounding the concrete. The warmth of the street against his face and body came next, followed by little points of stinging pain on various spots of his body. The rest of his senses began to return one by one. His nostrils filled with the smell of smoke, a distinct odor of burning rubber and petroleum. The blonde hair on his head was matted down with dirt and a little blood. He blinked his eyes and the chaos around him started to come into focus.

Sean was lying on the ground in the middle of a city street, though for a moment he couldn't remember which one. People were scattered everywhere, panicking in every direction. He squinted hard at the light and tried to push himself off the ground. His head spun and he had to stop momentarily.

Thirty feet away, a woman dressed in black was screaming something in Arabic, tears streaming down her face into the lower part of her burka. She seemed to be frantically saying something, maybe calling for help, but Sean couldn't make out the words.

Slowly, he pushed himself up into a sitting position while the chaos around him continued to spin out of control. He noticed several places where his khaki pants had burn holes, a few of them stained with blood. His white button-up shirt was dirty, and torn in multiple places. It, too, had several blood spots.

Across the street, only a few dozen feet away, he saw the source of the smoke and his memory started to piece the events together. He and Adriana Villa were meeting Tommy outside the hotel. They were going to investigate something at the Museum of Antiquities. There'd been an explosion. Then everything had gone black.

He was hit by a terrible thought. *Adriana.* It was quickly followed by concern for his friend, Tommy Schultz. He began to scan the area of devastation. Black smoke swirled around, blown by the desert winds that rolled through the city. There were people everywhere, running in every possible direction.

Sean felt the chill of fear creep inside of his mind as he struggled to regain his balance. His head still spun as he braced himself on the post of a streetlight nearby. Suddenly, someone grabbed him from behind. He started to react defensively, but stopped himself when he realized the person was trying to help.

It was Adriana.

"We have to get out of here," she said as she hooked his arm over her shoulders, supporting his weight.

"Where's Tommy?" he asked, not wanting to leave his friend behind.

The whining sirens of emergency vehicles were drawing closer. Adriana urged him to move. "Sean, we have to go." Her Spanish accent was thicker than usual. He'd noticed it got that way when she was very serious about something.

Sean's icy gray eyes peered through the mayhem. Then he saw something across the street, about fifty feet away, laying in a huddled mass on the ground.

It was Tommy.

He let go of Adriana and staggered through the onslaught of rushing people. She followed close behind as they made their way across the crowded road. He had to push and pull a few of the crazed citizens out of his way until he finally reached his friend.

Tommy's gray cotton pants were torn and tattered with singed holes and spots of blood all over. His white shirt was in similar condition. A small gash on the side of his head was bleeding slightly. Sean knelt down next to the wounded man and checked his pulse and breathing. Sean let out a sigh of relief. He was still alive.

"We have to get him out of here," Sean looked back to Adriana, hovering over the two.

She nodded sharply, then reached down and hefted up Schultz, swinging one arm over her shoulders, with Sean doing from the other side. Tommy's head hung down to his chest, unconscious from the blast. Sean and Adriana quickly carried him down the street, away from the scene, dragging his feet as they moved. They ducked around a corner just before the Cairo police arrived at the anarchic area.

"We need to get him to a hospital," Sean said.

The two laid Tommy down on the ground, leaning his torso up against a building. More sirens could be heard in the distance.

"I'll take him," Adriana volunteered. "Whoever did this may not know who I am. But they are definitely going to be looking for you." The Spaniard's conviction was sincere, but he knew they'd be looking for her too.

Sean shook his head and paused to take a breath. "I can't let you do that. You know they will be looking for you too." He looked down at his friend. "We need to get him out of the country, somewhere he will be safe."

Adriana looked puzzled. "How?"

He removed the black phone from his pocket and checked the touch screen. He was relieved to find it wasn't cracked. After a few seconds, the phone was ringing on the other end.

"Sean?" A familiar woman's voice answered on the other line.

"Emily, I need your help," he cut to the chase. "Do you have anyone in Cairo right now? I need an evac two minutes ago."

There was silence on the other end for a moment before she spoke up again. "Sean, what happened? Are you okay?"

"Emily, do you or don't you. There was a bombing outside our hotel in Cairo. Tommy is unconscious. Someone tried to kill us, Em. We need to get Tommy out of here now, somewhere safe."

"Give me one second, Sean," she answered. The other line was silent for nearly a minute before she came back on. "I have someone in the area. I'm tracking your exact location."

Another twenty seconds went by while he waited. Two more police cars passed by, but their progress was slowed by the throngs of people running through the street.

"I'll have someone there in less than three minutes, Sean," Emily's voice came back on, stealing his thoughts away from the police and back to his current objective.

"Thanks, Em. He'll need a flight out of the country." He looked down at his friend again. Tommy still wasn't moving, but his chest was heaving up and down. *That was a good sign.*

"Do you need one of our planes?" she asked.

Sean shook his head. "No, he can take the IAA jet. You'll have to scramble the pilot. He should be nearby. What's the closest city to Cairo where we have friendlies?" he asked.

On the other end, Sean imagined Emily Starks typing furiously on her computer, somewhere in Atlanta. She'd always been good at directing. In the field, she'd been an effective agent, and a good partner, but her true calling was administration. When she'd been made director of Axis, her true talents blossomed. In recent months, she'd pushed for Axis headquarters to be moved from its tight little space in Washington, D.C. to a more upscale area of Atlanta, Georgia.

"I have an asset in Athens right now. That close enough? Flight time is about an hour from Cairo."

"That will have to do," Sean answered. "Have your person notified when our plane will be landing, and have them take Tommy to the hospital immediately."

"Are you sure you shouldn't just take him to get treatment there?"

"Not an option," he replied determinedly. "I think he's going to be fine. Probably has a concussion, but he'll live. Though we still need to get him looked at and kept safe. Whoever did this won't just take one shot."

"Understood. I'll have a medic waiting at the hangar for you in Cairo," she answered.

"Thanks again, Em."

Sean hung up his phone just as a black SUV pulled up next to them on the sidewalk. The tinted window in the front rolled down and revealed a twenty-something, dark-skinned man. He appeared to be of Arab descent. His black hair and eyebrows framed deep, java eyes.

"Sean Wyatt?" he asked in an English accent.

"That's me."

"Emily said you needed a ride. Hop in," the man ordered.

Sean opened the back door to the vehicle and Adriana helped him lift Tommy into the back seat. Sean got in the rear with him as Adriana slid into the front. The moment the doors slammed shut, the driver took off.

He weaved his way through the flood of pedestrians and vehicles, honking the horn in an attempt to get them to disperse faster. After a few quick turns, they were out of the madness and onto a less crowded street, heading toward the airport.

"My name is Jolian," the driver introduced himself as he steered the vehicle through the city.

"We appreciate your help," Sean replied. Then he looked down at his friend. Tommy groaned slightly, something Sean took as a good sign.

"What happened back there?" Jolian asked.

Sean shook his head. "I don't know. It's all still really hazy to me." He'd been fighting his own problems the last ten minutes.

"We were meeting at the museum to investigate some ancient writings," Adriana answered. "We thought they might lead to the location of an artifact we're searching for." She was clearly in the best shape of the three who'd been rocked by the blast. "I was standing inside the building when it happened. The car sitting outside exploded. Tommy was closest to it." Her face was grim as she looked out the windows, watching the buildings whiz by.

"Someone knew we were going to be there, at that exact moment," Sean stated. He tried to contain his anger at the thought.

"Emily said you are going to the airport," Jolian interrupted. "Where will you go?" he asked.

Adriana looked back at Sean. "We need to get Tommy out of here. If someone knew that we were meeting at the museum, they can find us again. He won't be safe in a hospital here. The plane will fly him to the nearest city where Axis has people on the ground. They can keep him safe there."

"You're not going with him?" the driver wondered. He turned the wheel sharply, and the airport came into view in the distance ahead.

Sean shook his head. "No. We're staying here." His face was full of resolve. "And we're going to finish this."

2

CAIRO

"Now that we have our only potential problems out of the way, we should be able to proceed with relative ease." Alexander Lindsey looked over at a man in a gray, pinstriped suit.

The man nodded. His thin, brownish hair was combed over to one side on top of a narrow face and a long, hooked nose. His tired, greenish eyes were sunken back into his face. A caramel-skinned woman dressed in a form-fitting pair of cargo khakis and a tight black shirt stood off to the side. Her espresso hair was pulled back into a tight ponytail. She watched the discussion intently with deep chocolate eyes. Her face was strong and narrow.

The men were sitting in an old laboratory. Lindsey had procured the building before flying to Cairo six days ago. He'd had his best asset, Will Hastings, following Sean Wyatt and his cronies for several weeks. Thanks to the tenacious work of Hastings, Lindsey had known everything Wyatt was planning to do, and just when to strike.

Lindsey had maintained a distant supervision of operations during their search for the golden chambers. His old age had led to a desire not to be burdened with the rigors of chasing down buried treasure. So, Hastings had been in charge of the hands-on details.

The game had changed, though. Initially, he had made the first move, kidnapping Tommy Schultz and forcing him to lead the way to the first chamber. But Sean Wyatt had interfered.

Lindsey's crew had taken a different approach in the search for the second chamber. Since Wyatt and his group possessed the clue to the chamber's location, Lindsey had been forced to wait and follow. He'd lost some of his best hired guns during the fiasco. *A necessary sacrifice.*

He stood and walked slowly over to one of the nearby windows and looked out. The late afternoon sun was pouring in through the glass, and he squinted against the light. He wore a pair of brown trousers and a lightweight, olive green jacket. The weather had been beautiful since he'd arrived. He hoped it was a sign of things to come.

"When will your man be here?" The gangly man in the gray suit spoke with a French accent.

Lindsey turned around. "Soon," he answered. He had brought Luc DeGard in as part of the operation three weeks before heading to Egypt.

The Frenchman was one of the top researchers on the planet when it came to ancient history and languages. Lindsey wished the man could have been brought on sooner, but DeGard had been experiencing some personal troubles. Once contacted, DeGard accepted the offer eagerly. Lindsey wondered how much less the man would have taken, but the deal was done.

Rumor had it that Luc DeGard had come upon hard times. He'd been a professor of archaeology at University College in London for several years. The institution had a highly respected program, one that DeGard had disgraced when he had been caught in his office with his pants down, with one of his younger male students.

After his dismissal from the college, he spent much of his time gambling and drinking, a combination that had led to the lowly end in which Lindsey had found the man, in debt up to his eyeballs and desperate for anything. DeGard may have been a degenerate, but he was a ruthless researcher, and his desperation provided the perfect motivation for Lindsey.

The door at the end of the room opened and a young man with thick, dark hair appeared. He wore a brown leather jacket and tanned pants. The man glanced over at the woman with mocha-colored skin, exchanging a momentary stare before he turned his attention to the old man.

Lindsey looked over at him expectantly. "Did you get it?" he asked.

Will Hastings nodded and held up a small, stone disc. "Yes, sir. I got it."

3

CAIRO

The plane's engines were already warming up when the black SUV pulled up to the private hangar. The jet with three giant black letters on the tail belonged to Tommy's International Archaeological Agency.

Sean had checked his friend several times en route to the airport. Tommy had not regained consciousness, but was still alive. A dark-haired man in a blue button-up shirt stood just outside the plane with a stethoscope around his neck and a briefcase in one hand. Sean realized Emily must have called a physician, too.

Jolian parked the vehicle next to the plane, just outside the hangar. The doctor rushed over immediately and assisted in getting Tommy out of the SUV, onto a stretcher, and into the plane.

Once they had him secured, Sean turned to the physician, who was already opening up his briefcase and removing devices Sean didn't recognize. "Take good care of him. He's like my brother."

The man answered in a Middle Eastern accent. "Your friend will be fine, Mr. Wyatt. He's in good hands."

Sean nodded, satisfied with the answer, and looked down at Tommy one last time before leaving. His eyes narrowed. It tore him apart to see his close friend lying there, helpless. Sean had witnessed some terrible things in his career with the government. He'd seen agents killed, strangers murdered, and had done his fair share of killing. Tommy was his best friend, though. When the whole thing was over, Sean was going to have to have a serious talk with him about sticking to an administrative position.

He said a silent goodbye and started to exit the plane. Then he remembered something. He stepped back over to the gurney and searched Tommy's pockets. The only thing he found was his cell phone, hotel key, and wallet. Sean's face became immediately concerned. The stone was missing. He thought for sure Tommy would have brought it with him to the museum. He must have left it in the room. That, or their only clue to locating the third chamber had been stolen.

In his head, Sean ran through the short list of possibilities as to where the object could be. Nothing added up. And he was fairly certain Tommy had the stone with him when he'd left the hotel room.

That meant only one thing. Someone had taken it off him after the explosion. Sean realized that maybe the explosion hadn't been too early; it had happened exactly when it needed to. The timing had been perfect. If Tommy had been in the car, retrieving the stone would have been nearly impossible. He shook off the theory; still choosing to believe that maybe they had just been lucky.

The point still lurked in the back of his head, though. Someone was trying to kill them, and would do whatever it took to find the last chamber.

4

CAIRO

The Frenchman snatched the stone away from Will and held it up to the light. He examined one side of it, and then the other, carefully inspecting the inscription.

"I have seen this writing before," he announced. "And the image on the other side has only been discovered in one place."

Lindsey appeared hopeful. "And where is that, Doctor DeGard?"

DeGard smiled. His crooked teeth made his grin appear more like a crocodile's than a human's. "It's a temple, to the south. I've been there one time on a dig. It must have been twenty years ago. But I have no doubts that the images on this stone are an exact match for what I saw there."

Lindsey moved closer. He wasn't entirely convinced. "How can you be sure? You must have seen tens of thousands of hieroglyphs and ancient writings. Yet you're telling me you remember these from twenty years ago, after just one glance?"

DeGard shrugged. "I can take you to the site or you can pay me my money and I will return to London. I don't care about your little treasure hunt. As I remember it, there wasn't anything significant about that location. We unearthed a few clay jars, but the temple had been stripped of any treasures long before we arrived."

Lindsey seemed to consider it for a moment. They could ill afford to waste precious time on the Frenchman's hunch, but it was all DeGard had to go on, and he was the only expert in the room on the subject.

"Fine," he said at last. "Take us to the location. If you are right, I'll give you another ten thousand." He eyed the birdlike man suspiciously. "However, if you have wasted our time, my men will bury you there in the desert."

DeGard raised an eyebrow. "I assure you it is the correct place, Monsieur Lindsey."

"Will," Lindsey turned to the younger man. "Get the others ready. We will leave at once."

Will nodded and started to leave the room, but Lindsey stopped him. "Wait." Lindsey turned and pressed for one more answer from DeGard. "Is there anyone else you know of, who knows about the temple or could decipher the language from that disc?"

DeGard thought for a moment. "I can only think of a few people with such knowledge. One of them is in Cambridge, England. I believe there is one other, here, in Cairo. He could have been the one your enemies were going to visit today."

"What is his name?" Lindsey asked intently.

"His name is Richard Firth. He does a great deal of work for the Museum of Antiquities."

Lindsey glanced at Will. "Take care of it. Send the rest with us." Will nodded and left the room.

Then Lindsey returned his attention back to DeGard. "I pray, dear Doctor, that you are right."

DeGard shrugged again. His demeanor was either certain or arrogant. "You think threatening my life will motivate me, Monsieur Lindsey? The only thing that motivates me is money. So, you keep writing the checks and I'll show you where you want to go. Bien?"

"We shall see."

5

CAIRO

Adriana sat in the corner of Sean's hotel room, watching him go through his things. Jolian had driven the two of them back to their hotel after leaving Tommy at the airport. The ride had been a silent one, save for their driver asking where they needed to go. Adriana had kept quiet, knowing that Sean was trying to think. He'd appreciated that about her. She seemed to know when he needed to process things.

Now, he was looking frantically around the room for any sign of the stone they had found in Ecuador. Their expedition to South America led to the discovery of a second golden chamber, but they'd had to leave quickly, and barely managed to escape with their lives. Before exiting the chamber, though, they'd taken the stone disc that would lead them to the next marker, and hopefully, the final clue to the location of the final chamber. The disc was missing, however, and Sean feared the worst.

He found a piece of paper in one of Tommy's bags and unfolded it. On it were etchings from both sides of the stone disc.

"What is it?" Adriana asked. She stood up next to him to get a better view of what he'd found.

"It's a drawing of the stone. We make precise copies or document every artifact we find in case something happens to the original. Everything appears to be on it in exact detail." He examined the sheet of paper closely.

"That's good, right?"

"It's a start," he answered. "But Tommy said that the person we were meeting at the museum could help us find the next chamber, based on the clues from the stone."

"It sounds to me like we need to find that person before someone else does." Her comment was right in line with his thoughts.

"Yeah. And I'm guessing we don't have a whole lot of time."

He picked up his phone from the workstation in the corner and pressed the screen. After a few rings, a tired-sounding Emily answered.

"Sean, I heard Tommy arrived safely in Athens. Looks like he's going to be okay. The doctors said he's regained consciousness but still doesn't remember what happened."

"That's good news, Em," Sean said. He didn't try to hide the relief in his voice. "But, I have another favor to ask."

"Two in one day?" she laughed. "What's this one?"

"We were supposed to meet a man at the museum by the name of Richard Firth. He's an Egyptologist living in the area. Can you get us his address?"

He could hear her punching keys in the background. "Didn't realize I was running an information center here," she said sarcastically. "Ever heard of Google?" Sean gritted his teeth, but didn't respond.

"I got him," she said, finally. "Sending the directions to your phone now."

"Thanks again, Em. I owe you two."

"Don't think I'll forget," she responded jokingly. "We still have a position open here at the agency if you ever consider coming out of retirement." She'd not stopped pestering him about returning to his former job since the day he'd quit several years ago.

He snorted a quick laugh and ended the call abruptly. A few seconds later, a new message popped up on the screen.

"I've got the address," he said to Adriana. "We need to get there now. I just hope it isn't too late."

6

CAIRO

A light, evening breeze brushed through Will's hair as he knelt down on the grass just outside of Richard Firth's home. The structure's appearance was like many of the homes in the Garden City district of Cairo, featuring a more contemporary, elegant design. Garden City was a glaring contrast to many other areas of Cairo, especially the Islamic district.

Will had sat patiently in his car, one block from the professor's house, and watched as the gray-bearded man had arrived home from work. Apparently, Dr. Firth's finances were in good order, considering the comfortable house and the late model Jaguar parked in the driveway.

Once Firth was inside the building, Will had made his way casually down the sidewalk amid the evening's few pedestrians. As soon as there was a lull in foot traffic, he hopped the stucco wall into the yard just behind the house.

Normally, killing a target would have been a less hurried affair. Will preferred there to be as little chance of resistance as possible. His favorite way to execute a mark was while they slept. And there were so many ways to do it: knife, bullet, strangling, or occasionally, arson. This particular outing would most likely be messy. He didn't have time to wait around for the professor to go to sleep. That meant he would have to be as efficient as possible and hope the man didn't make too much of a scene.

Shouldn't be a problem, Will thought. The old man was just a historian with no training or background in combat.

He removed the small 9mm Glock from his jacket and attached the sound suppressor, then moved toward the side door and squatted next to the steps leading into the door's alcove. He could hear his target moving around in the kitchen, rattling pots and pans. The man was probably about to make dinner. With all the extra noise, Will would be able to enter unnoticed.

Just as he started to ascend the steps, he noticed a pair of headlights approaching a block away. He crouched back down, assuming the car would pass by harmlessly. Instead, he was surprised to see the SUV slowly come to a stop and park on the curb just on the other side of the backyard wall.

Even when the vehicle's engine shut off, he figured it was just a neighbor or someone coming to visit another one of the many homes in the area. When the passenger door opened, what he saw sent a confused shock through his system.

Sean Wyatt and his female friend, Adriana Villa, exited the vehicle and approached the front door of Richard Firth's home. Will thought Wyatt had certainly been killed or incapacitated by the car explosion, but there he was, alive and well, ruining everything.

SSSSS

"WHAT IF HE ISN'T HOME?" Adriana asked as they walked past the sleek black Jaguar sedan.

Sean pointed at the car with his thumb. "British historian living in the nice section of Cairo? Pretty sure that's his car," he replied with a smirk.

She nodded. "Good point."

They reached an unlocked wrought iron gate and made their way through it and up sandstone steps to a dark wooden door with a small, barred window near the top. Sean pushed the doorbell button and stood back.

A few moments later, a balding man with a white rim of hair answered the doorbell. He wore a tan, tweed jacket, navy blue slacks, and brown shoes. Round glasses atop a short, thick nose and splotched face completed the picture of man who'd spent his life dedicated to the study of ancient history. He was taller than Sean had expected, standing close to 6'2" as best he could figure.

"Dr. Firth?" Sean asked.

"Yes," he answered politely in a sophisticated English accent. "How may I help you?" The man looked down at Sean curiously.

"My name is Sean Wyatt. I'm with the International Archaeological Agency. We were supposed to meet with you and Tommy Schultz earlier today. May we come in?"

Firth raised an eyebrow. "You were supposed to meet me at the museum." He seemed thoughtful for a moment. "I was running a few minutes late to our meeting. By the time I arrived, the whole area had been barricaded. Apparently, there was a terrorist bombing at one of the hotels nearby."

"No, sir." Sean shook his head. "They were not terrorists. It was a deliberate attack aimed at us. Fortunately, they mistimed their little explosion, though not by much."

The professor's eyes grew wide. He was about to make a move to shut the door, but Adriana was quicker and braced it with her foot. "You should let us in, Professor. We're here to help you."

His head turned from her to Sean and back to her. "Help me?"

"Professor, we really should get in the house. You're going to have to trust us on this," Sean insisted.

The old man appeared to consider his options for a few seconds, and then backed away from the door. The two entered and Sean closed the door behind them after giving a quick look up and down the street.

"What is all this about?" Firth asked with a scowl.

"We think someone might try to kill you," Adriana said.

The blunt force of her words confused the professor. "Kill me? Have you gone mad? Who would want to kill me? I haven't any enemies." His voice was indignant.

"She's right," Sean agreed. "We have reason to believe that a group known as The Order of the Golden Dawn is sending someone after you. We need to get you out of here as soon as possible."

Firth looked at Sean as if trying to figure out whether or not he was telling the truth. "Golden Dawn?"

Sean nodded.

The older man scoffed. "They haven't been around for nearly a hundred years."

"I know," Sean replied. "But they're back. And they're after something big. Apparently, they're looking for an ancient treasure related to the four chambers of Akhanan. Up until earlier today, we were ahead of them. Now, they may have caught up."

Firth shook his head in disbelief, still stuck on the part where someone was coming to murder him. "I don't understand. Why would anyone come after me?"

"As far as we know, you are one of the few people who can translate this." Sean pulled a piece of paper out of his jacket and handed it to Firth.

The professor reluctantly took the sheet, clearly suspicious. "What is this?" he asked and started moving slowly toward the living room. He stopped under a row of track lights pushed his spectacles up his nose a little further.

"It's a copy of the stone we found in Ecuador. We were going to meet with you to see if you could decipher the inscription on the back."

Firth nodded slowly. "This is a very ancient form of writing," he said quietly. "I've only ever seen anything like this once or twice in my entire life." His voice was full of awe. Then he turned to face Sean. "Where did you say you found this?"

"Ecuador. A few weeks ago."

Sean and Adriana had followed their host into the living room and were standing a few feet away.

"Ecuador?" the man asked. "You're sure?"

Sean grinned and snorted a quick laugh. "Pretty sure. I was there when we found it."

The professor shook his head quickly, trying to process what he'd just heard. "That makes no sense," he began. "These writings come from a very ancient culture. They have only ever been found in two locations."

"Where?" Sean pressed in closer.

Firth shrugged. "Well, one of them is an Egyptian temple, but it is a day's journey by train. That whole place is an enigma. There are a lot of strange writings and hieroglyphs there. It's unlike anything else we have unearthed, thus far, in this ancient land. Not surprisingly, it is the location of some of the oldest artifacts that have ever been discovered in the region."

He looked down at the paper again. "These symbols have no business being in South America." The professor emphasized his point by tapping the paper with his index finger.

Sean nodded with a grin. "I've heard that before," he commented wryly. "I can tell you all about it. For now, we need to get you out of here."

"Where are we going?" he asked.

"Well, that's kind of what we were hoping you could tell us. We need to know what that sheet says. You think you can work it out?"

The professor nodded. "I already have."

"What do you mean, you already have?" Adriana jumped in.

"I mean, I know the exact location this sheet is talking about. The ancient temple of Nekhen."

SSSSS

WILL LISTENED to the conversation with his ear pressed against the side door of Firth's home. He couldn't hear everything, but he heard enough to know that his employer would not be happy.

He slid back into the shadows and waited until he heard the people in the house leave. A few minutes later, he heard car doors shutting and saw the lights of the SUV pulling out of the parking spot on the street. Will took off across the yard and hopped the little wall just in time to see the vehicle veer right and disappear around the corner.

The good news was that if Firth could figure out where to go, he knew where they would be headed next.

7

CAIRO

Sean steered the SUV through the quiet streets of the Garden District, past some of the most elegant homes in the city. The sun was disappearing in the west, setting the sky on fire with a searing orange glow.

"Alright, Mr. Wyatt," Firth began. "I've agreed to come with you. Now, I would like very much to know what is going on." The professor sat in the back seat, leaning forward as he spoke.

Sean could understand the man's agitation. He could also see why them showing up at Firth's door and telling him someone was going to kill him seemed a little crazy. Sean made a quick left turn and aimed the vehicle toward downtown. He looked back at the professor in the rearview mirror.

"Recently, we discovered two of the four lost chambers of Akhanan." He let the words sink in.

"I am aware of your recent discoveries," Firth retorted. "That was one of the reasons I'd agreed to meet with you and Thomas to begin with." It always sounded strange when people called Tommy by his real name.

Sean continued. "During the search, two professors were

murdered by someone working for the Order. The men were foremost experts in ancient languages and codes, just like you."

The new bit of information caused Firth to think for a moment. He sat back in his seat and seemed to consider the circumstances.

Sean went on. "We believe the Order is being run by a very wealthy and powerful man named Alexander Lindsey. The agency I used to work for is investigating him, but apparently Lindsey has left the country."

Firth absorbed the information quickly. "Do you think that this Lindsey is in Egypt?"

Adriana nodded. "Probably. We think that he is only interested in finding the fourth chamber. Now that he has the clue to the third, he is close to that goal."

"What do you aim to do?" the professor asked.

"We have to stop him. And we have to reach the final chamber before he does," Sean said plainly.

Firth sat quietly, contemplating everything he'd just heard. Then he shook his head. "I'm sorry. I don't understand why you don't just let them have the treasure. I'm sure the IAA doesn't need the money that kind of find would provide, even if it was in the hundreds of millions."

Sean forced a laugh. "We don't keep much from any of our finds, Doctor. Everything is returned to the governments of the area in which the artifacts are found. The money isn't the reason we need to stop Lindsey."

The older man shrugged. "Then why?"

Adriana turned around and held up an old canvas with a painting of an oddly shaped tree on it. "How much do you know about the Bible, Dr. Firth?"

He grasped the painting gently and looked at the name signed at the bottom. His face washed in disbelief. The old, gray eyes glanced at her, then at Sean's in the mirror.

"Where did you get this?" he asked in awe.

"I retrieved it in Germany. It was stolen during the war. My intentions were to steal it back and return it to the rightful owners, or to a museum. Instead, the last owner gave it to me shortly before he was killed by the Order." Adriana's words hung heavy in the cabin of the SUV.

Firth looked back at the painting. "I've never heard of this piece before. The shape of the tree is so strange, two trunks forming into one."

He continued to stare at the canvas as Sean steered the vehicle into an underground parking garage. The professor noticed where they were. "What are we doing?"

"We need to change clothes and get our things, Doc," Sean answered as he pulled into an empty parking space.

"I'm sorry," Firth said, forgetting about the painting for a moment. "What does this painting have to do with the sheet you showed me earlier? And what does any of it have to do with the temples in Nekhen?"

"Actually, Professor," Adriana interrupted, "that is what we need you to tell us."

He raised his eyebrows at her statement. "You don't know where you're going and you don't know what you're looking for? Not a very well thought out plan, eh?"

Sean ignored the jab and shut off the ignition.

Firth shook his head slowly as he returned his gaze to the painting. "I cannot believe you have been driving around Cairo with a Van Gogh in your car."

8

NILE VALLEY, EGYPT

Alexander Lindsey's phone rang in his jacket pocket. He reached into the folds and answered it quickly.

"Is it done?" he asked.

"No," Will's response on the other line was not what Lindsey had wanted to hear. "Sean Wyatt and his female friend got there before I did. They've already left."

"Do you know where they're going?" Lindsey asked, concerned.

There was a moment's pause. "They're headed your direction. But they're travelling by train, so you will have a few hours head start on them."

Lindsey appeared concerned. "Take care of it," he ordered.

"I'm already on the train, sir. I've got two of the men with me. We will handle it."

"See to it that you do."

Lindsey hung up the phone and put it back in his jacket.

"Problems?" DeGard asked from the other side of the back seat.

Lindsey shook his head. "Nothing we need to worry about." He changed the subject. "How much longer until we get to this place?" he asked.

He and Luc DeGard had been traveling south for nearly two

hours by car. They hoped to arrive in the early morning. Behind them were two SUVs with a total of eight armed guards.

"We should be there in another seven hours," said DeGard.

Lindsey sighed. He wished they could have taken a plane, but with all the extra men and equipment, it would have taken longer to make the arrangements to fly.

"It appears we may need to hurry once we arrive in Nekhan. Sean Wyatt has Dr. Firth, and they are on their way. So, when we get there, be sure you don't piddle around."

DeGard seemed to resent the comment but said nothing.

Outside the vehicle, the Nile Valley whirred by silently in the early evening darkness. Even though he was in the lead, Lindsey looked perplexed as he stared through the window. Sean Wyatt had caused enough trouble and Lindsey hoped Will could take care of him once and for all.

"If I may ask," DeGard interrupted his thoughts. "Why are you seeking the lost treasures of Akhanan? You are obviously a wealthy man. You have power. The treasure may be of significant value, but I would think a man like you wouldn't need it."

Lindsey continued looking out the window as he listened to the Frenchman's question. "How much do you know about the lost chambers, Professor?"

"They are ancient rooms of gold, thought to be legend until recently. Apparently, your enemies with the IAA found two of them," DeGard shrugged after his statement. "I would have turned your offer down three months ago. The chambers were the stuff of legend, myth. But, now that they have been discovered, I am willing to take the chance that we can find the next one, for a share of the spoils."

"You shall have a large share, indeed," Lindsey added.

"So, that begs my question, Monsieur. What is it that you are after?"

The question lingered in the car for a moment. A large shipping truck zoomed by on the other side of the road, interrupting the quiet hum of the road.

"There are some things, Monsieur DeGard, that are far more valuable than money."

"Ahhh," the realization hit DeGard. "So, you believe the fairy tales after all, Monsieur Lindsey." The old man ignored the comment so DeGard continued. "I supposed it is what every man seeks when he is near his end: the fountain of youth, the cup of Christ, or in your case, the tree of life." His last sentence was lathered in derision, emphasized even more by his accent.

"I see you are the right man for this job, Monsieur DeGard. But you are obviously not a believer. The tree of life was never mentioned after the great flood in the Bible. No one ever uttered a word of its existence until thousands of years later. Now, I believe are on the trail."

"The trail? The trail to what? Another chamber full of gold? I am certain you will find the chamber, but searching for immortality is folly, Monsieur. Death is the only certainty in this world."

"Perhaps. What do you care, though? As long as you get your money, correct?" It was Lindsey's turn to be contemptuous.

DeGard smiled broadly, revealing his crooked, stained teeth. "Something like that. And I'm sure I will." He laughed heartily as the car entered into the darkness of a tunnel.

9

NILE VALLEY

Sean sat next to Adriana, across from Dr. Firth in a first class cabin of the train. He watched the shadows and outlines of the landscape pass by, deep in thought. The professor was asleep, and Adriana was nodding in and out of slumber as well.

He hadn't been able to sleep much, despite the monotonous click-clack of the train tracks beneath. Tommy was in a hospital in Athens and it was all Sean could think about. He'd wished he had gone to the museum early to check things out, make sure everything was clear. Even if he had, there would have been no way to know there would be a car bombing. He forced himself to let go of the blame.

He turned his head away from the window and glanced over at Adriana. She'd fallen asleep again. Her head was cocked to one side and her dark brown hair draped over part of her face, reaching down to the nape of her neck.

They'd returned to their hotel with the professor in tow, and had changed out of their dirty, singed clothes, and hurried to the train station. Fortunately, they had caught the last train of the night out of Cairo.

Sean looked down at his watch. The local time was just passed

midnight. They'd been on the train a few hours. The bar car would
still be open. *Maybe a drink would help to get a little rest.*

He slipped out of his seat, careful not to disturb his travelling
companions, and headed toward the rear of the train. He passed from
one car to the next, unnoticed by anyone. From what he remembered,
the bar car was one more over.

Halfway down the aisle of sleepy travelers, he looked through the
door window that led to his destination. The hairs stood up on the
back of his neck, and for a moment, Sean thought he'd seen a ghost.
He rubbed his eyes to make sure he was seeing correctly. On the
other side of the window stood a man he thought was dead. Will
Hastings.

Sean's eyebrows lowered, still trying to comprehend the situation.
It couldn't be him. He'd watched as the police officer had been gunned
down inside a cave in Ecuador. Yet there he was, alive and well. But if
he was alive, why had he not contacted Sean or the others? Will stood
in the intersecting area between the passenger car and the bar area,
looking down at his phone.

Sean noticed a gun, dangling loosely in a holster on the inside of
Will's jacket. He still couldn't believe it was Will, and that he was in
Egypt. It couldn't be coincidence.

Suddenly, the apparition looked up and through the window. His
eyes locked with Sean's and, for a moment, there was a strange pause
as if the world around him had stopped. Before he could do anything,
Will pulled the gun from his jacket and squeezed off three muffled
shots. All Sean heard was the bullets thudding into the wall
behind him.

Six years of fieldwork for the United States government couldn't
have prepared him for the odd turn of events. But when the gun was
drawn, Sean's instincts to drop and find cover kicked in instantly.
After rolling to a stop, he removed his own weapon from his jacket
and ducked behind an empty seat to his right. When no more shots
came, he risked a peek around the corner of the seat.

There were three bullet holes in the glass window but Will was
gone.

Sean tried to piece everything together in his groggy mind. *Will was alive? Why was he shooting?* Nothing made any sense. He looked around to make sure none of the other passengers had been hit. Everyone was asleep and hadn't even noticed the entire altercation. Thankfully, the sounds of the train rolling along had covered up the low pops from Will's weapon.

Cautiously, Sean made his way down the aisle toward the rear of the car. When he reached the door, he pressed his back against the corner wall. Standard procedure from his days with Axis. He held his weapon close to his chin before stepping out from his cover, leading with the barrel. A quick look through the window revealed that the apparition was gone.

He slowly turned the handle on the door and pushed it open. The sounds from outside grew instantly louder as he stepped through into the intercessory area between cars. A sliding door to his left was open, filling the area with cool desert air. Sean had a bad feeling, like he was being led into an ambush.

But he needed answers. He stuck his head out the door and looked down the length of the train in both directions, but couldn't see anything. A train stop whooshed by with red lights flashing, causing Sean to jerk his head back inside. At the same moment, a bullet sent sparks flying off the corner where he'd just been standing.

Will was on top of the train. *What was he doing?* Sean moved over to the door on the opposite side of the little room and eased it open. He pushed his weapon out through the opening and checked above to make sure the area was clear.

Things started to come together in Sean's mind. Will had been with them every step of the way during their search for the lost chamber in Ecuador. He'd thought it odd that the policeman had taken such a keen interest in their adventure. *But who was he to tell Will he couldn't tag along?* Now things started to make sense. Will had never been on their side. He probably wasn't even a real cop. *Did that mean the other Atlanta police were in on it too?* Sean shook his head at the thought.

He remembered what he'd heard a few weeks before. *Golden*

Dawn has people everywhere, in every form of government. They've infil-
trated so many organizations; it is hard to know how many operatives they
have. So, that was it, he realized. Will was working for Golden Dawn.
He kicked himself for not figuring it out sooner.

Sean cursed under his breath. He wondered who Will really was.
At the moment, that was a question that would have to wait. His eyes
narrowed as he reached a hand out and grabbed hold of a ladder
rung on the side of the train.

SSSSS

WILL HAD BEEN SENDING Lindsey a text message when he looked up
and saw Sean Wyatt standing thirty feet away in the next car. The
shock on Wyatt's face had told Will he had the element of surprise.
He'd pulled out his weapon quickly and managed to get off three
shots, but he assumed the rounds missed. The sound suppressor on
his barrel was bulky and made accuracy less than reliable from that
distance.

Sean had hit the floor and rolled out of sight before he could fire
any more shots. Will's initial thought was to pursue, but he knew
Sean would do the chasing, if for no other reason, out of curiosity.
The IAA agent had thought him dead, so, there was no doubt he was
trying to figure out what was going on.

Still, Will knew that Sean would come after him. He'd opened the
side door of the car and climbed out into the cool, windy night air
and onto the roof. As he expected, a few moments later, Wyatt's head
had poked out through the door.

He'd fired another shot, but his target had been startled by a rail-
road crossing and jerked back inside the train, causing the bullet to
narrowly miss the head.

He wondered what Sean's move would be. Whatever it was,
staying out in the open on the roof was probably not a good idea.

Quickly, he turned and started moving toward the back of the train.

SSSSS

SEAN REACHED the top of the ladder and, hanging on with one hand, raised his weapon above the line of site on the roof. Will was moving quickly toward the rear of the car. Sean pulled himself up onto the top and started jogging in the same direction, careful to keep his balance on the constantly shifting train car.

Will had almost reached his destination when Sean knelt down and took aim. He trained his sights on the small of his target's back and was about to squeeze when he heard the engine's horn blast.

Sean turned to see the front of the train disappear into a mountain tunnel. He dropped down flat against the roof, pressing his body against the ridged metal, just as the train car entered the tunnel.

The roof of the burrow rushed by, mere inches above him. He forced himself to lie perfectly still in the darkness amid the pungent smell of diesel exhaust. The short time the train was in the tunnel seemed to last forever. Suddenly, the night sky opened up above him and the air became clean again. He stole a quick look toward the front of the train to make sure there wasn't another tunnel up ahead.

Returning his focus to the back of the train car, he saw that Will was gone. He stood up again and started making his way in the direction Will had gone.

A silhouette popped into view at the end of the roof. Sean raised his weapon as the other figure fired off three shots. He dove to the right and rolled to the edge of the roof, nearly falling over the edge.

He managed to stop himself with his left hand and extended his gun out in front of his face. He fired off a quick succession of shots, sending his target ducking for cover. Two rounds sparked off the upper edge of the next train car.

Sean rolled over and pushed himself up. He sprinted down the rooftop in Will's direction, his gun in the lead. He closed the gap quickly and jabbed his weapon over the edge where his quarry had just been.

Will had disappeared into the car's side door. Sean deftly descended the rungs and swung into the open door, catching Will off guard with two boots squarely in the back.

The force of the blow sent Will sprawling forward toward the other door. Sean had landed on his tailbone, momentarily shocking his system. Will spun around and extended his gun at arm's length. Sean simultaneously did the same.

"What are we going to do, Sean? Kill each other?" Will sneered.

"I thought you were dead," Sean replied. "I also thought you were one of the good guys. Guess I've been wrong a lot lately."

Will shrugged, "What can I say? I'm a hard man to figure out." He'd torn his jeans in the fray and his leg was bleeding, slightly. His dark, emotionless eyes stared fearlessly at Sean.

"So, you're working for the Order," Sean shouted above the wind. "How much did they pay you?"

Will laughed. "More than you'd make in two lifetimes. But I enjoy the work," he smirked.

Sean kept up the poker face, his voice and nerves remaining calm. He'd been in that situation before. Losing his cool would only make things worse.

"They gave you a policeman's funeral. It was a beautiful service," he said sarcastically.

Will cocked his head to the side. "How sentimental. Let's stay on task, though, shall we? I pull my trigger and you pull yours, neither of us gets what we want."

Sean nodded. "True."

Will's head turned slightly as if he saw something out of the corner of his eye. As he did, he squeezed his trigger. The weapon clicked. Wyatt's didn't.

He reacted instinctively and fired his weapon when he saw Will's finger move. The shot rang out in the tiny space, instantly causing both of his ears to ring loudly.

The bullet's impact sent Will staggering backwards, his gun clanked to the floor. A dark, wet stain formed around a hole in the right side of his North Face jacket. He leaned up against the door for a moment, looking down at the bleeding wound.

"You should have killed me," he said, his voice trembling slightly.

Sean said nothing. His ears were still ringing from the shot. But kept his weapon raised, and stayed a safe distance from Will.

"You're going to be apprehended as soon as we arrive at Luxor," he said.

"By who?" Will laughed, sickly. "You? You don't work for the government anymore. The Egyptians don't know you. If anything, they'll arrest you!" He clutched the wound in his upper abdomen, wetting his fingers with blood.

"I'm not giving you to the Egyptians," Sean said, in a scathing tone.

Will's face had become ashen, and he coughed a few times. He knew there was no escape. Then again, there was always one option. His hand slipped onto the handle of the door and jerked it open. Sean lunged forward to grab him but it was too late. Will's legs pushed hard and he jumped out of the room and disappeared into the desert night.

Sean rushed over to the opening stuck his head out. In the pale light of the moon, he could see Will roll to a stop in the dust far behind the train. He wasn't sure whether the bullet wound was fatal or not, but without medical attention, he would bleed out within the hour.

Sean reached over to the handle and pulled the door closed. He stuffed the gun back in his jacket then knelt down and grabbed the one Will had dropped. He reopened the door for a moment before tossing Will's gun out into the darkness. After reclosing the door, he headed back toward his car.

No way I'm going to sleep now, he thought.

10

NEKHEN, EGYPT

"W e're here, Sir," the voice of the driver woke Lindsey from his slumber. He wondered how long he'd been asleep. Sleeping in cars wasn't something he could normally do. However, travelling so much lately had finally taken its toll. He yawned and stretched out his arms. Apparently, his French companion had also fallen asleep and was rubbing his face in an attempt to wake up.

One of the security team members from the other vehicle opened the door for Lindsey, and the older man stepped outside into the cool, early morning. He gazed up at the sky for a moment, taking in the view of billions of stars. He'd heard the desert provided an amazing panorama of space. But seeing it was a whole other thing.

"Always darkest before dawn, eh Monsieur?" DeGard also looked up into the dark canvas above before returning his attention to the matters at hand. Nearby, ancient ruins of some of the earliest temples known to man sat quietly among the rocks and hills. The details of the formations were hard to make out in the darkness, but Degard had seen all of that before. What interested him was something that he doubted many others had taken note of.

"Lights over there, if you please," he ordered the men who were gathering equipment from the other vehicles. "Around the base of that rock formation. Two flood lights outside and then take the rest inside the cave." He was in his element, back in the field, where he belonged.

Off to the right, about a hundred feet away, a light breeze played with a canvas tent. Just outside the shelter were several tables and an old Range Rover.

"Should we dispose of them?" one of the men asked Lindsey, pointing with a sub-machine gun in the direction of the excavation camp.

"Not yet," the older man answered. "They should leave us alone. Just set up a perimeter in case they wake up and get nosey."

The muscular man nodded and trotted away to help the others.

Half an hour later, small generators quietly hummed, and the ruin's formation began to take shape in the glow of the floodlights. A rocky hill rose up about sixty feet, to a sharp point. A cave entrance had been adorned with stone sculptures, cut out of the rock face itself. Time and weather had made it difficult to tell to which gods the giant beasts paid homage.

Lindsey followed DeGard over to the sand-colored stone. The Frenchman gazed at it with narrowed eyes. "It has been a long time since I have been here," he said distantly. "The place has not changed a bit in all these years. Let us hope the inside is just as equally intact."

DeGard strolled toward the cave entrance as more lights began to come on inside. When they entered, the two men were greeted with walls painted in pale colors from blue and red to black and gold highlights. The atrium of the cave was a rectangular room, around thirty feet long and fifteen feet wide. The place smelled of stale air and ancient dust. Any artifacts that had been discovered there had long been removed. Fortunately, what DeGard needed was still there, right where he had remembered it. He walked slowly to one wall and ran his finger along some of the hiero-glyphics.

"These are some of the oldest writings we have ever discovered on the planet," he said quietly. Lindsey looked on, clearly confused as to what any of the inscriptions meant. He didn't need to know. That was why he had hired DeGard.

"What are we looking for?" Lindsey asked impatiently.

"Of course. You want to get on with it. Please forgive me for taking a moment to appreciate the enormity of where we are standing. What we are looking for is through there." He pointed a slender finger toward a door at the other end of the room. He motioned for a one of the guards to hand over a flashlight. DeGard switched on the beam and led the way through the dark portal.

Along the narrow passage were more wall paintings and hieroglyphics, similar to what they had seen in the first area. DeGard paid them little attention, and kept walking steadily forward. He passed several other doors as he went.

"What are all these rooms?" Lindsey wondered, as he forced himself to keep up with the Frenchman. The guards behind Lindsey kept their flashlights on the floor as their employer continued walking.

"Funerary chambers," DeGard informed without looking back.

Lindsey scowled at the answer, but said nothing else. After a few minutes of trudging through the primordial corridor, DeGard came to a stop. He stood under an archway, pointing his flashlight into a grand chamber.

The room's walls were completely bathed in ancient texts and pictures. Images of men, animals, and gods decorated the smooth, stone surfaces. DeGard stared at the impressive sight for a moment before proceeding further. He strode confidently over to the far wall, passing by two stone boxes.

"What are those?" Lindsey asked as he passed the crates.

"The exterior sarcophagi. The mummies and their more valuable inner sarcophagi were taken long before we got here."

"Mummies? Who was buried here?"

DeGard stopped before he reached the far wall and turned around. His flashlight shone on Lindsey's face, irritating the older man. "A few moments ago, you seemed to have no interest in the history of this place, only what secrets it may hold. Now you want to know everything?"

Lindsey shook his head, but he did not appreciate being reprimanded. "Just find whatever it is we need," he scowled.

"That's what I thought," DeGard said as he turned around and stepped over to the wall. "But just so you know, they aren't sure who was buried here." He got down onto one knee and started brushing away the sand on the floor. "Historians believe it was someone who predated the first pharaohs. But this place is so old it predates any records of ancient Egyptian society. There is a theory that a few of us in the field have come to believe may be correct. I believe that they come from a different race of people."

"What do you mean, a different race?" Lindsey wondered.

DeGard ignored the question for a moment while he continued to scrape away dust and sand from a particular spot on the floor. After a few minutes of working, he found what he was looking for. Engraved in the ground was a symbol that looked very similar to the one on the stone disc Lindsey had in his pocket. A little more brushwork revealed that the images were identical.

Lindsey's eyes grew wide as he realized what he was seeing. DeGard pointed to one of the symbols embedded in the center of the disc. It was a triangle with a circle in the center.

"I mean they were not Egyptian," he finally answered after catching his breath. "They were pre-Hebrew settlers."

"Pre-Hebrew," he repeated in a whisper. "The legend is true."

"If you are talking about the legend of the tree, perhaps you are getting ahead of yourself. But we will see what this means."

DeGard brushed away more of the dirt and found a small hole in the center of the floor's engraving. The indention was almost the exact size of the stone disc Lindsey had given him. Degard placed the object into the recession and took a step back, looking expectantly at the little space. Nothing happened.

Lindsey glanced over at the French archaeologist for a moment, wondering what he was doing. "Is that supposed to open some kind of secret passage or something?"

DeGard frowned. "I don't understand. That's obviously where the disc was meant to go."

He got back down on his hands and knees and investigated the piece. He pressed on it with his index finger but, still, nothing happened. After another minute of trying in vain to figure out what the problem was, DeGard pried the disc out of the hole and put his face down close to it.

"Ah," he said, finally. "That explains it." He put the object back into the recess and slid it forward.

There was a click followed by a deep rumble. A portion of the wall began to slide sideways, revealing a seam at first then a narrow opening, just wide enough for a man to fit through. After less than thirty seconds, the massive doorway stopped and the rumbling ceased.

"Sir," Kaba stepped into the room touching her ear. "We have a problem with the other encampment. They're demanding we leave at once. Something about being the only ones with permits to do excavations on this site."

Lindsey's eyes were still wide with wonder at the opening that had just revealed itself. "Tie them up and have two of the men watch them." She nodded and took off toward the entrance of the ruins.

DeGard had shuffled over to the opening in the wall and was shining his light into the dark area beyond. "It looks like the passage goes to the left up ahead." There was an eagerness in his voice. Greed had begun to take over, and he was obviously anxious to reap his reward.

"Lead the way," Lindsey ordered.

The Frenchman's eyes narrowed slightly. "How do you know it is safe? I, for one, do not feel like dying down here as the result of some ancient booby trap? Perhaps we should get one of your helpers to go first, just in case."

"Very well, get out of my way." Lindsey nudged passed a surprised DeGard and wedged through the portal.

He held his light at shoulder height and investigated the walls and floor as he moved, carefully mindful of the words his hired professor had uttered. While he doubted that there would be anything like that in the tunnel, he didn't want to die underground either, so he proceeded with caution. DeGard's flashlight cast a little more illumination to the passageway that was otherwise pitch dark. The two turned left as the path led and they found themselves walking another twenty feet before the floor began to slope downward.

Lindsey shone his light down the sloping corridor, and couldn't see the bottom. "How far down do you think it goes?" he asked, pointedly.

DeGard raised his eyebrows. "I have no idea. As you American's say, there is only one way to find out." Made braver by the older man's courage, the Frenchman set out trudging down the long tunnel with renewed vigor.

The slanted corridor took them a hundred feet down before coming a stop and continuing on a little further to the right. When they shone their lights into the new direction their eyes caught a glimpse of some objects on the floor. What the pale glow of the flashlights revealed was a treasure of astonishing measure. Three, three foot wide and five foot long chests, full of gold coins, chalices, crowns, necklaces, bracelets, and jewels lined the walls. DeGard's face lit up as he led the way into the rectangular room. The chamber was only twenty to thirty feet long and about twelve feet wide. The Frenchman stepped quickly across the threshold and dug his hands deep into the first chest.

"I cannot believe it, Monsieur Lindsey." He looked back at the older man who seemed to be ignoring the treasure chests. His eyes were focused on something at the end of the room.

Lindsey eased past his elated partner and moved toward the back of the chamber.

DeGard kept yammering as Lindsey stopped at the end wall. "You know, I thought I could perhaps help you find something. But I had no idea it would be this easy. Honestly, I almost feel guilty taking such a high percentage of this find. Well, almost." He let a necklace slip through his hands as he realized his employer did not seem interested in the fortune they'd just discovered.

On the wall directly in front of Lindsey were inscriptions, carved into the stone. "What does this say?"

DeGard reluctantly left the treasure at his feet and shuffled over to where Lindsey stood with arms crossed. He produced a pair of brown spectacles from his jacket and placed them on the tip of his nose.

"This is the oldest form of Hebrew we know of. It dates back to before the time of the earliest Egyptian communities."

"What does it say?" Lindsey persisted.

The Frenchman ran a finger along the engravings. His lips moved silently as he translated the symbols. Finally, he reached the bottom and removed his glasses. He kept his flashlight on the wall as he spoke.

"It is a story about three brothers," he began. "Their family had been on an incredible journey and settled in a valley just outside of some mountains. One day, the boys' father drank too much wine and became drunk. The father ripped off his clothes and was dancing around in his tent, naked. It seems one of the sons discovered him and started laughing. The other two saw what was going on and clothed their father. When the old man awoke, he knew what had happened and cursed his youngest son's child. In the curse, he said that his grandson would be a servant to all his brothers forever. Then it goes on to talk about the three treasure chests, a curse, and a reward.'

Lindsey's eyes were wide. "I know this story."

"You do?" DeGard was surprised.

"Of course. It is from the Old Testament of the Bible. It is the story of Noah and his three sons."

DeGard nodded in agreement. "But what is that story doing here, in southern Egypt?"

Lindsey turned his head and shone the flashlight onto the three chests. "What did it say about these? You said it mentioned them and a reward."

"Oui," he agreed in French. "It reads that the curse will be on the other two brothers and that his son will be blessed with the wealth of the father."

Lindsey was perplexed. All three chests looked the same. They each contained similar treasures, and were crafted in an identical fashion. DeGard slid past his employer and squatted down on one knee, shining his light on one chest and then the next.

"Do you see something?" Lindsey asked impatiently.

"Perhaps," DeGard cocked his head to the side in the briefest of seconds. "There are some unusual markings on the front of each chest."

"Can you decipher them?"

DeGard twisted his head around, "Of course, Monsieur, I already have." A shady grin crept onto the right side of his face. "They are the names of the three brothers. It would appear that if we move the correct chest, we will find an even greater treasure than this."

"You said the wealth of the father would be there for the cursed son. Ham was the one who defiled his father's presence. Noah cursed him. Which one is Ham's?"

"There isn't one," DeGard informed in a matter-of-fact tone.

"What do you mean there isn't one?" Lindsey spat. "There has to be. One for each of the three brothers, the sons of Noah: Shem, Ham, and Japheth."

"Yes, I am aware of that. But we are not looking for the name of Ham. We are looking for the name if his son, Canaan, which is the one on the end." He made his point with a jab of the finger.

Lindsey looked over at the stone box filled with precious metal and jewels. "Of course," he gasped. "Noah didn't curse Ham. He cursed Canaan, his own grandson, to a life of servitude." The older man knelt down before the chest and ran his finger across the strange inscription on the front. "Ham wouldn't have it, though. He wouldn't let his son be a servant to anyone." Lindsey cut himself off, wary he would say too much. DeGard didn't seem to pay any attention.

"How are we going to move that thing?" he asked in a snooty tone that suggested he wouldn't be doing any lifting.

"Not to worry," Lindsey ignored the man's lazy attitude. "We have help."

Several minutes later, a few of the men they'd brought entered the chamber carrying crowbars. Kaba was right behind them. "We need you to move this chest away from the wall," Lindsey said.

Kaba gave the order in Arabic and the two dark-skinned men immediately obeyed. They wedged their tools between the wall and the heavy chest then pushed back. The box moved slightly, grinding on the stone of the floor as it did. The men continued to leverage their weight for a few minutes until a hole, nearly the same size as the box, had been revealed in the floor.

The men stepped back and Kaba moved forward. "Would you like me to go first?" she asked without hesitation.

Lindsey nodded and she quickly dropped down on her knees and stuck her head and a flashlight into the cavity. She swung her legs around and dropped into the darkness with the deftness of a gymnast. The men stood over the recession, looking down as her light flashed around under the floor. A moment later, her face appeared as they shone their lights into the hole.

"It's safe for you to come down," she reported in a smooth tone. "Tie off the ropes the men brought down in their packs and lower yourselves down." Her face cracked with a rare smile, her dark chocolate eyes alive with wonder. "You are going to want to see this."

The men rigged the ropes and a few minutes later, helped lower their employer into the opening. Kaba grabbed him and eased the older man onto the floor. He shone his flashlight around in the room. In the pale glow of the electric bulb, she could see his face filled with awe. The entire room was paneled in pure gold: the walls, the ceiling, all but the floor, which was stone carved from the earth. He stepped over to the nearest wall and ran his finger along the engravings. Images of people and animals covered nearly every inch. He turned and looked down the expanse. The chamber ran about forty feet in length and was around twenty feet wide.

"What do you see?" the Frenchman asked from above, trying to see into the chamber.

"Lower him down, men," Lindsey ordered. "Let him see for himself. Words cannot describe it."

A few moments later, DeGard was touching down on the floor of the golden chamber. His expression was one of disbelief. He stepped quickly over to a gold panel and pressed his hands against it. "I will never be poor again," he stated in whispered jubilation. If he could have hugged the wall he would have.

Lindsey ignored him. He was focused on something at the other end of the room, in the center of the floor. A stone pillar stood just over three feet high. On the top of it, rested a round stone, four inches in diameter and about one inch thick. He glided over to it and paused a moment then reached down to pick it up.

"Perhaps you would like me to?" Kaba offered. She'd sauntered over to the plinth and was standing a few feet away from him.

"It is alright, my dear." He gently lifted the stone off of its altar and held it up in the light. On it, was engraved a picture of several mountains, and in the center, between two of the angles, was a man holding his hands up in the air.

"This is impossible," DeGard was mumbling behind them. "This cannot be real." Lindsey and Kaba turned around to see the Frenchman shuffling sideways along the wall. "This entire thing," he waved a hand around, "is talking about the flood story from the Bible. And there," he pointed at the end wall near the pillar, "is that the ark of Noah?"

The other two turned and looked at the image. Their flashlights gleamed off of the shiny yellow surface. In the center of the end wall, engraved in gold, was a picture of a long, strange looking vessel, resting between to mountain peaks.

Lindsey stared at it for a moment. Kaba looked to him expectantly, curious as to what he would say. The older man stepped away from the stone pillar for a moment and studied the disc in his hand. He turned it over, revealing ancient Hebrew script on the back.

"What does this say?" He spun around and held the object out to DeGard, who accepted it with interest.

"Again, very ancient writing. Difficult to make out. But I believe it says, 'where the mountain rises through the eye in the valley of eight the path home will be shone and there awaits life eternal.'" DeGard frowned at the last part. "Fountain of youth, Monsieur Lindsey?" He carelessly tossed the disc back to his employer who caught it carefully with both hands.

Lindsey chose not to acknowledge the barb. "The valley of eight? Where is that?"

"Monsieur, please hear what I am about to say to you," the Frenchman's birdlike face pleaded and he held his arms out, begging to be heard. "There have been many people who have tried to find these ancient things. They have lived and died searching for sacred relics that would give them immortality. What makes you any different? These things you search for do not exist."

"Those who went before didn't have this," Lindsey held up the disc. "You lack faith, Monsieur DeGard. But you will see. And when you do, you will believe. Now, answer my question, if you would be so kind." He produced a small pistol from inside his burgundy windbreaker and aimed it at the Frenchman's chest. "Do you or don't you know where this valley of eight is?" Kaba took the cue from her boss and produced a weapon of her own, training it on the same target.

DeGard took a deep breath and let out a long exhale. "Oui, Monsieur. I have heard of it. Please, put your weapons away. They are unnecessary. The compensation you offered is more than enough to lead you on this wild goose chase. So long as I get paid, I could not care less what we are looking for." His voice took on an air of warning. "The area is in eastern Turkey, around Ararat Mountain and the Valley of the Eight has been searched heavily over the decades, for the exact thing you are talking about seeking. No one has found anything except some giant stones and what one researcher claimed was the petrified roof of the ark."

Lindsey gazed at him through the peripheral illumination of the flashlights. "Good," he replied after a moment of consideration. "Then we should find little resistance when we arrive."

11

LUXOR, EGYPT

The train whistle blew, signaling that it was arriving at its destination. Sean was already wide awake, unable to get much sleep after the encounter with Will. He informed Adriana as soon as she had woken up, about thirty minutes outside of Luxor. She was shocked at the revelation, but not as surprised as he had thought.

"There was something not right about him," She stated after a long yawn. "I never fully trusted him."

"Well, thanks for the heads up," Sean said incredulously.

She smiled. "I thought he was dead. We all thought he was."

"Yes, but before that?" He held his hands out expecting an explanation.

"Look, you're okay. And he's probably dead. You said you shot him in the chest and he fell out of the train. I doubt he survived. And if he did, he will be out of commission for a while. That is if he made it to a hospital somewhere. Again, I seriously doubt that happened," her voice remained calm as she laid out the scenario.

"You're right. But I just can't believe I never made the connection. If he was a snake he would have bit me."

"He almost did," she quipped.

"To think that I was upset over his death. The city of Atlanta gave him a police funeral. They actually honored the guy," Sean sounded disgusted.

"You're going to have to let it go, Sean. We have other things to worry about right now." Her eyes were kind but determined as she stared intensely at him.

The group busily got their things together to make the exit a little quicker. The three stepped off the train onto the platform amid a flurry of activity. Stone pillars lined the landing, supporting an over-hanging roof. People were rushing around everywhere. There were a few disorderly lines of people waiting to board the train that would head back to Cairo within the hour. It was still early in the morning and the sun was still low on the horizon. Sean imagined in a few hours the place would be packed with travelers.

Sean had made a call over an hour before arrival, arranging for transportation and supplies. Fortunately, Tommy had left his little black book of connections in a Dropbox file the two of them shared. So, getting the contact information of drivers and suppliers hadn't been too difficult. He hated handling stuff like that. Normally, Tommy took care of all the little details. That wasn't an option for the time being, so he took matters into his own hands. He was relieved to find a couple of white Land Rovers waiting for them just outside the station. They were greeted by a short, Middle Eastern man standing on the sidewalk next to the vehicles.

"You must be Sean Wyatt," the man said with a broad smile that revealed bright teeth. "I am Sahid, your driver. I just spoke to you on the phone a little while ago."

Sean stuck a hand out, which the man shook vigorously. "Thanks for meeting us on such short notice."

"Not a problem," when the man shook his head, the black hair on top tossed back and forth.

Sean figured him to be in his mid-twenties. But it could have just been the guy's very friendly, almost jovial nature.

"May I take your things?" he offered to Adriana and Dr. Firth.

Sean only carried a book bag with a few necessities in it. Adriana carried similar luggage while Firth had only a courier bag.

Adriana shook her head, as did Firth. Sahid looked disappointed for a second, but picked up his attitude immediately. "We should probably get going before the sun is too high. The southern part of Egypt gets much warmer during this time of year than Cairo."

The group nodded and joined their driver in the first Land Rover. "You have the equipment I requested in the second car, correct?" Sean asked as he slid into the front passenger's seat. He looked back for a second and noticed the intricately decorated Egyptian bird that was placed over the three main doors of the train station.

Sahid nodded proudly. "Yes, Mr. Wyatt. We have all the things you requested." The young man started up the vehicle and steered it out onto the busy road amid box trucks, compact cars, and pedi-cabs.

Luxor City was a sprawling collection of buildings, most under ten stories high. It was rife with activity, even for such an early time of the day. Sean tried to recall visiting the area, but it was one of the few places his job hadn't taken him yet. His mind returned to the task at hand before he let it wander too much further.

"Dr. Firth, we may run into some hostiles when we get there. You and Sahid stay in the car until Adriana and I check things out." She flashed a quick smile with her eyes, grateful he'd not treated her like a helpless girl.

"I'm sorry, but I think it's time you fill me in on a few details," Firth leaned forward, gripping the back of the driver's seat with one hand.

Sean took a breath before speaking. "The Order of the Golden Dawn is being run by a man who calls himself 'The Prophet.' His real name is Alexander Lindsey. He is the man behind the bombing in Cairo, and the deaths of several innocent people, including two professors back in the U.S."

The professor frowned. "If you know who this man is and what he has done, why has he not been arrested?"

"Nothing can be traced back to him. He always comes out looking spotless."

"I see," Firth leaned back in his seat and looked out the tinted window at the crowded city. "So, Tommy found the trail to Akhanan's first chamber. People have searched for that for centuries, with no luck. Some said the chambers didn't exist." He laughed. "In fact, I was one of them."

"You did not believe in the golden chambers?" Adriana asked, curious.

"No," he shook his head. "It was a fool's errand to search for such a treasure. So much of it was surrounded by legend and myth. True archaeologists only search through the facts, the things we know, before trudging off into the wild world in search of something."

"I suppose it is a good thing that some people believe in the fairy tales. Wouldn't you say, Dr. Firth?" She raised an eyebrow. Her deep, brown eyes sucked him in.

"Perhaps," he cleared his throat and turned back to the window, clearly made uncomfortable by the Spaniard's comment.

Sahid guided the vehicle past the final few dilapidated buildings and the small convoy was suddenly out of the city, on the open plains leading to the ancient ruins of Luxor. Sean peered through the tinted windows; out on the flats, small convoys of camels were plodding along to and from the city to the outer reaches of the desert. The bright sun was almost near its peak in the cloudless sky. Off in the distance, several rolling hills of sand and rock eclipsed the horizon.

The convoy passed two tour busses, full of people. Sean hoped the tourists were headed for some of the more popular, mainstream historical sites. He didn't feel like dealing with a bunch of civilians. They always made things difficult, especially when bullets started flying.

Sahid interrupted Sean's thoughts. "We have word that there is a dig going on at the Nekhen site. A team of archaeologists is working close to where we will be."

Sean didn't like to hear that. "They aren't going to give us any trouble, are they?"

"No," the driver shook his head. "They should accommodate us.

Besides, they are digging just outside the ruins. We should be out of their way."

Sean acknowledged the information with a nod. But there was something else concerning him. "Do you know if anyone else arrived in town today? Have you noticed anything suspicious?"

Sahid reflected for a few moments, trying to remember if he'd seen anything strange. "Not that I can recall," he answered. "But in this part of the world, suspicious things happen all the time."

The comment didn't exactly fill the passengers' hearts with confidence. Sean pulled out his new black Springfield XD, and check the magazine to make sure it was fully loaded. He knew it was. He'd put the rounds in it himself. But old habits die hard. Sean had been trained to always check and recheck his weapon. As soon as one got careless, that was when bad things happened.

The drive to the Nekhen ruins took a little over twenty minutes. Upon arriving, the group noticed the tents of the other archaeology team set up off to the side of the hillside ruins. A cool dry breeze washed over the area. Something was amiss. Sean couldn't put his finger on it, but he knew things were too quiet, especially for an active dig site.

"Where is everyone?" Firth asked as he exited the vehicle. "Digs are usually very active places to be."

"Yeah," Sean agreed. "Something's not right." He looked around, peering into the desert for any signs of a potential problem.

"The ruins are over here. This cave entrance is what I believe we are looking for," the Englishman informed them, leading the way toward a hill with an opening in the center. On either side of the entrance, obelisks had been carved into the rock, a permanent reminder of an ancient culture that had long since disappeared.

Sean and Adriana followed Firth as he headed straight toward the opening. The professor said nothing, seemingly in a trance as he marched across the desert floor. Off to the right, several large white tents, lighting equipment, and many other tools of the archaeology trade were sitting silently in the bright morning sun. Sahid and a few of his assistants made their way to the biggest tent to see if anyone was home.

Sean and his companions were only twenty feet away from the entrance to the cave when Sahid stopped them. "Sean! You need to come over here."

Adriana cast a quick, worried glance at Sean. He had stopped and hesitated for a moment before obeying and trudging over the rocks to the tent formation. She stayed close behind while Firth seemed bent on getting into the cave, but he fell in line, curious to see what had gotten the driver's attention.

The young Arab held back the fabric of the opening to the tent. Sean gave him a look of uncertainty before stepping cautiously inside. What he saw was completely unexpected. Three young men and women were bound to wooden chairs throughout the room. A stout, older man of Arab descent was also tied up by a small workstation in the corner. He spoke up, seemingly the least afraid of the group.

"My name is Dr. Omar Abdulkarim," he stated. "Please help us." Sean nodded at Sahid and Adriana.

The three quickly made their way around the room, untying all of the people. Finally, Sean reached the man in the corner who had spoken up. "What happened here?"

Dr. Abdulkarim's dark eyelashes and eyebrows blended with his deeply tanned skin. He stood up after Sean untied him from a wooden chair. He rubbed his wrists as he spoke with a heavy Egyptian accent. "We have been at this site for the last few weeks. We have a permit from the Egyptian government to do light excavations for ninety days." The portly archaeologist was sweating through his white cotton button-up, and his thick gray hair was a soaked mess. "I have never seen those men before in my life. They came into our tents, dressed in black, carrying assault rifles. Then they tied up the whole group. I thought they were going to kill us. After around an hour or so, though, they just left. The guards in the tent with us simply walked out and never looked back."

Sean scratched the back of his head. "I wonder where they went," he said in a low voice, almost to himself.

"And why they left so quickly," Adriana added.

Firth had been silent, standing near the entrance to the tent for the last few minutes. He finally decided to speak up. "Would it be alright if we examine the ruins in the cave? I am a professor working out of the university in Cairo. We will not disturb the site. But perhaps we can find a clue as to what these people were doing here and what they were looking for."

The Egyptian man looked around and his younger assistants. They all appeared to be college kids, young women and men from universities in the U.K. and U.S. He nodded. "Certainly. If there is anything we can do to assist you in finding these men, I would be happy to help. So, please, do whatever you need. You will need lights, though. We haven't run any lamps up there since most of our work has been outside the temple area."

"Thank you," Sean offered then turned his attention to Firth. "Professor, lead the way."

The group exited the tent and followed Firth up the slight hill toward the cave entrance. En route, they all grabbed some flashlights out of black duffel bags Sahid had brought. They reached the edge of the rock formation and continued over the threshold, into the darkness of the cave's atrium. When the professor entered the room, he scanned it carefully, as if he were seeing it for the first time, while the others waited patiently behind.

His flashlight stopped at a spot on the floor off to the side. He became instantly perplexed. Firth took a few long strides across the stone floor and reached the spot that had caught his attention. Abdulkarim stood just behind him, looking over his shoulder staring at an indention in the floor.

"This wasn't here before," Firth remarked in a surprised tone. His Egyptian counterpart shook his head in agreement.

Sean and Adriana had moved further into the chamber and were standing near the far wall. "Where does this go?" Sean asked, shining his light into a narrow doorway.

Abdulkarim and Firth looked up at what had caught their interest. A perplexed frown washed over their faces. "I don't understand. That passageway, this recession in the floor, neither were here before," the Egyptian stated, confused.

"He's right, Sean," Firth confirmed in a baffled tone. "I have been to this location at least half a dozen times. That was never here." He jabbed his index finger at the opening to emphasize his point.

Adriana shone her beam into the black corridor and, without hesitation, stepped through the portal.

"Are you certain that's safe?" Firth asked, concerned.

Sean grinned at him. "Pretty sure she knows what she's doin', Doc." Sean disappeared into the darkness right behind her.

The two professors looked at each other and then at Sahid and decided they should follow along as well.

"I'm going to stay outside," Sahid said tentatively. He clearly had no interest in going into the forbidding passageway.

The two archaeologists didn't acknowledge his comment and carefully passed through the door into the ancient tunnel.

"I cannot believe that all the times I have been to Nekhen, I never knew this corridor existed," Firth remarked as they followed Sean and Adriana around a sharp corner.

"I have been here many times as well," Abdulkarim commented in a reverent voice. "I wonder how they knew about it? Or how the door opened?"

The group plunged ahead, winding their way into the mountain until they reached a point where the path began to slope down more dramatically. Sean and Adriana both shone their lights down the long shaft, carefully watching for anything suspicious or potentially dangerous. After a few minutes of creeping down the corridor, they reached the end.

Sean's eyes narrowed as he saw a chest of gold and jewels on the floor. His eyes scanned forward, seeing the other two chests in the room. He cast his beam on the wall at the end and noticed the ancient writing. Adriana stopped at a hole in the floor and flashed her beam into it.

"Another chamber," she stated and set a black backpack on the ground next to the cavity.

She knelt down on one knee and peered into the darkness below as Firth and Abdulkarim eased their way past the first treasure chest. The two men's eyes were wide at the site.

"It isn't that far down," she stated. "Let's tie off this rope to the stone boxes and see what we can find."

"I'm not going down there," Firth protested. His face contorted in disapproval.

Adriana had already pulled a climbing rope out of her bag and was hurriedly tying it around the two closest stone chests.

"You don't have to, Professor," Sean said. "This is what we do at IAA." He helped their female companion finish testing out the rope then hooked his flashlight onto his belt and repelled down the rope into the darkness.

Adriana copied his movements and descended just as quickly below. The two archaeologists stared at each other for a moment in disbelief then rushed over to the hole and got down on their bellies to peer through the opening.

Sean was standing on the floor shining his light around the room. The visual the four were treated to was nothing less than spectacular. Gold panels covered the walls around the entire chamber. Each piece of the shiny metal was engraved with ancient writing and pictographs.

"What do you see?" Firth shouted down into the lower level.

"The walls are covered in plated gold, just like the ones we saw in the other chambers." At this report, Firth leaned his head forward and twisted his head around. His eyes were huge as the beams of the flashlights bounced off of the yellow element.

"It's breath taking," Firth commented reverently. "I've never seen anything like it in all my life. How did they do it?"

The Egyptian archaeologist had poked his head through as well and was enamored by the sight. "All these years I have worked this area and never realized what lie beneath my feet." He shook his head.

Sean moved quickly through the room toward a pedestal he'd

illuminated with his flashlight. When he arrived at the stone structure, he became immediately disconcerted.

"It's not here," he sighed. "I was afraid of that." He ran his hands
along the sides, hoping there might be a hidden button or something
their predecessors may have missed, but he found nothing.

Adriana leaned her head around on both sides of the object, but
likewise found nothing of note.

"I can't believe they beat us to it," Sean was exasperated.

"What's going on? What are you looking at over there?" Firth
shouted from the other end of the room.

"Lindsey and his group have already been here," Sean replied.
"And they got the only clue that can lead us to the next chamber." He
lowered his voice and stared at Adriana. "We've lost the trail."

12

EGYPTIAN DESERT

Lindsey's caravan of vehicles sped along the desert road leading back to Cairo. DeGard sat silently, staring out the window into vast, empty landscape. He'd not said much since they had left the Nekhen Temple. It seemed the incident where his employer pointed a gun at him had resulted in an adverse effect.

The older man was busily tapping on the touch screen of his phone, attempting to send a text message to Will. Will Hastings had been his most trusted and loyal agent. The fact that Lindsey hadn't heard from him since they'd left Cairo was troubling. Based on their last conversation, Will had followed Wyatt and his companions onto a train bound for Luxor. He'd said the problem would be taken care of. If that were the case, Lindsey would have heard from him. But he hadn't. And in the old man's mind, that was disconcerting. He'd called a few times and sent a text message, all with no reply.

He slipped the phone back into one of his pockets and let out a deep sigh as he peered out the tinted window.

"Problems?" DeGard asked cynically.

Lindsey decided to ignore his question and ask one of his own. "You're entirely certain that this is the place we are looking for?" Lindsey interrupted DeGard's thoughts, pointing at a map on an iPad.

The Frenchman turned his head slowly and glanced at the image then nodded. "Oui, that is the place." His voice was low and he turned back to staring out the window after his short reply.

"It's just that, well, it doesn't look like there is much in that entire region save for an old monastery that was built nearby." He scrolled around the area on the map with his finger, zooming in occasionally to examine a new point of interest.

"You don't pay me a ridiculous amount of money to be wrong, Monsieur. You asked me if that was the place described on your little rock. It is the only one on the planet that makes sense. If you wish to continue on without me, pay me my money and I will be gone. I will bid you adieu and good luck." He never stopped looking out the window while he spoke.

Lindsey caught his irritation, but offered no apology. Instead, he just shut off the iPad and stowed it in the seat back in front of him.

Outside the car, the sun baked landscape whirred by. Everything had a light tan color to it, the color of sand. There were a few occasional trees, but most of them were over near the riverbanks along the Nile. The only sound in the cabin for several minutes was the clacking of the tires when they'd hit a piece of road that had been patched with tar. Otherwise, it was the monotonous whine of the engine.

"Why do you seek immortality?" DeGard's snide voice cut the silence and he looked over at Lindsey with accusatory eyes.

Lindsey raised an eyebrow at the unexpected query. "My reasons are my own," he responded in an ominous tone. "But unlike those who came before and failed in their quest for eternal life, my purpose goes beyond the mere desire to live forever. It is my purpose. It is my destiny to shape the world into a better place, void of wickedness and wrongdoing. With immortality, comes time. And with unlimited time, I will someday be able to create a better world."

DeGard frowned at the answer. It sounded like the ravings of a madman, but he dare not say that. Instead, he decided to be subtler.

"There have been great leaders throughout history who sought various sources of immortality and spoke of a better world. Along the way they murdered millions of people they thought would not fit in with the plan of the future. Do you have such intensions, Monsieur Lindsey? Will you kill millions to make the world what you believe to be better?"

"I will do what is necessary!" the older man snapped. "I do the work of God. There can be no questioning His orders. I am his ambassador to a dying planet full of thieves, rapists, murderers, whores, and filth. I will do whatever it takes to make the Earth new again." His voice continued to heighten until he finished the last few words. His wrinkled, ashen face had flushed red and a vein popped out on his forehead. DeGard gazed at him, beyond words at what he'd just witnessed.

He calmed himself down before he spoke again. "In the book of Revelation, it talks about a new earth that God will bring. My mission is to create that new earth." Lindsey turned his head and glanced out the window as they passed a small train of camels. "To you, I'm sure it must sound insane. You probably believe me to be a mad man, power hungry and hell bent on a pointless venture. I assure you, I am quite sane. And I will see my mission through to the end. It was for a great purpose The Order of Golden Dawn was created."

"Golden Dawn? That group has been gone for nearly a century," DeGard snorted.

Lindsey shook his head slowly. "No. It was merely sleeping. And like the sleeping church in Revelation, it has been awakened to perform a great task: the cleansing of this world."

"Cleansing?"

"Yes," the older man nodded. "We will purge the world of the wicked and begin it anew. The Order of Golden Dawn will establish the true one world government."

DeGard scowled. "As long as you pay me my money, I do not care what you do with your little group. Just see to it that I get what I was promised."

"You will. And more, I assure you. Check your account if you wish. I have already made sure the order has made a significant deposit into the bank you specified before." Lindsey handed the tablet to the archaeologist who took it with some hesitation.

DeGard glanced cautiously at his employer then pulled up his bank account on the device. After entering in his security information, he was greeted with an astounding number at the top of the page. His eyes grew wide.

"And there is more where that came from, my dear professor. Imagine all the carnal pleasures you could buy." DeGard ignored the last comment.

"I wondered why we didn't take some of the treasure from the chamber. It would have been worth millions," his voice trembled.

"As you can see, money is not an issue for us, Monsieur," Lindsey turned his head again and looked off into the distance. A few jagged hills rose up from the desert, brightly illuminated by the mid-day sun. "There is plenty more where that came from, I assure you." He took the iPad back from DeGard whose face still seemed shocked.

"Now," Lindsey changed gears, "Tell me about this Valley of the Eight."

DeGard rolled his eyebrows and shrugged. "There is not much to know. Obviously, the area is the alleged resting place of the ark of Noah from the Bible's Old Testament. The story claims that after the great flood, it came to rest high on the mountain. No one has ever been able to confirm it, though. With the severe weather patterns the mountain surely experiences, an object made from wood could not have lasted very long. If there is anything left, it would be buried."

"I would think that satellite photos would reveal something of such an enormous scale," Lindsey commented thoughtfully.

"Precisely. If there were anything to be found, it would have been seen by satellites, planes, something. Despite centuries of decay and erosion, there should be substantial evidence of something that size."

"Evidence? What kind of evidence?" Lindsey leaned closer across the back seat.

"We would at least see an outline of the wreckage. Imagine you are walking on the beach and the ocean waters wash up to your bare feet. When the water withdraws, your foot has sunken into the sand a little. If this happens several times, your foot will be a few inches deep in the sand." He demonstrated with his hands as he explained the process. "When you remove your foot, the outline of it remains in the sand until the water returns and washes it away."

Lindsey's eyebrows knit together, trying to comprehend what the Frenchman was saying. "Just what is your point?"

"The point, Monsieur, is that on the top of that mountain, there was no other source of water. If the flood story were true, the waters would have receded and left a major indention in the soil, soil that eventually would have petrified into stone or rock formations outlining the shape of a large boat."

"Interesting," Lindsey seemed to contemplate the new information. "So, if the ark is not there, where could it be?"

"Who knows? I, for one, do not believe in fairy tales, Monsieur. That story is a legend, a myth. There are many cultures around the world with the same plot. What should make the one from the Bible any different?"

Lindsey let out a derisive snort. "You see, Monsieur DeGard, when you say many cultures share the story, that fact makes me believe in it even more."

"Each person has their own beliefs. But if the ark truly does exist, I highly doubt it will be found on the mountain of Ararat. I will say, though, that based on the stone you have in your hand we may very well find something else." DeGard pointed at the disc Lindsey was holding loosely in his fingers.

"What might that be?"

"I do not know. I suppose we will find out, although we may have trouble climbing the mountain. It will be cold this time of year. We do not know in which area to look. And then, of course, there is the problem with the government."

"Problem?" Lindsey asked naively.

"Oui. The government does not take well to westerners climbing the mountain and digging around. And if the government does allow it, the locals will not."

"I see," Lindsey gave a slow nod. "Well, I suppose we will just have to figure something out that will take care of those little issues."

13

NEKHEN

Sean scanned the inscriptions on the golden panels. Adriana did the same. Their progress was slow, but the images that had been engraved into the shiny metal helped cover up any deficits they had in reading the ancient language.

"What are you doing?" Dr. Firth shouted down through the opening.

"You know, Doc, it would really speed things along if you two were down here helping," Sean answered back. "Adriana knows a good bit of this stuff, but I don't have the background in ancient Hebrew that you have. From what I can tell, these images seem to be a timeline of the flood story from Genesis." His last jab was half-humorous, half-true.

The two older archaeologists gave each other an apprehensive glance. Unwilling to miss any more, Firth grabbed the rope and began to descend. "Very well," he grunted, straining to lower himself down into the chamber. He somehow managed to make it to the floor and clumsily landed on his feet, though almost falling over in the process.

"I think I'm going to stay up here until I can get a ladder brought down," Abdulkarim chimed after seeing the much more fit professor barely make it without breaking his neck.

Dr. Firth brushed off his pants and jacket as if he'd accumulated some dust on the way down the rope, probably an act of habit more than anything else. He pulled the small, aluminum flashlight out of his jacket pocket and stepped slowly over to the nearest wall.

"Pretty amazing, huh?" Sean commented as he noticed the professor analyzing the brilliant panels.

"Amazing," Firth turned toward him and produced some reading glasses from within another pocket, placing them gently on his nose, "hardly does it justice, my boy." His voice was full of reverence. "We are seeing something that was designed and crafted thousands of years ago. We are the first people to see it since it was closed up and hidden."

Sean smiled as the older man ran his fingers along the panels, carefully reading the symbols as he moved down the wall toward the other end where Adriana stood. Sean rejoined her, watching the professor as he finished on one side and made his way to the other.

"It seems this chamber is the final beacon, pointing to the last one," as he spoke, he stepped sideways along the other long wall. "The people who built this were pre-Egyptian. They were the founders of the first civilization in this region of the world. The pharaohs, the pyramids, all of the great things the subsequent empires left, were as a result of the people who created this room." He paused his speech for a moment as he finished reading the symbols. "It seems they came from a land far to the east of here."

"How far east, Professor?" Sean asked eagerly.

Firth was still staring at some of the symbols. His forehead wrinkled, perplexed at something he'd read. "That is preposterous," he commented vaguely. "There's nothing there to find."

"Where, Doctor? What does it say?" Sean pressed and stepped a little closer.

The professor removed the glasses from his face and rubbed his nose for a second. "You were right about the timeline of events. Either this is the most elaborate hoax I have ever seen," he jabbed a thumb at the nearest wall, "or we may have stumbled upon evidence of Biblical proportions. Quite literally, it would seem." He chuckled at the last part.

Sean turned to Adriana for a moment then back to Firth. "What are you saying?"

Firth drew in a deep breath and rolled his eyebrows in surrender. "The inscriptions suggest that the people who left this room here were direct descendants of Noah."

"Now, that is interesting," Sean agreed and took a closer step to the golden wall. Then his eyes became wider. "It's all starting to make sense." The declaration piqued the interest of the other two.

"We found references to a great flood when we found the first chamber in Georgia. Mac said that there was a plausible theory that ancient Egyptians could have colonized the Americas thousands of years ago," he ignored Firth's skeptical raised eyebrow and continued. "We found more Biblical references to the Genesis account in South America. And now this."

He seemed to be trying to recollect something, and stepped away. Adriana could see the gears turning in his mind.

"What is it?" She wondered.

"The stones," he responded vaguely. "That is the secret of the stones."

She shook her head. "I don't understand. What secret."

"The first stone Tommy found had two birds on it, divided by a line. According to the ark story, Noah released two birds from the top of the boat to see if they were near dry land. The first was a raven, the second, a dove." His face became perplexed as he crossed his arms and continued to think. "But I don't understand the connection. Why the Americas? Why would they go through all that trouble to colonize a land so far away? And I don't understand the need to leave these golden chambers like a series of ancient bread crumbs to lead them back."

"Perhaps they didn't leave to colonize a new world," a new voice came from the other end of the room. A man stepped from the darkness as they spun and shone their lights on him. He wore black, loose fitting pants and a matching tunic and turban. His face was dark, contrasted only by his darker hair, eyebrows, and beard. The man's appearance wasn't what Sean paid the most attention to. It was the gun in the stranger's hand.

He considered reaching for his Springfield that was holstered around his waist, but he had a feeling the best he could do was get his hand on it before he was cut down. So, he stood still with both hands to his side.

"Who are you?" Sean inquired. "What did you do with Dr. Abdulkarim?"

The man smiled a sinister grin as he stepped closer. He was only ten feet away. "Who do you think called us?"

"Us?" Adriana asked.

Dr. Firth had begun slinking away toward the wall but had run out of real estate.

"We are the protectors of the ark, Miss Villa. We have been following your exploits for some time," he redirected the latter sentence toward Sean.

"I'm flattered," Sean quipped sarcastically.

"You and your friend were able to stumble upon something that has been hidden for over five thousand years."

Sean was incredulous. "I wouldn't say stumble. It took a lot of hard work and research to—"

"Silence," the man ordered and brandished the weapon threateningly. "We will protect the ark at all costs. It must never fall into the hands of man. Immortality is only for the righteous."

Sean's eyes narrowed at the last statement. "I've heard that phrase before," he spoke in a tone full of curiosity more than fear. "It was one of the clues Tommy and I found. What I want to know is what is so special about that boat that you and your friends seem hell-bent on protecting it, and Alexander Lindsey will do anything to find it."

The last statement caught the man off guard. "You speak of the man who came here before? He is of no concern. Several of my brethren are en route to intercept this man, Lindsey. Before the sun sets tonight, he will be in our custody."

"I hope you sent a lot of men, because Lindsey sure will," Sean stared threateningly into the man's eyes.

He wasn't sure who he would cheer for in a fight like that. But he had a gut instinct about the man in front of him with the gun. "You said your job was to protect the ark. What does that gig pay?"

"We have protected the ark of Noah for thousands of years. To serve the order is a great honor," the man inched closer still. "Every one of us would die to keep it safe. And we would kill as well." He finished the last sentence and lifted the barrel of his gun.

"All for some ancient boat," Sean prodded.

"It is more than a boat, Mr. Wyatt. Your lack of knowledge concerning the contents of the ark proves that you are unworthy."

"That may be," Sean's words came out just above a whisper. "But you should never get too close to your target."

He dipped to his left and brought his right leg around in a swift kick. The gun barrel fired, sending a bullet pinging off of the metal walls. Firth ducked down and tried to protect himself with his arms over his head.

Adriana reacted instantly, launching herself at the mysterious man and wrapping her hands around his neck. Sean gripped the man's arm and twisted it in an awkward direction, causing the victim to scream and drop to his knees.

The weapon fell to the floor with a clank. Sean reached down and grabbed it immediately then stretched it out toward the man in the tunic who was struggling to breathe with Adriana's strong arms around his neck.

"Stop squirming around," Sean ordered in low tone. "A bullet to the head is better than her snapping your neck. And I guarantee you she knows how." His warning seemed to catch the man's attention and he ceased his escape efforts. "Now, who are you?"

"My name..."he tried to speak but his voice was cut off by the tight forearm around his throat.

Sean motioned for Adriana to loosen her grip a little. When she complied, the man let out a desperate gasp.

"Try again," Sean's sarcastic tone carried no empathy.

"My name matters not, American. Our mission is the only thing of importance. You can kill me if you wish. You will never get out of here alive."

If there were others like him waiting above ground, leaving would be a difficult task indeed. Something about Sean's instincts told him the man wasn't bluffing.

"I don't want to kill anyone," he responded. "I never do."

"Empty words from a man with so much blood on his hands, Sean Wyatt," the captive spat.

Sean ignored the barb. "We've all done some things we're not proud of. I'm sure you have too. But right now, I am trying to figure out where Alexander Lindsey is headed. He has the only clue that will lead to the final chamber."

The stranger's dark eyes became slits. "And why do you seek the last chamber, Sean Wyatt? For glory? Wealth? Fame?"

"I don't give a crap about any of that," Sean laughed.

"All you Americans are the same. You only seek the temporary pleasures of this world."

"No," Sean shook his head. "I've had money. Still have some. And I don't care about fame. What I care about is history, good coffee, football, motorcycles, family, and friends. Not in that order. I don't know why Alexander Lindsey wants to find the last chamber so badly. We heard there might be something that can make humans immortal. As far as I know, that's an old fairy tale that has been the cause of way too much pain. But if you know something about it, and you want to help us stop a bad person from finding your precious ark, then I would speak up now before I put a little more blood on my hands."

The Arab's eyes peered unwaveringly into Sean's soul, searching for a crack, a weakness that would give away his true intentions. It was a game Sean had played many times, and his poker face was the best around.

"I am Jabez," the stranger blurted out finally. "I am the leader of The Order of Guardians."

Sean lowered the weapon to his side and motioned for Adriana to let him go. "See, that wasn't so hard. Was it?"

The man slumped forward, coughing for a minute on one knee. He regained his composure and his breath, and stood back up in an attempt to look more dignified.

Dr. Firth had watched the exchange from the safety of his corner. He had been silent the entire time. "I have heard of your group," he spoke with fearful reverence. "Only rumors about shadows and ghosts."

Jabez turned his attention to the old man. "We try to remain as invisible as possible," he sneered.

"We need your help," Sean stated plainly, regaining the Arab's attention. "We don't know where the next marker is that points to the final chamber. If Lindsey gets there before us, he will have access to whatever it is he's looking for. I have a feeling that will not be a good thing."

"We do not know the exact location of the ark of Noah. That is not our purpose. Our mission is only to keep the wicked at bay. If this Lindsey has the final clue to the ark's location, they will most likely be headed to the Valley of the Eight in eastern Turkey."

"Eastern Turkey?" Sean wondered. "Why would they be headed there?"

"Because," Jabez smirked, "that is the location of Mount Ararat. I assume you have heard that story." The stranger seemed to relax a little.

"Yeah," Sean nodded, "I've heard it. Big boat on top of a mountain. Doesn't seem feasible to me. I don't think there is enough water on this planet to cover twenty thousand feet of mountain."

"What you think is irrelevant. This Lindsey will not find the last chamber on Ararat."

"Just to be safe," Adriana eased over to Sean's side. "We'd still like to make sure they don't." Her dark, piercing eyes were mesmerizing and intimidating all at once.

Jabez studied the two of them, largely ignoring Firth who still stood cautiously off to the side. Sean could tell he was weighing his options, which were not great at that point. He cursed himself under his breath for letting Wyatt take his weapon. But there was nothing he could do. Sean had shown an act of good faith by lowering the gun. But distrust was written all over the Arab's face.

"Do you three know what treasure awaits in the final chamber?" he asked after several moments of consideration.

Sean and Adriana glanced at each other before Sean spoke up again. "The clues suggest that the tree of life is there, though, I am skeptical at best on that. However, if there really is some kind of fountain of youth-type thing there, we cannot let Lindsey get to it."

"And why not?" Jabez raised an eyebrow. For a guy with no gun in a gunfight, he was pressing his luck as far as he could.

"Because anyone who is that desperate, calculating, and cold blooded, cannot have righteous intentions for something so powerful. And like you said, immortality is for the righteous."

"And you do not wish to be immortal?" he asked boldly while taking a step forward. His loose black clothes ruffled around him dramatically.

"No," Sean shook his head, grinning to one corner of his mouth. "I don't think I want to be around forever in this old world. And I'm definitely not righteous. I'm a sinner."

They were lost without the clue to the next marker. But it seemed like the mysterious stranger could help. He knew where Lindsey was headed. Even though the stranger had given up that little tidbit, Sean had a feeling there was something he was keeping back. Sean decided to take one more leap of faith. He flipped the gun around in his hand and gripped it by the barrel then slowly extended it out to the Arab.

Jabez nodded slowly as he reached out and grasped the weapon. "Your trust has earned my allegiance, Sean Wyatt. I will honor that trust. Your eyes are honest. I believe that you do not seek the treasure for selfish gain. You have my gun, and my sword." He bowed deeply in a dramatic gesture.

Firth's mouth was agape. "You mean you're going to trust this...

this man, who moments ago, was going to kill us and leave us for dead in this...this tomb?"

Sean twisted his head around. "Oh, hey, Doc. I honestly forgot you were there for a second. And it isn't a tomb. No one was actually ever buried here."

The sarcastic comment cut the tension with the other two, but only served to rile the professor. He pulled Sean close by the sleeve of his shirt and lowered his voice. "How do you know you can trust him?"

Sean was still grinning the mischievous smile that made his cheeks dimple on both sides. "I can't, Doc." He slapped the professor on the back.

A few minutes later, the group was trudging back through the darkness of the tunnel, the only light was the spotty glow that came from the flashlights. For the first few minutes, no one said anything. Dr. Abdulkarim seemed to feel particularly awkward. Sean had given him a cold glance when they'd climbed back up the ladder to where the man had waited.

"So, are you one of them?" Sean had asked the portly, dark-skinned man. He didn't try to hide the fact that he was annoyed by the betrayal from earlier.

"No," he shook his head and continued pressing forward through the darkness. "I am a friend to their cause," he replied. "The Brethren are very influential. Their connections help get me permits to do excavations in places I normally wouldn't be allowed. In short, they help eliminate the red tape that usually surrounds my line of research."

"And all you have to do is call them whenever you find something or someone goes snooping where they aren't supposed to," Sean's words carried a snicker of derision.

In truth, he wished more of the world's decent archaeologists could be afforded similar luxuries. It was something he'd grown tired of during his time with IAA. There were several things he'd grown tired of, the more he thought about it. He had been hoping to have a job where he got to travel, study ancient cultures, and use some of his less-violent skill sets. But he had found that travel seemed overrated. There were no real free moments for him to get out into the communities and dig into the local cultures. It had become a routine, just like anything else. Except for the last few months.

Being shot at and nearly killed on several occasions were just the kinds of stress Sean was trying to get away from when he left the agency. The more he thought about it, the more he considered telling Tommy what he'd been planning.

No one knew about his little retirement scheme. At the moment, it was rattling around in his head like a pinball. He'd purchased two pieces of land, one in the mountains near the Tennessee/North Carolina border, and the other a few miles east of the busy beach town of Destin, Florida. The cabin in the mountains would be finished within the next few weeks. But the bungalow in Florida was already completed. It was within walking distance to the beach, and in a small area where traffic was low, and tourists were non-existent.

He'd thought about different things he could do to keep busy. While there were several surf shops around the region, he found there were surprisingly few paddleboard and sea kayak shops. Kayaking had been something he'd had a vague interest in for a while. But once he'd gotten out onto a lake and tried it, he was ready for more. The plan had started formulating in his mind to open up a kayaking shop that also had paddle boards. Making money wasn't the point. He'd saved up enough over the years to live on the rest of his life. He just wanted to get away yet still have something to occupy his time.

A draft of air blew into the passageway, forecasting that the group had nearly reached ground level. A beam of sunlight poured into the entry chamber through the portal in the front, illuminating one portion of the chiseled wall on the other side. When they exited the ruins, each member of the party was forced to shield their faces from the bright Egyptian sun. After a few minutes, their eyes began to adjust. Sean looked around at a group of men dressed similarly to Jabez, all surrounding them in a semi-circle. Each man held a black, sub-machine gun. Instinctively, Sean put his hands up as the men in black clothing came into focus. Adriana and Firth did the same as their eyes began to clear up.

"Jabez, I thought we had a deal," Sean said. He noticed his driver, Sahid, sitting on a chair nearby, being watched by another one of the brethren.

The young Arab seemed terrified. Sean had seen that look on a lot of faces the first time they'd had a gun pointed at them. He wondered what his own face had looked like on his initial experience.

Jabez turned around and ordered the men in to lower their weapons in something that closely resembled Arabic. They did as he commanded then he spoke a few more words. Seconds later, they were hurriedly loading up into tan-colored Range Rovers. The two who had been guarding Sahid also ran off to one of the nearby vehicles, leaving their captive confused and somewhat bewildered. The leader of the strange group walked over to a thick, mustached man who stood next to one of the vehicles. They exchanged words for a minute, ending with Jabez giving a few quick nods.

He stalked back over to where Sean and the others were standing. Firth's arms were crossed, clearly annoyed with whatever was going on. Adriana seemed to be a little more patient, standing with one hand on a hip. A few of the men in the trucks were staring at her with wide eyes. She was probably the first woman the men had seen in a while, assuming they were nomads of some type. Though, it was possible they had wives somewhere, and they just weren't used to seeing a woman not being covered from head to toe.

"My men said that the ones you spoke of are on their way back to Cairo. We have three cars in pursuit. The clue will be in our possession before nightfall." Jabez's confidence was genuine.

But Sean had a feeling it wouldn't be so easy. "I hope you're right," he warned. "Lindsey has surrounded himself with a group of mercenaries who follow him religiously. They even call him The Prophet."

"And why do they call him that?" Jabez scoffed.

"I don't know. I guess they think he's some kind of a religious guru. All I'm saying is your men should be careful. I've come face to face with some of his group. Taking him down won't be easy. And these mercenaries are like weeds. You pull one and three more pop up."

"My men can handle themselves."

"Fair enough. Still, I think we'd both feel a lot better if we were on a plane headed to Turkey."

Jabez nodded and turned, heading back to one of the Range Rovers. Sean motioned to Sahid and the young Middle Easterner bounced up out of his chair and jogged over to one of the big tents. A few moments later, he and the others from Sean's convoy appeared through the flaps of the tent in the blinding sunlight, and began loading up their vehicles. Sean cast an apologetic glance at Sahid as the young man headed toward him.

"I didn't sign up for this," Sahid complained in a whiny, heavily accented voice.

"I know," Sean held his hands up in a pleading manner. "I didn't think any of this was going to happen."

"Your company pays us well, Mr. Wyatt. But we are going back to Cairo. No amount of money is worth dying for."

Sahid turned around and stormed off, headed toward the SUVs that had brought them over from the Luxor train station. Jabez twisted his head with a smug grin on his face.

"Need a ride back to Cairo, my friend?"

Sean gave a questioning look to Adriana and Professor Firth before answering. "Seems that way."

"Not to worry," Jabez had a playful glimmer in his eyes, a strange site for such a hardened exterior. "I know a way we can make up for lost time."

14

Will woke up to a searing bright light. His face felt warm, telling him the sun was the cause of the brightness. He ached in several places, particularly on the side of his head where a constant pounding was taking place. He grimaced as he tried to sit up. The surface underneath him was hard. He realized he lying on a mixture of dirt, sand, and rocks. His vision was blurred, at first, and he wondered how long he'd been unconscious. Fifteen feet beyond his feet, train tracks stretched out for miles in two directions. It was then he began to recall the events of the previous night.

His thoughts jumped to the man who'd pulled the trigger. The scruffy-faced blonde had been lucky. *Why had Wyatt been up at that time of night on the train?* Will guessed Sean likely had problems sleeping. It was one thing they must have had in common. Will hadn't had a decent night's sleep in years, and he figured his enemy was probably wired the same way. Thoughts of sleep caused his eyes to get groggy again. Irrational ideas began seeping into his mind. *Just lie (should this be lie?) down over by those rocks and rest for a bit.* He shook his head, forcing himself to sit up a little more. Sean Wyatt had gotten the better of him. He couldn't let that happen again.

His plan had been to enter the train car where Wyatt and his friends were sleeping, and execute each one with a toxin that stops the heart. It would have been simple enough. A quick injection into the neck and the victim would be dead before they could feel the prick of the needle. He wouldn't have even had to dispose of the bodies. Will could have simply gotten off the train at Luxor and met up with The Prophet. Instead, it had been his body that rolled onto the rocky sand in south Egypt. He counted himself fortunate to be alive.

The thought reminded him of the round that Wyatt had fired, reminding him of the terrible soreness on the right side of his chest. He pulled a cell phone out of his inner jacket pocket. The device had been equipped with a titanium case, and was nearly indestructible. A bullet from Wyatt's gun had disproved that, putting a huge dent through the back of the case. The phone would be useless. But it had saved his life. Will stared reflectively at the warped bullet imbedded in the keypad then tossed the device in the dirt.

He leaned over on one knee and tried to push himself onto his feet. He wavered for a few seconds, the world spinning around him suddenly. He got back down on his knees again to let everything settle before attempting to stand. His head continued to throb, and he felt a large bump on the side of it, just an inch away from his temple. There was a little blood, but nothing life-threatening. He must have hit a rock on the tumble out of the train, which also explained the dizziness.

Will knew he had to regain his senses, and find a way to contact his employer. The Prophet was, no doubt, expecting his report, and knowing Lindsey, the old man had probably called several times throughout the day.

He glanced down at his Bulgari watch to check the time. Many people didn't even wear watches anymore. They simply went by the time on their phones. Will had always felt a connection to some of the more old-fashioned ways, in some regards. At present, he was thankful for that, otherwise he would have no clue as to what time of day it was. The hands on the watch face claimed it was a little after noon. He'd been out for a long time.

Beyond the train tracks, he noticed a car speeding along in the distance. *A road.* He doubted there would be a lot of traffic on the lonely desert highway, but someone would come along sooner or later. His eyes searched the warm earth as he found the strength to stand up straight. His coordination had finally returned, and the spinning had stopped. A few feet away, he found what he was looking for. It was a rock, just the right size to hide in his jacket. He wondered if it was the culprit responsible for his incredible headache.

Will removed his windbreaker and reached down for the stone then wrapped it up in the fabric. He headed for the road several hundred yards away. His hand involuntarily clutched his chest where the bullet had struck. It was possible he had a cracked rib, at best a bad bruise. His knee was a little tight. He'd probably hit it on something on the way down. But he didn't have time to think about diagnoses. He had to catch a ride.

Which direction, though? He considered the problem as he slowly made his way toward the stretch of highway. If Lindsey and his lackey Frenchman had been able to secure the clue they sought, they would no doubt be headed back to Cairo. The Prophet's private plane was still there and they would need to take it to wherever they were headed next.

However, Will had failed in his mission to eliminate Wyatt and his friends. If the IAA agent had arrived while Lindsey was still investigating the site, everything could have gone haywire.

Will shrugged off the thought. He reminded himself that The Prophet's mission was doing the will of God: to cleanse the earth of the wicked. And some former government agent turned treasure hunter couldn't stand in the way of that.

As he neared the highway, he saw a beat up Honda hatchback rolling his way. The gray car was old, but it would do the job. He limped hurriedly, covering the last fifty yards as quickly as possible. He reached the asphalt with a few seconds to spare and stood in the middle of the lane to wave down the driver. Will put on the most helpless expression possible, and attempted to look desperate.

The car rolled to a stop; Will hobbled over to the driver's side. An older, Middle Eastern man with thinning gray hair and sporadic facial hair rolled down the window. His skin seemed to be hanging off his facial bones. He looked up at Will, but said nothing.

"Thank you so much for stopping," Will smiled as meekly as possible. Even in his weakened condition, Will knew the man wouldn't be much of a struggle.

The driver must not have spoken English, but pointed to the passenger's seat: a ragged, torn upholstery with one of those beaded cushions over top of it. Will grabbed the door handle, holding the concealed rock in the other hand. His smile turned to a wicked grin. The man's dead eyes just stared back at him, unaware of what was about to happen.

"No," Will shook his head. "If you don't mind, I think I'll drive."

15

EGYPTIAN DESERT

Kaba steered Alexander Lindsey's SUV down the highway. She touched a finger to her ear, checking in on the two vehicles behind her.

She had been born of Middle Eastern decent, born and raised in Syria. But she had left the religion of Islam behind. She had always felt the belief system to be harsh on women, and longed to be free of it. She was also repulsed by fundamentalists. Both of her parents had been killed in a terrorist bombing by a radical Islamic group. They hadn't been the targets, just innocent bystanders in the wrong place at the wrong time. But it had been the last straw for her.

Young Kaba spent several weeks in mourning before swearing to avenge her parents' death. She first trained herself in the arts of self-defense. When she wanted more, she found a man in the city who was rumored to have knowledge of more advanced training. She spent two years under his tutelage, learning a vast array of fighting and weapons techniques.

When she'd finished her training, Kaba traveled a little, wanting to see the world outside of her homeland. She had wandered into a bar just outside of Istanbul, and bumped into a group of men there. She overheard them discussing something about their next job, and noticed they were dressed like they were either private security, or some kind of terrorists. Since they were white, she figured it wasn't the latter.

While the men were having their drinks, an assassin leapt out from the shadows behind her, a long blade wielded from his hand. His target was the man nearest her, a guy with short, black hair and streaks of gray through it. The man had his back to her and the assailant. For some reason, she felt the need to assist.

She stepped out with one foot and brought a hand up to knock away the attacker's hand that carried the knife. Kaba spun around and brought her other elbow into the neck of the assassin, sinking it deep into his throat beneath the scarf that covered his skin. The man gurgled for a few seconds, dropping the blade and clutching at his crushed larynx.

The man with the peppered hair spun around, gun drawn. His two companions slid off of their stools, ready for a fight. Instead, they saw a Middle Eastern woman in black pants and a ruffled blouse standing over the would-be attacker.

The group's leader gave her a grateful glance with an eyebrow raised then nodded his appreciation. She said nothing, and watched as the others grabbed the assassin off of the floor under his arms and drag him out a side door.

"Thanks," the middle-aged man said before following the others outside.

Kaba didn't respond, partially because she didn't speak a lot of English, but also because she didn't know how to respond. Instead, she waited for the door to the bar to close, then left out the same exit, leaving the few remaining patrons and the bartender standing with mouths and eyes wide at what had transpired.

Outside, she trailed the men into a dark alley. She ducked behind a trash bin and peered around the corner. The man she'd struck in the throat was lying motionless on the wet pavement, surrounded by broken glass, and trash. She wondered if he was dead, not because she was concerned. It was more out of curiosity.

The leader of the group stood off to the side as the others

searched the pockets of the unconscious man. They found piece of paper, but she couldn't tell what was on it. One of the men handed the paper to the guy in charge who looked at it with contained curiosity. He stuffed the piece in his back pocket and pulled out his pistol. She stared at him as he attached a long, black tube to the end of the barrel then extended the weapon out toward the man on the ground. He fired two shots into the assassin's head then ordered the others to dump the body in the trash bin. When he did so, he noticed her watching and grinned. Unsure if she was in trouble, she ducked back for a moment. Her breath came in quick gasps and her heart pounded in her chest as the black boot of the man she'd saved landed just in front of her feet.

"You saved my life back there in the bar." His voice was gruff, and carried years in its tone. "Where did you learn how to do that?"

His eyebrow was still raised as it had been inside the bar. His mouth parted in a thin crease of a smile, an attempt to put away any thoughts of danger.

"We could use a woman like you," he went on. "Let me know if you're interested in some work.

The loud sound of the body hitting the bottom of the trash bin caused her to shudder for a second. Kaba looked up into the man's eyes. She didn't know what kind of work he was offering, but she guessed he could show her the kind of world she was looking for. One where she could utilize her uncommon skills in a way that could benefit her most.

Kaba joined up with the man she came to know as Don, though she doubted that was his real name. None of the other men in his little group used their Christian names. They were mercenaries, guns for hire. Most of the work they ended up doing was dirty work the western governments of the world didn't want to do themselves. After a few years, she had gained a reputation in the darker circles of the mercenary world. It was a reputation that had led Alexander Lindsey to hire her on to lead his security team.

Her mind snapped back to the long, desert road ahead. She heard something in her earpiece and touched her hand to it again.

"Handle it," she ordered in a thick accent.

Lindsey had been staring out at the desert landscape on the way back to Cairo. They were only a few hours away now. But something was wrong. He'd over heard the communication by his driver and leaned up to find out what the problem was.

"What is it?"

The woman glanced back in the rear view mirror, her eyes concealed by wire-framed sunglasses. "Someone is following us," she answered plainly. "Three tan Range Rovers. They caught up to our last vehicle pretty fast. Looks like they may be a threat."

"Are they Egyptian government?"

"Don't think so, Sir. We'll take care of it."

Lindsey leaned back in his chair, but said nothing else. He seemed unconcerned, which was a stark contrast to DeGard who appeared very uncomfortable.

"There are people following us?" He asked in his nasally accent.

"Not to worry. My men will take care of it," Lindsey responded casually.

DeGard shifted in his seat, looked back for a moment, then tightened his seatbelt. He felt in his pocket to make sure the small bag of treasure he'd filled in the Nekhen ruins was secure, just in case.

Lindsey's black-clad men in the third vehicle of the convoy rolled down the back windows and leaned out on both sides, automatic sub-machine guns aimed at the first of the tan Range Rovers. They didn't hesitate, opening a barrage of bullets at the trailing vehicle. The Range Rover swerved, trying to dodge the hail of metal coming their way. The evasive maneuvers almost took out one of the other vehicles in their group. A flurry of bullets struck the hood, a few cracked through the windshield. The Rover slowed down to regroup and get out of range for a few seconds. The men in the back and in the passenger's side mimicked Lindsey's men and stuck their weapons out of open windows to return fire. The driver stepped on the gas and quickly caught back up to the last vehicle of the convoy.

Their AK-47s fired loudly back at the black SUV. But the recoil and difficulty of shooting from a moving vehicle made accuracy a problem. One or two rounds found their way into the back gate of their target, but did little damage.

"Aim for the tires!" the driver shouted in Arabic as they drew closer.

The words had no sooner come out of the man's mouth when another volley of bullets came from the barrels of the car in front of them. Three rounds struck him in the chest, causing him to lose control of the truck. As he leaned over the wheel, a thin trail of blood oozing from the corner of his mouth, the Range Rover lurched sharply to the right. Before it could run off the road, it flipped sideways, tumbling down the asphalt in a barrel roll, spilling the occupants in different directions.

The remaining two Range Rovers slowed momentarily to avoid hitting the wreckage then sped back up, returning fire as they neared. They approached side by side, taking up both lanes with no oncoming traffic in site. A bullet caught one of Lindsey's men in the chest, and he dangled lifelessly out of the window for a moment before gravity pulled him down. The body rolled off the pavement and into the desert sand.

The Rover on the left pulled up alongside the trailing SUV and opened fire, sending dozens of bullets through the gunman on that side and the back of the driver's seat. The SUV suddenly jerked sideways and launched over a nearby hill, disappearing in a cloud of dust and smoke.

Lindsey's driver looked back again in the rear view mirror, slightly more concerned than she had been before. "Take them out," she commanded in a stern tone.

The men in the left lane were reloading when a new wave of bullets came from the second vehicle in the convoy. They were forced to slow down for a moment, keeping at a safe distance until they could return fire. The other Rover took their place and began to pull alongside the black SUV. Lindsey's men poured rounds at the tan vehicle until suddenly, the front right tire burst. The truck wobbled back and forth for a few seconds, skidding across both lanes, finally coming to a stop on the side of the road.

The lone remaining Range Rover sped past with men and guns protruding from both sides. The gun barrels popped rapidly, peppering the back of the target vehicle with holes. One bullet struck a gunman on the driver's side in the neck. The man dropped his weapon and grasped his neck before tumbling out of the window and onto the road. The brethren's truck ran over the rolling body, and kept in pursuit. With no threat on that side of the car, the driver of the Rover pulled the hood of his vehicle up next to the back of the target. The other SUV swerved left, trying to keep the attackers at bay, and force them to approach from the passenger's side where two gunmen were taking aim. The tan truck's driver accommodated and quickly jerked the car back into the right lane.

The move by Lindsey's man would have been a good idea, had the driver been paying more attention to the other lane in front of him. But he was more occupied with the gunman to the rear, and never saw the big rig speeding his way. The black SUV crashed into the heavy tractor-trailer truck with a loud boom, leaving little left of it other than a pile of smoking, twisted metal.

Kaba looked back at the wreckage and the last remaining Range Rover approaching quickly.

"You two should get down," she said, matter-of-factly.

For the first time in the scenario, Lindsey had taken on the same concerned expression as his French companion. Both men ducked down behind the leather seats, DeGard covered his ears with his hands.

The tan Rover approached, guns blazing from the passenger's side. A blizzard of bullets riddled the back and side of the vehicle, shattering the window above the crouching Frenchman and pounding the metal door just next to him.

"Take the wheel," the driver ordered coolly to the man in the passenger's side.

The younger, blonde man in the other seat did as he was told and gripped the wheel, holding it steady as Kaba pulled a Glock .40 from a shoulder holster and rolled down her window.

The Range Rover was pulling up alongside them when she

whipped the pistol up with both hands and squeezed off one shot into the head of the driver in the other truck. The attacker's vehicle slow immediately and veered off the road, going airborne over a dune, and flipping violently front over back in the desert sand.

Kaba re-holstered the weapon and took back the wheel.

"You're safe now, sir." She said, keeping her eyes forward. She never even glanced back at the two men crouched in the rear seat.

DeGard rose up hesitantly, and looked back at the now empty road. A pillar of smoke wafted up from the accident with the 18-wheeler but was out of sight sixty seconds later. Lindsey straightened up and pressed down his jacket, removing the wrinkles.

"Well done," he applauded his driver, impressed at her composure. "Well done, indeed. You see, Monsieur DeGard, nothing to worry about."

The archaeologist looked back again at the empty road then at his employer. He wanted to say so much, but thought better of it and bit his tongue. Several men had just lost their lives, some of them Lindsey's, and the old man seemed relatively unaffected. Expendable resources. That's how the man so many called The Prophet viewed them, and probably him too.

He was beginning to regret signing on for the job. But a quick check in his jacket pocket reminded him of what awaited if he could see it through.

16

EGYPTIAN DESERT

Will slowed the gray hatchback to a stop. A tan SUV lay on its side, a tangled mess of twisted metal. Coolant, gasoline, and other fluids had leaked all over the road. A reddish trail of blood mingled with it. The driver was dead, his body lying on the shattered window against the ground. There were three other bodies strewn along the road within a fifty-foot radius of the wreckage. Will got out of the car and took a closer inspection of the trashed vehicle.

It was a Range Rover. The occupants were all wearing matching outfits, scarves, and turbans. There were AK-47s lying around near the wreck, too. *The men were armed*. Will searched what was left of the vehicle and found a few pistols, then stuffed them in his pants. They weren't the quality he'd grown accustomed to, but a gun was a gun at that point. And he needed one, but he wasn't about to carry around one of the AKs. He found them bulky, unreliable, and inaccurate. Precision, particularly, was something he valued desperately.

Upon closer inspection of the Range Rover, Will noticed something else that was peculiar: bullet holes. He ran his finger along the metal and into the indention where the paint flaked off. He looked down on the asphalt and noticed something metallic shining in the bright sun. He picked up the object and examined it. *I recognize this shell.* His eyes gazed north, up the highway. He could see some smoke on the horizon, bringing a smile to his face. From the looks of it, The Prophet's team was holding its own. But he needed to make sure.

Will started to get back in the car then remembered the body still stuffed in the hatchback. The accident site seemed like a logical place to drop it off. After all, the mortal wounds left by the rock would seem like a natural occurrence due to such a violent crash.

He carelessly dumped the body out on the ground then sped off down the road. Will had only gone about another mile when he saw one of Lindsey's SUVs off on the side of the pavement. He pulled over again, this time to see if it was the car his employer was in. The bodies lying around were hired guns. No sign of The Prophet.

Will immediately knew what had happened. There had been some kind of a chase. The men in the tan Range Rover had attacked Lindsey's convoy. *But why? Who would have done something like that? Random terrorists?* It was certainly possible. And with the country's political state in an upheaval, it could be highly probable that Lindsey's caravan had fallen prey to bandits or terrorists.

Will got back in the car and pushed up the road until he came to an empty SUV. There was no one around, but he did notice one of the tires was flat. Probably shot by one of his boss's mercenaries. He kept moving, only slowing down slightly as he passed the vacant vehicle. Then, he saw the source of the smoke that was wafting into the dry, desert air. One of Lindsey's black SUVs had been crushed like a can, running directly into an 18-wheeler. The big rig had been hauling steel I-beams, and when combined with the momentum of the truck, the SUV hadn't stood a chance in that game of chicken.

A corpse lay on the road, dead hands still clutching his sub-machine gun. Both legs stuck out at awkward angles, and a blunt-force head wound oozed a line of blood down the black road. Another body, nearly bent in half, dangled out of one of the back passenger windows. The driver and front seat passenger couldn't be seen for all the metal, plastic, glass, and wires. Safe to assume they were dead. No one could have survived that. The driver of the rig had, apparently, hit the windshield. He was slumped over the wheel underneath cracked glass and a smeared blood stain.

Still no sign of The Prophet.

Will was glad for that, but he tempered his relief. Up ahead, off to the side of the road was another wrecked vehicle, just over a rocky dune. A man clad in loose-fitting black clothes was standing nearby and saw the car approaching.

Must be one of the men who'd attacked Lindsey's convoy. Probably a good idea to finish the job.

The man hobbled out in front of the car hoping Will would slow down and offer help. Will Hastings did the exact opposite. He stepped on the accelerator and steered the car right at the injured stranger. The man's eyes grew wide as he saw what was happening, and tried to lunge out of the way. Upon seeing his target's sudden movement, he made the corresponding steering wheel adjustment and guided the car to where the man had dived.

The left side of the vehicle rose and dropped two times in quick succession, like it would have going over a speed bump. Will slowed down slightly, only to look back in the mirror to make sure the man was dead. The body lay completely still on its side, so he kept on driving. A few miles passed with no other signs of battle. Will suspected that meant his employer had made it through the gauntlet safely.

He remembered the rendezvous point that he and Lindsey had discussed before departing for Luxor. At the time, Will had thought the idea of a meeting place in Cairo to be moot. If things had gone according to plan, they would have met up in Luxor. Now, he was glad they'd made precautions. His phone was gone, which was a problem. Fortunately, he remembered how to get where he was going. His foot pressed harder on the accelerator, and the car picked up speed, rolling down the empty highway. He hoped Lindsey would wait for him. One, because he needed to be paid. And two, it was time for Will to finish off Sean Wyatt, once and for all.

17

EGYPTIAN DESERT

Sean had been on his share of airplanes. From small, one-prop puddle jumpers, to jet fighters, he'd pretty much seen it all. He had never traveled in the back of an old cargo plane before, but it didn't seem to bother him much. Professor Firth, on the other hand, was quite uncomfortable.

Jabez and his men had hurried them over to a local airstrip, if it could be called that. The airport was little more than a flattened out field of dirt and sand. Their new acquaintance had a pilot in their group, along with an old twin-prop plane, a DC-3 if Sean hadn't missed his guess. Sean had seen lots of those kinds of planes in the movies, but he had never had the chance to get up close to one in real life. Now he was flying in one.

Despite the plane's age, it flew fairly steadily, though the few times they hit pockets of turbulence, the metal body creaked and moaned as if it might bend, and eventually snap in two. Sean was unconcerned about that. The professor was an entirely different story. The older man leaned over with elbows on knees, trying not to get sick.

Adriana seemed unaffected, completely absorbed in a worn, leather-bound book. It carried a similar appearance to the diary they'd used to help find the chamber of gold in Ecuador. But it wasn't the same book. This one displayed Greek lettering on the outside, and had a strange marking in the center of the cover. The symbol looked like an ancient clock, or maybe a compass. It was hard to tell.

"We should arrive in Istanbul within a few hours," Jabez interrupted Sean's thoughts suddenly, approaching from the cockpit. "From there it is only a few hours drive to the Valley of the Eight."

Sean thought about the city. *Istanbul*. It was an odd mix of cosmopolitan life and old world tradition, thrown into a blender and set on puree. Very few places in the world had people's lives on display the way that town did. The poor, the wealthy, and the huge middle class were all out for everyone to see.

He hadn't been there for pleasure or people-watching though. Sean had been there on a mission with Axis. Those were memories he'd rather not relive. But as the plane cruised through the sky, he knew it was a distinct possibility.

"Have you ever been to Istanbul," Jabez sat down and looked over at him.

"Only once," Sean nodded.

"It is fascinating place."

"I didn't really get a chance to look around. I was trying to not get killed."

"Oh?" Jabez asked, puzzled.

"Yeah. I was there on a mission. Not as a tourist or a treasure hunter." He added air quotes to the last few words, remembering what had been said about his current agency.

Sean's Middle Eastern companion smirked at the comment. Six of Jabez's men had come with them on the plane. Each one of them stared straight ahead, like the guards outside Buckingham Palace.

"How did you, and all these other guys come to be in this order of guardians?" Sean waved a finger at the men on the other side of the plane.

"One does not choose to become a member. We were each chosen, picked by former members." As he spoke, Jabez stared across at his men with reverence.

"How did the Brethren come about? I think it's a little weird that you guys are the protectors of the ark, but you don't know its true location." Sean didn't try to hide his skepticism.

"We are direct descendants of Japheth, one of the three sons of Noah. When Canaan, Noah's grandson, left the Valley of the Eight, he swore that, someday his children would return and claim their rightful inheritance. Japheth made his sons take an oath to never let that happen. We are to keep the children of Canaan from finding the ark. The safest way to do that was to keep the true location of Noah's ship in total secrecy."

Sean frowned, clearly lost. Adriana had closed her book and scooted closer to listen in on the conversation. Seeing Sean to be a little confused, she spoke up.

"You are referring to the curse, aren't you?" The question seemed random, but Jabez's eyes widened slightly, telling her she'd hit the mark.

"What do you know about it?" His eyes continued to pierce hers.

She merely shrugged. "I have heard things."

"In your line of work, I am sure you hear many things. Don't you?"

She cocked her head sideways but never gave in to his stare, holding it firmly in her own. "It is advantageous to keep aware of whisperings in the shadows. That is where I get most of my information."

Sean listened intently to the conversation, wondering where it would lead.

Adriana went on. "The legend of the curse comes from the Bible, in the book of Genesis, to be precise." Jabez nodded, so she kept talking. "As the story goes, Noah became drunk one night. When his son, Ham, came into his tent, the scriptures say Ham laughed at his father. The other two brothers, Shem and Japheth, heard a commotion and came to see what was going on. Upon entering the tent, they saw their naked father and Ham, apparently shaming him. The other two boys clothed their father and took care of him."

The plane hit some turbulence, and dipped down quickly for a few seconds. The professor leaned over even further. His face was bright red, clearly on the brink of vomiting. He reached over and grabbed a small paper bag from a nearby rack then held it in front of his mouth, just in case.

Adriana ignored Firth, continuing her tale. "The texts said that God placed a cursed on Ham, and his descendants. In particular, his son Canaan would be the first to feel the curse, and all of his generations after."

"Very good," Jabez nodded. His eyes were slits, studying the Spanish woman. "I am impressed. You have learned your Bible stories. But what do you know of the stories not in the old books?"

Sean was basically on top of the two of them, as he pressed in further to better hear what she knew.

Adriana rolled her shoulders. "Just myths and legends."

Jabez continued his stare, as if willing the words to come from her mouth.

She finally submitted. "It is said that Canaan left the sacred mountain and the Valley of the Eight. He took his wife and children, moving southwest." The Arab nodded as she went on. "Canaan's family traveled far, going through what is now Jordan and Israel, to settle in Egypt."

Sean finally interrupted. "So, the first settlers of Egypt were the grandchildren of Noah from the Bible?" He sounded skeptical, though based on the things he'd seen over the past few months, anything was possible at this point.

"That's the legend," Adriana agreed.

Jabez cut in. "It is more than a legend, my friends. It is a historical fact."

The plane surged again. This time was the straw that broke the camel's back for Firth. He stumbled toward the back of the plane and heaved into the bag. Jabez raised a suspicious eyebrow.

"It seems the professor does not enjoy flying."

Firth was doubled over in the rear of the plane, but he heard the comment and twisted his head over his shoulder to cast an annoyed gaze. "I am sorry if I am just not used to flying in a cargo bay," he replied in a barbed tone.

Sean was intent on finishing the story. "So, Canaan left and came to Egypt. What does that have to do with the chambers, especially the ones in the western hemisphere?"

"Do you not see?" Jabez almost seemed sympathetic.

"No," Sean shook his head, clearly not connecting the dots.

Jabez took another deep breath. "When Canaan reached southern Egypt, he established a community there, in Nekhen. His ancestors became the first settlers of the ancient land."

Sean interrupted. "That would explain the old age of the site."

"Yes. But the ruins at Nekhen are only part of the story," Jabez apprised. "By the time they had settled the village, Canaan was a fairly old man. He had grown tired of running. So, he stayed in southern Egypt, where he died.

"After a generation had passed, many of the people in the area referred to Canaan as a minor deity. A few even claimed his father, Ham, was a god of gods. Many of the original Egyptian myths were derived from the stories of Canaan and his father. There were many, though, who remained true to the one God. And they remained afraid of the curse that had been placed upon their family."

"It all makes sense, now," Sean cut in again.

Adriana's eyes stitched together. "What do you mean?"

"All the stuff we found back in the U.S. down in South America. Tons of Egyptian artifacts." Sean could see she still didn't follow what he was getting at. "Before we found the first chamber, Mac told us that he believed the ancient Egyptians had built boats, capable of travelling vast distances. His theory was that the Egyptians travelled to the Americas in search of a new life and possibly more resources."

Jabez grinned slightly at the revelation.

Sean went on. "But what if they weren't coming over to establish a colony? What if they were running from something, something that was so powerful, it would mean the end for their entire existence as a people?" He thought for a moment, rubbing the right temple of his head to hone his thoughts. "The pyramids. The symbols. Even the language. All of it made its way to the Americas. We found pyramids in Georgia for crying out loud. I can't believe Mac was right about all that." The last part came with resignation.

"Yes, Mr. Wyatt. Now you see. Many children of Canaan built boats. It was easy for them since their ancestors had pioneered the idea." Jabez gave a good natured grin as he spoke.

Sean still seemed in a daze of hurried thoughts. "Mac said they found an ancient navy out in the middle of the desert not too long ago."

Jabez confirmed with a nod. "They went as far away as possible to escape the curse, traveling through what is now the United States and South America. The native cultures that were established are all descendants of the line of Canaan."

"And they left clues as to where they came from and how to get home," Adriana included.

"That is correct." Jabez wringed his hands for a minute in quiet contemplation. His fingers were worn, and dark, probably from years in the sun. The man was visibly concerned. On his face, Sean and Adriana could see the wheels were turning.

"How does your group fit in to all of this?" Sean voiced what his thoughts had rolled over for a few hours. "You said you were the descendants from the other sons of Noah. Then, you said you were chosen. Which is it?"

Jabez's face creased slightly at the question. "Good question. We believe every person in the world comes from one of the three sons of Noah. We are chosen based on that lineage. Though, now it must have surely been diluted. We consider ourselves descendants based on our creed more than blood at this point."

Firth seemed to have gotten over his nausea and was leaning back against the wall of the plane in an attempt to relax. His chest still heaved huge breaths, and his face was pale. The paper bag hung loosely in one hand.

He spoke up for the first time in a while, his eyes staring up at the ceiling as he did. "You still haven't told us how we will be able to find the ark. You said you don't know the location of it. If Lindsey has the clue, and we get there before he does, it won't make a difference. What are we going to do, sit around and watch where they go and simply follow?"

The grin on Jabez's face grew a little bigger. Wrinkles creased under his eyes. "Mr. Lindsey may not have the only clue to the ark's location."

18

CAIRO

A tin-colored airplane hangar sat off to the side of the main airstrip to Cairo's international airport. Inside, Alexander Lindsey's private jet, a white G6 Gulfstream, was revving up its twin engines, getting ready to depart. Lindsey had called ahead for the pilot to make preparations, so they could depart immediately upon arriving in Cairo.

Kaba whipped the vehicle around on the tarmac and stopped it inside the cavernous shelter next to a black Yukon Denali. Lindsey didn't wait for anyone to open the door for him, even though there were six men in tight, black outfits standing by when they pulled in. He had a plane to catch, and time was of the essence.

The old man flung open the door and shuffled toward the plane, moving faster than DeGard expected possible. The Frenchman took his time, allowing one of the bodyguards to open his door.

"Load everything up immediately," Lindsey ordered over his shoulder to Kaba.

She nodded and began issuing orders to the six men standing in a forward facing line near the other SUV. They simultaneously broke rank and began opening doors and unloading black plastic cargo boxes. They systematically carried the units over to the underside of the plane where a nearly empty storage bin awaited with a door propped open.

DeGard watched as the men busily emptied the vehicle and loaded the plane with the supplies. He frowned and raised a suspicious eyebrow. "Are you planning on starting a war? Or starting a colony?"

Lindsey had already begun his ascent of the stairs to board the plane. He looked back down at DeGard and frowned. "We are already in a war," he said loudly over the whine of the jet engines.

DeGard wasn't sure how to react, and simply stood at the base of the staircase, watching the older man as he disappeared into the innards of the plane. After a few moments, he followed reluctantly up the steps and into the cabin.

Inside, the interior of the G6 was luxurious. Every seat was upholstered in tan colored leather. The floor was a dark hardwood, contrasting the color tone of the leather seats. DeGard slipped into one of the backward facing seats across from his employer and fastened the seatbelt.

Lindsey was deep in thought, staring out the nearby window. His chin rested on the two middle fingers as his index finger slowly scratched the skin on his cheek. The white hair on his head was disheveled and scraggily, showing parts of his freckly skull beneath.

"What are you thinking about?" The Frenchman's voice was huskier than usual.

Lindsey snapped from his thoughts suddenly, slightly surprised. "It is a shame that Will hasn't reported in. I fear the worst has happened. It isn't like him to go more than a few hours without checking in."

DeGard offered no sympathy. "He is expendable. Just like all the other grunts who work for you." He shrugged and played his hands as if he were throwing away a piece of wadded up paper. "Let it go."

The old man's face boiled. His tired, gray eyes filled with fury, and he leaned over the space between the seats so he was close to level with DeGard's knees. "You shut your mouth, Frenchman, or I will shut it for you permanently. Do you understand? Will is not expendable. He is my most trusted asset.

Kaba entered the cabin of the plane and saw Lindsey's blushing face hovering close to DeGard. She interrupted their exchange with a rare smile. "Someone is here I think you will be happy to see."

Lindsey's expression turned curious. "Who could I possibly want to..." Before he could finish, Kaba stepped out of the way and allowed a young man, probably in his upper twenties, to walk by. He was lean and athletic, with shortish brown hair that looked like it hadn't been washed in a few days. His jacket was torn, and the dust on it matched the grime and dirt on his pants.

"Sorry I'm late, Sir. I had to catch a ride out in the desert." Will staggered in, but remained standing.

The old man's face lit up in a fraction of a second, but he squelched the emotions just as quickly. The brief joy that Lindsey had shown was strange for DeGard to behold, and he wasn't quite sure what to make of it.

Lindsey stood up and offered the younger man a seat next to where he'd been. Will slouched down, exhausted.

"What happened to you?" Lindsey asked, sounding slightly annoyed. "I've tried calling you but your phone goes straight to—"

"I got shot," Will interrupted. "Sean Wyatt shot me, and I fell off the train."

Lindsey appeared genuinely concerned for the briefest of seconds. "Shot? Where? Do you need medical attention?"

Will shook his head slowly and pointed to the side of his chest that the bullet had stopped. "Those phones you gave us, they're pretty tough. The thing stopped the bullet. Otherwise I'd have a ripped apart lung, and probably be dead."

The realization hit Lindsey. "The phone stopped the bullet?" Again, Will nodded. He doubted his employer would bother him about the phone calls anymore. A bullet explained everything.

"You're quite fortunate," the old man stated. "We need to get you some food and water." He turned his attention to the young woman still standing at the front of the plane. "Kaba, could you get something for Will to eat and some water."

She gave a quick nod and started to head to the back of the plane, but Will reached out and grabbed her leg, stopping her in mid stride. The move would have been one that could have gotten an ordinary man killed, or at least the arm bent in an awkward and broken direction. For Will, she would allow it.

"Along with that water, could you bring me a scotch on the rocks. I need a drink in the worst way." She passed him a sliver of a grin and continued down the aisle.

Will turned his attention back to the other two who were looking at him like he was a breathing dead man. "So, where are we going?"

"Turkey," the Frenchman spoke up. "I believe that the clue we discovered points the way to the mountains of eastern Turkey. Not that we'll find anything of interest there." The last part he nearly said under his breath, but both counterparts heard the jab. They also both decided to ignore it, Lindsey merely casting a snide glare.

Will leaned back in the leather chair and put his head against the headrest. "So, that's where this journey will end and a new one will begin." Before he could begin to relax, a thought occurred to him and he sat back up quickly. "What about Wyatt and his little group."

Lindsey waved a dismissive hand then stuck it into his jacket pocket. "They will be left far behind. We were able to retrieve this from the third chamber." He produced the small, round stone and handed it to Will.

Will cradled it gently as he eyed the piece. He didn't understand the writing on it, nor what it could all mean. But the French archaeologist knew what it meant. At least, he hoped the guy did. DeGard seemed to know his stuff, so if he said that the place they needed to go was Turkey, Will and his boss would have to go with what the man said.

He handed the object back to his employer. "So you got the only clue that could tell Wyatt and his friends where the next chamber was?"

Lindsey gave a quick sideways nod that seemed to say a sarcastic, "Oh well."

"I was looking forward to finishing off that self-righteous has been. Perhaps I will see him again someday."

Kaba returned carrying a tray with a roast beef hoagie on a French roll, and a rocks glass with yellowish-brown liquid and three ice cubes. She cast him a quick smile before heading to a seat a little farther to the rear of the plane. The six men from outside entered the cabin and closed the door just before the jet started moving.

Will took a huge bite out of the sandwich, and chewed it slowly like it was the best thing he'd eaten in his entire life. He put the food down on the silver platter and reached over for the drink then took a long, slow sip before letting out an "ahhh."

"Nothing but the best. That's one of the things I love about working for you, sir." Will set the glass back down and took a less aggressive bite of the sandwich.

Lindsey crossed one leg over the other and sat back in his chair. "Speaking of best, I was wondering, how was it that Sean Wyatt got the best of you?"

Will nearly choked on his food, but managed to gulp it down before speaking. The few seconds it took him to get the bite down gave him enough time to gain his composure. No one ever questioned him about his methods or his effectiveness. To be fair, he'd never screwed up before, so there'd never been reason to. That was probably one of the biggest reasons he hoped to meet up with Sean Wyatt again someday. From the sound of it, that rendezvous wouldn't be soon. But it would happen eventually. Of that he was certain, even if it took him out of his way to make it happen, he would see Sean Wyatt again.

"I was going to take them all out while they slept. It was three in the morning when I approached their car where they were sleeping. For some reason, Wyatt was awake and moving through the train cars. I don't know. Maybe he couldn't sleep or something. I took some shots at him when he realized who I was. He got lucky. It won't happen again." Will stopped talking for a minute and stared down at the floor. Then, he reached over suddenly and grabbed his glass of Scotch, downing the thing in one swallow.

Lindsey remained calm, but concerned. "I don't think we will be having any more problems with Mr. Wyatt. As stated, we have the only link to the location of the final chamber. I fail to see how Wyatt and his companions could ever conclude as to where its location could be without this stone." He held it up proudly for a moment before placing it back in his pocket.

Will was somewhat surprised by Lindsey's reaction. The Prophet had been ruthless to people who failed him. He recalled the man Lindsey had thrown out of a helicopter into Lake Mead, and the two men on his council that had been placed into the brazen bull. He'd seen the contraption once when he was visiting Lindsey's mountaintop mansion. Will had never heard of anything like that before that day. He imagined it to be an excruciating way to go. Such was the price of betrayal.

Lindsey's two right hand men had gone behind his back and sought to override his power. It was a move that had cost them their lives. Despite getting tired of being ordered around, Will had become a strong believer in what The Prophet was trying to do. He had seen too much evil in his lifetime. Criminals roamed free to rob and murder as they pleased, almost unchecked by inept police departments. Prisons were overcrowded, and the prisoner population continued to grow every year. It seemed every time Will turned on the news, there was some story about rape, murder, theft, something.

But his employer had a plan for all of that. And it started with finding the last golden chamber. If the old man was right, and he usually was, the ancient Biblical source of immortality was hidden somewhere in eastern Turkey. It was gamble, but only one of money and time. The old man had plenty of the first, much less of the second. Will had bought into his grand plan and believed it could be achieved. But he also thought there must certainly have been some personal reasons Lindsey was searching for the lost tree of Eden and its mysterious power.

It was a story Will knew well. He'd read all the books about men who had searched for the Fountain of Youth or a magical pool that could restore a human's vitality. Those explorers searched only for a way to live forever. Lindsey was the first person he'd heard of who considered using it for other purposes. The world had become sick. And Alexander Lindsey had stumbled on an idea that could cure it.

Will had grown up in an environment without love or compassion. He'd grown callus to the way the world had become. For most of his teenage and adult life, he'd lived a life of self-serving pleasure seeking. He'd had no purpose, no direction. Then, he met The Prophet. Alexander Lindsey had given Will something he'd never had before. He showed him the error of his ways, and a way to make the world a better place.

That sentimental stuff hadn't really resonated with Will. But he played along. He told Lindsey what he wanted to hear. The fact was, Will enjoyed killing. He enjoyed being given carte blanche to do whatever he wanted, with nearly unlimited resources. The old man paid well. Will got to travel all over the world, meet exotic women, and kill anyone Lindsey wanted dead.

From time to time, Will hated being bossed around. Lindsey was a persistent manager of things and resources, always prying his controlling fingers into whatever was going on. The man expected constant reports on nearly every situation. The Prophet was the only person, though, who had ever been a father figure to Will. Lindsey had taken good care of him, and always would. Occasionally, he wondered if he would be included in the old man's inheritance. Wild thoughts about beaches, women in bikinis, mansions, fast cars, and drinks that never ran out, would run rampant through his mind. While he had to play by Lindsey's rules at the moment, that wouldn't last forever. If his employer left Will enough money when he kicked off, he would live the life he'd always wanted: one of hedonism and leisure.

Will watched Lindsey put the stone back in his pocket as the multitude of thoughts began to wind down to the warm internal glow the scotch provided.

"I could use another one of those," he held up the empty glass toward Kaba, who was sitting with her legs crossed in the seat across the aisle.

She smiled politely, but her tone was snippy. "The bar is in the back," she replied.

Will let out a snort of laughter. "Fair enough."

He'd had plenty of fun with the young woman since she'd signed on with Lindsey. It had only taken one night of drinking together for them to find themselves waking up next to each other the following morning. Will wondered if their employer knew anything was going on, but he seemed oblivious. At least he acted like he was oblivious. Maybe he wouldn't care.

The jet engines strained outside the cabin as the plane taxied onto the runway, pausing briefly. There was a moment's pause followed by the sudden thrust of acceleration. They whined louder as the vehicle tilted upward and pierced into the sky. Lindsey laid his head back against the headrest, eyes closed. DeGard was gazing out the window, moving his head around to better see the world dropping away below. A look of childlike curiosity covered his face.

Had The Prophet told the Frenchman about their grand scheme? It wasn't exactly something Will could just ask the man. He would probably have to wait and ask Lindsey later on when they were alone. For some reason, Will felt like DeGard most likely did not know what their real reasons were behind finding the ark of Noah and the ancient source of immortality. He would find out soon enough, provided they had correctly interpreted the clues. Things were still unclear in Will's mind as he found himself drifting away in random thoughts. His eyes became heavier as sleep dragged him away from the world of the conscious.

19

TURKEY

S ean stared questioningly at Jabez. "What do you mean he
might not have the only clue?" When they had left the third
chamber, the room was vacant.

Jabez leaned back in his seat and stretched out his arms. He could
tell what Sean was thinking. "Lindsey retrieved the only clue from
the third chamber. However, we believe there may be another clue
that points the way to the ark's resting place."

Sean and Adriana were huddled close, listening intently.
Professor Firth seemed to be over his queasiness and had scooted
back toward the group to hear what the Arab had to say.

"There is an ancient monastery on the border of Armenia and
Turkey called Khor Virap. It was built in the seventh century, but the
site's usage goes back all the way to the years following the time of
Christ. Some have said that the apostles may have even visited the
location." He looked at each person of his audience directly in the
eyes before continuing.

"In the late third century, Saint Gregory the Illuminator was
held prisoner there by the pagan king, Tiridates III, for thirteen
years. In the end, Saint Gregory became a mentor for the king,
and was eventually given acceptable quarters in the palace. The

two of them ended up proselytizing communities all over the country."

Jabez could see Sean was attempting to tie everything together in his head. The Arab beat him to the punch. "History books give a few reasons for Gregory's imprisonment. But the legend gives another. It suggests the reason for Saint Gregory's imprisonment was that he knew an ancient secret, the location of something that could grant eternal life to anyone who found it."

"He knew where the ark was." Sean injected.

"So it would seem," Jabez agreed. "The king had imprisoned Gregory in some of the deepest parts of the ancient fortress. It surely must have been a hell on earth. Thirteen years passed, during which the pagan king persecuted many Christians as well as anyone who refused to do his bidding. During the years of his imprisonment, Gregory suffered many forms of torture. The monarch became fond of Gregory and eventually gave up on the idea that the priest was hiding something. He resigned to the fact that Gregory would either never give up the information or had nothing to hide."

The airplane's engines strained a little outside the cabin as it tipped a little to one side, altering its course before flattening out again. The maneuver caused Firth's nausea to return, but he held it back, not wanting to miss anything Jabez was saying.

"During Tiridates's reign, he was said to have gone mad at some point, behaving like a wild boar and living with pigs. His sister had a vision in which she saw Gregory healing the king. She told the king's most trusted counselors about the vision immediately. The council thought the priest must have surely died in the pit of the prison. But when they went to find him, the man was still alive. They pulled him out to discover him in terrible physical condition. After nursing the priest back to health, Gregory was able to heal the king and return him to a normal state of being.

Adriana looked confused. Something didn't add up. "How did Gregory survive that long without any sort of food or water? If he had been forgotten in the dungeon, he would have died within days, a week at most."

Jabez raised a finger to emphasize his point. "Precisely. He would have surely been dead if they had forgotten him in the dungeon, as the story suggests. Saint Gregory must have been sustained supernaturally to still be alive after all those years."

Sean was leery of jumping to conclusions. That was how people got their hopes up or found themselves searching for buried treasure in uncharted jungles. He'd seen and heard a lot of crazy stories over the last few years. But this one was different. *A priest that lived for thirteen years without sunlight, proper food, and water? It didn't make sense. Unless he had eaten from the tree.* Sean shook off the thought for a moment. Something inside his head told him that was impossible. Even though everything he had seen up to that point pointed to the reality that the tree of life was a real thing, he couldn't bring himself to believe it.

A silent moment had taken over the conversation as everyone considered the implications. Sean broke it with a question. "So, the question is, what does this have to do with finding the fourth chamber? I mean, clearly you are suggesting there is a connection between the priest and the last chamber. Aren't you?" He wanted to be sure he was following the Arab's line of thought.

"That is exactly what I'm saying," Jabez nodded. "There can be no other conclusion. Clearly, Gregory found the chamber and the sacred tree. If he ate of it, the power within could have sustained him through those years in the darkness of the pit."

Lightning flashed outside the windows, illuminating the wing directly behind where Jabez was sitting. He sped up the pace of his tale. "It is no coincidence that Saint Gregory was a missionary to the area around the Armenian and Turkish border. He was an avid researcher and spent countless hours in the scriptures as well as ancient documents. Gregory was convinced that the reason that the tree of life could not be found after the Biblical flood was that it had been moved, not destroyed or covered up. His theory was that Noah removed the tree and placed it in the ark to keep it safe."

"So, the tree is in the ark?" Sean tried to clarify.

"That is what we believe. And if Gregory found it, he may have left a clue as to its whereabouts."

Firth had heard enough. "You mean to tell us that you're dragging us half-way across the Middle East on a hunch? It sounds as if you aren't even sure there is a clue."

Jabez was briefly taken aback by the criticism, but he remained calm. "Saint Gregory left behind strange markings on the walls of the pit where he dwelled for those thirteen years. To date, no one has been able to explain them. I believe in those markings, Gregory gave us the location of the ark in case he did not live through the ordeal in the dungeon of Khor Virap."

It was a huge leap of faith their new friend was taking. Making the assumption that Sean and his colleagues could figure out what the inscriptions meant was a gamble, if there were any markings to begin with. Still, it was worth a try. They'd come too far to let Lindsey just walk away with whatever was to be found at the end of the trail.

Firth was much more resistant. "Are you telling me that through all the centuries, no one has been able to make heads nor tails of the inscriptions you're taking us to, yet we are supposed to magically come up with some answers as to what they could possibly mean?"

Jabez looked at the gray haired professor for a few seconds then at Sean and Adriana. Both his eyebrows rose as he smiled. "Yes. That is exactly what I'm telling you. It seems to have worked for Mr. Wyatt so far. Wouldn't you agree?"

Sean couldn't help himself and burst out into open laughter. "You know he's right, Professor. We really do seem to be on a pretty good streak right now." He shoved the professor's shoulder playfully. Adriana smiled to one side of her face.

"When we get there," Jabez began again after a few more moments of laughter, "we will meet a friend who has access to the fortress prison. He will allow us to look at the pit without the distractions of other tourists."

It sounded like a plan or at least some semblance of one. Sean wished Tommy was there, knowing that his friend's expertise would make things a lot easier. Sean hadn't received any word on Tommy's condition from the Greek hospital since before they left Cairo. He would have to check again once the airplane arrived in Istanbul.

Second time in Istanbul. The first time he'd been there, things were different, and similar. Several years prior, an Axis assignment had taken him to the city that had long been the crossroads of so many cultures. Sean's eyes narrowed as he recalled the mission.

Axis had received information on a possible deal involving former Soviet nuclear weapons and a terrorist organization known as Red Circle. The intel had come through as a result of heightened interest in terrorist activity following the September 11 attacks. Word was that Red Circle planned on acquiring an old Russian nuke, and somehow getting into London. Most of the attention was focused on the United States in the months following the attacks on New York and Washington. The terrorists must have figured no one would be monitoring the safety of the UK.

They'd been wrong. Axis was called in to assist British special ops and take down Red Circle before they ever had a chance to get their hands on the device. In Sean's opinion, there'd been too many moving parts. There were so many people involved; it was a disaster waiting to happen. And it did. Several agents were killed from both agencies. The disaster, however, was averted. And the nuclear device was secured. In Sean's mind, the lives lost could have been avoided. It was the last mission he'd served for Emily Starks before turning in his resignation.

Sean realized he was staring at the floor and quickly regained his composure. "When we get to Istanbul, is your friend going to set us up with a place to stay? It sounds like he's taken care of transportation."

Jabez nodded. "Yes, everything is taken care of. We will be staying at a hotel that is friendly to our cause. Our brother, Omar," he pointed to one of the men on the other side of the plane toward the tail of the cabin, "his family owns a place. Arrangements have been made. We will stay the night in Istanbul and leave for the Armenian border early in the morning."

"Sounds good," Sean said and leaned his head back against the wall near a window.

Firth snorted a quick protest but returned to focusing on not getting sick. Adriana seemed satisfied and was once again reading her book. The conversation was, apparently, over because Jabez got up and went back to the cockpit, closing the door behind.

Sean closed his eyes and went back to where he'd been in his mind only a few moments before.

The deal for the nuke was taking place in an abandoned fabric warehouse on the outskirts of town. It was a logical location for the people making the deal. And it also made intervening a huge tactical problem. Line of sight was covered by men on the roof and in the windows of the old building. That meant a direct approach was nearly impossible. They would see a frontal assault coming from a mile away. Literally.

Sean had gone over the layout of the facility and found a way in through an underground drainage system that ran under the walls. The plan had been to go in from the inside then bring in support from the outside, effectively surrounding the culprits.

It all sounded like a great idea. But as Sean had predicted, it all went haywire.

The entire operation depended on timing, which Sean hated. He preferred to have the ability to audible out of a situation, or at least have enough flexibility to make a judgment call. British special ops wouldn't hear of it. They'd insisted on everything being done on their timetable.

When the demolitions expert on their team, a heavily muscled guy named Vince, had trouble setting off the explosives imbedded in the floor, the whole operation was thrown off kilter. Sean had tried to radio the units outside the building and tell them to wait, but there was too much interference. With no warning, the units on the outside moved in too soon and were immediately pinned down by the snipers stationed around the building.

By the time Vince finally blew the floor out from under the terrorists, they were already in full panic mode, trying to load up and make their escape. Sean slung his grapple up quickly and hauled himself up the rope into chaos. The first thing he saw was the back of a white delivery truck's doors being closed with a large wooden crate concealed in the back.

The explosion had drawn the attention of the terrorists who weren't trying to get away quickly, and a hail of gunfire ensued from four men on the other side of the warehouse. Sean fired off three quick shots, taking down two of the gunmen before ducking behind a nearby steel support beam.

He pointed to several wooden boxes on the other side of the hole Vince had blown in the floor and yelled at the other three members of his team to take cover in that position when they got topside. Bullets pinged off his protective barrier; a few hit the tin wall behind him. He spun around and fired his AR-15 four more times, dropping the remaining two gunmen.

Another threat appeared on the upper catwalk that encircled the warehouse. Several more men with assault rifles were firing down on his position and on the rest of his team who were coming up through the cavity in the floor. Two more appeared on the ground from behind the truck that was now starting up and trying to turn around so it could go through the large hangar doors at the end. Sean also noticed a man in a slick gray business suit with peppered gray and black hair jumping into the back of a black SUV. For a split second, Sean thought he recognized the man, but the barrage of bullets kept him focused on the immediate threats.

The SUV sped off, cutting past the delivery truck as men were still trying to get the doors locked down. Sean had to find a way to stop the truck. He laid down covering fire as his support team continued to appear through the hole in the floor. When all of them had made it to cover, he signaled for them to take out the guys on the catwalk first. He could handle the two on the ground.

Mere seconds after he'd given the order, one of the men on the catwalk fell over the railing and smacked into the floor. His support team on the left picked off the gunmen one by one in quick succession. Sean wasted no time. He pulled out his Berretta and ran toward the first of the two terrorists on the ground, squeezing of three shots as he sprinted to a concrete cylinder. The target dropped to the ground leaving one guy remaining. The delivery truck roared to life as the loan terrorist continued to fire his weapon recklessly in Sean's direction. He gave a quick nod to Vince who was still tucked behind the crates. Vince popped up and fired twice with his AR-15.

The gunman's assault rifle went silent as the truck started to pull away. Sean dropped his pistol and put the butt of his assault rifle against his shoulder. He would only have one chance to hit the driver as the truck made the turn to go through the door. If the vehicle reached the exit, he doubted the team on the outside would be able to stop it.

He closed one eye and breathed slowly as he watched the front edge of the truck. It swerved to the left then turned sharply to the right. The driver, a man in a black turban with a thick black mustache appeared in his scope's crosshairs. The truck would be gone in less than three seconds. Sean let out a long, slow breath, and squeezed the trigger.

He'd received commendations for valor and leadership. But none of that mattered anymore. Taking lives was something he was good at. And he wished he wasn't. Sean longed for a life in which he didn't have to kill, didn't have to hide, or worry that someone was watching him. His friend, Tommy had given him a standing offer to join the International Archaeological Agency. It was a security position, the main task of which was to secure artifacts for transport to research facilities. The pay was good. The hours were great. And the risk factors were much lower. It was exactly what Sean had been looking for. Since he had a long-time interest in ancient history, it pretty much sounded like the perfect gig.

His resignation from Axis had been difficult. He'd worked with Emily a long time. She had become one of the few people he trusted in the world. But she would be okay without him. Or so he hoped. There was a group of recruits that looked promising for the small agency. The realization that he wouldn't regret leaving, but he might regret staying, was the biggest influencing factor.

Emily had begged him to stay on. But too many things were telling him to get out. So, he did. And he never looked back. That wasn't to say he ever lost touch with his former boss. They'd helped each other out several times since he left. And he imagined that cooperative exchange would continue well into the future.

"We'll be landing in Istanbul in a few minutes," the pilot's voice cut through his thoughts, and he opened his eyes. Everyone was securing their seatbelts in preparation for landing.

Sean hoped this visit to the ancient city would go better than the last.

20

ISTANBUL

The untamed scents of the eternal city filled Alexander Lindsey's nostrils as he stepped out of his car, onto the sidewalk. The dry air outside his lavish hotel was filled with the smell of spices, herbs, roasting meat, onions, and garlic; all of it wafted in his direction from the bazaar a few blocks away. Istanbul was a wild parade for the senses. The sidewalks were a river of people dressed in a vast array of clothing from the bland to the extraordinarily colorful. Lights flashed from a thousand directions. The sounds of cars, music, and laughter filled his ears.

DeGard exited the vehicle and gazed around at the sites of Istanbul at night. The city was a cornucopia of historical significance. The city had been the economic center between Europe, Asia, and the Middle East for thousands of years. It was dead center of the famous Silk Road, and was the only connection between the Black Sea and the Mediterranean. Over the course of its history, Istanbul had been the capital city for four major empires. In the early 1920s, when Turkey became a republic, it was passed over as the Turkish capital in favor of Ankara. Still, the city had grown immensely during the twentieth century, boasting the second largest population within a city limit in the entire world.

Everywhere DeGard looked he could see the mingling of modern humanity, ancient architecture and design, and Islamic influences. Each time he visited, DeGard felt like he was in a cultural playground.

Lindsey didn't seem nearly as impressed. A scowl covered his face, and he hurriedly trudged into the hotel, past the doorman in a costume that reminded him of the story of Aladdin. Inside the hotel, he was greeted by more smiling faces and a world of opulence that would appease the most particular of tastes. His scowl still prevailed.

Will followed him in with wide eyes staring around at all of the sights. He had stayed in luxurious hotels during his employment with Lindsey, but this one might have topped them all. Lavish burgundy curtains flowed from the ceiling of each end of the white marble concierge desk. The glass elevator was in the center of the enormous lobby, ferrying patrons up and down the twenty-story facility. In front of the elevator, a wide semi-circular fountain displayed an amazing water show like a miniature version of what one could find at the Bellagio in Las Vegas.

Lush greenery hung from the balconies and ledges. Enormous pottery lined the orange-tan marble floor with various trees from the region.

Kaba had entered the building before the others and secured the checkout, knowing that Lindsey did not wish to delay. The Prophet was tired from his extensive journeys. He would need a good night's rest before moving on to Ararat the next day. It would be a journey of several hours, and he would need all the energy he could muster. She stepped away from the mocha-skinned woman behind the concierge desk and handed Lindsey his room key, sure to point out which room he would be staying in. She also handed a key to Will, but gave him a knowing, flirtatious glance as she did.

DeGard had finally dragged himself inside and spun around in circles as he inspected the hotel's interior for the first time.

"I have to say, Monsieur Lindsey, you certainly know how to travel in style." The old man simply grumbled and shuffled away toward the elevator. DeGard looked at Kaba with a confused expression. "Was it something I said?"

She shook her head. "No. But he detests Islam. And we are in the heart of a city that is built on it."

"Ah," the Frenchman realized. "I see. And how do you feel about that?"

A quizzical expression passed over her face. "I do not believe in religions," she said in a matter-of-fact tone that suggested he should already know.

DeGard seemed somewhat surprised. "Yet you follow a man who is obviously religious?"

She crossed her arms, the tight white turtleneck she'd put on accentuating her muscular figure. "I do not follow The Prophet because he is a Christian. I follow because he pays well, and he will rid the world of all wickedness."

There it was again: a cryptic reference regarding getting rid of the wicked. DeGard wondered if his employer was planning some kind of holocaust or ethnic cleansing. He watched as Lindsey and two of his other men stepped onto the elevator and ascended the many stories to his floor. Kaba and the others had grabbed some of their luggage and were walking toward the next elevator.

The Frenchman wanted to get to the bottom of things. He felt like he'd been kept in the dark long enough. He caught up to Kaba and pulled on her shoulder. As soon as he'd done it he knew it was a bad move. She spun around quickly with a defensive frown on her face.

"I'm sorry," he tried to make the peace in his meekest, nasal tone. "But what is all this I keep hearing about getting rid of the world's evil doers? That isn't the first time I've heard about it. What is the old man planning?"

Her eyes narrowed, sizing him up to see if she should apprise him of what Lindsey was planning. "I think if you want to know about what The Prophet intends to do, you should speak to him about it." She turned around as the elevator doors opened then stepped inside with Will and the remaining men from their group. DeGard watched the doors close with an annoyed stare.

"Fine," he said to himself, and pressed the button between the elevators.

A few minutes later, DeGard was knocking on the door to Lindsey's room. The old man had reserved a room on the top floor of the hotel. DeGard imagined his employer preferred the space so he could look down on everyone else. The thought brought a disfigured smile to his wiry face. He wiped away the grin when the door opened.

Lindsey stood in the doorway. He had already put on a black smoking jacket, and poured himself a bourbon in one of the hotel's rocks glasses.

"What do you want?" he asked, clearly annoyed. Lindsey took a sip from the bourbon and barely flinched as he swallowed. He'd been in a foul mood since arriving in the city.

DeGard decided to be blunt. "Monsieur Lindsey, if I am going to be an integral part of this operation, I want to know exactly with what I am involved." He almost literally stomped his foot as he was metaphorically putting his foot down. Lindsey seemed unimpressed so the Frenchman continued. "I want to know what it is you and your little group are up to. You are the head of The Order of Golden Dawn, non? This is a well concealed organization that very few people know of. But you are planning something on a global scale, and from what I have heard you and your associates saying, many lives will be lost. Is that true? Are you planning some kind of holocaust or genocide?"

Lindsey listened as patiently as he could. He almost seemed amused by the archaeologist's clown-like mannerisms. The man's thin pasty frame didn't help. Lindsey took another sip of the bourbon and chopped his lips after he swallowed, savoring the taste of the oak-aged liquor.

"My dear DeGard," Lindsey smiled at his visitor. "Am I to understand that you are developing a soft heart for the degenerates of the world? I certainly understand, knowing full well the reputation that precedes you."

DeGard bit his lip for a second while his face flushed red at the barb. He cocked his head sideways for a second then responded. "A soft heart? Non, Monsieur. However, if you are planning some kind of massive attack on humanity, I want to make sure I will not be harmed."

Lindsey snorted a short laugh. The loose skin under his chin shook as he responded, and his hollow eyes stared back with sincere deprecation.

"You will be spared, Monsieur DeGard, but only because you are working for me."

"That is all I needed to know."

The old man closed the door before the Frenchman could say thank you or goodbye. Not that he needed to. Alexander Lindsey was a strange man. That was certain. And he'd not come clean about what he was planning. DeGard was still frustrated about that. At the moment, there was nothing he could do. He would find out what the crazy old man was scheming soon enough. As long as he was safe, that was all that Luc DeGard cared about.

He'd learned a long time ago to always watch out for number one. It was what he did best. And no matter how much money he was being paid for this wild goose chase, he wanted to make sure he would live to spend it.

21

ISTANBUL

Driving through the streets of Istanbul was almost surreal to Sean. Most of the buildings looked the same, with a few, more modern exceptions sticking out here and there. Bright flashing signs lit up the night sky and illuminated the streets and sidewalks like a strange, electric sun.

The plane had landed a few hours before, but the man Jabez had made arrangements with for pickup arrived thirty minutes late. Based on the thick traffic, Sean didn't pay much mind. Of course Firth had complained the entire time they'd sat in the lonely hangar off to the side of the airport. Sean wished he'd had one of the tranquilizers he'd used on more than one occasion with Axis. In fifteen seconds the professor could be out cold, the only problem being that they would have to carry him into the hotel, which might look somewhat conspicuous. Sean laughed to himself at the thought.

Adriana hadn't said much on the flight or after they had arrived. She seemed deeply interested in the leather bound book she had been reading. Her eyes glimmered in the lights of the city as she stared out the window.

Their host, a squat Turk named Khalil, zipped the small caravan of SUVs through the busy evening traffic of downtown Istanbul. He didn't say much, probably because of the reaming he'd taken from Jabez on account of his tardiness. But Sean got the impression he was more a man of action rather than words. He wore a short red fez, a linen long sleeve shirt and matching pants, and sported a Fu Manchu style moustache and goatee. His dark hair was slightly receded, giving Sean the impression the portly man to be roughly in his mid to upper forties. Since Khalil hadn't said a word on their drive into town, it was unclear whether the man spoke English or not.

The vehicle turned into a driveway that was blocked off by an ornate, bronze gate. Palm trees and shrubbery lined the pavement beyond the entrance, leading to a five-story hotel overlooking the Mediterranean. The gate opened slowly and the two SUV's passed through, zipping their way down the driveway and to the front of the hotel. Several valets waited under a giant awning made of plaster, accented with cedar cross beams and paneling. The valets were dressed in uniforms that almost looked like Turkish military garb, with gold tassels and medallions dangling from their shoulders and chests. They quickly opened the doors for the new arrivals and began busily asking which things they could take.

When Jabez exited the vehicle, a younger valet stared at him with uneasy apprehension. Jabez was an imposing figure, and when he wasn't smiling, that sense was only amplified. The young man got over it quickly and asked if there was anything he could take in. Jabez shook his head but never broke the stern look on his face. The valet rushed off to help someone else.

Firth was clearly used to a life of convenience, and all too happy to allow the men to carry his few bags. He carried himself with an exhausted dignity through the bronze-framed doors.

Inside the hotel, the guests were greeted by tan marble floors and matching pillars. Hundreds of thousands of mosaic tiles covered the walls in dramatic fashion. Signature domed archways hung over openings in a hexagonal lobby. The portals led to the different sections of the facility containing the hotel quarters, dining and entertainment areas, exercise and spa area, and the lobby in which they were standing.

Sean's head spun around a full 360 degrees as he admired the craftsmanship that had gone into creating the palatial hotel.

"I guess your friend has a decent connection here, huh?" he quipped at Jabez.

The Arab cocked his head for a second as if making such arrangements were just another typical day at the office. A few moments later, his driver was handing out room keys and giving directions for finding their rooms.

Adriana noticed that Jabez and his four men didn't receive a key.

"Where are you and your men staying?" she prodded.

He turned and smiled at her. "We will be in a home not far from here. A place like this is far too grand for simple men like us. Humble quarters are all we require. And we must also pray for strength tonight." He smiled wide with the last part. "All of this would be an easy distraction," Jabez waved his hand around dramatically showing off the extravagant interior of the lobby.

The Arab turned back to Sean. "I will return in the morning to pick you up at 8:00 o'clock, Istanbul time. So, be sure you have eaten a big breakfast. It will be a few hours drive to the border. Arrangements have been made so the Armenians will know we are coming, and should not give us any trouble."

"That's good to know."

Firth was still frowning. Sean had figured the man had grown tired of all the intrigue. The older professor was what Sean and Tommy called a "classroom archaeologist." They rarely got out and did any exploration in their twilight years.

"I don't mean to be rude," the older man said, bobbing his head and fedora as he spoke, "but I am going to bed. I shall see you in the morning." He waved a dismissive hand and plodded off in the wrong direction through the entryway of the spa.

Sean snorted a quick laugh, knowing in a moment the professor's dramatic exit would be ruined with a U-turn and an embarrassing walk to the other side of the lobby.

Sure enough, thirty seconds later Firth re-appeared and stalked quickly across the marble tiles, past the lavish beige couches, and through the correct portal. Adriana snickered slightly.

"I suppose we should turn in as well," Sean put out a hand for Jabez, who took it and gripped it appreciatively.

"We will see you tomorrow. I pray the Father keeps us safe."

The man spun around and ushered the rest of his men out the doors. His last sentence lingered in Sean's mind, though. He couldn't help but wonder why they wouldn't be safe. It was doubtful Lindsey was on the same trail. But experience had taught him to never get too comfortable. As soon as you did was when the enemy could rear its ugly head.

He followed Adriana across the room and into a great hallway lined with bronze candle sconces. A thick burgundy carpet ran the length of it atop more of the marble tiles like the ones they'd seen in the lobby. A set of elevator doors opened up to the left as they neared.

A few moments later, they had reached their floor and were walking down a hall that mirrored the one they'd just left.

They'd been silent since leaving the lobby, but Adriana broke the quiet. "Sean, my father does covert operations for various governments of the world."

The sudden confession caught him off guard. "I'm sorry. Your dad does what?"

"Technically, you could consider him to be a spy. Now, he mainly does contract work for different agencies connected to the United States government."

They stopped walking at an intersection of two hallways. A glass-ceilinged dome loomed above them. Enormous pots with small palm trees dotted the corners of the circular intersect.

Sean's eyebrows stitched together. "Espionage? Your father?" It was rare when someone surprised him. But he had to admit to himself this was one of those times that really caught him off guard.

Adriana could tell he wasn't sure about the idea. "It isn't as bad as you make it sound. He doesn't work for any bad people," she defended with a slight pout.

He shook his head, still confused. "I'm sorry. Why are you telling me this anyway?"

"Because. He may be able to help us uncover whatever it is Lindsey is up to. My father has connections in places some of your friends may not. It could be worth a try."

Sean nodded slowly, finally understanding the connection. "Okay," he agreed. "See what he can find out. I will contact Emily and see what she has turned up. Call me if you hear anything interesting."

She smiled wryly. "I texted him over an hour ago. If father can find anything, he will be calling soon."

He gave an impressed smile and walked the remaining twenty feet to their rooms. Hers was across the hall, and she looked back after unlocking it with her card key. Sean had turned around as well to watch her for a second. He cast an awkward smile across the six-foot space.

"You don't have to stay in your room if you don't want to, Sean." Her voice was confident and hopeful. The Spanish accent was intoxicating and filled his ears like music. Her figure beckoned to him as she stood with one hand on a hip. Every instinct told Sean to step across the hall, wrap his arm around her slender waist, and press his lips into hers. He could tell from the look in her chocolate, almond-shaped eyes that she was hoping he would.

For a few seconds, Sean imagined what her firm, tight body would feel like. The outline of her athletic legs in those tight pants she always seemed to wear was almost too much to bear.

But something made him hesitate, made him decline every natural instinct that was roaring inside his head. "I need to get cleaned up," he basically ignored the invitation. "It's been a long day, and we should get some rest. Please, though, let me know if you hear anything from your father."

Her face was the picture of disappointment and confusion. She'd thrown herself at him, and he had rejected her.

Sean doubted many men would have done the same thing. She was better than that, though. And she deserved better. He'd met her several weeks before, and they had gotten to know each other fairly well so far. But he didn't want to ruin that. He hoped that, someday, they could venture into a physical relationship. Maybe he was old-fashioned. At least he thought he was, more so than most people in an age of Internet dating and sexting. She pushed open the door and disappeared inside, a dejected look washing across her face. The door clicked shut, and Sean remained standing on the threshold of his own room. He owed her an explanation. He knew he did. Maybe later he would try to tell her how he felt, what he wanted.

He banged his head against the door slowly a few times. "What is wrong with you, Wyatt?" he said quietly to himself. "What are you doing?"

Sean unlocked his door and slipped inside.

The room felt like many other hotel rooms he'd stayed in before. At their core, they were all the same: just glorified bedrooms. Sure, there were different coats of paint or fancy wallpaper, tiled floors or hardwood, lush sofas, and dozens of decorative pillows. In the end, though, he just wanted a decent place to sleep. None of that over-the-top stuff really meant much.

He had to admit that the room was different than most he'd stayed in. The interior decorator had decked out the Arabian architecture with an array of colors and hues that pleased the eye, but wasn't so distracting one couldn't relax.

Sean turned on the shower, one of the more ordinary places he could find in the hotel. The tiles were beige, filled in with a dark grout. It had no doors, only an entrance into the shower with a short, tiled wall going up one side to protect from splashing onto the floor of the rest of the bathroom. He let the hot water soothe his senses for several minutes before cleaning up and getting out to dry off.

He threw on a t-shirt and boxers then noticed his phone lighting up on the dark cherry oak dresser across from the bed. It was a text message from Adriana. Sean hesitated before unlocking his phone to read it. He wondered if she was going to say something about the uncomfortable exchange in the hallway from earlier. Shrugging it off, he opened the phone's interface and read it.

"I have information on Lindsey you need to hear. Come over ASAP. PS, I'm sorry about earlier."

Sean smiled at the text, glad she wasn't angry at him. Putting himself in her shoes, he actually felt a little bad for her. It had to be awkward.

He pulled on some jeans from his bag and went across the hall. When she opened the door, she was dressed in a snug, red t-shirt and some gray pajama pants.

She still looked a little uncomfortable, and bit her lower lip in a cute gesture. Before she could say anything, he beat her to it.

"Look, Adriana. I want to...I really like you. And I am definitely attracted to you." His words made her face light up slightly. "But we have a lot going on right now, and I don't want to jump into anything with you. I just want to get to know you and not have this turn into some one-nighter because we got caught up in the moment. Understand?"

"Yes," she nodded, still smiling. "I do."

"When all this is over, I think we should just get away from everything and get a little alone time. Sound good?"

She nodded again.

"Okay," he still beamed at her. "Now, what did your father say?"

Sean stepped into the room that looked almost identical to his own. He was almost a little disappointed at that fact. A tiny part of him had hoped each room was uniquely decorated.

Adriana sat on the edge of the bed and picked up her phone. Sean assumed a casual seating position on the nearby sofa.

"Father has many contacts in the United States. It turns out, our friend Alexander Lindsey has his hands in many pies, as you Americans say." Sean raised an eyebrow, impressed with her use of the expression. "No one has been able to prove anything in regards to Golden Dawn and their direct operations, but it seems Lindsey and the same collection of men have accounts that get distributed into a network of investments and legitimate businesses."

"I'm listening," Sean crossed a leg over his knee and leaned back.

"These men have a secret meeting place, much like the Bildeburg group, with the exception that they meet in the same place every time and the Bildeburg group always changes the location, annually."

Sean's interest was piqued. But he wanted to know something more specific. "You said these men and Lindsey are all wealthy, and they have lots of businesses. Anything I might have heard of?"

She nodded slowly, accompanying it with a sly grin. "Most of their network is small to medium-sized organizations. Some are even at the local level. But there is one that stands out far above all the rest. Father believes that this umbrella company feeds into most of the others, providing them an in house way of laundering money and increasing their distribution channels." She paused for dramatic effect, but Sean didn't bite. He waited patiently for her to finish.

"Have you ever heard of Biosure?" she asked, crossing one leg over the other and resting both hands on a knee.

"Yeah. They're one of the top producers of different kinds of pharmaceuticals or something like that."

"True," she confirmed. "But they are also the largest provider of influenza immunizations in the entire world. Biosure distributes sixty-five percent of the world's flu shots to more than thirty-four countries."

Sean uncrossed his legs. His mind had started working on what Lindsey was up to in conjunction with the information Adriana's father had provided.

He rubbed his face while he verbalized what he was thinking. "It's flu season right now. That would mean Biosure will be shipping out tons of the stuff as we speak." He couldn't quite connect the dots on what all of it meant, though.

"What do you think he's planning?" Adriana wondered aloud.

He wasn't sure. There was something missing from the equation, and it was driving him nuts that he couldn't figure it out.

"We have to think about what it is that Lindsey is looking for," he said after a moment of silent contemplation.

"The tree of life," she shrugged. "A source of immortality. But how does that figure in?"

The lights went on in Sean's mind. He stood up and went over to the sliding door that led onto a small balcony then paced back and forth in front of it. He stopped in the middle and looked over at her.

"What if this thing that is hidden in the ark, this tree, what if it can heal anything? Sickness, disease, anything."

Adriana uncrossed her legs then re-crossed the other leg over top. "A cure for everything," she realized.

Sean pointed a finger at her. "Exactly. We need to find out what is in those flu shots."

"I doubt my father can do that, but I can see."

"Don't bother," Sean stopped her. "I have someone that might be able to do a little snooping around for us. Did your father say where Biosure's main distribution facilities are?"

She confirmed with a nod. "He said they have one in Utah, Los Angeles, Atlanta, and Chicago."

"Atlanta?"

"That's what he told me."

Sean's grin grew wider. "I think I know just the person for the job."

22

CARTERSVILLE, GEORGIA

The phone rang on the old wooden desk next to the cabin window. A floppy-eared, reddish brown hound started bellowing loudly on the floor. The dog did it every single time the phone rang. His owners knew it was the animal's instinct to alert the log home's inhabitants that they were receiving a call. But it was an annoying instinct.

A bearded man in a flannel shirt and a fleece North Face vest burst through the front door, rushing across the room to the phone.

He spoke in a commanding tone to the animal over its howling and the annoying ringing. "Calm down, boy. I hear it, ya crazy dog."

The canine must have understood because he silenced almost immediately and sank back down to the floor with his chin on big front paws.

"Hello," Joe McElroy put the phone up to his ear, his breath coming quickly. The strong southern accent was still evident, though, even with the heavy breathing.

Joe had been outside helping his wife get the leaves out of the landscaping when the phone rang.

"Mac? You sound a little out of breath. Everything okay?" Sean's voice came through the earpiece in an almost mocking tone.

"Hey, buddy! Are you okay?" Joe's face lit up instantly at the sound of Sean's voice. "The explosion in Cairo has been all over the news. I knew you were going to be in that vicinity, and I wondered if you were nearby."

The other end of the line was silent for a few seconds before Sean spoke up again. "We were the targets of that bombing, Mac."

"Targets?" Joe's eyes squinted, sending crow's feet across the upper parts of his cheeks. "What do you mean you were the targets?"

"The Order of Golden Dawn tried to eliminated us."

Joe let the words sink in as he considered what Sean was implying. He could hear his wife raking leaves outside the front door. Satisfied she would be occupied for several minutes, he continued his conversation.

"Is everyone okay? Adriana? Tommy?" he was clearly concerned.

Joe had been friends with Sean for a long time. He had become a park ranger near the town of Cartersville, but had helped Sean and Tommy find the first golden chamber, and took a bullet to the shoulder in the process. His arm was no longer in a sling, but it wasn't the same as it had been before. There had been some nerve damage, and that was something that would take time and new medical practices to heal.

"Adriana and I are okay. Tommy is in a hospital in Greece, but I think he is going to make it. We had him flown there after the attack. I didn't think it wise to keep him in Egypt. Security would have been too big of an issue."

Joe agreed. "Good call. Where are you now?"

"Adriana and I are in Istanbul."

"Istanbul?" Joe almost shouted, but kept his voice low so the wife wouldn't hear the conversation.

"Yeah," Sean replied. "We flew here earlier today from Luxor. It's a long story. Don't ask right now. I'll tell you all about it when we get state side. The reason I'm calling is I need you to do something for me."

Joe cast a quick glance out the front windows. He could see the top of his wife's head just beyond the railing on the porch. It was cold out, so she was wearing a thick cap to keep her head and ears warm.

"Sounds interesting," Joe said in a hushed, secretive tone. "How can I help?"

"Have you ever heard of Biosure?"

Joe thought for a few seconds before responding. "Yeah. I've seen their commercials. I think they have some kind of alternative to Viagra or something like that. Right?"

Sean laughed for a second on the other line. "I don't know about that. But I do know they are one of the world's largest suppliers of influenza vaccinations."

Joe wasn't sure where this was going. "Okay. So?"

"They have a distribution center in Atlanta. Adriana and I believe the guy behind Golden Dawn is also the main stock holder in Biosure. We think he is getting a shipment of bad flu shots ready to send out."

"Bad flu shots? What do you mean?" Joe was lost on the idea.

"We think he has created some kind of super virus or something. We don't really know. That's why we need you to get a sample and get it to the lab to have it analyzed."

Joe's face twisted, perplexed by the proposition. "A sample? What do you mean a sample?"

Sean cut through the bull like he usually did with Joe. It was something his long-time friend appreciated. "I need you to sneak into their facility, steal a sample of a shipment of flu vaccinations, and get it back to our friend Jenny Solomon at the CDC. She will take care of the rest."

"Wait. I don't even know how I'm going to get into this place. You want me to just break into a high security pharmaceutical company and steal a sample of their flu shots?"

"Pretty much," Sean confirmed what Joe feared. "You're the only one who can pull it off, Mac. This thing could be huge. If Lindsey is up to what we think he may be up to, there could be a worldwide epidemic coming. We have to find out what is in those shipments and shut down Biosure from sending them."

Joe took a deep breath and exhaled slowly. He had another idea. "What about Emily? Why can't she send in some of her agents to snoop around and get a sample?"

"No good," Sean countered. "She is still part of the Justice Department. There's no way she can get anyone on it that fast, and even if she could, I'd wager there would be too much red tape. But if we can get a sample to CDC, and it proves to be something bad, she can send in the cavalry."

Joe's dog looked at him with droopy, sad eyes. They always looked like that, even if he was getting his belly rubbed. Joe scratched his beard for a moment, contemplating his options. He was a government worker. If he got caught breaking and entering a pharmaceutical company, it would mean his job. Not to mention the bigger issue, who was outside raking leaves. His wife had put the quietus on his adventurous activities for the last few years. Recently, when he'd been shot, he thought his wife might actually finish the job that the gunman hadn't. That's how angry she'd been.

Back in her day she had worked for the FBI, and had seen enough to know that she didn't want to be in that world very long. He wished she wouldn't be so overprotective. In a strange way, Joe took it as a compliment.

As far as Sean's request, Joe had a few days off coming up. It wouldn't hurt anything to cruise down to Atlanta and check out the Biosure facility. He had a uniform that closely resembled a private security outfit. All he would need was clearance codes to get into the building. One of the tech guys with IAA could probably help with that.

It was starting to seem like Joe was running out of excuses.

"Okay, Sean. I'll do what I can."

"I really appreciate it, Mac. I'll be in touch."

Joe hung up the phone and looked over at the dog then let out a long sigh.

A female voice cut through the silence of the rustic living room. "Just what is it you're planning on doing?"

Joe started at the sound of his wife's voice, and looked over to see her standing in the doorway that led into the laundry room. She must have come in through the garage though he never heard her. She had her hands on the hips of her work jeans, and an accusing look on her face. Dark hair hung down to the shoulders of a gray jacket.

"Hey, dear. You scared me," Joe tried to stall. He could tell from the sustained glare that there was nothing he could do to get out of it.

"What is it Sean Wyatt wants with you now?" she took a menacing step closer.

It wasn't that Joe was afraid of his wife. She was his best friend. And that was why he didn't want trouble. He just didn't want to make her unhappy or cause her to worry. And she was the queen of worriers.

"You know, I can't do this anymore," he said after a moment of thought. "I am a man. And I don't need you bossing me around or telling me what I can't do." He was a little surprised at the tone he'd taken.

So was Mrs. McElroy. She froze in place, hearing Joe speak like that to her for the first time.

"Sean needs my help, Helen. And honestly, I could use a little help on this one, too."

Her eyebrows pulled together slightly, and the expression on her face was slightly disarmed. "What has Sean gotten himself into?" Helen's southern accent was something Joe had loved about her immediately. When she was angry, it was terrifying. But right now, she seemed to have taken on genuine concern. Maybe she also appreciated being included.

Joe decided to tell her everything, thinking a little transparency might go a long way. He calmed his tone as he spoke.

"We aren't sure, honey. But it sounds like it could be something big. That bombing we've been seeing on the news over in Egypt? Sean said that was a direct attack on him. Tommy is in a hospital in Greece right now. Sounds like he will be okay. Sean and Adriana are in Istanbul right now. And they need our help."

Helen shuffled sideways over to the edge of the big leather couch and propped herself on the armrest. She seemed more worried than angry. "What is all this about?"

"A man named Alexander Lindsey, the head of a secret organization known as Golden Dawn, is also the founder and primary shareholder of a company called Biosure. They have a distribution facility in Atlanta." Joe let out a long breath before continuing. "Sean said they might be about to send out a large shipment of bad flu shots to several countries. We need to get a sample of whatever it is he is sending out and get it to Jenny Solomon over at the CDC. She can get it analyzed and tell us whether or not there is a threat."

Helen was having trouble understanding. "So, you are just supposed to sneak into a pharmaceutical company and grab a sample of some flu shots? How are you even going to get in?"

"I thought I could get one of the tech guys at IAA to work out the access codes. Then it would just be a matter of getting the sample."

She shook her head. "Joe, I never told you this before, because I didn't think I could. But you know I worked for the FBI for a few years before going into teaching." He nodded. "Well, I worked in the electronic crimes division. One of my jobs was to hack into secure sites to test out how strong their defenses and fire walls were." She crossed her arms as she finished.

Joe was flabbergasted. He knew she was proficient on the computer, but he had no idea she was a hacker. Helen had kept it hidden from him for the years since she'd left the bureau.

She spoke up again before he could say anything. "I could probably get you into the building. But it will be difficult to get in and out without being noticed or setting off any number of alarms. And if you are dealing with something that could be a biohazard, you'll need to be careful." She stopped talking for a minute. Joe could see her mind was running through other options.

"I think I have an idea," she said finally, her face twisted with a mischievous grin.

Joe hadn't seen this side of her. And he was shocked and surprised all in one. Still, he had reservations about involving his wife in what was turning out to be an international conspiracy.

"Helen, this could be dangerous."

Her eyes narrowed in a broad smile. "Not with my plan. It will be like takin' candy from a baby."

23

NORTH EASTERN TURKEY

The enormous, snow-capped peak of Ararat loomed ominously up ahead. It hadn't taken long for Lindsey's rented helicopters to take his team and equipment out to the eastern edge of the country, near the border with Armenia.

The land was a hodgepodge of contrasting scenes. Much of it appeared to be desert, but was mingled with rich, fertile farmland, vineyards, and hillsides dotted with olive and fig trees. The plains leading up to the mountain were a picture of desolation. At least, that's the way Lindsey saw them. He wondered how anyone made a living off the land in certain places of the world. This was certainly one of them.

There were several small shanty dwellings here and there, most likely homes of shepherds, considering one of the few signs of civilization they'd seen were the flocks of sheep and goats milling around in large groups.

DeGard pointed to an area where a small church had been erected on a hillside. It was built out of stones from a nearby hillside and topped with a tin roof. The pilot took it down in a flat area a few hundred feet away from the little structure. The second chopper followed suit and landed nearby.

A few moments later, Lindsey, DeGard, Will, and Kaba were moving across the dirt field toward the church and several large stones that appeared to be some kind of monoliths. The other four mercenaries stayed back with the other chopper.

The helicopter engines had quieted down somewhat, and the group was far enough away that they could hear each other without having to yell.

"What are these?" Will asked DeGard, pointing at the odd stone that jutted up from the earth.

DeGard had done a small amount of vague research concerning the Valley of the Eight. He knew about what many called "the anchor stones." But he wasn't completely convinced. Supposedly, there were several large stones in the area, much like the one he was staring at currently. In ancient times, it was purported that boats used giant stones to keep them balanced in rough seas. The stones would be attached to long rods underneath the bow and would serve as a stabilizer. While DeGard had seen several such counter weights before, the fact that there were several in an area so far away from a major body of water caused him both skepticism and curiosity.

"They are anchor stones," he answered. "At least, that is what they are said to be. I have a difficult time believing that for certain since there is no sea near this location. Nor have any ancient boats been discovered here."

A dirty boy in shepherd's clothes and a ragged turban stood near a wooden fence about twenty feet away. He watched the newcomers with wide eyes and mouth agape, as if they were some kind of aliens come down from the heavens.

Lindsey moved closer to the monolith. The object towered over him at seven feet high. It featured several crosses engraved on the surface.

"Who put these here?" the old man asked, pointing at the carvings.

DeGard shrugged. "No one is certain. But they are done in the style of the Templars. Many believe that this location was important to early Christians because a significant Biblical event occurred near here. Of course, it could just be superstition."

Lindsey cast him a warning glance for a brief second. Then ran his hand across the smooth stone. He traced the outline of the largest cross reverently.

"There are several more of these anchor stones in the area," DeGard added. "However, this one is the most prominent. Some of the others are near the town cemetery," he pointed off to the east, "over there. And I believe there are a few more just on the other side of that hill. If the clue we discovered in Luxor was referring to a single anchor stone, this would be the one."

"You're sure?"

The Frenchman's shoulders rose slightly at the question. "Monsieur, I do not know anything about this for certain. It is speculation. But if the clue from the Nekhen ruins is pointing to something in this region, I believe it is this stone."

Lindsey examined the object for a moment then stepped around to the other side, scanning every inch of it. Will and Kaba stood back as their employer circled the monolith and returned to his original place.

He let out an exasperated sigh, and put his hands on his hips. "So, what are we supposed to look for?" DeGard shook his head and threw his hands up as if to say he was clueless.

"Do you have the stone?" Will asked, finally speaking up after watching in silent frustration for a few minutes as the other two men spun their wheels.

Both men turned around simultaneously. Lindsey spoke up. "Yes, Will. I have it right here." He fished it out of the navy blue blazer he was wearing and held it out.

"What does it say, Professor?" Will had been absent during the discovery of the round disc in the ruins of Nekhen. And he couldn't read Ancient Hebrew, like most of the normal world.

DeGard chimed in from memory. "Where the mountain rises through the eye of the needle the—"

"What?" Will cut him off in mid-sentence. "The eye of the needle?"

"Yes. That's what the man said, Will. What are you getting at?" Lindsey's voice was gruff as he spoke.

Will spun around and faced Kaba. "Come here for a second. I want you to look at something." She raised a suspicious eyebrow, but did as he requested and followed him over to the stone.

There was a hole in the top of it that immediately caught Will's attention. It had been drilled through all the way to the other side of the stone and was almost perfectly smooth. He thought it interesting that something so old could have been done with such precision. More than just being a point of curiosity, it gave him an idea.

"Here," he said to Kaba and cupped his hands near his thighs. "I'll give you a boost. I want you to look through that hole at the top and tell me what you see." She gave a quick nod, understanding what he was getting at, and a second later she was peering through opening.

"I just see a spot on the mountain," she reported, unimpressed. Will let her back down for a moment and stepped over to one of the black duffle bags they'd brought from the helicopter.

He fished out a pair of binoculars and handed them to Kaba. "Try it again, this time looking through one of those lenses."

They repeated the procedure, but this time she peered through the cavity with one eyepiece of the binoculars. She breathed slowly to try and keep steady as she peered through the stone at the mountain. She made a few adjustments of the lens to clarify what she was seeing.

"There is an indention. It might be a cave." Her voice was audibly excited. "It is up near the snow line, but there is definitely something there. Seems like there might be a place to land the helicopter near the anomaly." She looked down at Lindsey with a jubilant expression. He smiled up at her. Will's arms were shaking, so he let her down to the ground once more.

"Good thinking, Will," Lindsey said proudly. The old man beamed, actually looking happy for the briefest of seconds. "Can you remember where that spot is on the mountain?" He turned his attention to Kaba.

"No. But with this we won't need to," she pulled another device out of one of the bags. It was a small, black box with what appeared to be a lens on one end and a viewfinder on the other. "This will tag the location with a laser and guide us to exactly where we need to go."

Kaba motioned with a quick nod of the head for Will to boost her up one more time. He obeyed, and hoisted her up to the hole in the rock. She placed the device in position then pressed a few of the buttons before looking through the viewfinder. Holding the thing steady, she pressed another one of the buttons then hopped down. She looked at a small LCD screen on the top of the object. A small red dot appeared in the center of it with a green dot off to the right.

"That is where we are going. When we get there, this dot will be right on top of the other. I suspect we won't have to wait until we are that close before seeing what we are looking for." At her explanation, a corner of Lindsey's mouth curled into a smile.

DeGard stared at the mountain, dumbfounded. He was in nearly complete disbelief that a non-scholar had been able to so quickly figure out the meaning of the riddle. The rest had already started back to the helicopter, so he fell in line behind them, trying to maintain his dignity by walking upright and taking huge strides.

Lindsey made a twirling motion with his finger for the helicopter pilot to start up the engine again. Moments later they were lifting off the ground and moving toward the mountain. The dusty village passed below them, a patchwork of stone homes, muddy roads, and old wooden fences. There were a few antennas and telephone poles, evidence that the people at least had some form of electricity, however unreliable it might have been.

Up ahead, the mountain grew larger in the windshield as they came closer to the rocky slopes of Ararat.

"Head up that way," Kaba said, now in the front seat next to the pilot. Will, Lindsey, and DeGard had assumed positions in the back.

Off to the right of the helicopter, Will noticed a stone structure on a hill in the distance. It resembled a fortress or a castle. He couldn't tell for sure.

"What is that?" he pointed out the window.

DeGard was sitting across from him. He leaned forward to see what Will was asking about. It only took a second to recognize the old building.

"That is Khor Virap, just on the other side of the Armenian border. It is a monastery for the apostolic church of Armenia." He leaned back in his seat as he answered.

"It looks old," Will commented, still intrigued by the building. He could make out the outline of a central facility encircled by a high rock wall.

DeGard let out a deep breath. "That's because it is old. Khor Virap was originally built at the time of Constantine, somewhere around 300 AD. It was a castle and a prison, if I remember correctly. And I usually do."

"Oh." Will sat back and relaxed, letting the ancient church fade from his memory.

The helicopter covered the expanse from the tiny village to the foot of the mountain in a short amount of time. Then, it began the ascent up the side. Kaba kept a close eye on the device, making sure they kept aimed in the right direction. Random gusts of wind rolled down the slopes, causing the pilot to have to work a little harder at his task. He made it look easy, moving his feet and hands only a little faster to keep the machine flying level as it zipped up the mountainside.

They passed 8,000 feet, and the wind picked up again, pushing the helicopter sideways. But it kept pushing on.

"It's just up ahead," Kaba said and pointed out the windshield.

Snow was blowing down on them from above and decreased visibility. As they reached 8,200 feet, a ledge cut deep into the side of the rock and opened up a large, flat area.

Kaba tapped the screen on her device. "This is it."

The pilot held the flying machine steady for a second before deciding on a place to set down. There was plenty of space for them, but not the other chopper. As the runners touched down on the rocky plateau, he radioed the other pilot to turn back.

The rock landing ran to where the mountain sloped up dramatically. There was, however, a huge chunk of rock that appeared to have been ripped out, providing for a deep recess into the face of the mountain.

Lindsey and the others exited the helicopter and were immediately greeted with bone-chilling winds that cut through their lightweight jackets and coats. The pilot stayed with the chopper as the rest of the group quickly scurried across the landing and into the cavity in the stone. As they neared, the wind died down, blocked off by the overhang in the rock.

Kaba and Will both had bags with them and produced flashlights after seeing how dark the inside of the cavern was. They continued deeper inside with DeGard and Lindsey close behind. Once out of the blustery cold of the cliff, they let go of their coats they'd been holding tight against their bodies.

"What is this place?" Lindsey wondered aloud. No one answered. Instead, they pressed slowly on into the darkness.

Kaba handed him a flashlight so he could look on his own. Will did the same for DeGard.

The four beams flashed around on the walls of the cavern as the group continued to move further into the mountain. The walls were cut roughly into the ancient stone. DeGard noted the extraordinary difference between the carving here and at the ruins of Nekhen.

"It almost seems as if this place was created in a hurry," he scanned the jagged walls with analytic eyes. "It is nothing like what we saw before."

"Maybe it was done with cheaper tools," Will offered jokingly.

The humor was lost on DeGard as he ran his hand along the rough surface. The room was twenty feet wide at its opening and maintained that width for fifty feet, at which point it began to narrow toward the center. By the time the group had reached the back of the cavern, it had slimmed to a five-foot wide passage.

Will led the way with the other three falling behind him in single file, creeping deeper and deeper into the dark. The walls became moist the farther they went.

"Is it possible," Lindsey began, his voice bouncing off the corridor walls, "that this place is much older than the one we found outside of Luxor?"

"That is certainly likely," the Frenchman answered. "But there is no way to be certain. And where are the carvings, the inscriptions? There is nothing here but cold, wet rock."

The passageway made a sudden turn to the right and as the four moved forward, the last remnants of outside light disappeared at the lip of the entrance. They were plunged into complete darkness, save for the flashlights in their hands. Like before, the cavern path began to descend downward, something Lindsey took to be a good sign since the passageway in Nekhen had done the same.

They continued down for another fifty feet, the air became more damp and musty. Without warning, the floor leveled out, and they could see a wall at the end of the tunnel. Will wondered if it was another turn in the path. When they arrived at the dead end, they were greeted with the first signs of humanity they'd seen since entering the cave.

Dramatic lettering, almost like calligraphy, stretched from one side to the other. There was an object also carved out of the stone, just below the words. It was a tree with two trunks stretching over what Lindsey imagined was a river.

DeGard was behind the other three and pressed forward to get a look at what they'd found. His expression turned pale for a moment. Then he began to laugh. The others didn't know what was so funny, seeing that he was the only one of the four who could read the engraving.

"What is it" Lindsey demanded. "What is so funny?"

The Frenchman took a step back and tried to catch his breath. "I tried to tell you...that it was only a legend." He barely got the words out between laughs. "I knew there was something fishy about this cave. It was clearly created much later than the one we found near Luxor."

Lindsey's eyes narrowed in the faint residual light of the beams. "What? What are you saying, man? Make some sense, will you?"

DeGard got a hold of himself and shone his flashlight onto the lettering again. "This says 'Immortality is only for the righteous.' It is written in Latin. And I would say it was probably done around the late third to early fourth century."

24

ARMENIAN-TURKISH BORDER

The yellowish rock walls of Khor Virap rose up from the hill as if they were carved from the earth itself. Sean peered through the windshield at the almost eerie spectacle of the ancient fortress against the backdrop of Mount Ararat. The snow-capped peaks and dramatic slopes of the mountain loomed ominously off in the distance.

Crossing the Armenian border had been little to no trouble, which explained why there were so many Armenians living in the major cities of Turkey. They had apparently immigrated, looking for work.

They had veered off of the asphalt thirty minutes ago, now bouncing along the bumpy dirt road toward the ancient citadel. In the center, the round tower of the chapel extended up three or four stories, built of contrasting red blocks.

The small caravan of SUVs had passed a few farms en route to the fortress. Nothing was growing, though, due to the cold weather in that part of the country. Sean imagined during the summer months the region exploded with greenery from the different crops that were grown. Still, he'd never really liked flat lands, preferring mountains and forests to anything else.

A few minutes later, the trucks stopped in front of a gate at the foot of the hill near the monastery. Jabez had claimed that the location was a sacred pilgrimage spot for many Armenian Christians, but during the winter months it was almost completely empty, save for the monks who maintained it. From the looks of, he had been right about the low tourism during the cold season.

Jabez exited the driver's side of the vehicle and walked casually over to a small, wooden guard shack. A monk appeared in the doorway and spoke for a few seconds with Jabez. The man in the brown robes then nodded his head and floated over to the gate, unlocking it and moving it out of the way for the vehicles to pass through.

The Arab returned to the convoy and hopped back in the SUV, shaking off the outside cold as he did. Sean had noticed the remarkable change in temperature just a few hours outside of Istanbul. He figured a climb in elevation was probably the main culprit.

Jabez steered the SUV onto the winding road that led up the hill to the fortress. "They are going to let us drive to the top. Usually, visitors are required to park down here and walk up. Thankfully, there aren't many people here this time of year, so making an exception for us is not a problem."

The narrow street only had two turns before they reached the top of the hill where Jabez parked next to a low, stone wall. Adriana hopped out of the vehicle and looked out across the plains, holding one hand over her forehead. Her dark brown hair flapped in the cold breeze that swooped up from the flatland and over the hill. The main peak of Ararat and its smaller sibling towered over the land from the Armenian western border.

Jabez trotted back to the other truck and gave the other men some instructions before returning to the front of the lead vehicle. One of the men in the back of the other SUV got out and climbed into the driver's seat of the other vehicle.

"I told them to go over to the town and fill up the fuel tanks to save time. They should be back by the time we finish here," Jabez explained.

Firth grumbled about something while zipping up his coat. Sean and the others followed Jabez up a slight rise to a wide-open gate leading into the monastery. The trucks disappeared around the bend, heading back down the mountain.

Sean had never seen anything quite like it. The external wall was clearly built as a protective barrier from invasion, or possibly to keep people in. On the inside, instead of a castle or a garrison, the small chapel stood as a stark contrast to the facility's original purpose and infamous history.

The long, boxy design of the chapel was accented by triangular gables, and a twelve-sided tower jutting up in its center, topped by a dome. From a distance, the building seemed to be more reddish in color. But up close, Sean now saw many charcoal-hued blocks, and a few lighter ones as well. There seemed to be no rhyme or reason for the differentiation, which added more curiosity to the place.

Jabez acted as the tour guide as the small group neared an atrium made from gray stone, another odd contrast to the rest of the building.

"This chapel was built in the year 642 A.D. by Nerses the Builder." He raised a hand as if to display the building. "It has been an Armenian Apostolic Monastery for much of that time. The name Khor Virap means 'deep well' in their traditional language. It was given that name because of the pit that Saint Gregory was cast into."

Sean noted that some of the construction seemed more recent than the date their Arab friend had given. "It looks like some of this was built later than 642."

Jabez nodded. "The original chapel was built in that year. More was added, as we see it now, in the mid-17th century."

"How do you know so much about this place?" Firth chimed into the conversation with his usual, snide demeanor.

The Arab stopped just short of the entryway and spun around. A bearded priest in dark robes and black shoes stood under the arch near the doorway, smiling at the visitors as they approached.

"In the thousands of years since the ark's disappearance, there have been but a handful of people who sought to uncover its location.

In between those few travelers, it can become quite boring. So, we study." There was a glimmer in his eye that told Sean the man was attempting humor. Though, Firth didn't really appreciate it.

Sean burst out laughing for a few seconds while Adriana and Firth watched on with rapt curiosity.

A moment later, Jabez was laughing too, and grabbed the professor on the shoulder. "Of course I am joking, Doctor. We make it our business to learn as much as we can about this region and surrounding areas. It is part of our calling."

"And here I thought you were just nomadic assassins," Firth said sardonically.

Jabez's laughter ceased and his face became serious again. "We are that when necessity requires it." He turned around and stalked toward the priest who had opened his arms in greeting.

Firth glanced at Sean, who shrugged off the comment. "Don't look a gift horse in the mouth, Professor," he added and followed just behind their Arab guide. "He's helping us. And try and remember, you could be dead right now if we hadn't come by your house. So, try and lighten up a little." Firth stopped in his tracks, briefly appearing insulted.

He thought for a moment before following Adriana to the threshold of the chapel.

Jabez introduced them all to the still-smiling priest, who now had his hands folded behind his back. His name was Sarmen Ovesian. Jabez said that he had been at the monastery for over twenty years. Sarmen had come to serve in the ministry as a young man of only 16 years. He was now nearly forty and had specks of gray in his thin, black hair. A life of service had suited him based on the smile on his face.

"Welcome to Khor Virap," he said in thickly accented English. "It is a rare pleasure to have visitors this time of year. Please, follow me in out of the cold."

Sarmen led the way through the dark wooden door and into the sanctuary of the little chapel. The expanse of the room was fairly small with only a few rows of pews on either side of the aisle. From front to back, the sanctuary only stretched about thirty to forty feet. Dark walls were dotted with candle sconces, dripping with wax. The light from the tiny flames flickered against the stone and some ancient paintings of saints, priests, and patriarchs, just as Sean imagined it would have centuries before. The altar was a simple white stand draped with red velvet cloth. Matching material hung from the wall behind the altar in two places. It was much different than many of the flamboyant cathedrals that dotted the European landscape.

After heads spun around for a moment, taking in the sanctuary, the priest ushered them toward a door just off to the right of the altar. "Through here is where you will find what you are looking for," he explained.

They passed through opening into a room that was much smaller. It was a tiny alcove, lit only by a few candles on the floor. There were a few crosses painted in gold standing against the walls. What lay in the middle of the room, though, was what really caught their attention. In the center of the floor, an iron set of steps descended into the ground through a hole about three feet wide.

Sean stared, wide-eyed at the depression. "So this is the pit," he said, more statement than question.

The priest nodded. "Gregory spent thirteen years of his life down in that place, with very little food or water. Only divine power could have sustained him for that long."

Sarmen's words hung in the cool, musty air. It would have been a living nightmare to be kept prisoner in such a place. There were no sources of natural light, just complete and utter darkness, twenty-four hours, seven days a week. In the ancient world, there weren't many things worse than being kept in a dungeon. This pit, however, was one of those worse things.

Standing over the cavity, Sean gazed down into the darkness. There was a faint shimmering light mixing with a steadier, whitish light at the bottom of the steep steps.

"We burn candles to honor Saint Gregory," the priest explained. "There is also a light bulb to provide better illumination. Please, you may take as long as you like to look around. I have a few other tasks I must attend to." He smiled and motioned for Sean to go ahead and climb down the steps. Sarmen's flowing robes followed him out of the alcove and back into the sanctuary in dramatic fashion.

Sean was dubious. "He's just going to leave us here?" he asked Jabez.

"Sarmen is a very trusting person. And he is especially sympathetic to the brotherhood." The Arab stepped past Sean and began climbing down the almost ladder-like steps, disappearing beneath the floor.

Sean twitched his head to the side for a second. The answer was good enough for him, so he followed Jabez down into the hole. The ladder-like staircase dropped almost straight down for about twenty feet then cut off at an angle the rest of the way down until it reached the floor. The vertical passage also became narrower below the mouth, slimming down to a two foot wide cubed shaft.

In the bottom of the pit, it took a few moments for everyone's eyes to adjust to the darkness, even with the light the solitary bulb was putting out. In a small, arched recession cut into the wall, a painting of Saint Gregory stood alone.

Firth examined the canvas for a few seconds. "This painting is around four hundred years old, he declared in shock. "It should be in a museum, not down here."

Sean wasn't about to get in an argument about where the artwork should be. It belonged to the monks, and they could do with it as they pleased. Though, he was somewhat distressed over the graffiti that lingered on the rock above the painting's alcove. It was a wonder the canvas had never been tampered with.

The pit had been carelessly hewn out of the mountain in some places, but braced with large blocks of stone and mortar in others. Whoever had done it wasn't concerned with aesthetics. This place was meant to be a place of torture and death. The walls had become blackened over the years, though there were still flecks of white here and there displaying the original color of the rock. The hard floor was jagged and uneven with a coating of dirt over the top of it. Sean had expected it to smell worse than it did. But the stench of the ages had worn away. He imagined when the place had been transformed from a prison to a sacred site, some cleaning must have occurred.

"It is hard to believe someone lived down here for thirteen years," Adriana commented reverently as she gazed around at the dismal setting. Her voice hummed off the rock walls.

Jabez agreed. "It was a difficult trial, for certain. And yet, after he was released from it, he ministered to the man who put him here. Above that, Gregory served the king for the rest of his days. I do not know many men..." he corrected himself for Adriana, "people who would do something like that after being so poorly treated."

The portrait of Saint Gregory stood quietly off to the side in its little archway. He was adorned in priestly garments and a miter, standard for someone in the employ of the church in those days.

Even Dr. Firth seemed to be impressed by the gravity of such a tortured existence. He crossed his arms and rubbed his stubbled face with one hand, wiping his nose a little as he did. "I couldn't imagine living in this place for a month, one year, much less thirteen."

No one else said anything for a few moments, letting the somberness of the room fill their hearts and minds. After a minute had passed, Sean moved over to the wall near the little alcove where the portrait rested. A small, stone cross sat next to it. He touched it reverently for a second then pulled his hand back. He knew it had probably been there for a thousand years. The gravity of historical facts like that always hit him heavily.

"If there's a clue for us to find here, we should get to it quickly. Lindsey may already be on his way to the ark. We may not have much time."

The others spread out as much as they could in the tiny area, scouring the walls and ceiling with their eyes.

Sean spoke under his breath, just to himself. "I just hope Mac can buy us some time."

25

MOUNT ARARAT

"What do you mean it was done in the early fourth century? And how is it in Latin?" Lindsey's voice boomed through the tight corridor.

DeGard's laughter ceased as he sensed the serious nature of the moment. "Monsieur, I tried to warn you that chasing this treasure was folly." His French accent sounded even tinnier in the narrow confines of the cave. "It is clearly a fool's treasure. There is nothing here, and probably never was. You have been chasing a fairy tale. There is no tree of life, Monsieur Lindsey. I am sorry, but you have wasted your time and money searching for this."

It was the first time Will had ever seen devastation on the face of his employer. Alexander Lindsey had been a strong, ruthless man to work for. He'd ordered kidnappings, executions, and bombings, never once flinching in the slightest. Most recently, Will had discovered the fate of Lindsey's betrayers. The men had been executed in a brazen bull within the confines of Golden Dawn's secret council room. Lindsey was certainly not a man of weakness.

Now, though, as Will stared at the old man in the yellow radiance of the flashlights, Lindsey's white hair seemed whiter, his wrinkles more pronounced. The old man appeared defeated.

Lindsey started coughing violently, probably a combination of the damp air and the sudden realization that he'd been duped on such a grand scale. He stepped away from the others, covering his mouth and bracing himself on the rough-hewn wall.

Kaba put her hand on his shoulder for a moment, but he jerked himself away. After a few more seconds, the coughing finally subsided.

He stared hard at the writing on the wall. "All the money. All the time. Everything we've done. To come this far…all for a hoax." Lindsey's voice was filled with regret and bitter resentment. He shook his head slowly, still staring at the wall. His breaths were coming quickly in big heaves. "Why would someone leave this here?"

DeGard looked back at the inscription for a moment. "I do not know, Monsieur. Why do people create giant rings in corn fields and then claim Aliens did it?"

The words went in one ear and out the other as the old man shuffled close to the wall. As he neared it, he felt something shift underneath his feet. There was a clanking noise deep from within the mountain then silence again. The four stepped back away from the wall, scanning the walls to see what was happening. Will's flashlight fell on the spot where his employer had been standing only a moment before. Suddenly, the section of the floor dropped away, sending a gust of warm air up into the space.

Will put his hand against the wall to maintain his balance, and crept closer to the gaping hole in the floor. He leaned over and shone his light down into the abyss, but the beam never reached a surface, only deflecting off of dust and steam.

"There's nothing down there," Will said in an even tone. "It's an old booby trap. Whoever built this place didn't want anyone coming out of it."

Lindsey's face lightened slightly despite the terrifying realization that he had nearly died. He moved back toward the cavity in the floor, investigating it carefully from a safe distance. His eyes narrowed as the dust settled.

"It must have surely been designed to collapse sooner than that," he realized out loud.

"But it didn't," Will comforted.

The old man nodded and rose back up. "The question is, why someone would go to the trouble of putting a trap here, if there was not something to hide elsewhere?"

DeGard let out an exasperated sigh. "Are you suggesting you are going to continue this ridiculous charade? Because if you are, I am going to ask that you pay me my fee and let me go."

Lindsey's eyebrows raised in surprise at the Frenchman's bold comment. He'd had enough of the foreigner's doubt, his lack of conviction, and his tedious fear.

"If that is what you wish, Monsieur DeGard, then we will let you go." Lindsey gave a quick nod to Will.

Kaba understood the unspoken order and grabbed DeGard from behind as her partner snagged the suddenly panicked professor. They forced the man toward the hole then spun him around, each gripping one of his wrists.

"What are you doing?" he screamed, sounding more like a terrified little girl than a grown man. "We had a deal!"

Lindsey stepped toward him, menace covering his face. The wrinkles on his skin seemed to frame wicked emotions fueled by anger.

"You said you wanted out, and to be let go. So I will let you go." The low voice was rough, and the loose skin beneath his neck shook as he spoke. "Unless, of course, you wish to continue your employment with me."

Kaba and Will shoved the skinny man out over the abyss, holding his life by thin wrists. His head went back and forth, trying to look down yet desperately not wanting to see what waited below.

"Please!" he pleaded. "I'll do whatever you ask. Just don't kill me!" His voice sounded like a whimpering, nasally dog.

Lindsey thought he saw tears welling up in the Frenchman's eyes.

"So, you will continue to assist us in this charade?" The last word carried a sarcastic air with it.

DeGard nodded frantically. "Oui! Oui! I'll do whatever you say."

Lindsey nodded and his two associates jerked up the trembling professor, and pulled him to safety. DeGard quickly moved away from the hole and put his hands on his knees. Bile rose up through his esophagus, and for a moment, it appeared he might vomit.

"Now," Lindsey spoke in a commanding tone again. "What are we missing here? We know that someone set this trap. And we believe based on the good professor's earlier assessment that it was probably built around the late third century. That is what you said, correct Monsieur DeGard?"

The Frenchman was still bent over his knees catching his breath and trying hard not to throw up. "Yes," he nodded, breathing heavily. "The Latin and the style of the engraving would suggest that time frame."

"That means that the people who built this cave, knew about the ark. And they also knew about what the ark contained, based on the contents of the message."

Will's eyes opened wider. He could see where his employer was going with the line of thought. "So, you think the people who carved out this cave found something. But where is it now?"

"The monastery," DeGard gasped and leaned back against the craggy rock wall.

His flashlight had fallen on the floor and was now aimed at his feet. The other three shone their lights on his face, causing him to shield himself from the brightness with one hand.

"What did you say?" Lindsey demanded and shuffled over to where the shaking Frenchman stood. "What monastery? You better start making sense quickly."

DeGard began to regain his composure, becoming angry over the fact that his boss had threatened to drop him into a bottomless pit. When he spoke, his voice was still shaky. "We flew by a monastery on the way here. Khor Virap. Your assistant here asked about it." He pointed a crooked finger at Will.

Lindsey turned his attention to Will then back to DeGard, as if trying to size up whether or not the man was telling the truth. Will confirmed it with a nod, but that still didn't explain what the monastery had to do with the missing clue to the ark. The old man was irritated, angry, and growing tired of the search. He had come to the eastern border of Turkey believing he would find the greatest treasure ever known to man. Only a few people ever even believed it still existed.

Now, to be so close only to get presented with another obstacle was almost more than he could bear. Lindsey's patience was running out. And his last hope was in a Frenchman who had been ex-communicated by his profession for unethical behavior. Despite Lindsey's belief in his own mission, the irony was not lost on him.

His eyes peered deep into DeGard's soul. When he spoke, it was nearly a hiss. "Why are you bringing up this monastery now? What is it about that place that is so special?"

DeGard took a deep breath and exhaled slowly. He bent down and picked up his flashlight while he spoke. "As I told your associate before, Khor Virap was initially built around the turn of the same century I believe this passage was constructed. It would make sense that the people who built it may also have taken the clue and hidden it somewhere."

"Go on."

"Khor Virap was originally a prison. Saint Gregory was kept in the dungeon there for over a decade. He is the patron saint of Armenia and was responsible for converting the king, and eventually the entire nation as a result of his ministry."

Lindsey was beginning to lose interest in the story about the priest. "I don't care about any of that. What is so special about that monastery? And I warn you, if you are wasting my time, I will not hesitate to drop you in that hole."

The Frenchman swallowed hard while trying to convey a look of disdain. "It was said that Saint Gregory had miraculous healing powers. That he was able to heal the king. Rumors suggested he had access to some ancient power. To many, it was evidence that he had the power of God at his disposal. The healings made it easy to convert tens of thousands of Armenians."

Lindsey took a step back, lowering his flashlight. He looked over at Will, whose face was barely illuminated by the whitish-yellow glow of the beams. Will cast him a glance that basically said they didn't have any other play at that point.

"How far away is this place?" Lindsey asked finally.

"Not far," DeGard shook his head. "But we will have to cross the border to get there."

Kaba spoke up. "Not a problem. The border is not heavily patrolled in an area not far from Khor Virap. We should be able to cross over without any problems if we fly low."

The old man hesitated for a moment, deciding the best course of action. He couldn't afford any more mistakes. Back in the United States, over two thousand crates awaited his orders to be shipped all over the world. The longer it took to find what he was looking for, the riskier the entire mission became. If the legends about Saint Gregory were true, he may have had access to the fruit of the tree from Eden. The story description certainly aligned with every bit of research he'd done through the years.

The ability to heal, energize, and grant immortality were all components of the tree God had placed in the Garden of Eden. With it, he would be able to live forever and destroy all the sinful people of the world.

Lindsey raised one eyebrow, but his face remained stern. "Very well. Let's investigate the monastery. Perhaps our friend, Saint Gregory, left us something of interest after all."

26

CARTERSVILLE

"So, tell me again what it is you're doing?" Joe watched as his wife scanned through what looked like a complicated spreadsheet.

Helen had accessed the Biosure database using a bunch of terms he'd not understood. She'd said something about going in through their back door, but after that, everything had been mumbo jumbo to him. Whatever she did, it had worked, and now they were staring at hundreds of order manifests for Biosure influenza vaccines.

"It looks like they're shipping these all over the world," Helen remarked as she scrolled down the list of shipping addresses and orders. "I wonder why all the dates are open. Wouldn't they all be queued to leave on specific days and times?"

Her face expressed the same confusion as Joe's. It didn't make sense. Hundreds, maybe thousands of orders were listed there on the screen. But none of them had a shipping date. Joe's mind was turning as his wife continued to look through the spreadsheet.

"If what Sean said was correct, it sounds like Lindsey is planning to use Biosure to distribute some kind of super virus out into the world. But he wouldn't do that unless he could protect himself from the virus." Helen could tell the wheels were turning in Joe's head.

He rubbed his beard for a few moments before continuing. "So, that is what he's looking for. He's trying to find the tree of life from the Garden of Eden because he thinks it will make him immune to whatever it is he's going to unleash. He must believe it has some kind of medicinal properties that can override the virus."

Helen looked up from the computer while Joe finished his thought. She glanced back at the computer for a second then returned her gaze to him. "These shipments are all some kind of super bug?" Her face contorted, disturbed at the idea. "They are ready to be sent to major cities all over the globe. It will be a pandemic within days.

Joe nodded. "So it would seem. We have to make sure those shipments don't go anywhere until we can get a sample to the CDC, and confirm what it is we're dealing with."

Helen acknowledged what Joe had said with a quick nod. She turned her attention to the computer screen and began typing furiously. Several different windows popped up while she worked, but before he could see what they were, the boxes disappeared. He had never seen anyone type as fast as his wife. Come to think of it, he had never really seen his wife do anything on the computer. Joe assumed that she used it for browsing the Internet or Pinterest, typical things. Now he could see there was a layer to his wife he'd never known about. She was a government trained computer hacker. The thought actually excited him for a second before he redirected his focus back to task.

She hit the "enter" key and watched as a flurry of numbers and letters passed across the screen. At last, a window popped up that read, "account created."

Joe leaned over and saw the message. "What does that mean?" he asked over her shoulder.

Helen smiled at his reflection on the monitor. "I just created an all access pass for us to get into Biosure's headquarters."

"Are you serious?" his face was in utter disbelief. "You just broke into the Biosure computer system and gave us access to the building?"

"Yep," she nodded. "I figured it would be safer to send it there than to our house."

"Honey," Joe beamed. "Did I ever tell you you're amazing?"

"Not as often as you should," she grinned as she looked up at him.

Up until that point in their relationship, Joe had never seen such guile from his wife. And they had been married for twenty years. He had always assumed she was overprotective of him out of fear of being alone. Now, he realized she had probably seen and done things that showed her a world of trouble. Her way of keeping him out of that trouble was to nag him.

Another thought occurred to Joe, interrupting the ones about his wife and her mysterious past.

"But will they know we hacked into their system? I guess what I'm asking is, will someone be able to track where the order came from?"

Her face became slightly more serious." Maybe. That is always a possibility. That is why we need to move fast. I doubt anyone at Biosure will notice, but I'd rather not chance it. We will have to act quickly and get a sample of whatever that stuff is over to Jenny."

"Did I say you were good?" Joe smiled broadly from behind his beard. "I mean, you are really good."

"Thank you. Now, we need to think about how to navigate that building," she stated in a thick southern drawl.

"Right."

Her expression turned serious as she switched back to the computer screen. The huge list of addresses on the manifest stared back at her. "I just hope we get to this in time."

27

TURKISH-ARMENIAN BORDER

The helicopters cruised over the border separating the two countries. Patches of snow dotted the plains in a few places. It had been a warmer season than the region was accustomed to. Even so, there had been a few snowstorms that had come through a little earlier than usual leaving traces of white in spots where the sun didn't shine as long.

It hadn't taken long to fly from the dramatic slopes of Ararat Mountain to the rolling plains of Armenia. The silhouette of the strange monastery rose up in the distance, almost as if it had been carved out of the hill on which it sat.

Lindsey had ordered the two pilots to swoop around and approach Khor Virap from the south. As the helicopters passed by the ancient site to the west, it seemed the lonely monastery was fairly empty. Seeing any vehicles was fairly difficult from the safe distance they maintained, but Lindsey had insisted they approach with caution. In the back of his mind, he continued thinking that it was still possible someone else might be on the same trail. And he didn't want to spook anyone.

The pilots steered the flying machines around and landed them in a field near a small parking lot at the base of the hill. The occupants noticed a small guard shack at the foot of a narrow driveway that wound its way up to the top where a thick, rock wall wrapped around the premises. Engines began to shut down as the group exited the cabins and headed toward the flimsy gate.

A smiling monk appeared in the doorway of the shack, wearing dark robes and matching shoes. The priest welcomed the group in his native Armenia. There were a few other words he fired off, but no one in the group understood.

"Do you speak English?" Lndsey asked gruffly.

The monk ignored the older man's rude demeanor, continuing to speak with a smile. "Of course," he said in a strained accent. "Welcome to Khor Virap. Are you here to worship or just see the site? We will be having a service in a few hours."

"We just want to take a look around," Will answered for his employer.

"Very well," the monk kept smiling. "It is rare that we get many visitors this time of year. Your group is the second in the last few hours. This must be a first." He beamed at Lindsey with an overly-eager grin.

The young priest turned to open the gate, but Lindsey grabbed his arm, stopping him in his tracks. The gesture was the first thing that had taken the stupid smile off the monk's face since Lindsey had laid eyes on him.

"Wait. You've had other visitors today?" the old man demanded.

The monk nodded, shaking the thin layer of brown hair that rimmed a shiny, pale head. "Yes," the smile returned. "I believe they are Americans like you. You are American, yes?" He raised an expectant eyebrow.

Will's eyes narrowed. "These visitors...did they have a woman with them, and an older man?"

"Yes," the monk confirmed emphatically. "Do you know them? I can take you to where they are if you like. I believe they are viewing the—"

"No," Lindsey cut him off before the monk could finish. "I think we may have to come back later."

The monk seemed confused, momentarily. "So, you do not wish to see the chapel?"

Again Lindsey insisted. "We will return at a later time. Thank you." He turned around and started walking toward where the helicopters were sitting.

DeGard was just as confused as the priest, unsure of why they were leaving. "You have them right where you want them. What is it you plan to do? Are you going to force them to give you whatever they have found?" he questioned insistently.

Lindsey ignored the query and motioned for Will and Kaba to come close as they walked away from the still gawking monk. The two sped up and leaned in close, listening carefully to his employer's instructions.

"Get rid of the monk. Tell the men to grab their weapons. We will surround the chapel, and when Wyatt and his friends leave, kill them. Kill them all."

Will nodded and turned around, heading back toward where the young monk was standing while Kaba sprinted in the direction of the helicopters.

As he neared the young monk, Will put his arm around him and ushered the young man toward the little guard shack. To the naïve witness, it would have appeared Will was sharing a secret or maybe a request with the priest. As soon as the two disappeared from sight into the confines of shack, there were a few faint pops. A moment later, Will reappeared in the doorway, concealing his pistol within his wool pea coat.

The other mercenaries were already following Kaba back from the helicopters, trailed by Lindsey who had added a black trench coat over the top of his other layers. A cold breeze rolled across the plains, cutting through to the bone. Will imagined the old man must have been affected by it more than anyone in the group. But Lindsey was driven, and would not accept failure, even if that meant personally overseeing the mission through to the end.

They walked through the gate, marching up the hill toward the entrance to the fortress. The wind picked up the farther they went up the hill. When they reached the top, Lindsey and DeGard were holding their coats tight against their torsos to keep warm.

"I wonder where their transportation is," Will wondered in a low voice through clenched teeth. He pressed his hand against the gun in his coat, anticipating that his revenge was close at hand. It was time to end this little game once, and for all. Wyatt had been lucky before, but his luck was about to run out.

Kaba scanned the area, searching for movement. "No sign of their cars. Maybe they left."

"That priest said they were still here," he disagreed. "There's only one way in and one way out. If they had left, that monk would have seen it."

As they neared the entrance to the monastery, another monk greeted them with a hearty smile. Lindsey nodded at Will who stepped in front and put his arm around the shoulders of the monk, much the same way he had the young man at the gate. Repeating what he had done before ascending the hill, Will took the priest into a doorway just on the inside of the wall. He re-emerged a few moments later, alone.

He gave a quick look at Lindsey then motioned for the other men to follow his lead. Will kept his gun concealed within the folds of his jacket as he ducked into a corner of the entryway into the courtyard of the fortress. Across the way, the entrance to the chapel stood quietly. A quick scan of the area revealed no other visitors. He assessed that the monks must have been somewhere else on the premises. The bitter wind picked up again and funneled through the archway where he and the other men were standing. Kaba looked at him from the other side of the portal, waiting for an order.

Lindsey and DeGard watched from a short distance as their team moved swiftly through the archway and into the courtyard, checking every corner before taking up positions surrounding the entrance to the church.

Will sprinted back to the archway where his employer and the Frenchman now stood, safely concealed behind the corners of stone.

"There is no other way out of the chapel, Sir. We have the entrance surrounded. When they come out it will be like shooting fish in a barrel."

Lindsey's eyes narrowed. "Good. Make sure there are no survivors."

28

KHOR VIRAP, ARMENIA

Sean and his companions had scoured the entire pit for over an hour, searching for a clue to the whereabouts of the lost ark of Noah. The rough walls and dusty floors had not given up their secrets, if there were any. Firth sat down on a small, semi-circular platform near the painting of Saint Gregory. He'd grown tired of the search and had, once again,S become his grumpy self.

It was a battle Sean was growing tired of fighting with the professor. He understood the frustration, though. There wasn't anything to be found in the depths of the pit. At least nothing of profound clarity. Sean would have given almost anything for a simple x that marked the spot.

Adriana stood close by. Her hair had been pulled back in a ponytail, revealing her smooth, thin neck. For a moment, Sean was distracted by her natural beauty and caught himself staring. When she turned her head, he quickly diverted his gaze to the wall just behind her.

"What are you thinking?" Jabez interrupted from across the room. "Have you seen anything that might resemble a map?"

"No," Sean shook his head, disappointed. "Maybe we are thinking about this the wrong way." He stepped into the center of the room and slowly spun around in circles, eyeing the walls carefully. "If you were Gregory, and you wanted to make sure you left a clue for someone in the distant future to find the ark, you wouldn't want just anyone to find it. Right?"

Jabez and Adriana nodded. Firth had his hands on his knees, listening with vague interest.

"So, who would you want to find it?" he asked in his most cynical, English accent.

"What is the recurring theme we keep running into?" he asked, but got no response other than blank stares. "Righteous. Immortality is for the righteous. Who are the righteous?"

"Priests?" Adriana offered.

"Followers of God," Jabez included with only slight confidence.

Both of their answers made sense, but didn't help with the question as to where the clue might be, if Saint Gregory had even left one at all. For a minute, silence returned to the dimly lit chamber as the four occupants considered the question.

Sean stared at the ground near Firth's feet while he tried to think of an answer. It came to him suddenly as he observed the strange undulations in the floor. Near the Professor's feet, it wasn't as flat as the rest of the rest floor. There were small ridges and dips, as if the stone tiles had been carved away by miniscule rivers of water.

Firth noticed his curiosity and wondered what Sean was looking at. "What is it?"

"Move your feet, Professor," he ordered. Firth did as requested and stood back up, moving off to the side.

Sean got down on one knee and ran his hand along the dirty floor then felt along the stone nearby. There was definitely a difference. He could see it more clearly now that he was down on his knees.

"Adriana, could you hand me the brush out of my backpack?"

She nodded and stepped over to his black bag that he had set on the floor against the wall. A moment later, she fished out what looked like a small broom, typically used on excavations or archaeological digs. She passed him the tool, and he immediately got down on his one hand, and with the other began sweeping away the ancient dust.

"What is it?" Jabez reinforced the professor's question. "What do you see?"

Sean never stopped brushing vigorously at the floor, increasing a small pile of dirt with each stroke. "The righteous are penitent, Jabez. The penitent kneel before God. So, the righteous kneel to find their way to immortality. Saint Gregory left his clue here in the floor where only the most humble, penitent person would find it. The years of dust have covered it up, but not entirely."

He continued sweeping away the dirt and debris until a strange mark appeared in the floor a foot or so away from ripples in the stone. Sean worked faster after seeing what his efforts had produced, and a few minutes later, he stood back up and stepped away.

The other three crowded around and stared down at the cleaned space on the floor, mouths dropped to their chest, eyes wide with wonder.

An X had been carved out of the dark stone near the platform. A line was also gouged out that led from the center of the X to a place in the middle of the miniature ridges and valleys.

Sean smiled broadly, but was still a little astounded. "Well, that is interesting."

"Incredible," Firth got down close to the floor and examined the oddity. "It would appear that Saint Gregory left us a clue after all?"

"Yeah, but what does it mean?" Sean asked. "Those look like mountains. Is that Ararat? I mean...we are pretty close to it."

Jabez shook his head. "No. Ararat Mountain only features two main peaks. And the area surrounding it is flat. This is a range of mountains." He waved his hand around the area of hills and valleys. "There is another possibility I had not considered."

All eyes in the room went to Jabez as he thought about the idea. "Ararat Mountain is not the only Ararat in the region." The others stared at him, begging with their gazes. "There is a small city to the northeast of here by the name of Ararat. For as long as history goes, there has been a settlement there. Some people have claimed that it was established by Noah's ancestors." His voice lowered slightly as if he were concealing a secret. "That town is on the edge of a mountain range much like this one designed by Saint Gregory. It would appear that he has left us a direct path to the ark of Noah, somewhere in those mountains."

"Good enough for me," Sean stated, pulling his phone out of his pocket.

He snapped a few pictures of the map Gregory had left inlaid in the stone floor.

Firth stood up. A scowl crossed his face once again. "Wait just a minute. That is hardly a definitive map. Even if it is correct, we could find ourselves wandering through those mountains for weeks or months without finding something. We need a reference point."

"This is it," Sean pointed at the X carved into the stone floor. "This is our reference point."

"That could be anywhere," Firth argued. "It could be this prison cell, or a town to the northeast, or it could be in the Himalayas."

The room fell silent again after the professor made his point. Jabez stared hard at the ground.

When he spoke, it was full of conviction. "This is definitely that mountain range, Professor. It is not far from here. We can take the town as the center point of the X and use that to figure out which way to go into the mountains."

Sean was still sold on the idea. "Those mountains accessible by SUV?"

"In many areas, yes. There are lots of old roads that go through them, all the way up to the north part of the country."

"Gentlemen," Firth interrupted. "This could be nothing. What if we get out there into those mountains and get stuck or don't find what we are looking for?"

Sean turned to the professor. "Doc, you're a man of science. Right?" Firth nodded. "Well, sometimes, even scientists have to take things on faith. That's just the way it is. And right now is one of those times. Now, if you would prefer, we can drop you off in the next village and leave you there until we come back. Or you can find your own way home. But if I were you, I would be extremely interested in taking a chance on this. Because if we are right, this will be the most incredible archaeological discovery in the history of mankind." He watched as his speech sunk in to the professor's head.

The older man was stunned at first. But as he considered the possibility, ambition reared its head in the back of his thoughts. Sean made a good point. If the ark of Noah was real, and there were evidence, he would be one of the most renowned archaeologists in history. He would be famous the world over, able to write his own ticket no matter where he went. Speaking engagements, book deals, and anything he wanted would be there for the taking. Firth wasn't a greedy man. He simply enjoyed the good things in life: nice cars, single malt scotch, and homes that catered to his particular tastes.

"Very well, Mr. Wyatt," he agreed. "You make an excellent case. I will accompany you into the mountains. I hope the venture is not in vain."

Sean shrugged, giving the professor a look of indignation. He wished he could just leave Firth in the pit or at worst, the next town. But he had a feeling that they might need the professor's help again if they did find the Ark. Just to be safe, Sean wanted him along for the ride.

"Only one way to find out, Doc," he replied and slapped the man on the shoulder. "Now, we should get going. If Lindsey is on his way to the ark, we will need to hurry to catch up."

One by one, the group ascended the steep stairs, back up to the alcove on the side of the small chapel. Sarmen was waiting for them at the top with the same welcoming smile on his face.

"Did you find what you were looking for?" he asked in a hopeful voice.

Jabez nodded. "We think so, my friend. We will know soon enough."

"Would you all like to stay for the afternoon meal?" the priest invited as he stepped through the archway and back into the main sanctuary of the chapel.

"Thank you," Sean offered. "But we really have to get going. Maybe another time."

"Very well," the monk replied in the same, kind tone. "Please, let me know if I can be of any assistance in the future. And I would like to know what you find wherever this journey takes you."

"We will, brother," Jabez assured.

Sarmen turned to lead the way back toward the entrance when a splash of blood shot out of his upper back. He wavered for a moment before dropping to the floor in a heap.

Jabez's face changed instantly to one of shock as he crouched down to check on his friend. Sean put his arms out wide, pressing the professor and Adriana backwards into the safety of the alcove. Shards of stone exploded off the wall just behind his head. For the moment, the Arab was protected by the rows of church pews as he knelt beside the priest.

A wet spot was forming around a hole in his dark robes, just above the right side of his chest. The smile that had seemed permanently on his face was now gone, replaced by a look of horror as he gasped for breath.

Jabez tried to comfort him as he hovered over. His face had become calm. "Relax, my old friend. Slow your breathing." He placed his hand over the wound, feeling just inside of the robes with his fingers.

Another bullet smashed into the wall near the front of the presbytery. It was a few feet away from where Sean had taken cover at the edge of the alcove.

"How did they find us?" Adriana asked from just behind him. She had moved Firth back closer to the pit entrance in order to get a better view of what was going on.

Sean didn't have the answer. "It has to be Lindsey's people, right?"

"Who else would it be?" she replied with a question of her own as she removed a black, Springfield .40 caliber from the inside of her jacket.

Even under duress, the vision was somehow sexy to Sean. Seeing her standing there next to him, ready to unleash hell on their attackers, was strangely attractive. He shook off the thoughts and withdrew his own matching weapon.

"I see you went with the XD," he said coolly.

"XDM," she corrected.

He flashed his eyebrows at her, impressed. "It's going to be tough for us to shoot through the door from here. One miss and we could send a bullet bouncing around in this place. We need to get to a better firing position."

She nodded in agreement. "It is unfortunate there is no other way to get out of this place. If those are Lindsey's men out there, they will have the entire building surrounded. I am not sure we have enough bullets for that kind of siege."

Adriana brought up a good point. It was one he was already concerned about. There was a reprieve from the shooting for a moment. Sean figured the shooter didn't have a clear target. Sarmen was coughing on the floor while Jabez tried to comfort him. The Arab's hands were covered in blood.

The monk gathered his composure for a few seconds, long enough to gasp out a few short sentences. "There is a passageway, under the chapel. Under the altar." His body racked with another fit of gurgled coughs. "It leads to the outside of the fortress walls."

The priest's eyes fixed onto the ceiling and never blinked again. Jabez was holding the man's head that suddenly became heavy. He gently laid the monk's head onto the floor and looked back at Sean, a fiercely angry expression on his face.

"They will pay for this," he said in a trembling voice.

Sean nodded. "They will. But for now, we have to get out of here." His eyes shot over to the altar in the center of the presbytery.

The object featured a cubed stone base that narrowed into a column, stretching up to an angled podium. It would take both of the men to move the thing, if they could move it at all. The bigger problem was that moving the altar would put them right into the sniper's line of sight. It would be like shooting fish in a barrel in that position.

"We need to set up a barricade that will give us enough cover to get that thing out of the way."

He glanced back down at the pew in the first row nearest to him. They had been bolted down, anchored into the stone floor with what he apprised to be one inch bolts. Last he checked, they hadn't brought a wrench with them. Jabez noticed what he was looking at and produced his Desert Eagle .45 caliber from within the folds of his nomadic clothes.

"Don't," Sean stopped him. Jabez had pointed the barrel of his gun at the base of the pews. "You'll send bullets everywhere. We need to find something else." His eyes panned across the small sanctuary and found another alcove on the opposite side of the space. The pale light that poured into the dark cavity played on something that caught his attention. An old, wooden desk sat flush against the wall. It would be tight, but it might just give them enough protection from the hail of fire to get the altar moved out of the way.

"That will do," he stated. Jabez's eyes followed Sean's across the room. He looked back over and gave a quick nod.

Sean turned to Adriana. "I need you lay down a little covering fire from behind that first pew." He pointed over at the spot with his gun. "You wouldn't mind would you?" he added a wry grin with the last question.

She responded in kind. "It would be my pleasure." Adriana crouched down and crawled into position. She held the gun close to her face as she leaned up against the edge of the seat, looking back at Sean, waiting for his signal.

He readied himself to sprint across the front of the chapel in a pause of silence thick with anticipation. Then, he nodded quickly at her and darted across the floor. Simultaneously, she whirled around from her position and fired five shots through the chapel entrance. It wasn't until after the second round left the barrel that she saw the sniper dressed in black, crouching on one knee in the fortress court-yard. Her first two shots kicked up dust around the man with the sound-suppressed assault rifle. The last three were closer but missed, crashing into the block wall behind him.

She ducked back in under cover as, out of the corner of her eye, she saw Jabez clear the room right behind Sean. A few seconds later, the two men were sliding the massive desk through the opposing archway. Adriana gave a quick check back at the professor to make sure he was okay. He was still tucked away inside the alcove, clutching his small bag with both hands like a helpless child. Sean and Jabez were almost back to the middle of the room. To give them additional cover, she stuck her pistol around the corner of the pew and led out with a few more volleys before taking aim with the last two. This time she hit closer to home and saw the sniper jumping out of the way, at least for the moment.

It was all the time the movers needed to get their makeshift barricade in place. Both men jumped around behind it and flipped it up on its side, making the top a protective shield. They ducked behind it in the nick of time as more rounds pounded into the thick wood from the sniper's gun. The bullets were coming faster now, most likely because the men outside had converged on the opening to the chapel to double their efforts.

The flurry of bullets ceased and she could hear a deep grinding sound resonating off of the ancient sanctuary stones. She crawled back around to the other side of the chapel and could see around the desk that Sean and Jabez were slowly inching the altar to the side. Firth was still gripping his bag in the alcove, obviously not about to lift a finger to help so, she tucked her weapon away and slid behind the new obstruction to help pull on the heavy altar. An opening began to reveal itself underneath where the foot of the object was. Adding her strength to the task made the thing slide much faster, and a few moments later, there was a gaping hole the size of a large person in the middle of the floor.

Sean inspected inside it but couldn't see anything. It was completely dark. He retrieved a small flashlight from one of his pockets and shone it down into the abscess. A dusty smell wafted up from inside a roughly hewn passageway.

"Looks like this is our only way out," he looked up at Jabez then Adriana.

The Arab didn't wait for orders. He withdrew his weapon again and readied himself to fire through the entryway. "You three go on. I will be right behind you."

Sean knew there would be no winning that argument. But he

would at least let Firth and Adriana go first. "Professor. Time to move."

The older man had a terrified look on his face. He shook his head vigorously. Right on cue, a chunk of the desk was blown away near the top edge. Sean had a bad feeling the man would be tough to coax out of his hiding spot. Now that more bullets were flying, he imagined it would be nearly impossible.

"Professor, if you stay there, they will kill you. This is our only way. Duck down and crawl over here as fast as you can. It's your only option, Doc," Sean re-emphasized. Firth's face still seemed uncertain.

He must have realized that he was running out of time. And there weren't really any other means of escape. It was either, die there in the chapel, or suck it up and get to the secret passage as fast as he could. Adriana held out her hand, beckoning him to hurry.

More rounds shattered the stone around the altar. One of the crucifixes behind the presbytery was quickly becoming a mangled piece of wood, filled with splintered holes.

Firth moved cautiously over to the edge of the alcove and got down on one hand and his knees. He scurried quickly over behind the altar where the other three were taking cover. Adriana dropped down into the opening first then reached up, ready to steady the professor as he descended into the corridor. The older man carefully lowered his legs down into the darkness one at a time.

Jabez and Sean gave each other a quick glance. The Arab motioned toward the hole with his eyes, reminding Sean once again that Jabez would be the last one standing in the chapel.

"Go," he ordered in his thick accent. "I will be right behind you."

Sean eyed him suspiciously. "Ok. But next time, you go first."

Jabez's eyes narrowed, accompanied by a mischievous grin. "Deal."

Sean holstered his weapon within his jacket and dropped down into the hole like he'd done it a thousand times before. He looked back up at their companion who still had the same grin on his face.

"Go!" Jabez yelled down at them.

Adriana and Firth took off, disappearing into the darkness, their flashlights bouncing off the walls as they ran. Sean waited for a second then darted after them.

Jabez took a deep breath then let it out long and slow. He turned his head to the left and stared at his friend Sarmen whose body lay in pool of blood on the stone tiles of the chapel just a few feet away. The Arab gripped his Desert Eagle with both hands, holding it close to his nose. He closed his eyes and whispered a few prayers in a hushed tone. Tears welled in the corners of his eyes, but he clenched his teeth and squelched them. Jabez was not afraid to die. He'd been taught not to fear death. And when one worked for the Almighty, the end was not a concern. But his heart was heavy for his friend. The monk was innocent, and it was the Arab's fault the man had died.

His thoughts turned to Sean and his companions. They were truly good people, seeking to do the work of God whether they knew it or not. But they would need time to reach the SUV's. If the attackers didn't believe they were still inside the chapel or were already dead, their escape might be cut short.

He took another deep breath and sighed. "For the honor of God and the brethren," he said with conviction. Jabez spun around and stood up, unleashing a hail of bullets at three men in black outfits, forty yards away on the outside of the chapel. The first one fired his rifle but his barrel was aimed too high, giving Jabez a second to line him up and plant a round directly into the man's chest. The impact of the .45 caliber bullet sent the sniper a few feet backwards, knocking him into the other two. Jabez didn't stop firing, sending bullets into the dirt and walls around the remaining gunmen. They tried to recover, firing off some random shots, but their aim was panicked, confused by the sudden offensive by the tall, dark-skinned man in the nomadic clothing.

Jabez's weapon clicked, signaling he was out of ammo. He twisted back around and ducked behind the desk to reload. He only had a few spare magazines. It would have to be enough. At least he hoped it would. The empty one clanked on the floor next to his feet and he slipped one of the fresh ones into grip. It clicked, and he pulled the slide back, chambering a new round. Just as he did, a new onslaught of bullets poured through the entryway of the chapel, splintering the desk, and sending rounds ricocheting dangerously around the room. He ducked his head, afraid for the first time since he was a little boy.

He forced the fear to the back of his mind and leaned around the corner of his tattered shield. The desk wouldn't last much longer. Jabez took aim at one of now four men who were positioned in a side-by-side line in the courtyard. He let out another long breath and squeezed the trigger again.

29

KNOR VIRAP

"What is going on?" DeGard asked in a panicked tone.

Lindsey glanced over at him with disdain. The two men were standing at a safe distance, watching the battle unfold before their eyes. One of his men had been shot in the chest and was lying on the ground; Lindsey assumed the man was dead.

"Relax, DeGard. Will knows what he is doing. There is only one way in and out of that chapel." His finger pointed at the entrance. "And they won't have enough ammunition to hold out for very long. We have plenty. It is only a matter of time until they surrender or do something desperate."

DeGard looked back at the entrance. Lindsey had five men in position now, firing bullets precisely through the small entryway. Whoever was inside must have also had the added danger of rounds bouncing off the walls, creating a cauldron of metal projectiles. The Frenchman nervously glanced around, seemingly fearful that the authorities would show up at any second. He reminded himself that they were in the middle of nowhere, and there probably were no authorities nearby.

Dust kicked up around the men firing into the chapel as bullets struck the ground near their position. A few stuck the wall behind them. Whoever was firing from inside the little church was severely outgunned. From the sound of it, it was a .45 caliber. If Will made his guess, it was probably a Desert Eagle.

Kaba stood near him as the gunfight roiled, their team exchanging volleys with the hidden gunman in the building. She kept her hands on her own weapon, just in case she needed to jump into the fray, or in case Wyatt and his companions thought it a good idea to go on the offensive.

The muffled pops of the assault rifles stopped for a moment, though the men kept their weapons trained on the entrance to the chapel. The men positioned on the other sides of the building also kept their guns level, just in case. A chilly breeze rolled the gun smoke through the courtyard and up over the walls. An acrid smell still hung in the air. The men positioned on the other sides of the building also kept their guns level, just in case.

The tension was palpable for a few moments. The only sound being the breeze blowing over the walls and through the ears of the observers. Will kept one hand up off to the side of the men positioned to attack the entrance. He had signaled them to stop firing, but DeGard couldn't tell why. He assumed they were waiting to see if anyone inside the building would continue shooting back.

Will pointed at two of the men in the front of the formation and motioned them to circle around to the front edge of the entryway. They immediately obeyed, sprinting to both sides of the door leading into the chapel. Both men kept their guns high and at the ready with their backs against the wall. The two other remaining men near the wall moved forward slowly, careful not to run head first into a hail of bullets. No more rounds came from inside the chapel, though.

At Will's signal, the two at the doorway spun around and poked their barrels through the opening, checking both sides of the room, and all the corners before proceeding inside. The two men behind them followed right behind. A few seconds later, one of the men inside yelled out the all clear.

DeGard smiled. "They are all dead?" He guarded his enthusiasm.

Lindsey said nothing. The old man didn't seem happy for some reason, which was baffling to the French archaeologist. He reflected the expression on Will's face, which was one of suspicion.

Will boldly walked toward the entrance with Kaba following close behind, and the two disappeared into the shadowed entrance. Several minutes passed before Will reappeared in the sunlight.

"Sir, you should come look at this," he suggested.

The old man walked slowly across the courtyard and into the dimly lit interior of the chapel. A few of his mercenaries were checking something on the floor in the front behind a stone altar. Another one was on a knee off to the side, looking at something else. The pungent smell of gunpowder hung in the air. Bullet holes riddled the wooden church pews; the first few were a tangled mess of splinters. Lindsey neared the front of the room and saw what the man to the side was checking. It was the body of a monk. The dark robes were soaked in blood. Lifeless eyes stared at the ceiling.

Now he could also see what the other two were looking into. A dark hole had been cut into the floor just behind the heavy altar. They seemed uncertain about going into the dark cavity.

Another man appeared with Kaba in an alcove off to the left. They both held their guns down at their sides. "Sir, the pit is empty," she informed.

Will's face was perplexed. The men near the hole looked up at him awaiting orders.

"Should we pursue?" one with a shaved head asked. He had a black scarf around his mouth that matched the rest of his clothes.

Will thought for a moment. "Everyone, back outside! Now!" He ordered suddenly.

"Where are they," Lindsey asked sternly.

"I don't know, Sir. But I have a bad feeling we need to get back to the helicopters."

30

KHOR VIRAP

S ean and Adriana ushered Firth as quickly as they could through the passageway. There was a light up ahead, peaking through some cracks. They reached the end of the corridor and realized there was a large, wooden door wedged into the floor and ceiling. Sean pushed hard against it, but the barricade barely budged. Adriana leaned into the obstacle as well, causing it to grind a little further against the floor. Firth gasped for breath a few feet behind them.

Sean looked back at him in the pale glow of the flashlight. "Professor, if you don't mind, could you lean into this thing with us. A little help would be nice."

The older man fired off a quick look of derision, but stepped over and put his shoulder awkwardly against the façade. The extra weight was just what they needed, and the door lurched forward and toppled over. Light poured into the darkness through a cloud of dust. As the dust settled, they realized they were beyond the walls of the fortress, at the base of the hill. In front of them, two black helicopters sat silently on the Armenian plain. The pilots were nowhere to be seen.

"Come on," Said to the others and warily started across the span between the foot of the hill and the closest helicopter.

Firth looked skeptical but fell in line behind the other two. He questioned Sean as they moved. "Do you even know how to fly one of these contraptions?"

"No," he answered. "But she does."

"You do?" Firth cast Adriana a questioning glance.

She shrugged as they reached the flying machine. "Aviation is a hobby of mine," she gave a whimsical grin. "And it also comes in handy in my line of work."

She opened up the pilot's door and climbed inside. Sean and the professor climbed in as well, with Firth in the back. There was enough room to carry at least six people in the chopper, and it reminded Sean of ones he'd seen in pictures and movies from the Vietnam War.

Adriana quickly turned knobs and flipped switches. It didn't take long before the rotors above the cockpit were whining to life.

"What about Jabez?" Firth yelled into the cockpit over the rising sound of the engines. "Are we just going to leave him?"

Sean turned around and stared into the professor's eyes. It was probably one of the single most intense, determined stares Firth had ever seen.

"Jabez wanted us to go without him, Doc," he explained. "I could see it in his eyes." Sean was clearly distraught, but he also knew there was nothing he could do to save their new friend.

"You're just going to leave him?" The professor asked again, disbelieving what he'd just heard.

"We'll wait for him for a minute, Doc." Sean spied the top of the hill where the driveway ended near the fortress entrance. If there were any signs of the enemy, they wouldn't have much time before the chopper would be peppered with bullets.

The engine continued to gain momentum, and the propeller blurred overhead. "Ready whenever you are," Adriana said through the headset. "Just say the word."

Sean tried to watch the top of the hill and cave entrance simultaneously, his eyes jumping back and forth between the two. Worry set in when he saw the first of the black clad mercenaries at the top of the hill. Fortunately, they were at a fairly safe distance, but even so, he didn't want to chance it. His attention went back to the rock wall and the corridor they'd left a few minutes before.

"Come on, Jabez. Where are you?" he said quietly through clenched teeth.

Puffs of dust started kicking up as the bullets started to rain down from the hilltop. It looked like six men lined the edge of protective barrier that ran along the driveway at the top.

Sean had just given the signal to Adriana for her to lift off when he noticed some movement out of the corner of his eye. It was Jabez running at a dead sprint toward the helicopter.

"Wait a second," Sean ordered just as she was beginning to get the machine airborne.

Sean flung open his door and yelled out at the Arab. "Hurry. We have to move!"

Jabez never looked back up. He could see the rounds of metal pounding the dirt all around. Some of the snipers had noticed him and now the trail of gunfire was chasing him toward the helicopter.

Sean jumped back inside as Jabez neared the open back door. As soon as he reached the open back door, Adriana began to pull the aircraft off the ground again. Jabez launched into the floor of the back part of the chopper as it lifted off the ground. Adriana pulled the stick gently, veering the helicopter away from the small mountain. A few bullets panged off the metal shell of the cabin for a moment before they gained some distance and altitude.

Jabez breathed heavily in the back of the helicopter, taking in huge gasps of air while he put on a headset that had been hanging on the wall.

Sean turned around and looked back at him. "I thought you weren't going to make it," he said into the microphone that wrapped around near his mouth.

"I didn't think I would either," the Arab replied. "But I appreciate you waiting on me."

"What about your men?" Adriana interrupted the mushy conversation.

"I will let them know not to return to the fortress. We will certainly need the trucks to navigate the mountains north of Ararat. We could fly, but I seriously doubt there will be many good places to land. Not a lot of level space in that mountain range."

Adriana leveled out the helicopter high above the Armenian plains. Off to the left, the two peaks of Ararat Mountain loomed ominously. There had been something mysterious about the place, like it had long held a secret that the world needed to know. Now that mystery was mostly gone. If the ark of Noah was somewhere else, Ararat would become just another mountain.

"It is beautiful," Adriana commented as the soared by in the afternoon sky, leaving the mountains behind and pulling up new ones in the distance.

Sean thought about it for a few minutes. Firth stared out the window at the enormous peaks. He must have been cold because he pulled his jacket tighter around his torso.

"There is another problem you have yet to consider," the professor said after a long period of silence.

The headsets were filled with the strange background noise associated with flying in a helicopter.

"What's that?" Sean twisted his head to look at Firth. He had almost reached his limit with the professor's negativity.

Firth faced him while Jabez leaned forward, finally having caught his breath. "Even if the map we found in the pit was legitimate, we don't have a starting point." He cocked his head back and gazed at the Arab. "How big is this town of Ararat?"

Jabez shrugged. "Maybe thirty thousand people. Perhaps more."

The professor raised his hands as if demanding an answer. "You see? While that is a small town, it will still cover a considerable amount of land. How do we know the center point for where Saint Gregory started his journey? You can't exactly draw a line with a map if you don't have a starting point. And if you begin with just anywhere in the city, you could end up being far off course in the middle of the desert mountains."

Sean realized his point and turned around to face forward. He could see the outline of the city up ahead in the distance against the backdrop of the mountains.

"He must have left another clue," Adriana said, her eyes still locked on the horizon in front of her. "Gregory doesn't seem like he would have just scribbled some information on the floor of a dungeon without having first created a waypoint."

That had to be it. Sean scratched his face while he considered her statement. He hadn't shaved in a few days and his stubble had become a little itchy. For a second he was distracted by wondering how men with beards could tolerate the irritation. He refocused his mind back on the task of figuring out what Saint Gregory could have left behind to guide them to the ark.

"Jabez," he said and turned around again. "Do you know if there is a something in the town of Ararat like a monument or some kind of tribute to Gregory?"

He shook his head. "No. I do not know of anything like that. However, there is a statue in the middle of the town that is very old. Some people have said it has been there longer than the city itself, that the first inhabitants placed it there."

Sean's eyes narrowed. "What kind of statue?"

31

KHOR VIRAP

Lindsey's mercenaries ran down the hill in front of him and DeGard with Will and Kaba in the lead. The old man couldn't move very fast, which wasn't an issue at the moment considering the helicopter would take a few minutes to start. He just hoped Wyatt and his friends hadn't tampered with anything. It was unlikely they'd had time since their escape had been narrow. The chopper would be tight with Kaba and Will, plus his four remaining men. It would have to do. He didn't want to leave anyone behind. Or did he?

The Frenchman was nearing the end of his usefulness. Lindsey wondered how much more he could get out of the former professor. At this point, they were simply following Wyatt.

He and DeGard rounded the bend at the bottom of the hill and approached the helicopter. Kaba was already warming up the engines and the other men had taken seats in the back.

Will was walking swiftly toward the two slower movers. "I'm pulling up the transponder right now. We will know exactly where they are and where they're headed in a few minutes."

"Excellent," Lindsey responded between labored breaths. A cold gust of air picked up and rolled across the flat, carelessly flipping his white hair around.

He was still considering the fate of his French employee. While he would be more than happy to have him tossed out of the helicopter as he'd had done to another man a few weeks before, it would be a shame if the need for his expertise arose on the final leg of the journey. He would let DeGard live...for now. It was a certainty, though, that the man's usefulness would run out soon. Then he would give the Frenchman his reward.

As if hearing his name in Lindsey's thoughts, DeGard spoke up. "Where do you think they're going?" he asked above the noise of the helicopter's engine.

"We'll know shortly," Lindsey shouted back.

He left the Frenchman standing alone for a moment before the bird-like man caught back up again. The two climbed into the chopper. The men on board made room for Lindsey, and were sure to give him enough space. For DeGard, however, they did not, forcing him to squeeze into a small space on the edge of the seat next to a man with a wide jaw and a piercing set of grayish blue eyes that seemed to stare straight through.

DeGard tried to make himself comfortable but was clearly unable to, so he resigned himself to the fact that he was just going to be ill at ease for the foreseeable future. He hoped that their destination wasn't far away.

Will turned around and shouted into the rear cabin. "Looks like they are headed toward a small town to the north. Won't know until they stop if that is where their destination is. But it's the only town in the area."

"Why would they go there?" Lindsey asked into the headset. "Unless they think there is something of significance in the town."

"The ark wouldn't be there?" Will reasoned. "You don't think the city was built on top of it, do you?" He didn't sound like he was convinced that was a plausible idea. But anything was possible.

DeGard shook his head on the edge of the opposite seat. "I don't think that is why they are headed there. It must be because of another clue. What is the name of the town?" His nasally voice was even more grating through the radio than in normal conversation.

"The town of Ararat," Will answered.

"What?" Lindsey turned back around and stared in disbelief at his chief assassin. "What did you say?"

"The name of the town is Ararat."

Lindsey faced DeGard again, this time with a glare of righteous indignation. "Did you know that this town existed?"

DeGard's face was full of confusion as he shook his head. "No, Monsieur. I swear it. I was not aware that there was a city by that name in this region. I only knew of the mountain."

The old man wasn't sure whether or not to believe him. But the sincere expression on his face was genuinely confused as to Lindsey's line of questioning.

"Do you not realize what this means?" he pressed.

The epiphany hit DeGard, and his eyes showed it by growing wider. "Do you think Wyatt found a clue that leads to the city of Ararat instead of the mountain?"

"It makes perfect sense."

Kaba interjected as she lifted the helicopter off the ground and guided it toward the northeast. "There are series of mountains there that begin just outside the city. There is a legend about those mountains, though."

Will looked over at her, but she kept her eyes forward as they pulled the darkening sky to the east into view. "What legend? You knew about this place" he pushed.

"I didn't think there was any connection to what we were looking for. The ancient scriptures suggested that the ark of Noah came to rest on Mount Ararat. It did not say anything about the city or the mountains outside it. Given the current circumstances, it certainly seems like the little town could hold another clue as to the location we seek." She still kept her eyes straight ahead, never wavering in her voice or her gaze.

Lindsey let out a deep sigh. His irritation at DeGard had left him for now. But he still wanted answers. "What about the legend, Kaba. Leave nothing out."

"There isn't much to tell. The locals believe there is some kind of power in the mountains. They generally don't go there if possible. Some say there are rebels camped there, and when people stray, they are kidnapped and forced to serve as soldiers. Others, though, believe there is something more sinister at work."

The old man's eyes practically glowed at the new information. "That must be it."

Her eyebrows lowered. "I'm sorry. I do not follow."

"Don't you see? If anyone happened upon the ark, they could have been killed by any traps that had been left by the ancient ones."

DeGard took a turn at throwing in his two cents. "Or it could have been much worse, if you believe the tale in the Bible."

Kaba kept her eyes on the horizon while everyone else in the chopper turned to the Frenchman with the long, pointy nose.

When he continued, his tone was lathered in sarcasm. "It says in the book of Genesis that the Lord put an angel at the gates of Eden with a flaming sword to protect the way. Is it possible that the angel still guards the path to Eden and that is what happened to all the victims who disappeared in the mountains?"

Lindsey's eyes narrowed. "I sense your cynicism, Monsieur, and I understand that you do not believe. But now that you mention it, I think it could be entirely possible.'

DeGard prodded. "And just how do you think you are going to get by an angel, Monsieur? If that is what you think you will find."

Conviction filled the man's old eyes, and the wrinkles around them tightened slightly, producing more on other parts of his face. "I don't believe it is an angel guarding the gates of Eden. I think it could be something else."

The Frenchman's eyebrows stitched together, unsure where his employer was going with the line of thought.

"So, if not an angel, what was it?"

Lindsey had a glint in his eyes. "What if the angel was actually some kind of ancient security system?"

DeGard was unconvinced. "You mean something like booby traps?"

"Could be," Lindsey didn't disagree. "It is very plausible that the ancients simply decided to call the device or devices an angel to further sway others from seeking the location of the garden and the forbidden tree, as the Bible says, 'lest they live forever in sin.'"

The idea seemed to settle in DeGard's mind for a few moments. It made sense. He'd seen things throughout history done the same way. Ancient Egyptians had harnessed the power of geological static electricity and made it look like the power of their gods. The Greeks and others, including some from Scandinavia, had claimed lightning and thunder was the result of Zeus or Thor. Over exaggerating things had resulted in a greater amount of control over the populace. People, after all, were ignorant, especially if an expert or a religious leader were telling them what to do and what to believe. Better safe than to incur the wrath of the gods.

"So you think the angel and the sword of fire was an exaggeration, conjured up to keep the people from thinking about sneaking into the garden?" He wanted to make sure he understood what the man called The Prophet was insinuating.

"I think it's more than plausible, Professor. I am almost certain of it."

Will interrupted the conversation from the cockpit. "Looks like they have stopped moving, Sir. The other bird should be just outside of town. Either they have ground transportation or they'll be going on foot to wherever they're headed."

"It will be difficult to sneak up on them in the helicopter," Kaba added. "They will hear this contraption coming from miles away."

Lindsey went into deep thought at her point. She was right. They would need to hang back if they wanted to make sure Wyatt and his friends were unaware they were being followed. But if Wyatt ditched the helicopter and proceeded in ground vehicles, there would be no way to track them. The old man knew he needed to be on the ground to effectively track Wyatt's group without being spotted.

"Surely there must be a place we can acquire some ground transportation." Lindsey said finally.

Will took his employer's meaning and immediately began searching on a tablet for the necessary information.

They would have to move fast to avoid losing Sean Wyatt and his little band. Something kept tugging at the back of his mind. What were they trying to find in the town of Ararat? It had to be another ancient clue, something that would point the way toward the final destination in this long, crazy journey.

"Sir," Will interrupted his thoughts. "I think you might want to take a look at this." He handed the electronic device back to Lindsey.

The old man gripped it with freckled, old hands. His eyes stared at an object in the center of the screen. It was an overhead view of the town of Ararat. And the thing he saw in the middle of it caused hope to arise anew in his heart.

"Triangulate a path from that point," he ordered Will. "It looks like our problem is solved."

32

ARARAT, ARMENIA

The two SUVs bumped along the road heading into the little city. Sean wondered what people did for entertainment around the area or if it was simply like a third world country where survival was all that mattered. They didn't see many people as the small convoy passed through the first array of buildings.

Jabez had radioed his men and ordered them to the location where Adriana landed the helicopter. They had proceeded in the land vehicles to cause less of a fuss with the locals because Jabez had said they would likely need ground transport to investigate anything in the mountains to the north.

They zoomed along the bumpy, dirty street headed for the middle of town. On one of the sidewalks, they passed an elderly woman walking with the assistance of a cane. She had a white and blue shawl pulled over her head that draped halfway down her back. Many of the buildings were dilapidated or in ill repair. Some of the structures seemed to be abandoned.

Jabez answered the unspoken questions that lingered in the vehicle. "This town was officially founded in 1927. The cement factory here has kept people working for many decades. Unfortunately, between the dust from that factory and the poisonous gases from the gold factory, the quality of life here is very low."

"That's fairly young for a town," Sean commented. "Are you sure there is a connection to what we're looking for?"

"While the town was officially founded in 1927, there have been inhabitants here much longer. The village itself actually dates back several thousand years. From what I understand, the statue we are looking for could be that old, dating back to a time before the Bronze Age."

The convoy turned sharply down a side street, then made a left, heading back to into the direction they were going a few moments before. Sean peered ahead through the windshield, impatiently searching through the run down city. Up ahead, the street came to a point where they could only turn right. It was a small town square. Across the street in the center of the square a black iron fence wrapped around a small area no larger than two thousand square feet. There were a few small trees and benches giving it the look of a miniature park. In the center of the little area was what they had come to find, though the object wasn't at all what Sean had expected.

"Stop the car," he ordered. Jabez did so immediately and pulled off to the side of the street. The car with the four men behind them did the same.

A piece of granite shaped like a sword stood seven feet tall. The tip of it was melded into the rock from which it had been cut. The weapon was designed in a style from ancient times with a broad blade and a small, flat hand guard just above the hilt.

Sean and the others got out of the vehicles and checked both ways before crossing the street, though he wasn't sure why. They hadn't seen another moving vehicle since arriving save for a donkey pulling a cart. A few shoddily clad children were sitting on the side-walk a hundred feet away, busily playing with what looked like homemade dolls. The kids had a grimy appearance as if they hadn't bathed in several days, maybe longer.

The group trotted toward the black fencing, scanning it for an entrance. Off to the right, a small gate hung slightly open. Jabez's men looked up into the vacant windows of the surrounding buildings, checking for any potential danger. They basically had to push Firth along to keep the older man moving, something that he clearly didn't appreciate, but took with a small amount of dignity.

They arrived at the base of the huge sculpture and stared up at it. Years of vandalism and neglect had left graffiti on most of the surface. Only at the very top, near the hilt of the carved sword, did the stone remain clean albeit weathered by the centuries.

The sidewalk circled around a small patch of dirt where the base of the statue anchored into the ground. The westward sun cast a long shadow along the ground in the shape of the stone weapon.

"What are we looking for?" Adriana asked as she examined the piece closely.

Sean shook his head. "I don't know. Look for anything that may look like words or symbols," he suggested as he bent over and tried to scan the surface of the stone for any clues.

Firth took the approach of standing back with his arms crossed as he gazed at the piece, while Jabez copied what the other two were doing. The men from the brethren had formed a perimeter and were keeping an eye out for anything suspicious.

Suddenly, Sean perked up and looked around, a paranoid expression on his face. "Do you hear that?"

Adriana looked up into the sky. "It sounds like the other helicopter."

Jabez's eyes shot upward as well, scanning the partly cloudy sky. His men did the same, cautiously looking about the rooftops of the town. For a few moments, the tension was as thick as mud. Everyone around the odd statue could feel it.

Then, as quickly as it had arisen, the choppy sound of the helicopter faded away into the distance. Jabez's men continued to search the skies suspiciously for another thirty seconds, just in case.

"They're gone," Firth announced with a level of certainty. "I wonder where they went."

Sean's eyebrows tightened slightly. "Yeah," he said in a disconcerted tone. "I wonder that too."

"Do you think they found something we may have missed?" Adriana asked.

It was a possibility Sean had considered. But he didn't think so. They had been thorough, despite their rush at the ancient fortress. "Doubtful. It's probably more likely that they went the wrong way. Still, I don't want to be around if they turn back and come this direction."

"Agreed," Jabez chimed in, and immediately began scouring the stone sword again.

Several minutes passed without any revelation or discovery. Jabez, Sean, and Adriana had all done circles around the ancient object without finding so much as a scratch that seemed out of place. Firth had never moved, simply resting his chin on one hand with the one arm tucked underneath the other.

"Got anything?" Sean sounded exasperated.

The others shook their heads and joined him on one side of the monument. Firth stayed put, still staring at the object the same way he had been for the last several minutes.

"What are we missing?" Sean asked the group. "Is there anything else at this site?"

Jabez looked around the fenced in area but didn't see anything of note. "It does not appear so."

Sean noticed the professor hadn't moved since they got there. Something had gotten Firth's attention, but what it could be was still a mystery.

"What is it, Professor?"

The older man remained still a few more seconds before responding. Finally, he let his hand down from his chin and pointed at the long shadow running along the ground toward the east.

"It's a sun dial," he said matter-of-factly. "If I had to guess, I would say the shadow points to the area in the mountains you are looking for. Of course, you would need to know the time of day. That could be a problem."

A grin crept across Sean's face. He put his hands on his hips for a moment, impressed with the professor's assessment.

"Well, Doc. There you go. Welcome back to doing some field work."

Firth scoffed. "This is hardly real field work," he emphasized the word *real* with a sarcastic beat. "And like I said, you have the problem of not knowing the time of day required."

"Yes," Adriana interrupted. "But we know the general direction from the map in the prison pit. Sean, pull up the picture you took in the dungeon."

He had already begun fishing the device out of his pocket before she'd finished her sentence. A few seconds later he was tapping the screen and spreading his fingers, zooming in on the image Saint Gregory had left so many centuries before. Adriana and Jabez peeked over Sean's shoulder as he analyzed the picture on the screen.

The line extended out at an angle, leading into the mountains. Those mountains ran from the northwest to the southeast for hundreds of miles, which presented a problem. If they guess wrong, Sean and his companions would end up out in the middle of the wilderness mountains.

Another cold breeze rolled through the center of the town, kicking up dust along the way. Dark clouds were beginning to sneak up from the west. While the southern part of Armenia and eastern Turkey didn't usually experience drastically cold temperatures, there were times when the weather could reach some extremes. Snowfall wasn't a typical thing. But as cold as the air was, Sean wondered if the approaching storm might bring some precipitation.

The bigger problem was that if Firth was right, and the sword sculpture was a type of sun dial, they would be up a creek without a paddle if the clouds covered up the source of light. They needed to figure out the direction, and quickly. Otherwise, hours could be lost, maybe even days. That was something they couldn't afford.

Sean closed the picture out and pulled up his Google maps app. He entered the location and zoomed into the center of the city where they were currently standing. He twisted the overhead view a little and zoomed back out, peering with narrow eyes at the image.

"What are you looking for?" Adriana asked. Firth had moved over to where the other three were huddled around Sean's phone and tried to lean in to see what he was doing.

"A road, a path, a trail, anything leading out of the town that could coincide with the line that leads into the mountains." He pointed at the screen. "The problem is there are several roads that lead out of the town, heading into the mountains. It could be any of them."

Adriana's face crinkled slightly as she considered the problem. "What if the direction we should take is still part of the clue, the one about the righteous?"

Sean shot her a quick grin. "Could be. But how does it relate?"

"Before, it had to do with kneeling. I doubt there is another map hidden under this dirt, though," she traced a finger around the area circling the monument. "It would have been found long ago. Or it might have even washed away after being exposed to the elements."

"So, what could it be?" Jabez wondered.

Adriana began slowly moving around the sculpture, staring at it as she spoke. "Muslims are required to pray at certain times of the day. In the ancient times, the Judaic ancestors of Abraham kept a similar tradition. There was a time for morning and afternoon prayers, while the sun was still up, nearing the end of its journey across the sky." Sean nodded as she spoke. He was beginning to see where this was going. "It is estimated that the afternoon prayers took place around five o'clock. If we assume the sun would be at that point," she extended a finger into an empty place in the sky, "the shadow would be cast across the ground in that direction." She pointed at the sword, but her eyes were gazing beyond, into the high mountains outside the city.

Sean checked the direction she indicated then got back his phone to see if where she was pointing had any discernible paths. There was one faint outline of a dirt road that trailed away from the town and wound its way into the Mountains.

He looked up from the screen and smiled. "I think you did it," he praised. "I'm pretty sure this is our road."

Jabez and Firth peeked over his shoulder at where he was indicating on the screen.

"Pretty sure?" Firth returned to his dubious self. "If we are going into those mountains, I would hope that you are a better than pretty sure." He crossed his arms again and cocked his head to the side.

Sean slipped his phone back into his pocket. There was "It's the only way that makes sense," he responded as patiently as possible.

"And how far do we go into the mountains? Do we just keep going until we bump into some mythical boat?" The Englishman held his arms out to his side. "If it was there in plain sight, other people would have already found it by now. It won't be that easy."

For a moment, the only sound that interrupted the silence was the wind blowing across the surface of the sword and a through a few of the scraggly trees dotting the tiny park.

Firth had a point, as much as Sean hated to admit it. If ark was sitting in plain sight in the mountains to the north, someone would have already found it. Even if it weren't obvious, satellites or possibly airplanes would have noticed an anomaly and taken pictures of the ancient vessel.

Adriana interrupted his thoughts. "We need to think about this differently, Professor. If there were a large boat-type structure that came to rest somewhere, years of erosion and decay would have destroyed the entire ship. Correct?"

"Obviously," he answered emphatically. "Based on the geography, those mountains probably receive most of their rainfall in short bursts. That means flooding. So, after decades and centuries of rotting and decay, the remnants of anything would have surely washed away. If there was something there to begin with." He added the last part with a little sneer.

The dark clouds in the distance eased a shadow over where the companions stood. Without the warming light of the sun, the temperature seemed to drop about ten degrees. Jabez pulled his cloak tighter around his shoulders.

Adriana nodded in agreement to what Firth had stated. "Your assessment is accurate, Professor. But if there were a structure that large, it still would have left behind a trace of something else." To this, Firth's face curled in question.

"What do you mean it would have left something else behind? There is nothing. Even if it was there, it is gone now."

"Tell me, Professor. Have you ever been to the beach before?"

His face twisted further, clearly confused as to where her line of thought was headed. "Yes. But what does that have to do with anything?"

She set one foot out in front of the other on the loose dirt. The ground sloped slightly downhill running away from the stone sculpture. "When you were at the beach, did you ever walk along the line where the water met the sand?"

His frown couldn't get any deeper. "Yes. I supposed, so. I'm not much of a beach person, though." Sean snickered at the last comment.

Adriana ignored his skepticism and continued. "When you walked on the wet sand, did you ever let the water wash up over your feet?"

Firth was now exasperated. He put his hands on his hips and let out a deep sigh. "Look young lady, I don't know where you are going with this, but I hardly think we have time to be discussing long walks on the beach."

"I have," Sean chimed in, answering the question for the grumpy professor.

She smiled over at him. "And what happened when you let the water wash over your feet?"

Sean had to think for a second. He hadn't been to the beach in a while. Standing there in the cold made him long for it even more. The warmth of the sunshine, the calm sounds of the ocean waves crashing into the beach. Then he remembered.

"Your feet sink a little into the sand. Right? They sink and sand washes up around them. If you stand there long enough, your feet get covered with sand."

She nodded at him, her grin widening slightly. "Exactly." Firth crossed his arms, trying desperately to make the connection with what she was talking about to their current predicament. "Now," Adriana went on, "when you pull your foot out of the sand, what do you have?"

Sean's face lit up as he realized the answer. What she was saying suddenly made total sense. "A footprint," he said steadily, trying to contain the epiphany.

"Precisely," she said pointedly, moving her foot away from its spot on the ground.

The men imagined seeing the footprint in the sand, as they would have on the beach. Professor Firth still wasn't convinced.

"That theory is fine and all, but a wet footprint in the sand washes away eventually," he spoke almost as if he were happy to rain on her parade.

Adriana was undaunted, though. She'd overcome more obstacles than a grouchy English archaeologist in her life. And she'd prepared for his argument in the same moments she had come up with the idea.

"When the waters of the great Biblical flood began to recede," she began, "a massive amount of water dissipated quickly, just as it would on the ocean with the footprint. But if there were an extended period before rotting and decay began and the boat disappeared, the footprint the vessel would have left would have had more than enough time to solidify. It's likely that the area around it would have petrified into a rock wall."

Firth considered her thoughts for a moment in stunned silence. Sean and Jabez watched the older man intensely, waiting to see what he would say next. Finally, he uncrossed his arms and put them behind his back.

"When did you come up with this?" he asked in a less harsh tone than usual.

She waited for a second to see if there would be an insult accompanying the question. When none came, she answered. "Just now. But it makes sense. If the circumstances were right, after the flood waters receded, it is possible the ark sank into the muddy earth. Then it would have only needed time to do the rest."

"So we are looking for a giant footprint?" Jabez needed clarification.

"In the shape of a giant boat, apparently," Sean grinned. "I like it."

Firth remained dubious for a few more seconds. "That is actually a sound theory," he surrendered. "It might just be exactly what we're looking for." His mouth curled slightly into a narrow smile. "Good thinking, young lady."

Adriana appreciated the compliment. But she accepted it with a stoic expression. "We haven't found the thing yet, Professor."

33

ARMENIAN MOUNTAINS

T he helicopter swooped around another rocky peak only to find another on the other side. Below, the ridges and mountaintops sloped down into valleys that rose back up to similar peaks. The mountain range seemed an endless patchwork, extending far to the north and east, beyond the horizon.

Lindsey and his men had been flying around for the last hour, but with no luck. They hadn't found even the slightest resemblance of the ark.

DeGard spoke up from the rear of the chopper, filling the radio headsets with his nasally voice. "I am sorry, Monsieur, but if there were an enormous boat sitting out in the open, someone would have seen it by now."

The air in the cabin was getting much colder, despite having all doors closed. Lindsey pulled his coat around his torso just a little tighter. Kaba looked over at him to get his attention then tapped on the fuel gauge. It was getting low. They would need to set down soon, or head back.

Dark clouds had rolled in quickly from the west, and his concerns were realized when tiny white flakes began swirling around the windshield of the helicopter. They had brought supplies: food, tents, a little extra fuel, and several other items normal civilians might take on a winter camping trip. He had insisted upon it. Lindsey had always been of the mindset that it was better to be too prepared than under-prepared.

Kaba pointed to a flat area on one of the ridges nearby. "I think we should set down over there. It's one of the only flat places I've seen. Either we land now or head back, Sir. It will be dark soon, and we won't find anything after dark."

"Very well," he nodded his head. "Take her down over there. We'll set up camp for the night and hope this storm blows over by the morning."

His pilot nodded and steered the helicopter over to the appointed ridge. As they neared the landing spot, wind shear picked up and wobbled the chopper around. Kaba remained calm, making subtle movements with her feet and hands to keep the flying contraption steady until it was safely on the ground.

Lindsey's men opened up the side door, letting in a gust of frigid air. A few snowflakes swirled into the cabin and settled on the hard floor while the men pulled supply bags and containers from storage bins inside the chopper. The rotors eventually slowed to a stop, but Lindsey had no intention of going out into the freezing cold. Not yet. His old bones were already sending pain signals to his brain. He imagined if he were to step outside for very long, his entire body might lock up.

While two of the men were securing the helicopter with a few anchors, Will grabbed a long nylon bag and dragged it over to where the ridge began to rise toward the mountain peak. He figured up against the hill it would be at least a little less windy. He unzipped the large bag and began pulling out a beige-colored material similar to what the bag was made out of.

Once he'd piled up the fabric, he connected a small box with a knob on the side of it to a plastic hole in the fabric. He switched the knob and an electric motor came to life, sucking air through the box and pouring it into the fabric. In just a few short minutes, the inflat-able structure began to take shape. While the air compressor filled the walls, Will quickly moved around the perimeter to stake down each side of it so the wind wouldn't blow the thing away.

The other men had copied what he was doing and were inflating two additional structures, slightly closer to the helicopter. He didn't like the idea of camping up on the top of the mountain in the dead of winter, but Will knew that his employer was too old to try and make it down to the bottom of one of the valleys. The hills were too steep and rocky for the fragile Lindsey.

By the time he finished pounding in the last stake, the air compressor had completed its task. The inflatable domed structure stood about twenty feet square, enough room inside for several people. Will figured he and Kaba would sleep in that room with Lindsey. The old man seemed more and more anxious to keep Will close. He wasn't sure if it was because his employer felt a close connection to him, or if it were just a matter of paranoia.

Kaba had finished shutting down the helicopter and had joined Will on the far end of the quickly forming encampment. She carried a small black box in one hand and a nylon bag strapped across her shoulder. She stepped through the flap that served as a door and set the box down on the ground. Bending down, Kaba flicked a switch on the side of the device and warm air began to pour out into the inflatable dome. After the heater had begun warming the room, she removed an inflatable mattress from the shoulder bag and set about getting it ready.

A few minutes later, Lindsey was satisfied that his temporary quarters would be warm enough, so he carefully stepped out of the helicopter and shuffled past the two other, smaller domes. He stepped into the room and was greeted by surprisingly warm air. Kaba was busy in one of the corners inflating a second bed.

"I wonder if this storm is going to last long," she looked up, squatting near the inflating mattress.

Will had entered the quarters and shook his head. "I don't know. But the snow is really starting to come down. It's got to be pretty rare in this part of the world," he cast a wary glance at Lindsey. "We could be up here a while, Sir."

The old man grunted, and loosened up his coat a little. He was amazed at the amount of heat the heater could put out and at how well insulated the structure was.

"We are too close to turn back now," he said with conviction. "We know that, based on what we looked at on the screen, the ark should be somewhere near here."

DeGard stepped into the inflatable and looked around, inspecting the place for a moment before speaking. "I'm impressed. It seems you are a man who likes to be prepared." He strolled leisurely over to the far side of the tent and spun around in a dramatic fashion. "I wonder. Are you prepared for the possibility that we may never find what you are looking for?"

Lindsey coughed for a moment before peering at him through narrow slits. "The ark is here, DeGard. I know it."

The Frenchman threw up his hands. "Based on what? A hunch? If there were a giant boat in the middle of these godforsaken mountains, we would have found it by now. Someone, at least, would have discovered it centuries ago."

"It is here," Lindsey repeated and trudged over to the nearest mattress and sat down. He had a tired look on his face. Will wasn't sure if it was from the exhaustion of the journey or from the frustrating banter of their French companion.

"We will stay here for the night," Will interjected, seeing the conversation was going nowhere. "In the morning, Kaba and I will head up to the top of the mountain and see if we notice anything out of the ordinary."

Lindsey nodded then laid his head down on the mattress. He propped his feet up on the edge of the inflatable bed and closed his eyes.

Kaba gave Will a concerned look. DeGard, too, was somewhat thrown off by the old man's odd behavior. Lindsey's face had become pale, making him seem even older than his years belied.

"Is he going to be alright?" DeGard said with mocking empathy.

Kaba shot him a warning glance. "He will be fine, Monsieur DeGard. Your quarters will be with the other men. If I were you, I would get my bed prepared for the night. From the looks of it, this storm is going to keep us in until the morning."

DeGard appeared indignant, but didn't argue. Kaba clearly had no problem with taking physical action if necessary, and the look on her face expressed exactly that.

"Very well, Mademoiselle. I will leave you and your prophet. I only hope he lives through the night. It would be unacceptable if I did not receive my full payment." He threw in the last insult as he stepped back through the door and disappeared into the cold wind.

Will carried a blanket over to the bed where the old man was now sleeping. He draped it over him and stepped back. "I know you want to kill DeGard, Kaba." Will spun around slowly and stared at her.

She stood up from finishing the last mattress and stared back at him. "What do you care?" she asked.

Even in her winter coat, he could make out the outline of her taut body. She had felt amazing the other night. And part of him wished they could have a repeat performance. There was no privacy at the moment. He wondered if she was thinking about the same thing. Quickly, he diverted his thoughts back to her question.

"You should know that I get first dibs on him when the time comes. So, take a number." He smirked as he answered.

She strolled toward him deliberately, one step in front of the other. "And why do you get to have all the fun?"

"Because I saw him first."

"Fair enough. But at least let me watch when you do it."

She stopped a few inches from him. Her chest heaved slow, deep breaths. He wanted her. Suddenly, Lindsey coughed from behind where Will was standing, and he turned to make sure the old man was okay.

The old man's eyes were still closed. He must have just been racked by a fit of coughs in his sleep. When Will turned back around, Kaba was headed out the door into the cold.

"Where are you going?" he asked, curious.

"To get him a pillow and some more supplies. I hope we find the tree soon. I don't know how much longer he can make it." She slipped through the door and into the waning light of the early evening.

Will looked back over at the old man. Alexander Lindsey had saved his life, and had given him a future he could have never dreamed. He owed everything to Lindsey. And Will would do anything to save the man's life and bring his vision to fruition.

34

ARARAT, ARMENIA

"We should find a place to hole up for the night," Sean suggested as the group climbed back into the SUVs.

Snow had begun to fall, and from the looks of it, the storm wasn't going away anytime soon. Little snowflakes were settling on the windshield. While none was accumulating on the ground yet, Sean had a feeling that would only be a matter of time.

Darkness had begun to settle in as well, as if the clouds themselves had ushered it. The few derelict people on the sidewalks had disappeared, apparently unwilling to stay outside in the cold any longer.

"I suppose finding a hotel is out of the question," Sean joked with Jabez as they closed the doors to their vehicle and brushed off some of the snowflakes from their jackets.

Jabez must not have gotten the joke because he cast Sean a curious glance. "There are no hotels near here. But there is a church we might be able to take shelter in."

Sean let go of the fact that the Arab had missed the joke. "Do you think there will be anyone there?"

"I doubt it," he replied. "It looked like it had been abandoned when we passed it."

"Oh," Sean raised his eyebrows.

Jabez cast a wry grin and stepped on the gas. The two vehicles whipped around the town square and headed back in the direction they'd come. "Remember the direction we need to go. We will come back through this part of town on our way out in the morning."

Adriana was busy in the back seat with a tablet in her hands, scanning through aerial images of the mountains to the northeast. Firth couldn't help but ask.

"What are you looking at?" he said in a polite a tone as he could.

"These are satellite images of the mountains where we believe the ark may be," she pointed at the screen and made a circular motion. "I'm looking for an anomaly, the footprint that we discussed earlier. I imagine it would closely resemble a small canyon at this point. So, it would remain unnoticed to someone who didn't know what they were looking for."

The professor seemed impressed. He slid a little closer and continued staring at the screen as she scrolled through the regional view. It all pretty much looked the same. There were some spots where erosion had cut away deep valleys, but other than that, spotting anything unusual was more difficult than she had first suspected.

"What is that, right there?" he jabbed a finger at a point on the screen where there was something strange sticking out from one of the seemingly endless mountains.

She shook her head. "It's an old rock quarry." Adriana continued scrolling through the images for a few more minutes.

"This is it," Jabez announced and slowed the vehicle to a stop.

The little convoy was parked in front of a ragged old building. The sign dangling over the front entrance was barely hanging on by one point. Sean wasn't sure what the lettering said on it, but he wasn't impressed by the facility.

"Jabez, this thing looks like it's been closed for a long time."

"It probably has," the Arab shrugged. "Most of the Christian church members left this region a long time ago when Muslim influence became overwhelming. Some still clung to their homes, though, and their churches. This one was probably one of the last ones to be left behind."

To say the gray building was dilapidated would be an understatement. But the roof was intact, and except for a few spots where it looked like the paint had cracked and rotted, the walls seemed sturdy enough.

Jabez sensed Sean's hesitation. "It is either this or we head on into the mountains. My men have tents we can pitch. But it will be dark before we can get them ready, and by then the temperature will have dropped significantly."

Sean knew he was right. They didn't have many options. At least Jabez had prepared for the worst. "Ok," he said after a few more seconds of consideration. "This will do."

They stepped out of the vehicles into the darkening town. There were a few lights on in some of the buildings, but no signs of life. It was one of the strangest things he'd ever seen, like an entire city had been abandoned, but with some of the lights still on.

Snow flurries had been falling on their drive to the church. Now they were full-fledged snowflakes, dropping at an ever-increasing pace. The men in the rear vehicle began unloading black plastic supply crates and black bags. One of them marched over to the front door of the church, and after discovering it was locked, kicked the thing in.

Sean and his companions followed Jabez up the sidewalk and into the entrance of the little church. Inside, the smell of dust filled Sean's nose. But as he looked around, he was surprised to find things left in remarkably good shape. The pews were all in their rows. Church hymnals had been left in their slots on the back of the seats. And the cushions in the pews seemed to be in decent repair.

The sanctuary was minimally decorated, featuring white walls with dark window frames, and a few dark buttresses pointing up to the angled ceiling. Two bronze chandelier-style light fixtures hung from the roof over the center aisle between the rows of seats. In the front, the wooden pulpit sat alone with a cross emblazoned on the front of it. There were a few pots to each side, but they were empty. The plants that were in them at one point must have been removed long ago.

It was cold in the room, but not as cold as it was out in the elements. A few of Jabez's men had brought in small heaters. Sean had wondered how the things were going to operate on no power. Then he realized they had fuel cells in them. The men placed the devices on the floor in each corner of the sanctuary and turned them on, causing them to hum quietly in place as they put out warm air.

"We can sleep on the pews," Jabez stated. "Those cushions are much better than sleeping on the floor or an air mattress. And there are enough for all of us."

Firth let out a deep sigh and shook his head but said nothing. Sean wondered if the professor had reached his maximum output for complaining.

Adriana didn't wait for anyone to say anything. She dropped her gear off in the next to last row and started pulling out some of her things, making herself at home. When she was satisfied with her claim to a spot, she sat down on the pew and pulled out her tablet again, diligently trying to find the anomaly they were looking for in the mountains.

Sean watched her, mesmerized. She was an intriguing woman. Once her mind was set to something, Adriana wouldn't let anything get in the way of finishing. Since they'd met, there hadn't been much time to spend in a social-type setting. But something inside him ached to. He hadn't felt that way in a long time about anyone. There had been some flings here and there, but nothing serious. He had been intrigued by Allyson Webster. She, however, had done what he felt so many others had done to him, which was why he preferred to fly solo. Allyson hadn't been who she claimed to be, instead turning out to be some kind of international criminal only along for the ride to see what kinds of priceless treasures she could steal and sell on the black market.

There were any number of women he'd met through the years,

but there had only been one Sean had ever really trusted. Much less given his heart to. That was a long time ago. And she was gone. He blamed himself for it for years, only forgiving himself after drowning his guilt in work for the government. Axis had been a blessing in that regard. It was tough to think too much about the past when you had people chasing you, shooting at you, lying to you. Paranoia had become his best friend, and had made him alert, cautious, and tenacious. Maybe now he was getting soft. He'd let down his guard with Allyson. And now he found himself doing the same with Adriana.

Sean told himself that Adriana was different. She'd stuck around, and proven herself over and over again. Deep down, he wondered if he was simply justifying his feelings because of her good looks.

She looked up from the tablet, catching him in the act of staring at her. A crease reached out to her cheek in a little smile.

"What are you thinking about?" she asked innocently.

He looked away briefly, ashamed that he'd been caught staring, but quickly brought his eyes back to her. "Just impressed with how diligent you are. You don't give up easily. That's an admirable trait."

"I get it from my father," she replied and returned her attention to the screen.

Her face resonated in the glow of the electronic device's retina display. "He taught me to never give up on anything I set my mind to, even if he believed it to be silly."

"That's good advice."

She nodded. "It has served me well in my endeavors. Some people might call what I do a childish venture; that I am playing a fairy tale hero. But to be able to return great works to their rightful owners, or to a place where they can be shared with the rest of the world, is good work."

He shook his head. "I don't think it's childish at all." His face twisted slightly. "Although, I'm glad to be out of the game where people are chasing me and trying to kill me all the time."

Adriana smirked and glanced back up at him. "It would seem you are hardly out of that game."

Touche. He snorted at the comment. "Well," he hung his head for a second, "I guess I'm still trying to get out of it."

Her eyes returned to the screen again while she spoke. "For people like us, Sean, I am not so sure we can ever retire to a life of gardening and bridge. While I do not enjoy the dangerous aspects of what I do, I believe some part of me needs it."

"Not me," Sean disagreed and took a seat next to her. "I've got other plans."

She continued to scroll her finger across the screen, zooming in occasionally to get a closer look at a peculiarity then moving on.

"What kind of plans?"

He hadn't really talked to anyone about his retirement goals. But it was something that weighed on his mind, and had been even heavier over the course of the last few months. The thoughts reminded him of Tommy, and again his heart panged slightly. He hoped his friend was okay.

"I'm a man of two places," Sean began. "I've got some land up in the Blue Ridge Mountains in Georgia. Going to build a cabin there near a lake. I figure I'll spend some of my time there, and some of it at my beach house."

He could see her eyebrows rise in the glow of the tablet's screen. "You have a beach home?" she seemed surprised.

He shifted uneasily. "Well, no. Not yet. But I'm looking at some places down on the Gulf of Mexico. Nothing too touristy. Just a quiet beach town."

"And what will you do in your cabin and in your beach house?" she sounded dubious.

"I dunno. I've always enjoyed mountain biking. Tons of places in the mountains to do that. And I'm really interested in flat water kayaking. My cabin will be right on a lake, so I can do that anytime I want. It's so peaceful being out on the water, paddling, cruising along. Who knows? I may even open up a sea kayaking shop near my beach house. That looks like it might be fun, too."

There were a few moments of silence before she asked the question that was already stuck in his head. "Have you spoken to your friend about this?"

"Tommy?" Sean knew exactly who she meant. "No. Not yet. I haven't had the time. And now that he's...I guess I feel a little guilty about wanting to walk away."

"But do you not enjoy the work, the traveling, discovering ancient artifacts and secrets that have long been hidden?"

"I guess," he shrugged. Actually, he did love that part. But he was tired, and just wanted to be in one place for more than a few weeks at a time.

"That did not sound convincing," she said skeptically. "However, you must do what your heart calls for." Her words hit him in more than one way.

He wanted so badly to move a little closer to her. The outline of her face, the smooth texture of her creamy skin beckoned to him. He thought better of it, though. She could be like an untamed animal. If he moved too quickly, it might startle her. Maybe he had become gun shy with women. Or maybe he just didn't want to get too close to someone again.

Jabez's men had finished bringing the supplies in and closed up the front door and were busy making sure the building stayed as warm as possible for the night, repositioning the heaters and plugging up any holes in the walls. Firth found an empty pew near the front of the church where he placed his few belongings then headed back to where Adriana and Sean were talking.

The professor had overheard their conversation and decided to add his two cents. "You know, Sean, it isn't just about what your heart and mind want to do."

Sean looked up from the screen with a quizzical stare. "I'm sorry?"

Firth helped himself to a seat in the pew directly in front of his two companions and turned around awkwardly to face them. "In this life, there are always three parts to our path. The first is what our minds want to do. We think we know, and sometimes we use logic to uncover our way. But in the end, that isn't always the right decision.

"The second part comes from our hearts," he continued. "Like the young lady said, we long to make our hearts happy. Reason would make you think that if we make our hearts happy, our minds would be at peace."

Sean hadn't heard the professor talk like this since he'd met the grouch. Now, all of the sudden, he was a philosopher? Still, he listened patiently to see where the old man was going with his point.

"The last, and probably most important part has nothing to do with our hearts or our minds. In fact, it has very little to do with us as individuals. It has to do with the bigger picture, the grand scale of things. It is what we are called to do."

He let the words hang in the old sanctuary for a few moments. Sean understood what Firth was saying. Sometimes, what people wanted didn't really even matter. It was what the world needed of them, what life needed of them.

Firth narrowed his eyes. "What the universe needs of us takes all precedence. And sometimes, it may not be what is best for us. It may even call us to give up our lives. But if that is what is needed, that is what we must do."

It was a heavy thought. But Sean understood. Adriana had looked up from her tablet while the professor was talking. His words had caught her attention too, and clearly must have struck a nerve.

Sean spoke up. "What are you sayin', Doc? That I shouldn't retire? That I shouldn't try to relax? I think I've done my time helping out the universe."

The professor cocked his head to the side for a second and shrugged. "I'm not saying you shouldn't do those things. All I am saying is that when the need arises never turn your back on it. You must accept the call no matter what the consequences."

Jabez slammed the front door to the church and plodded into the sanctuary, effectively ending the conversation.

"I've never seen snow like this before. It's a good thing we stopped here for the night." He looked at the three grave faces, not sure why everyone was so glum. "Is something wrong?"

"No," Sean perked up. "Everything is fine. So, the snow is coming down pretty hard?" He stood up and walked over to a window.

Time had given the clear glass a grimy, dusty film. There were boards over most of the glass. But Sean could see out through a small opening in the wooden planks. Large snowflakes poured from the sky through the dim glow of the streetlights. In the short time they'd been in the church, a thin layer of snow had accumulated on the sidewalk and street. He wondered how long the storm would last and how much snow it would dump on the region. His thoughts returned to Tommy and his job with IAA . Was Firth telling him not to quit? Sean knew Tommy would be okay. There were plenty of good people who could do what Sean did for the agency.

Firth's voice startled him from a few feet away. He turned to find the professor standing right behind him.

"I'm not telling you not to quit," the professor said, virtually reading Sean's mind. "I'm just telling you that if you are called, you must answer. It's who you are."

Sean nodded, understanding. He understood what Firth meant. The professor gave a single nod.

Adriana's voice cut through the silence. "I think I found something."

Firth and Sean turned their attention back to where she sat; her face virtually glowed in the darkness. Jabez was leaning over the back of the pew, staring at the screen. Sean rushed back over to her and looked at the screen, the professor followed closely behind. The older man seemed to be letting curiosity get the best of him for a change.

The Spanish woman's delicate finger rested on the screen. It was pointing at a strange rock formation. The shape was a long rectangle canyon, cut oddly from valley between two mountains.

"I haven't seen anything like this before," she stated.

"How big is that area?" Sean wanted to make sure they were looking at the right spot.

She turned her eyes back to the electric glow of the display. "From what I can tell, it is only a few hundred feet long and about half as wide."

Sean turned to Jabez then the other direction to see what Firth would say.

His mouth was agape. He shook his head slowly. "It can't be," he whispered in awe. After a moment, he stood up straight and looked down at Adriana. She had moved her attention to the old archaeologist. "It would seem, young lady, your theory about the footprint in the sand might have been correct after all."

35

ATLANTA

The clock on the dashboard read a few minutes after four. Joe and Helen had hurried from their home in the foothills down to Atlanta. Helen reasoned it would be better for them to visit the Biosure facility during operating hours rather than after. With more people milling around, they would be better able to go unnoticed. Breaking in when no one was around would surely draw the attention of the building's security.

A little recon had revealed what Helen had suspected. While the company employees did have ID cards, access was granted via a five-digit code. Thanks to her nifty work on the computer, they basically had unlimited access to the entire facility.

A steady stream of people dressed in business suits flowed in and out of the main entrance. The gray building was immense. It rested on the side of a hill overlooking one of the main expressways. Hundreds of huge windows along all facades provided the interior with views and natural sunlight from every angle. Enormous concrete columns supported an overhanging second floor on the entire front side of the structure. The letters spelling out the company name jutted out just over the entryway.

"Hardly a small-time operation," Joe quipped as he and his wife stared at the monstrosity.

"Shows you how much money is in the pharmaceutical industry," she commented.

Joe laughed. "Looks like you and I went into the wrong line of work, huh?"

She shook her head and smiled. "I wouldn't trade my soul for all that money." Her southern accent carried a twinge of bitterness. "Especially with this company."

Joe and Helen had been married a long time, but he was starting to find out there was way more to his wife than met the eye. He stared at her for a moment as she peered into the building.

"We should head in," she interrupted his thoughts, "while there is a steady stream of traffic."

He nodded and opened the door while she exited out the passenger's side of the car. They had both donned business suits, hoping to look as professional as possible. Joe had wondered if they should have lab coats until his wife had apprised him that most of the people coming and going from the facility would be marketers, accountants, and other cubicle dwellers. He had dug out an old, navy blue suit from the closet that was probably five years out of style. His hope was that no one would notice. He hadn't had to wear a suit tie in years. Fortunately, he remembered how to tie the thing.

"You clean up pretty good," Helen had told him as he stared goofily at himself in the mirror.

Of course, she had looked stunning. For a country girl, Joe's wife could pull off the sophisticated city look whenever she wanted to. She was wearing a sleeved black dress that sported a dramatic v-neck. A few buttons on the side of the loose skirt added a unique element of style. Her matching high-heel shoes completed the look. When he'd seen her standing in the mirror behind him he couldn't help but gawk for a few seconds. She had even added some waves to her hair, making it cascade over her shoulders like a shimmering golden brown waterfall.

They passed several rows of cars, walking as casually as possible as they approached the entrance to the facility. A brown-haired man in gray suit pants and a white-button up shirt, probably in his mid forties, strolled out of the glass doors talking busily on his cell phone. He carried his jacket over his shoulder. The conversation was something about sales and advertising. His voice trailed off as he made his way into the parking lot.

Helen looked at Joe and prodded him to keep moving. "We have to look like we belong," she urged.

Joe smiled awkwardly and opened the front door for her. She nodded politely and entered the building ahead of him. Inside, the facility was a web of activity. A security desk sat off to the side where a guard was busy checking off a form. Men and women in suits, lab coats, and a few business casual outfits hustled up and down the stairs, and across the floor. In the center of two spiral staircases, a circular water fountain stood in the middle, sending water spraying into the air in a constant stream. The pool of water was surrounded by a short wall crafted from mountain stone. Different kinds of plants and foliage accented the corners and pillars in the atrium. And several long, metal cylinders extended down from the ceiling, each holding a bright white light bulb in the center.

Helen had done her research before the drive down to Atlanta. She had memorized the layout of the building so they would look like they knew where they were going. The longer they stood still in a spot, the more suspicious they would appear.

"This way," she said, making sure to keep moving.

He tried to keep up, staying close to Helen's side, but she was walking fast, like all the other people in the building appeared to be.

"The entrance to the packing facilities should be around this corner." Her assessment proved correct as they rounded a turn in the walkway. Straight ahead was a set of double doors with a keypad just to the left of them.

Helen went straight to the keypad and entered in the five-digit code she had enabled earlier on her computer. Joe shouldn't have been surprised when it worked, but he was. There was a quick buzz of an electronic lock then a click just before the door swung open. She glanced sideways at him with a smirk.

"Oh, you're good," he praised her as they passed beyond the threshold and into a more sterile-looking hallway.

It reminded him of a hospital corridor. As fantastic as the atrium had been, the hall was the polar opposite. The walls were bare, and the tiled floor seemed antiquated compared to the modern exterior. The two hurried along at a brisk pace, but tried not to look like they were hurrying. It was a fine line.

The passage wrapped around to the back of the facility. Along the way Joe and Helen passed several doors, none of which were the ones they were searching for. Helen's pace began to slow slightly, and she looked back a few times at some of the doors they had already passed.

"You remember which one we're looking for, right?" he tried not to sound panicked.

"Yeah," she didn't sound confident. "I thought it was right here but..." They came to a sharp bend in the corridor and were greeted by a steel door at the end of the hall.

There was a keypad next to it just like the one they'd seen at the entrance to the passageway they were currently in. The only difference was the man in the security guard outfit sitting next to it.

36

ARARAT

"It will have to wait until the morning," Jabez said as he stepped away from the group huddling around the electronic glow of the tablet. "And it may be later in the morning if this snow keeps up."

Sean turned his attention back to the image on the screen. "My concern is that even if we are able to get out on the road and into those mountains, will we be able to recognize this place?"

Adriana zoomed in on the key spot on the map then tapped a few other places on the screen. A green pin plopped onto the oddly shaped canyon.

"Now we have a digital waypoint to follow. GPS will guide us straight to it," she explained. "I just hope the roads are safe enough. With all the snow, some of the mountain passes could be potentially dangerous."

Sean's face blushed slightly. "Yeah, I should have thought of that."

The stress was getting to him. He should have slept well the previous night in Istanbul, but instead he had tossed and turned in the soft, luxurious bed. All he could think about was stopping the mad man, who called himself some kind of prophet. He thought about calling Mac to see if his friend had made any progress with the Biosure investigation, but he resisted. Joe would need at least a little time to figure out a way into the facility, and even more time to get the samples to Dr. Solomon.

"I suppose for now, we will just have to try and be patient," Adriana cut into his thoughts.

He snapped out of it and nodded quickly. "Yep. Guess all we can do is hunker down and ride out this storm."

"The forecast says it will clear out later tonight and that the late morning temperatures will be in the upper forties," Jabez informed the group before wandering away to talk to some of his men.

"Hopefully it gets close to that warm up in the mountains," Sean commented. "But the temperature drops three degrees every thousand feet you climb in elevation. So, it's unlikely it will be that warm up there."

Adriana's eyebrows crinkled together and she turned to face him. "How do you know that?" She wondered. "That is a fairly random bit of knowledge."

Sean let out a snort. "I learned it in a high school ecology class I took. Weather is something I'm fascinated by," he explained. "I don't know why. I've just always found it interesting."

"You really do have your mind's fingers in a lot of cookie jars, don't you?" she asked the question with a thin smile.

"I guess," he shrugged. "I'd like to have them in a few less jars."

She switched off her tablet and shoved it back into her small backpack. A few seconds later, she removed the leather book Sean had noticed her reading before. He let his curiosity take over and prodded.

"What is that? I noticed you reading it earlier."

She held it out to him. "It's a journal I found while I was in Germany." He took it out of her hand and examined it.

The inside was full of stuff he couldn't translate. He recognized many of the Greek letters, mostly from his days at the University of Tennessee. But what any of it meant was a mystery. Sean knew how to speak a few languages, a few of them ancient, but Greek wasn't one of his specialties. It was, however, one of Adriana Villa's.

"What kind of journal?" he asked as he fingered through the pages. "Obviously, it's very old."

"Yes," she agreed. "It is quite old. If I had to guess, I would say mid to late seventeenth century."

He nodded. "Looks that way." Sean had come up with the same assessment based on the materials used for the pages and the cover.

Scrolls, books, and tablets were all traceable to a specific period of time in history based on the materials used. Cultures could also be identified by whatever the message had been written on.

"It seems the person who wrote this was very interested in finding an ancient Greek device," she stopped his progress momentarily and flipped back to the cover.

Her finger rested on the image of the strange mechanism. It appeared to have gears and wheels, with a few hands on it, almost like a clock, but seemingly not a clock at all.

"I've seen something like this before," Sean said with a tone of uncertainty. "I can't remember where, though."

She nodded. "You are talking about the Antikythera mechanism. It was discovered in 1900 off the coast of the Greek island of the same name. No one could determine its use for over a hundred years. A research team claims that the device's use was to give captains of nautical vessels a more accurate way to chart the stars and planets. It is a logical conclusion, since seafaring ships used celestial bodies to guide their voyages."

"You don't sound convinced," he eyed her suspiciously.

Her eyebrows flicked up for as second. "I cannot say I am entirely convinced. Though that may have been the purpose of the one discovered near Antikythera, this book suggests there were others. And they were not created for a singular reason."

Sean's curiosity was definitely piqued. "So, what then?"

She smiled. "I don't know yet. I haven't finished the book." Adriana pulled the journal out of his hands with a gentle tug.

He returned the smile. "I'll let you get back to your reading then. But I'd like to hear what you learn about it."

Her expression changed to one of doubt. "I thought you said you were going to retire? That you were tired of all this?"

A snort of laughter escaped his nostrils again. He couldn't get anything past her. "Yeah. I know. But I'm not retired yet."

37

ATLANTA

The guard looked up from his computer screen and gave a nonchalant smile. The computer was positioned on top of a small desk in the corner of the wide hall. Joe imagined the guy must have had the single most boring job on the planet, to just sit there and check people's clearance for access to a room.

At the time being, that boring job presented a huge problem to what they were trying to do. Helen and Joe continued moving forward, hoping the guy hadn't noticed their pace slow upon seeing him. As they neared, he gave a single nod to them, and shot a quick glance at the ID badges that hung around their necks. Almost as quickly, he returned to staring at the computer screen while Helen rapidly entered in her five-digit code.

She pressed the *enter* button, but instead of getting a green light accompanied with the door opening, a red light appeared on the pad. Her code hadn't worked. Joe checked out of the corner of his eye to make sure the security guard hadn't noticed. For the moment he hadn't, his eyes still glued to whatever it was he was looking at on his monitor. Helen swallowed hard and entered her code again. She took a breath as she hit *enter*. A shot of fear ran through her as the red light beeped again.

This time, the security guard did notice. The man looked up from his computer with an irritated expression on his face. When he stood up, Joe realized how big the guy really was. The guard was easily three four inches taller than Joe and was built like a Mack truck, with muscles bulging out of the tight guard uniform. He had a military haircut, something Joe hoped was more related to fashion rather than a previous line of work.

As the huge man stepped out from behind his desk, Joe had a million thoughts run through his head. Some of them were wild, fanciful ideas of taking the guy out at the knees then knocking him unconscious. That might have worked, but to what end? They would still be stuck there in the hallway entering an invalid code. And if it didn't work, which was the more likely scenario, Joe would probably end up in a hospital or dead.

The tension built as the guard stepped closer to where they stood next to the keypad. "I'm sorry, ma'am. We've had problems with this thing all day. People have been entering their access code, and it isn't letting anyone through. The tech guys are supposedly working on it, but it may be tomorrow before they have it fixed." He smiled as he cut in front of them and punched in a different set of numbers. "They gave me an override code just in case anyone else had any problems."

"Thank you so much," Helen offered, forcing a grateful smile. "I was starting to think I was losing my mind for a second there."

"No trouble at all, ma'am." The guard tried to sneak a quick up and down at Helen, hoping she hadn't noticed. Joe almost couldn't contain his laughter.

Finally, the door clicked open. Helen made herself contain a sigh of relief. "Thanks again," she said and almost rushed through the opening. Joe simply gave the young man an appreciative nod.

Once the door closed behind them, they both let out a gasp.

"I thought we were done for sure," Helen related.

"Done? Did you see the way he checked you out?" Joe nearly exclaimed as they disappeared around a left corner in an even more sterile hallway.

She let out a doubtful hiss. "Honey, that boy is half my age."

"I don't know. You might qualify as a cougar to these young guys."

She shook her head and his comment as they rounded another bend in the corridor and came to a long, glass window. Through it, they could see a vast warehouse full of boxes, crates, and plastic containers. There were mechanical loaders moving about, lifting some of the plastic-wrapped shipments onto pallets for other automated vehicles to take to another part of the room.

"This is a high-tech operation they got going on here," Joe observed. "I only see a few people inside that warehouse area." He motioned to a few people in white lab coats. Each one of the workers wore a white mask over his mouth and nose.

Helen acknowledged the people inside with a short glance, continuing to push forward until they had reached a more elaborate doorway. It was an air-lock entrance, the likes of which Joe had only seen in movies.

On the wall next to one of the windows, a temperature gauge displayed red digital numbers that read 40 degrees.

"Is that the temperature in there?" Joe asked.

She nodded. "The flu vaccine needs to be kept cool. The temperature should be between thirty-six and fifty degrees. Forty is optimal." She pointed at the intricate doorway. "That will be a clean room," she said then stepped over to the other side of the corridor where a few lab coats and masks hung on a metal rack on the wall.

She grabbed a coat off a hook and started putting it on. "You'll need to wear one of these," she stated. "And we'll need to hurry."

Joe obeyed and quickly snatched a lab coat from the rack. He slipped it on over his coat then copied his wife, pulling a facemask over his nose and mouth.

"We have to go one at a time through this air lock," she said, pointing to a sign that backed up what she said. "I'll go first."

Joe watched as Helen pressed the button that opened the automatic door, and stepped inside. When the portal closed behind her, she pressed another button on the inside edge of the next door. A stream of mist and air sprayed out from jet nozzles imbedded in the ceiling. After a few seconds of the sterilization process, a green light flashed next to the second door before it popped open.

For a moment, Joe thought he heard footsteps tapping from around the corner. He wondered if the security guard had been alerted to who they were or the fact that they weren't really employees of the company. He had to wait until the other door closed before he could open the first, but the thing was moving slowly. The noise was growing louder, and he feared any second the guard or several guards would appear around the corner.

A green light came on next to the button and he pressed it hurriedly. As soon as the opening in the portal was big enough, he stepped inside and hit the second button, closing the door behind him and starting the sterilization process. The strange spray wasn't wet. It felt more like a cool, dry powder. Grates in the floor sucked air downward, pulling the smoky substance into an air duct below. A few seconds passed before the second green light came on, and the door opened for him as it had for Helen.

She was waiting on the other side as he entered the warehouse. "I thought I heard someone coming," he said in a weak attempt to stay calm.

Her face became concerned. "Quick, over here," she moved toward a stack of plastic boxes and ducked down behind them. Joe followed closely and looked back just in time to see another person in a suit walking around the corner.

"Crap," he whispered.

"Did you see anyone?"

Joe nodded, crouching next to her. "I don't think he saw us. He was looking at his cell phone. It was a guy in a suit, not security."

She looked relieved for a moment. "Still, we better get this thing and get out of here." He agreed with a quick nod.

"How do we know what we're looking for?" he wondered, silently.

She scanned the row of plastic wrapped packages across the aisle. There was a bar code on the top right corner of each one. "I guess we look at the labels."

"Right," he hoped he didn't sound like an idiot.

Helen shuffled over to the row and examined the first label. "This one is going to Russia," she said. "But it isn't what we're looking for. It's some kind of antibiotic."

A sudden noise startled her from the other side of the row. She peeked through the crack between the shipments and was relieved to see it was just the robotic forklift. The machine picked up a pallet then backed its way down the aisle, out of sight.

Joe put his hands out, asking if that was one of the shipments they were looking for. She responded by shaking her head quickly.

Another noise echoed from down at the other end of the aisle, causing Joe and Helen to jerk their heads in that direction. One of the machines had turned their direction and was rolling along the concrete floor. The machine took up most of the space in the row, meaning Joe and Helen were going to have to move.

Taking a chance, Joe eased his head back around the end of the row and stole a look through the glass to the corridor. The man in the suit had just finished putting on a mask and was taking the last remaining lab coat off the rack.

"That guy looks like he's coming in," Joe informed Helen. "We have to get over to that other row or that thing is going to hit us. Gotta go now."

He grabbed Helen by the wrist and jerked her up, careful to keep low as they moved. The loader was moving closer as he stopped at the corner of the next row and took another cautious glance back through the glass. The man had his back turned, which Joe took as the perfect opportunity to move. They both stood in sync and rounded the end of the row, ducking behind the other side of the stack of supplies. A few seconds later, Joe heard the sterilization chamber power up, signaling that the man was about to enter the warehouse.

While temporary danger had been averted, there was still the problem that the guy would likely find them eventually. And there were two other people in the room in lab coats. As soon as they were spotted, there would be no chance of escape. They had to move fast.

Helen stayed crouched low and shifted over to the next row of shipments. She read the label, but again was disappointed. She was beginning to wonder if they were going to find anything.

A buzzer made a sound from behind where Joe was crouching. It was followed by the click of the air lock door opening.

The guy in the suit was in the warehouse, and Joe and Helen were running out of time.

38

ARMENIAN MOUNTAINS

The temperature inside the inflatable tent was remarkably warm considering that just outside it, snow was piling up by the minute. The mountain winds combined with the storm to cause the sides of the temporary shelter to shake violently, testing the strength of the anchors Will had driven into the ground.

Alexander Lindsey sat in a chair near one of the heaters, still wrapped up in his coat despite the warmth pouring out of the device next to his feet. His eyes poured over the pages of an old book he held delicately in his hands. The cover of it was brown leather. Its edges had been worn away through the years. The pages within were still in fairly good condition despite the apparent age of the book. The old man read the contents of the book slowly, not wanting to miss anything important.

The room had been peaceful, other than the wind outside causing the nylon to flap back and forth. Will was busy cleaning one of his handguns, while Kaba did the same on a makeshift table they'd put together out of a few plastic crates.

Out of the blue, the peace in the room was broken up by a short gust of cold air through the door as it followed the French archaeologist into the area. Snowflakes covered his hair and shoulders like a dramatic case of dandruff. He shook off the accumulation and stepped further into the dwelling.

Lindsey looked up from his study with disdain. "Is there something we can do for you?" he asked in an impatient tone.

DeGard faked gratitude and tilted his head one way in a mocking bow. "Thank you, Monsieur. But I am merely tired of the idle talk that is taking place in the other tent. I decided I would come over here to see what you three were doing. However, now that I am here, I can see it is no more interesting than the chit chat of those brutes you call your guards."

"Well, I am so sorry to disappoint you," Lindsey lied, overdoing the sarcasm by a metric ton.

DeGard didn't seem to care. He reached down and pried up the leather book in his employer's hands so the cover became visible. The Frenchman's eyes narrowed as he tried to see what the man was reading. A curious expression crossed his face.

"What is this?" he asked after moment of awkward silence.

Lindsey eyed him suspiciously and pulled the book back a few inches. Will turned his attention to the conversation from across the room.

"I see no harm in telling you," the old man said, finally. "You may as well know. It's a diary. And it is very old."

"Obviously it is old," DeGard commented with a sneer. "There are not many books in existence from the period."

Lindsey stared up at DeGard over the tops of the wireframe glasses perched on his splotchy nose. He could tell the Frenchman was waiting for further explanation, but he wanted to make his employee wait for just a few more seconds. If he happened to beg, that would be even better.

"Who did it belong to?" DeGard pressed.

Lindsey lowered the book to his lap and closed it gently. "Its original owner was a man by the name of Sir Francis Drake. Do you know that name?"

"Of course. Every historian knows Drake. He was one of the greatest pirates who ever lived. How did you obtain this diary?"

"Privateer," Lindsey corrected.

"Whatever you want to call it, Monsieur. How did this book come into your possession?"

Lindsey shook off the desire to have Will shoot the man dead right there. "Sir Francis was not just a pirate. He was a world traveler and a very learned man. He did not spend all of his time at sea, though history teaches us that is where his expertise was most renowned." He took a deep breath before starting again. "On one particular journey, he and his crew sailed the Mediterranean to the coast of the Turkey. After securing their vessel, the men ventured deep into Islamic lands, something few Christians had done since the time of The Crusades."

Kaba looked up again from cleaning her gun. She had come from the area the old man was mentioning. While there were no fond memories for her there, cutting ties to one's homeland was something even bitter reminders could not do.

DeGard shook his head dubiously. Narrow eyes peered with suspicion at Lindsey. "Francis Drake went into Arabia? I have never heard this tale. Are you sure your sources are accurate?"

The old man held up the book, wagging it at DeGard. "I've had this analyzed by three different experts. Every single one of them has said this was certainly written by Drake. Now, do you want to hear the rest of the story or do you wish to return to the other tent?"

"I apologize. Please, continue."

Lindsey decided not to question the sincerity of the apology, instead going on with his tale. "While in the city we now call Istanbul, Drake and his men had found an inn to rest for the night, calling themselves traders from the west. The story says that even though the innkeeper was disinclined to harbor Christians, the gold Sir Francis offered far outweighed any misgivings the proprietor may have had.

"During the night, Drake awoke from a frightful dream, in which he had seen a bizarre vision. Fearful any of his men might consider him to have gone insane, he kept it to himself and recorded the contents of the dream in this diary." Lindsey finished by snapping the book like a whip to emphasize the ending.

"So, it is just a book about Captain Drake's dream?" the skinny man was unimpressed.

Lindsey gave a smile as one would have given an ignorant child. "That is not all that happened, my dear DeGard. After the dream, Drake was extremely troubled. He believed he had a vision but could not divulge any of the information to his men for fear they would mutiny. So, in the middle of the night, he left the inn and headed into the city for some night air. As he strolled through the streets, he passed a window that flickered with candlelight. He couldn't read the sign over the door because it was in Arabic, but the door was open despite the fact that it was late at night. For some reason, Drake was compelled to enter the building. Inside, he found an old man sitting on the floor next to a fire. Several candles burned in various places around the room."

A gust of wind rattled the walls of the inflatable tent, momentarily interrupting Lindsey's story. DeGard looked around, seeming worried the structure would collapse or blow away. But after several seconds, the wind died down again, returning the room to the steady ripple of the nylon in the breeze.

"As it turns out," Lindsey continued, "the old man Drake found in the room was actually an alchemist."

"Alchemy?" DeGard scoffed again.

"I am only telling you the story behind this diary and why it pertains to our journey now."

"By all means, Monsieur, go on."

"The Arabic alchemist told Sir Francis of a place where the eternal life could be found, where a substance grew from a tree that could sustain life perpetually."

Finally, DeGard understood the point of the old man's story. "Ah. So, the book is a map?"

"No," Lindsey shook his head. "If it were a map, none of this charade would have taken place. The stones, the clues, all of it would be pointless if I had a map. Don't you think?"

The Frenchman didn't react, feeling foolish for probably the first time in his life.

Lindsey held up the book again. "This book contains a warning and instructions to anyone who is brave enough to enter the final chamber."

"A warning?"

"Yes. Inside the final chamber, those who seek eternal life will face three tests. Those three tests must be conquered in order to gain access to the tree of life."

A deathly silence fell over the room again as DeGard absorbed the information. If what the old man said was true, it meant that Sir Francis Drake had kept a deep secret for most of his life. While the Frenchman was no expert on the history of the famous privateer, he believed he would have heard such an interesting tale as the one that had just been spun before him.

Still, he had to push a little further. It was part of being a historian and a scientist. "I must ask, Monsieur. Where did you discover this diary of Sir Francis Drake? Surely something like that would have been hidden away or locked in a vault somewhere."

The old man had a sinister twinkle in his eye. For some reason, he enjoyed toying with his French employee. Perhaps because he had felt like the man had been disrespectful since the moment they had met. It didn't matter anymore. Soon, DeGard would be dead, and Lindsey would have the key to eternal life.

"Someone found it for me," he said, trying to keep a mysterious tone in his voice.

Kaba looked over again from the corner but remained silent. Lindsey didn't acknowledge her glance, not wanting DeGard to know anything else.

When he spoke, the Frenchman turned up his nose in defiance. "Very well. So, tell me, what are these three tests?"

39

ATLANTA

Helen and Joe crouched next to one of the stacks of vaccination packages. Over the row across from where they crouched, the clicking sound of hard sole shoes clicked on the concrete. The man in the suit was walking down the aisle. Where he was going was a mystery they didn't want to know the answer to.

The machine in the aisle behind them hummed along before stopping. Joe felt the pallet vibrate suddenly and realized the robotic lift was picking up the stack. Helen had the same realization, and they both leaned forward for a second. A moment later, the entire pallet was a few inches off the ground and was being pulled away from them, creating a gap in the row of shipments.

At the same time the robot had centered the load and started moving back toward the back of the facility, Joe heard the voices of the two people in lab coats. The employees were about to round the corner of the aisle where Joe and Helen were hiding. Thinking fast, Joe grabbed his wife's shoulder and pulled her into the empty space that had just been vacated by the machine.

He leaned up against the stack of vaccinations with his back toward where the voices had come. They were continuing to move toward the entrance of the warehouse. For the time being, they were safe. But he didn't want any more close calls.

"We need to get out of here," he whispered.

She said nothing, but nodded in agreement. Taking his cue, she peeked down the lane in both directions to make sure the cost was clear. Seeing no danger, she slipped across the smooth floor and crouched next to another stack of vaccinations. Helen examined the white shipping label for a second then turned to Joe with a sly grin.

"This is it," she mouthed silently while jerking her thumb at the product. He gave a quick nod and shuffled over to where she squatted by the wrapped plastic containers.

Joe slipped a knife out of his pocket and in a quick motion had unfolded the blade. A few seconds later, he had opened up a long slit in the plastic wrap. The containers within were small, about the size of a shoebox, and were made from a thick, white plastic. Joe carefully slid one out, terrified that pulling one box out would cause all the others to tumble down onto the floor.

Joe was relieved when that didn't happen and placed the hard-shell box down on the floor between he and his wife. The company logo was on the top, as well as the description of what was inside. The label said it contained influenza vaccinations, though Joe and Helen feared it was something far more sinister.

They both had the same thought simultaneously. But Joe voiced the concern first. "If we open this, and we are right, and it breaks, we could die." His eyes carried his fear.

She tilted her head slightly and answered in a matter-of-fact tone. "Then let's not break it, sweetie." Her southern accent and casual demeanor relaxed him a little.

Helen reached down and unhooked the clasps that kept the box sealed. As she slowly opened the lid, a little cloud of mist escaped for a second. Joe looked up suddenly, worried they had already unleashed something. She shook her head, and continued to lift the lid. Inside were four, glass vials of clear liquid. Her thin, strong fingers wrapped around one of the tiny containers and started to pry it up out of its foam casing when a voice from the other end of the warehouse froze her in place.

"What's going on over there?"

Joe's face petrified, eyes wide. He eased his head slightly to the left to see beyond his wife. The man in the suit covered by a white lab coat stood at the other end of the aisle with a tablet device in his hand and a suspicious stare in his eyes. Joe only had a second to come up with an answer. So, he did the only thing he could think of. He told the truth, sort of.

"Something cut open this shipment, and one of the containers ended up on the floor." He folded the knife with one hand and returned it to his pocked as he stood, hoping the man hadn't noticed.

Helen looked up at him with a glare of death. "What are you doing?" she mouthed to him as she palmed the vial. She quickly closed the container and slipped it back into its place in the stack.

The man in the suit cocked his head sideways for a second as if contemplating whether or not he should check it out.

"The contents weren't damaged," Joe explained. "But we're going to need to re-wrap this thing." He hoped the suit would accept his explanation.

When the man started walking their direction, Joe felt his heart sink into his stomach. Helen stood up and spun around. He noticed the vial was no longer in her hand and wondered if she had put it back in the container.

"How did this happen?" the man asked pointedly. His nametag claimed he was Tom Thurmond.

Helen shrugged and answered. "We aren't sure. Looks like one of the loaders may have cut the plastic on accident as it passed by. It's kind of strange, though." She remained cool while speaking to the threat.

Tom barely paid any attention to them or the tags that hung around their necks. Instead, he focused on the cut in the shipping plastic. He reached out a soft hand and ran his finger along the edge of the cut.

"It looks like something sharp did this." He turned his attention back to Joe and Helen. "You didn't see how it happened, though?"

They both shook their heads in tandem.

He looked back at the opening then surprised both of them by holding out his tablet for Joe to hold. Joe gave a quick nod and grabbed the device.

"Which one fell out?" he asked pulling back the packaging.

Helen pointed to the container, which the man immediately began to pry out with a high level of care.

"You're sure none of the others fell out or were damaged?"

"That was the only one we saw," she clarified.

The man set the container on top of the stack and cautiously unhooked the clasps. Joe watched with apprehension, wondering what he should do. Thoughts of hitting the guy over the back of the head and making a mad dash for the door ran through his head. But he knew that had almost no chance of working out.

Tom Thurmond lifted the lid, again revealing the thin fog that emanated from within the little box. A second later the four vials came into view, all in tact in the foam casing, and in perfect condition.

He lowered the top of the container and locked it back into place before stuffing it back in its place among the others.

"Looks like the contents are ok," he said finally, taking his tablet back from Joe. "Glad you two noticed this," he said in a stern but appreciative tone.

"Me too," Joe said, trying to hide his relief.

"I will go ahead and alert the shipping department to fix this immediately before the send it out." He began tapping the screen on his tablet and turned to walk away.

The man was half way down the aisle when Helen and Joe turned the other direction to get out as fast as they could. They'd only taken a few hurried steps when the man's voice interrupted them again.

"Oh," Tom yelled at them.

They halted instantly and spun around slowly, fearful their identities had come into question.

"Thanks for finding this."

"No problem," Joe offered with a right-hand salute while Helen just smiled and gave a nod.

He could feel his wife mentally grabbing his arm to get the heck out of there. The two spun around again and walked casually around the corner of the row of shipments. Once they were out of sight, their feet picked up to a more hurried pace. The other two workers in lab coats were out of sight, but they didn't want to chance it. Joe hit the button to open the door to the sterilizing chamber and ushered his wife in.

"I'll be right behind you." He let the door close behind her and kept a careful eye on the man name Tom who was currently walking away from the anomaly in the shipping warehouse.

Joe noticed the robotic loaders had stopped moving about the time Helen had entered the cleansing chamber. He could hear the sound of the jet spray inside and couldn't help himself from wishing it would go a little faster. He was about to check to see how much longer the thing had when he noticed the two other people in lab coats from earlier round the corner at the other end of the room. They were busily looking through some sheets and talking. But if Helen didn't get out of the airlock soon, their identities might be compromised. Joe and his wife had been lucky to get away from Tom Thurmond. Joe didn't feel like pressing his luck again.

The buzzer sounded from behind him, startling him to the point he almost jumped out of the coat. He whirled around and pressed on the button to open the automatic door. He saw the two people in the lab coats look up and see him enter the chamber, but a quick side glance told him they hadn't paid him any mind and were back to chatting about something else.

What seemed like an hour, but was probably thirty seconds later, the other door to the airlock opened and he stepped out while taking off the lab coat. Helen was on the other side, already out of her costume and clearly ready to leave.

"What about the sample?" he mumbled as he shook off the lab coat, trying not to move his lips, wary of the camera in the corner.

"Let's just get out of here," she replied.

"But the sample. Millions of lives—"

"I said let's go."

He had heard that tone for a variety of reasons over the years. Joe knew when to fight a battle and when to let one go. This was one of those times where he had to surrender. He carelessly hung the coat on a hook and followed her down the hallway toward the front of the building.

A few tense moments later they arrived at the door where the guard was stationed at his desk. Helen pressed a button that would open the door, and the two walked through as casually as possible, desperately attempting not to look like they were trying to escape.

The young, muscular guard smiled at them as they eased by. They were nearly to the end of the hall when his voice echoed through the corridor, again freezing them in place.

"Hey stop," the words sent a chill down Joe's spine.

He imagined Helen was experiencing the same sensation, but to look at her face you couldn't tell. They turned slowly, expecting to see the friendly security guard with a gun in one hand and a radio in the other. Instead, he had a clipboard and a pen as he slowly walked toward them.

"I'm so sorry," he apologized in a sheepish tone, "but I forgot to have you guys sign in earlier and I need you to just put your names on here. It's something they've been making us do lately. With all the security they have, I think it's a little redundant. But you know how big corporations are."

Helen let out a long, annoyed sigh. "You know, it really is frustrating," she sympathized and took the pen from the guy, writing down her name in a left-hand column.

"Tell me about it," he remarked as Helen finished and handed the pen to Joe.

Joe said nothing, afraid his voice would crack. For a moment, he hesitated, trying to remember what the fake name on the ID card said. His fingers began to shake as he nearly panicked.

A few tension-filled seconds later, the name came to him, and he blew off his moment of trepidation by saying, "Oh, I sign here. I'm sorry. My eyes aren't what they used to be." He signed the name quickly and set the pen back down on the clipboard.

"Thank you. I appreciate your understanding," the guard smiled and waved, giving Helen one last glance before turning around.

This time, the both of them didn't worry about looking like they were in a hurry as they marched down the corridor and out the hall into the foyer.

When both of their car doors were shut, Joe and Helen let out a deep sigh of relief. She revved the engine to life and wheeled the sedan out of the parking lot and onto the road as quickly as possible.

"That was too close," she commented, steering the vehicle onto the interstate, heading south.

"Yeah," Joe said, looking back through the rear window of the car as if he were afraid someone was following. "But what are we going to do about the sample? If those shipments get sent, millions, possibly billions of people could die if there is some kind of super virus in those containers."

"Sweetie, you don't need to worry about that," Helen smiled over at him and merged into one of the middle lanes. She stuck her hand in her suit jacket pocket and removed a small, glass vial. "We got what we needed."

His face washed with disbelief. "How did you...but the guy in the warehouse...there were four vials in that container."

Her grin widened. "I slipped it in my pocket while I put the container back. Then, when he asked which one it was, I told him the one next to it. Just an old shell game, baby."

"Did I tell you, you were good?" Joe laughed. "You are really good. I do okay with bullets flyin' at me. But all that sneakin' around stuff is for the birds. About wrecked my nerves just now."

"You did fine," she encouraged. "But we are twenty minutes from the CDC, so hold that vial by its top in front of the vent to keep it cool until we get there. We ain't out of the woods yet."

40

DeGard helped himself to an empty chair near a stack of cargo boxes and pulled it over to where he'd been standing across from Lindsey. He eased into the seat and folded his hands together while crossing one leg over the other. He peered at his employer expectantly, eagerly awaiting the tale this supposed diary of Sir Francis Drake held.

Alexander Lindsey's patience was beyond thin with his French assistant. The man didn't seem to understand social cues. It shouldn't have surprised him that DeGard didn't know when he should stay or leave. All Lindsey had wanted was a few hours of quiet to analyze Drake's diary and try to figure out the riddles behind the three tests. In the short time he had been studying them, he had not found a solution. Not yet, anyway.

He wondered if the Frenchman would be able to lend any help on the matter, but he doubted it. DeGard was there mainly for his abilities to interpret ancient languages. And while he certainly had some other talents in terms of historical knowledge, Lindsey didn't consider DeGard to be a critical thinker when it came to riddles. Still, if by some miracle the man was able to help, it would be worth it.

"The three tests the alchemist told Drake about were designed to try the three parts of a human being's makeup. The spiritual, mental, and physical." Lindsey allowed his voice to trail off at the end of the sentence.

"So, what are the tests this supposed alchemist spoke of to Drake?"

"The first one tests a man's spiritual purity. The alchemist told Sir Francis that only the most righteous may eat from the table of God."

DeGard's eyebrows lowered slightly at the clue. "What does that mean?"

"I suppose we will have to see when we get there. But in the Bible, it mentions that the meek will inherit the earth. And there are many comparisons to humility and righteousness. Perhaps that is an additional clue." Lindsey shrugged as he offered the theory.

"Perhaps," the Frenchman stuck his thumbnail just inside his lip and bit down on it gently, considering the thought. "But what is the real definition of meek? Some interpretations of that could mean that the people who are mentally disturbed are meek."

"I hardly think that is what the verse meant by the word *meek*," Lindsey scoffed. "And besides, the notes in the diary clearly say that humility is the key. I'm merely stating there is likely a correlation between the two words, not some other crazy definition."

DeGard threw up his hands in surrender. "My apologies. I was merely offering an alternative point of view." He shut up for a few seconds, just long enough for there to be an awkward silence in the tent before speaking again. "So, what is that supposed to mean, about the righteous eating at the table of God?"

The older man nudged his spectacles a little closer to the bridge of his nose and proceeded to finger his way through some of the pages of the book until he reached what he was looking for. He turned it around so his archaeologist could read the ancient handwriting.

At first, DeGard's eyes were wide as he leaned forward, realizing that the book could indeed have belonged to Sir Francis Drake. Then they narrowed as he tried to read the faint words. After a several seconds, he leaned back in his chair again and pressed an index finger to his temple.

"The most righteous," he said to himself. "I suppose that the righteous proceed slowly, without arrogance. They take their time to move and are very calculated."

"Or it could be a death trap," Will interjected from the opposite corner. "And we could all end up dead."

Both of the men engaged in the conversation snapped their heads in Will's direction. He had never lifted his eyes away from the task of cleaning his gun. At present, he was busily running a cleaning tool down the barrel of a handgun.

"Of course," Lindsey attempted to ignore the cynical comment. "It must be some kind of test. There is a text in the Bible that mentions that as well. It says to the humble are wise, and the wise stand for the right."

DeGard nodded slowly, still uncertain. Lindsey could tell the obnoxious man was a little energized by the riddles, though.

"What is the next one," the Frenchman asked.

Lindsey flipped through a few more pages and stopped again. "The second is titled as the physical test and says that only the strong shall pass through to taste eternal life."

"That's all? I would think there would be something more than just that."

Again, the old man turned the book around so DeGard could see for himself. After he read it, the Frenchman moved his hand to his chin to process the new information. He said nothing, simply staring at the floor as he considered the problem.

"I haven't been able to figure that one out, either," Lindsey spoke for both of them. "It is vague, to say the least. But the last clue is even more ambiguous."

One last time he flipped through a couple of pages toward the end of the book. He craned his neck slightly to better read the faded words on the page. "This one reads that many shall wander in darkness, but the wise will reach to the heavens and find the path to immortality."

DeGard frowned, obviously taken aback by the strange riddles. "Did Drake not ask for a few more clues? This was all he wrote down?"

Lindsey nodded. "Pretty much. Though, there is one catch that Drake mentions."

"Which is?"

"He says that when one arrives at the entrance to the chamber, there will be three doors, not one. It says that the seeker will not know which test he will face first."

"So, the person who finds it will just have to be lucky," DeGard realized.

"He goes on to talk about an expedition into the mountains to try and find the entrance to the chamber, but he and his crew got lost. Several of his men died along the way. Eventually, he says they turned back and returned to their ship, and eventually home to England."

"So, Francis Drake tried to find Noah's Ark," DeGard said in a hushed tone, more to himself than anyone else.

"It would appear so."

The Frenchman still seemed full of doubt. "I still wonder about the authenticity behind this story. He could have been a raving madman by that point in his life. How do you know it isn't some fairytale told by an old sailor, who had spent too many years at sea?"

Lindsey cocked his head to the side like someone who had just won a chess match or proven themselves to be right in a debate. His chin wrinkled slightly as he grinned.

"Because, at the end of the diary, there is a line I have only seen in one other place on the planet. *Immortality is for the righteous.*"

41

ATLANTA

J oe and Helen waited patiently by their car in the parking lot of the Center for Disease Control. He had driven by the place on occasion when in the area, but had never gone inside. Something about a place that housed every major disease known to man, and probably some that weren't disclosed, made him more than a little uncomfortable.

They had both calmed down somewhat since leaving the Biosure facility, but their nerves were still on high alert. Each time a car entered the parking lot, they perked up and kept a wary eye on it until it had passed by or disappeared in the rows of automobiles.

Neither of them had said much until five minutes before arriving at the CDC building. Joe had called Dr. Solomon and asked her to meet them in the parking lot. He hadn't wanted to risk taking the vial inside. And they had already pressed their luck with security a few times that day.

A woman exited a side door of the enormous gray building and immediately headed their direction. Her sleek, brown hair was pulled back in a long ponytail. She wore a white lab coat, gray slacks, and a badge hanging from one of the front pockets on the coat. Her creamy skin radiated in the afternoon Georgia sunlight. She was a beautiful young woman.

"That her?" Helen asked as Dr. Solomon weaved her way through the cars.

"Yep." Joe nodded slowly.

Helen seemed confused. "Why hasn't Sean asked her out? She's stunning." It was a rare thing for Helen to offer admiration, and Joe let her know he was shocked with an awkward glance.

"They're better as friends," he commented. "Actually, they're better as casual acquaintances." He didn't say anything else on the topic because the subject of their conversation was nearly in earshot.

His wife wore an expression that clearly stated she suspected there was more to the story than met the eye.

"Hey, Jenny. Thanks so much for meeting us," Joe smiled as the woman approached.

He opened up his arms and embraced her. She accepted the hug warmly, and returned the gesture, wrapping her lithe arms around him.

"It's good to see you, Mac." She smiled wide as she let go of Joe, revealing the brightest teeth Helen had ever seen.

"This is my wife, Helen."

Dr. Solomon extended a hand, which Helen shook firmly. "It's a pleasure to meet you, Doctor."

"Please, call me Jenny." Her smile extended almost all the way to her brown eyes. "So, Sean says you have something I need to take a look at?"

Joe took the vial out of his pocket and placed it in the palm of her hand. She held the tube up in the sunlight, carefully inspecting it. The clear liquid shimmered in the light.

"Sean didn't say much. But I'm under the impression he believes this is some kind of virus." Her last comment sounded more like a question.

"That's what he said," Joe responded. "We did a little digging around after he called me and discovered a huge shipment was due to leave the Biosure facility."

Helen cut in. "The strange thing was that there were no shipping dates. It was as if all the shipments were on hold, waiting for something."

Dr. Solomon gazed at the liquid for a few more seconds before lowering it out of the sunshine. She then slipped the vial into one of her lower lab coat pockets.

"That's odd," her eyes went back and forth between Joe and his wife. "Usually, those kinds of things don't just sit around for very long. The pharm companies are all about profit. And the sooner they can get a product to market, the more money they'll make."

Joe and Helen exchanged a confirming glance.

"Biosure is a huge corporation," the doctor explained. "They have holdings in the billions, from what I understand. Their network is huge. I've only met a few people from there, no one high ranking. But even the lower level employees reek of something slimy."

"What do you mean?" Joe crossed his arms, interested in what Dr. Solomon had to say.

"I don't know, exactly. It's hard to put my finger on it. But I get this weird feeling like they run that business like it's a cult or something. Everyone I spoke to from there seemed like they had been brainwashed. It was really weird."

The married couple shared another suspicious expression.

"How long do you think it will take before you know something about that vaccine," Joe pointed at Dr. Solomon's pocket.

"I can do an analysis on it today. It will probably be a few hours. I'll need to run a few other tests to confirm whatever it is. But if it is as serious as Sean implicated, I want to get it done as quickly as possible."

Helen seemed concerned. "Joe and I speculated on that. But we aren't medical people. Just how dangerous would some kind of super virus be?"

"It's hard to say," the doctor took on a grave demeanor. "We've been on the lookout for this sort of thing for a long time. The Spanish flu was a superbug that killed nearly one hundred million people in 1918. The strange thing was that the people it killed were usually the stronger, healthier individuals. Their immune systems reacted to the flu virus by going into a sort of hyper mode, and ended up killing the people by causing too much damage to their organs and tissue."

"Any idea what caused it?" Joe cocked his head to the side and raised an eyebrow.

"Not really," she shook her head. "It was during World War I, so all the troops being in such close quarters didn't help. Plus they were constantly moving around from place to place, so that aided in the spread of the epidemic. No one really knows for sure, though, where ground zero was."

Joe pondered what she'd said for a moment before speaking again. "I remember reading about the Spanish flu as well as some other biological catastrophes that occurred in history. The plague was another such instance. No one was sure about the origin, but how it was spread was easy to identify."

"Correct."

"There was something else," he continued, "I remember reading about those epidemics that are still somewhat of a mystery."

Helen looked surprised as she turned to listen.

"Eyewitnesses in both accounts, with the plague and with the Spanish Flu, claimed to have seen dark figures outside their villages and towns before the illnesses struck. I don't know what that means. It could be nothing."

"Are you talking about extraterrestrials, Joe?" Helen made it sound like she was disappointed in him.

"Not necessarily. The accounts merely suggest that someone or something was behind the outbreak, that's all."

Dr. Solomon felt the pocket to make sure the vial was still there. "Well, I better get inside and check this out. If it is something like what happened in 1918, the implications would be far worse now. The world is so interconnected, a bug like that would have catastrophic effects on the population. Literally, billions could be at risk."

"Thanks for helping us with this, Jenny," Joe said and gave her a last, quick hug. "Call me when you know something."

He and Helen were getting in the car as Dr. Solomon walked away when she stopped and turned around. "By the way, Mac." He stopped just inside the passenger's side door. "Be careful. I've heard some strange things about people who tried to cross paths with Biosure. Nothing was ever proven, just stories. But when you hear something more than once, it makes you think."

"Will do," he assured. "Thanks again."

Helen started up the car as Joe slipped into the seat. "Looks like we ought to sleep with the light on tonight," She said and steered the car back out onto the road.

"Yeah," he agreed. "And with a bullet in the chamber."

42

ARMENIAN MOUNTAINS

DeGard had overstayed his welcome with Lindsey. But the annoying Frenchman didn't seem to take the hint. Will and Kaba had finished cleaning their weapons and had prepared a simple meal over a few small camping stoves.

"You really did come prepared," DeGard gazed at the supper with wide eyes.

Lindsey slurped some hot soup peered over his glasses at the archaeologist. "We were ready to set up a dig site. Don't you normally have things like this for an excavation?" He enjoyed seeing the epiphany smack DeGard in the face.

"Of course. I had not really thought of it that way. So you were ready to be here for a few weeks, non?"

"That is correct."

DeGard waited for Will and Kaba to get their soup from the small pot before helping himself to a bowl that had been set out on a makeshift table. He poured the rest of the steaming liquid into the bowl and grabbed a spoon from nearby.

"I suppose this isn't the kind of fare you're accustomed to, eh?" He dug the spoon into the noodles and broth, heaping it into his mouth like it was a shovel.

"Not at all," Lindsey disagreed. "When I was young, I was part of a boys group that went on many camping expeditions. And this," he motioned to the tent around them, "is much more luxurious than what we used to sleep in. And these mattresses are far better than sleeping on the hard ground like we did in those days."

"Ah," DeGard swallowed the soup, surprised at how hot it was and at the interesting back story to his employer's life.

Unexpectedly, Lindsey's cell phone began to ring on the cargo box next to him. He frowned for a moment, wondering who was calling him. Will was in the same room, and only a few people had his personal number.

"How do you get service out here?" the Frenchman interrupted the internal line of questioning.

"Satellite phone," Will answered for his boss.

Lindsey reached over and picked up the device then glanced at the number after re-adjusting his spectacles. It was an Atlanta area code. Biosure headquarters.

The people in charge of the pharmaceutical company had been ordered not to try and contact him unless it was an emergency. The vice presidents he had appointed were both members of his council, so he knew they could be trusted, especially after what had happened to his two adepts a few weeks before in Utah.

He hit the green button on the screen and put the device to his ear. "This is Lindsey, what's the problem."

"Sir, we have a problem," the man's voice on the other end reported.

"Well, what is it?"

"We had a security breach in our Atlanta facility. Somehow, the database was hacked. We believe it happened earlier today."

"They didn't wreck the system did they?" Lindsey asked in an almost dismissive tone.

"No, sir. Nothing was touched in the database."

Lindsey appeared wary. "Then what is the emergency?"

"It seems whoever hacked into the system created security codes and then broke into our facility. It happened about an hour ago. We still aren't sure how they got past our additional security protocols, but we are investigating every possible lead."

The old man's face turned even more ashen than was natural. "Who was it?" his voice carried a tone of righteous anger.

"We have a positive ID on the suspects and have a team en route to their location now." The voice seemed confident, but to Lindsey it felt like the man was leaving something out.

"What did they do?"

There was a momentary pause for a few seconds before the man answered. "It seems they broke into the warehouse and took a sample of the flu vaccine."

Lindsey said nothing at first. His face continued to lose color even though his blood boiled. Will and Kaba stared at him, concern filling their faces. DeGard seemed unaffected, continuing to slurp soup into his mouth.

When the old man spoke, his voice was gravely, carrying a sinister tone. "Kill whoever is responsible for this. And see to it that the sample is recovered or destroyed. We cannot let this get into the wrong hands."

"Yes, sir."

Lindsey hit the red button to end the call and laid the device back down on the makeshift table.

"Problems?" DeGard asked with half-full mouth of broth and noodles.

Old, tired eyes peered through the Frenchman's soul. "Everything is fine," he lied. "I have it all under control. At sun up, we need to continue the search. If we have to go back for more fuel, we will. We will do whatever it takes."

43

ARARAT

S ean stared at his phone. His feet were propped up on the church pew's worn cushions while his back was leaning against the armrest on the end of the seat. He figured his casual treatment of the sanctuary's facilities and furniture wouldn't do any harm. After all, it wasn't a church anymore. No one had probably held a ceremony in the room in the better part of three years.

His eyes were fixed on a picture of him and Tommy. It was a day the two boys had been dressed in their little league baseball uniforms. Their parents had thought it would be cool to take a few pictures. It was hard to remember a time when Tommy wasn't around.

He wondered when he would get another report from his friend, but that would drive him crazy. Sean had to put it in the back of his mind for the time being. Tommy was in good hands, he assumed. And he would be fine. But there was something else that kept nagging at Sean.

With all the talk about retiring and leaving IAA, he had started to feel somewhat guilty about the whole idea. A big part of him kept saying it was his responsibility to protect his friend and take care of him. Why, he had no idea. Even though he and Tommy had been great friends for much of their lives, they were both grown adults. Each could take care of themselves. Or so Sean believed.

The fact was, Sean had always watched out for Tommy for most of their lives. When his parents had been mysteriously killed, Sean and his family took him in, making the boys more like brothers than ever before. Sean had always treated his friend like a little brother and done all he could to protect him.

Several people were confused by the dynamic of their relationship. They had been the modern day Tom Sawyer and Huck Finn. Sean laughed quietly to himself at the thought, trying not to disturb anyone else in the room. A memory of a prank they'd pulled in high school rang in his mind.

It had been their senior year, and everyone in the class was racking their brains to figure out what prank they should play on the school. It had to be better than the ones from the past, but it couldn't be the same idea. And it couldn't be anything that would get them expelled. So, no permanent defacement of property or anything like that.

Sean and Tommy had come up with the idea of breaking into the school and unlocking the huge indoor swimming pool then letting all the seniors into the building for some midnight swimming. Neither one of them knew how to pick locks, though. Well, at least not at that point in their lives. So, the only solution they could come up with was to stay in the building late one night, and remain hidden somewhere until the school had been locked up.

At the end of the school day, they had hung around for some of the extracurricular activities that were going on at the time, trying to look inconspicuous. About thirty minutes before the custodial staff was to go around and begin their locking procedures, Sean and Tommy hoisted themselves up into the ceiling by way of a bookshelf in the counseling office. The ceiling tiles were easy enough to remove, and as their intel had belied, there were floors everywhere just above them. Sean had observed some maintenance workers climbing up into the space once before and had asked how they moved around. The unsuspecting man had explained that there was basically an entire floor hidden above the ceiling, from which all the inner workings of the school could be accessed.

The boys had replaced the tiles and sat impatiently, frequently checking their watches to see when the school would be locked up for the evening.

Sean smiled again in the church pew, thinking about how nervous he had felt while waiting for the custodians to leave the building. He and Tommy had told all the other students in their class to give it an hour before showing up to the school. They wanted to make sure it was dark and everyone was clear of the facility. Kids showing up in the parking lot while someone was leaving would have thrown up a huge red flag.

While they sat there in the dark silence of the school's underworld, Sean and Tommy didn't say much. They had been afraid someone would catch them. There was a little bit of whispered banter between the two of them about how epic the prank was going to be, and that no one in administration would even have to be the wiser. It could be something that went down in history with their class and became the stuff of legend.

Tommy had checked his watch for the thirtieth time, finally deciding they had waited long enough. The boys climbed down from the ceiling and made their way through the cavernous high school halls, the cafeteria, gym, and to the doors where they could unlock the pool.

Sean shook his head thinking about their surprise when they realized all the doors leading into the pool were locked. Through the door window, could see the first few students starting to arrive outside of the pool windows.

"What should we do?" Sean had asked. "We don't know how to unlock the doors. And if we go out, we'll be locked out there with the rest of them."

Tommy looked around for a minute and then realized the solution. "You think there's another space above those ceiling tiles?" He pointed up to the ceiling ten feet over their heads.

Sean followed his friend's eyes as he realized what Tommy was thinking. He was staring at the ceiling tiles that extended out over the pool, all the way to the far wall of the facility. The drop from the ceiling to the pool was easily thirty to forty feet, certainly a dangerous proposition.

"No way, man," Sean had said. "I don't think that's such a good idea."

Tommy had turned his head, spotting a ladder that just happened to be leaning against the wall not far from where they were standing. "Dude, the class is counting on us. This is our chance to do something amazing that no one else has ever done or will get to do again."

Sean stared at the image on his phone. His friend had been right. It was a mantra Tommy lived by. He based his life on treating everything like it was a once-in-a-lifetime opportunity.

As a result, the boys had climbed up into the ceiling and crawled on a narrow catwalk out over the pool. Once they had gone what they figured to be about half way, Tommy reached down and removed one of the ceiling tiles. Below them, the chlorinated water rippled in the darkness of the facility, lit only by a few orange outdoor lights just beyond the wall's windows.

Tommy had looked over at him with a grin on his face, dangling his feet over the edge.

Sean thought better of the idea, letting doubts swirl around in his head. "I don't think we should do this, Tommy. We could get hurt."

There would be no convincing him. Tommy patted Sean on the shoulder. "It's gonna be fine, buddy. It's only water." Those were the last words he said before shoving himself through the hole in the ceiling and plummeting into the water below.

His body disappeared for a few seconds before his head popped up in the dark water fairly close to where he'd gone in. He let out a yell, pumping a fist in the air.

"You okay?" Sean shouted down.

Tommy nodded as he dogpaddled in the middle of the pool. "I'm great, man! Come on down!"

Sean hung his feet over the edge for a few seconds. A familiar pain snuck back into his stomach, and his head swirled. He had been afraid of heights since he could remember. He was pretty sure something had happened when he was a child to cause the inexplicable phobia, but nothing concrete ever presented itself. The only remotely plausible explanation was that his mother had pushed him out of a swing when he was three, landing Sean on his head but unhurt, for the most part.

Sean took in a deep breath of the musty church air, remember how nervous he had been at the thought of jumping. In the end, he never took the plunge. He couldn't do it. Fear had overcome him, paralyzing him from taking any action.

Tommy had insisted it was okay that he didn't jump. But Sean had felt like a failure, instead electing to crawl back through the ceiling and let his friend unlock the upper door from the inside. By that time, most of the senior class had arrived outside and were clamoring for the two friends to open the doors.

The prank had been an incredible success. Students flooded into the pool area, thrilled at the fact that they were pulling off the greatest prank in school history. One kid had brought a boom box, and the music blared off the facility's walls. People danced on the concrete around the edge of the water, some of the couples made out up in the bleachers, while most of the group splashed around in the warm waters of the forbidden pool. They had had the time of their lives that night.

Sean smiled briefly as he remembered the evening. He looked around the darkened sanctuary. One of Jabez's men stood by the door, keeping watch. They had been rotating out every two hours, taking turns so each man could get some sleep. His eyes drifted to the pew where he knew Adriana was sleeping.

Tommy's voice from high school rang in his ears. "Jump, Sean. Jump."

He had messed up enough with relationships in the past. At the moment, Sean had a good working friendship with Adriana. He didn't want to jeopardize that. Then again, no risk no reward. That was the way Tommy had lived his life. Sean had, instead, chosen to take risks in other areas of his journey.

Every piece of his being told him to go back to where she was sleeping, wake her up, and tell her he wanted to see where things could lead. It wouldn't be a cheesy conversation where he told her he was in love with her or anything like that. He just wanted to let her know he was interested in seeing what could happen.

A twinge stuck him in the chest as he realized he was still sitting there on the catwalk, hanging over the pool in high school. Sean had always wanted things to be perfect. He took every precaution to ensure safety and success. It was one of the reasons he had been the best agent Axis had ever had. His methods had caused him to be the desire of several other government agencies as well.

He looked back one last time at the pew where Adriana slept, knowing full well he wouldn't take the leap, at least, not tonight. Letting out a deep sigh, he slid down into the church pew and rested his head on the bag he'd brought along. He slid the phone back into his pocket and pressed the button on the top to turn it off for the night.

Above, the cracked white ceiling stared down at him. He wondered what his friend would think of him at that moment, if Tommy had known what Sean was feeling and pondering. Tommy never said anything about Sean's unwillingness to jump into the pool. That wasn't his style. He had always been a supportive friend. They'd always had each other's backs, no matter what. Just like brothers.

As Sean closed his eyes and started to drift away, he could hear his friend's voice echoing through the sanctuary. "Jump."

44

CARTERSVILLE

T he clock on the McElroy cabin wall read 11:00 o'clock. It had been dark since 5:30. The moonlight was blotted out by a mostly cloudy sky, making the forest darker than usual.

Joe and Helen had been waiting on pins and needles, anxious to receive word from Dr. Solomon. Joe had reminded himself and his wife that those things took time. He imagined Jenny sitting over a microscope somewhere deep in the CDC trying to figure out what it was they had taken to her. He wondered if that was an accurate mental portrayal or if there were machines that would do the work for her. He believed that there had to technology out there that could do such a thing.

To pass the time and keep from worrying about what Dr. Solomon might discover, they were both reading silently in the faint illumination of a few lamps. The rest of the house remained dark. Helen and Joe enjoyed being in a room that wasn't so brightly lit, each feeling far more relaxed when things were a little darker.

Their hound rested his old chin on the floor, droopy eyes looking up occasionally or flicking to one side then the other when one of them turned a page or shifted in their seats.

The clock continued to tick, second by second, seemingly not annoying the home's occupants. Suddenly, a cell phone on the end table next to Joe began to vibrate violently on the hard surface. He set his book on his lap and picked up the device. The caller ID displayed Jenny Solomon on it. He gave a quick nod at his wife, who had an expectant expression on her face.

He hit the green button and answered. "Hey, Jenny. What did you find out?"

"I need you to listen to me, Joe. I don't know how much time we have." The grave tone in her voice caused him to sit up in the deep leather couch.

"I'm listening." He cast Helen a concerned look.

"This thing is worse than Sean could have ever thought," she began. "I have already alerted the authorities, but I'm getting blocked by red tape at every turn. They want search warrants, paperwork...I can't get into that right now. Soonest they could shut down Biosure would be a day, maybe two. And that's if they hurry."

"Ok, Jenny. Slow down. What is it we're dealing with here?" He could hear her rushed breathing on the other end of the line.

"The easiest way I can describe it is that this is a mutated form of the Spanish Flu virus from the early 1900s. It didn't take me long to recognize that the contents of that vial were live."

"What do you mean, live?"

"Typically, vaccines are made from dead or an inactive form of whatever it is that's desired to be prevented. The shots are given to the patient, and the patient's body learns how to fight off the virus by beating up on a weaker or dead form of it."

"Ok," Joe wanted her to know he understood that part.

"This sample wasn't dead at all. The virus inside it was alive and kicking. And what's worse, it was a strain like nothing I've ever seen before."

"I thought you said it was like the Spanish Flu."

"Only in what it will do," she explained. "It will cause a cytokine storm inside a human body, but unlike other forms of the flu, this strain is resistant to every antibiotic I've got. And I have them all." She let the last few words sink in.

Helen was staring at Joe, wanting an explanation. But she could tell that whatever he was hearing wasn't good.

"What should we do, Jenny?" he asked finally.

She didn't hesitate. "We have to shut that facility down. None of those shipments can be allowed to leave that building. If any of them get into the public, even a few samples, the results could be catastrophic."

"Maybe Emily Starks can help us out," he thought out loud. "She has been known to bend the rules on more than one occasion."

"Whatever it takes," Jenny agreed. "There's one other thing, Mac."

"What's that?"

"This virus doesn't just cause a cytokine storm to kill its victims like the Spanish Flu. It is almost as if this virus was developed to kill the healthy and the weak."

"Meaning?"

"During the epidemic in 1918, the Spanish Flu mainly killed healthy people. Their strong immune systems were their downfall. Those with weaker immune systems managed to survive because their bodies didn't overreact and attack the virus. With this one, it won't matter if their immune systems react or not. The virus actively attacks tissue, feeding off of it and replicating itself at an alarming rate."

Joe didn't need to be a biologist to know that didn't sound like a good thing.

Jenny kept talking. "Whoever developed this thing knew what they were doing."

"If this virus gets out into the public, what kind of damage are we talking about?"

"In terms of the human population? Ninety percent. Give or take five percent. I've already called my director. He is on his way down here right now. We may be able to get the authorities over to Biosure before morning. But we have to do something immediately."

"I understand. Thanks, Jenny. Keep doing what you can. I'll see what we can do from here."

"Alright, Mac."

He ended the call and began looking up Emily's contact info. His wife was still staring at him, waiting for an answer.

"It's the worst case scenario," he said, not taking his eyes away from the glass screen on his phone.

"How bad?" she wondered.

"Basically," he tilted his head slightly and peered straight into her eyes. "It could mean the extinction of the human species."

Her eyebrows lowered in a frown. "I don't understand. Why would someone want to eradicate the entire planet?"

"Sean seems to think that whatever it is Alexander Lindsey is looking for could be the ultimate cure for any illness, virus, even death itself. It could be that he is planning on killing off almost anyone so he can start the planet over, sort of like the story of the flood from the Bible."

Joe could tell a sickening feeling was creeping up in his wife's throat. He felt it too as the words came out of his mouth.

"What are we going to do?" she asked.

"I'm calling Emily to see if she can help. Apparently, Jenny is having some problems getting through to anyone."

"Isn't that why we have the CDC?"

Joe forced a quick snort of a laugh. His wife made a good point. "That's what I thought, too."

A second later, he held the phone to his ear. After a couple of rings, Emily's smooth, commanding voice answered.

"Hey, Mac. What's up?"

He decided to dispense with the pleasantries. "Emily, we need your help."

She yawned audibly over the phone before responding. "Sorry, I was already in bed. What's going on?"

Joe tried to relay as much of the information as possible to the Axis director. He wanted her to hear everything and understand the gravity of the situation. After he got done explaining it all, he sat silent for a few seconds to wait for her reaction.

"You're a hundred percent sure on all this?"

"Jenny wouldn't have said it if it weren't true, Em. It doesn't look good. We need to shut down that facility ASAP. And right now, you're the only one that can do it. Jenny's stuck in their protocol train right now. But she said we need to lock that place down immediately. Anything you can do to put Biosure under siege for a little while until she can get the cavalry there?"

The line went silent again as Emily contemplated what their next move should be. It was a dicey situation, and a huge leap of faith for her to take based on second hand information. But Joe wasn't one to overreact. She knew that if Joe McElroy was concerned, the threat had to be real, especially if it was coming from a researcher at the CDC.

"Okay, I'll get a team over there and get the facility secured. We'll do it quietly. No need to go inside with guns blazing. I think we can do it by simply blocking all the ways in and out. I doubt anyone will notice at this hour. We can keep a lid on it until the CDC gets what they need to go in."

"Sounds good, Em. Thank you," Joe offered.

"No, Joe. If this is as bad as you and Dr. Solomon believe, everyone will need to thank you."

He blushed a little and leaned back. As he did, something startled the dog, causing the animal to pick its head up quickly and snap to the left. Its ears perked up as well, and instantly, the animal began to growl. The old hound was a well-mannered dog unless there were strangers around. Over the years he'd stopped paying attention to the random animals that would frequent the wooded property. All were facts that caused concern on the faces of both the animal's owners.

"What is it boy?" Helen asked.

Joe shifted forward again to see what was bothering the dog. As soon as he moved, the clock on the wall shattered behind him. The sudden noise was accompanied by the cracking sound of glass from across the room. He instinctively ducked down, risking a quick look at the window. A bullet hole was in the center of it, and the round had barely missed his head.

"Joe?" Emily's voice carried through the speaker of the phone. He was still clutching it in his hand, having not yet ended their conversation. "Is everything okay?"

Helen had seen what happened and immediately took cover out of the window's line of sight, careful to stay low on the ground next to Joe.

"Someone's here," he answered Emily's question after a few seconds. "If I had to guess, Biosure's boss found out about the missing sample. And they've sent their goons to take us out."

"Can you hold out for a bit, Mac? I'll get some support there as soon as I can."

Joe gave a sympathetic look to his wife. He'd not wanted her to get into any danger. But the look she had on her face wasn't one of fear. It was resolve.

"We'll be fine," he answered. "Just get your team to the Biosure labs, and if you can spare a few, send 'em our way."

"Will do, Mac. Hang tight." The lights went out in the cabin just as he hit the red button to end the call.

In the darkness, they could see red dots scanning the walls of the living room from several angles. In the pale light of the cloudy sky, the dog still stood erect, pointing at the door.

"Easy, boy," Helen calmed the animal.

"Looks like they've got the place surrounded," Joe noted.

"You okay, honey?"

He grinned underneath his beard. "Yeah. They don't know what they've gotten themselves into."

Joe pushed against the heavy couch, sliding it toward the back wall and off the area rug covering that part of the floor. At the same time, Helen eased the coffee table toward the front of the house, also making sure the rug was clear of the furniture.

Joe belly crawled over to the end of the rug and sat up. He grabbed the end of it with both hands and yanked it back, revealing a portion of the floor with a distinct outline cut into it. The square had been cut about two feet wide, just big enough for a person to fit through. Helen stuck her finger into a little groove cut into the wood and lifted up the trap door. A narrow tube extended down into the footings of the house via a ladder of metal rungs.

An eerie silence crept over the house as Helen began to ease herself down the ladder. The dog began barking loudly, breaking the strange quiet. Immediately, windows started shattering as bullets rained through the panes and into the cabin. The dog continued to bark but jumped back, momentarily startled by the hail of gunfire. The only sounds coming from outside were muffled pops from the gun barrels. Joe figured they had sound suppressors.

He slid over on his butt and grabbed the dog, forcing the animal to submit by hugging it close to his chest. The canine struggled slightly but Joe held the hound firm until he hovered over the escape tube.

"Here," he said. "Take the dog." He lowered the animal down toward Helen who was already at the bottom standing in front of a metal door.

She stepped back up a few rungs and grabbed the dog with one hand, letting their pet down to the floor near her feet with care.

Joe was sure to stay low as he shifted into position in the makeshift hatch. He grabbed the edge of the rug and pulled it back in toward the center of the room as he ducked into the trapdoor, letting the thing shut over top of him.

45

CARTERSVILLE

J oe hung onto the rungs of the ladder while Helen punched in a five-digit code on an illuminated keypad. There was a quick buzz followed by a loud click, signaling the vault-like door had unlocked.

The dog shot through the portal as soon as the door swung open. Helen and Joe followed quickly behind, the latter sure to pull the door closed behind.

Fluorescent lights flickered on automatically as they entered a room constructed out of a steel shipping container. The space was twenty feet long and eight feet wide. As the lights came to life, rows of various guns became visible on the walls: shotguns, handguns, hunting rifles, and a few AR-15s. Helen didn't hesitate to start grabbing belts and straps, loading them up with pre-loaded magazines from shelves beneath the array of weapons.

Joe began to do the same, but hesitated for a moment as he buckled a belt around his waist. "Should we just stay down here and wait until they leave?" he wasn't worried for himself. Joe just didn't want anything to happen to his wife.

"And let them just wreck our home? I don't think so." The look that accompanied her statement left no question in his mind as to what their course of action would be. He strapped one of the assault rifles to his shoulder and grabbed a few handguns.

"You thought I was paranoid to have this place put in," she said as she grabbed a compound bow and a quiver of arrows from a corner. "Not so paranoid now, huh?"

"To be fair," he argued, "you wanted this bunker put in just in case the government collapsed. This is completely different." He smiled as he finished loading a magazine into a .40 caliber Springfield.

The dog sat on the floor, watching eagerly as his two masters hurriedly moved around the room.

"Stay here, boy," Joe ordered, extending his hand out to the dog. The animal obeyed, watching the two of them head to the opposite door.

They passed into another, longer container lined with more fluorescent lights on the ceiling. The second unit was empty, and much longer than the other, stretching forty feet. At the end was another metal door like the one they'd just gone through. Helen rushed to the other side of the bunker with Joe close behind. She swung open the door, revealing a set of wooden stairs and a storm door at the top. They quietly ascended the steps and eased open the hatch, flashing their weapons in every corner to make sure it was clear.

They climbed through the opening into the tool shed, still wary of any possible intruders. Various items like a leaf blower, rakes, sledge hammers, gardening tools, mowers, hedge trimmers, and other items lined the walls and floor of the 12x12 building. The muffled sounds of the gunfire could be heard through the walls. Joe tiptoed over to the door and eased it open to get a peek at the situation.

Outside, four men were in front of the house, and another four were in the back. The ones in front were still firing a barrage of bullets into the building while the men in the backyard were laying low on the ground, probably covering a possible rear escape. Had Joe and Helen gone out the back door, they would have been mowed down on site.

"There's four in front and four in the back," he apprised her.

"So, eight of 'em, huh? Well, the first two will be easy. The last six won't be when they see what's happening."

He nodded, agreeing with her assessment.

She slid the handgun back into a holster and took the bow off of her shoulder then removed an arrow from the quiver before placing the container on the ground. Fitting the arrow in place, she lifted it up and stepped over to the door.

"Grab one of those arrows for me. As soon as I let this one go, have the second one ready." He did as told and grabbed an arrow out of the quiver, holding it next to her as he prepared to open the door again. "Ready?"

"Yep," he smiled up at her from a crouching position.

She gave a nod and Joe slowly pushed the door open. The men were reloading on the lawn, putting fresh magazines into their weapons. One of them had started ascending the stairs with another guy in tow. The men were wearing black sweaters and matching winter caps. Their faces had been painted in dark camouflage. The last two guys in the yard spread out, holding the perimeter. Those would be her first targets.

Helen drew the bowstring back and put the farthest man in her sights. He had stopped in a position on the other side of the walkway leading up to the steps. She held the string steady for a moment and let out a long breath. Her fingers released the string, sending the arrow across the span in less than a second. Before the tip of the projectile went through the man's neck, she had already taken the next arrow from Joe and was reloading. The other man saw his companion drop to the ground out of the corner of his eye, and turned toward the body. He must have noticed the arrow sticking through the man's neck because he crouched down and began scanning the woods beyond the twitching figure.

His mistake was giving Helen a larger target. She wasted no time loosing the second arrow, sending the blade deep into the man's back. He groaned loudly for a second before collapsing to his knees and falling on his face.

Joe eased the door of the shed closed so they wouldn't be seen. "Did I tell you, you were good?" he whispered.

"About five times this week, honey," she said equally as quiet. "Now check the window over there and see what's going on. If those men start snooping around, we might be better of going back into the house."

"The old backtracking move. I like it," his teeth shone brightly in the darkness. "But I want you to stay here. I can go back in, take a few shots at them, and then you can pick them off from out here."

She contemplated what Joe had suggested, and finally agreed. "Okay, but be careful. Don't go back in through the trap door if you hear anyone inside." He kept a wisecrack comment about her obvious warning to himself. He quickly shuffled back over to the storm doors and disappeared inside.

Joe made his way back through the escape bunker, past the curious dog, and back up the chute to where the ladder led into the living room. He put his ear up against the bottom of the trap door and listened carefully, making sure there was no movement above. There was nothing. The men Helen had killed had probably distracted the ones who were about to enter the cabin. That meant they would be looking for her, which also meant he needed to act fast.

He prodded the hatch up and slipped out, whipping his hand gun around in a quick motion to make sure the room was clear. Everything was in tatters. Every window was obliterated. Lamps, their leather chairs and sofa, the computer monitor, it was all riddled with bullets. Even the logs of the cabin were in splinters. Joe didn't have time to worry about material possessions, though.

He climbed out of the cavity and crouched low, making his way over to one of the shattered windows. The men outside weren't saying anything, obviously aware that they should use silent communication. Joe stood slowly, careful to keep pressed against the interior wall. He took a peek around the edge and saw one of the men checking the body with the arrow through the neck. Another guy from the back of the house had come around and was checking the other corpse. Joe quietly slid the handgun back into its holster and pulled the assault rifle around from his back. He put the stock against his shoulder and winced for a second. It was where he'd been shot nearly a month ago. While most of the damage done had healed, the skin and tissue were still tender.

He raised the weapon put the man standing closest to the porch sights, aiming at the side of the man's torso. Joe took in a deep breath of air then let it out, much like his wife had done with the bow. He squeezed the trigger, cutting down the man almost instantly. The blast from the gun's barrel was the loudest thing he'd ever heard, causing his ears to ring painfully, but he remained focused on the attackers. Before the intruder closest to him could react to the sound, Joe had already fired the next round, sending the man sprawling over top of the corpse with the arrow in its back.

On the other side of the lawn, the last man remaining in sight dove toward the cabin in a desperate effort to take cover. Joe turned quickly in the henchman's direction, but his shot was blocked by the wooden railing on the steps. It must not have obstructed Helen's view, because a second later, he saw a blur go through his field of vision accompanied by a quiet whoosh. The man on the receiving end of the arrow shot yelped for a second then fell onto the grass just short of the walkway.

Joe allowed himself a devilish smile for a moment, despite his ringing ears. His wife was a woman full of surprises. Just as he was starting to feel better about things, he was reminded there were still three men left outside their home. Bullets started ripping through the house again. Joe hit the floor and tried to assess where the assault was coming from. It only took a second for him to realize someone was firing from the rear of the house.

He belly crawled through the broken glass and splintered wood to the closest end of the cabin, and into the laundry room. Joe sat up for a few seconds, allowing his back to lean against the clothes dryer. Deciding he needed more mobility, Joe set the rifle against the wall and withdrew his pistol again. A couple of seconds later, the hail of metal stopped, leaving the living room slightly more destroyed than previously.

Joe crept over to the nearest window and risked a peek outside. What he saw caused him a great deal of concern.

No one was there.

Back in the shed, Helen had heard Joe firing the assault rifle, picking off two men then dropping the fifth to the ground herself, the arrow catching him in the upper part of the chest. She'd kept the door to the tool shed cracked so she could see if anyone else came around to the front, but no one did.

A few moments had passed when she heard the sound of more gunfire coming from the back of the house. Bullets ripped through the remainder of the front windows spraying out into the small field in front of the house. Whoever was back there knew someone was inside the cabin.

Helen opened the door a little wider, shouldered the bow and quiver, and slipped out into the cold air, making her way back around behind the shed. Her eyes darted back and forth in the darkness, making sure there was no other danger lurking in the shadows. She retreated back into the darkness of the forest, taking cover behind a pine tree before moving further toward the rear of the house. One thing her few friends didn't know about her was that Helen's father had taught her everything he knew about hunting when she was a child. She knew to be careful as she moved through the woods, making sure she didn't step on any twigs or too many dry leaves. Exposed roots and soft dirt was the best thing to walk on. But in the middle of December, leaves and sticks were everywhere. Even as she snuck through the shadows, she kept the bow ready, still electing to go with stealth over the convenience of a handgun. As long as there were more of them than her and Joe, she needed to be as silent as possible.

The men she was hunting must not have had the same training because she heard a short snapping sound about thirty feet away inside the trees. Helen crouched down, peering through the trunks. To her right, she had a clear view of the back yard. Even with the cloudy sky, the full moon provided a little backlight. No one was on the lawn, meaning whoever had just been shooting had retreated into the woods.

She stayed low, keeping the bow horizontal with an arrow notched. She heard the sound of some leaves rustling from the same direction as before. The noise caused her to draw back the bowstring instinctively. Sure enough, one of the assailants was squatting behind a thick oak tree about thirty feet away. The man's face was painted black. He was gripping a small sub-machine gun, but she couldn't tell the make, not that it mattered. She drew the string back farther and took aim, putting the center of the man's chest in her sights.

The arrow flew true, through the tree trunks and undergrowth, striking the man just below the throat. He let out a groan and gripped the shaft as he fell over sideways. The noise drew the attention of the other two men hiding in the forest, and they immediately opened fire, spraying a barrage of rounds around the vicinity. Helen had ducked behind a pine tree's narrow trunk as soon as she'd loosed the last arrow, only risking a peak around the bark to ensure the man had gone down. She pressed her body tightly against the tree as the metal rounds thudded into the wood around her. A few struck one she was leaning into, but the wood was too thick for almost any bullet to penetrate.

After a few seconds, the attackers must have run out of ammunition again because there was a pause in the assault. Helen heard the familiar sound of one of the Springfield's firing from near the house. She risked a glance over and saw the flash from the end of the barrel as Joe popped off six shots.

Inside the cabin, Joe kept under cover until the men outside had stopped firing into the cabin. He thought he had heard the sound of someone grunting, followed by another stream of gunfire. Only this time, the bullets weren't coming his way. It could mean only one thing: the men were firing at his wife.

Angrily, Joe raised up from his hiding spot and, aided by the low flashes of gunpowder from the enemy guns, spotted both of the remaining men as the launched a volley of hot metal into the woods near the shed.

He quickly lifted up his weapon and popped off three shots into the closest man to what he assumed was Helen's position. The second attacker was trying to reload his weapon, a mistake given the fact that he was in a wide open space between trees. Joe fired three successive shots, landing two in the man's chest and one in the abdomen. The target staggered backwards for a moment before falling lifelessly to the ground.

"All clear, Helen," he shouted out the window. "That's all of them."

Helen heard Joe's voice, and was about to come out of her hiding place when she saw something troubling coming down the driveway. She couldn't tell the make or model, but three SUVs were rolling toward the cabin. And they looked like they were in a hurry.

"Joe, we may have more company," she yelled back, staying hidden in the shadows.

"Emily said she was sending support. Maybe that's them."

Helen shook her head, still leaning against the tree. "I don't think they could get here that fast. They're still fifteen minutes out, at best. And that's if they are coming in through the air. We could be looking at longer, Joe." There was an air of resignation in her voice. "Joe?"

"Yeah?"

"If we don't get out of this alive, you know I love you, right?"

There was a pause as the SUVs drew closer, the sound of tires on gravel starting to fill the air.

"Yeah, honey. I know. And I love you too. But don't say any of that goodbye, crap. We'll be fine."

She smiled in the darkness. Helen couldn't say what she wanted to. She knew she was okay at the moment. But she worried about her husband. She'd been training her whole life, since she was a little girl, exactly for something like this. If she wanted, Helen could run deeper into the woods and stay hidden until the trouble passed or until Emily's team arrived. But she couldn't leave Joe. She would stick it out with him no matter what.

"You might want to get the AR back out Joe, pick a few of them off as they get out. That should even the numbers."

"Roger that," he answered.

Helen moved stealthily through the darkness of the trees, getting into a position where she could be most effective with a frontal assault. The three SUVs were nearly at the end of the driveway. She hoped Joe was in position, but she knew he would be. Joe was the most dependable man she'd ever met. She could count on him for anything. And if he said he was doing something, he always kept his word. That was one of the reasons she loved him so much. Though, she regretted not telling him everything about her past. Maybe someday she could disclose everything, about what she had done before they were married.

The SUVs came to a stop in front of the house and the doors opened quickly. She notched another arrow and drew back the string on her bow, raising it slowly to line up the driver of the nearest vehicle. Suddenly, a twig snapped behind her. She started to turn around but a gloved hand wrapped around her mouth as a gun barrel was pressed to her head.

"Drop the bow, now," the gruff voice ordered. "And tell whoever is in the house to drop their weapon." She obeyed halfway, dropping the bow onto the ground. But she didn't say anything.

The barrel pressed deeper into the side of her head, causing her to wince slightly. She cursed herself under her breath for being so careless. They'd killed eight men. Which meant there must have been nine.

"Don't feel like talking? Fine," the man gripped her face tightly, almost to the point where it felt like he might break her jaw. He forced her out from her hiding place in the woods as he called out to Joe. "Whoever is in the house needs to drop their weapons and come out with their hands up, or I will splatter this woman's brains all over the lawn. And bring the sample you stole, too."

46

The sun had risen early in western Armenia. Sunlight poured through the cracks of the building, giving a little more illumination to the otherwise dark sanctuary.

Sean hadn't slept much. He'd grown accustomed to trying to sleep in uncomfortable places. It was part of what he did, both before working for IAA and at present. But his mind had raced with too many thoughts. In between insomniac productions, he dozed off a few times, maybe aggregating a total of two hours of sleep for the whole night.

Jabez and his men were already taking equipment out to the vehicles, allowing cold bursts of air to rush through the door each time it opened.

Dr. Firth was still sleeping when Sean made his way over to the older man and nudged him from his slumber. "Time to go, Doc."

Firth had woken slowly, seeming peaceful at first. Once fully awake, he quickly returned to his grumpy self. "What kind of food do we..." he started to ask but Jabez tossed him a plastic bag with something that looked like dried meat. "What is this?"

"Goat jerky," Sean answered for their new Arab friend. "I suggest you eat some. We have a long day ahead of us."

The professor looked down at the plastic bag with an air of disgust. He apprehensively reached into the sack and pulled out a wide piece of the dark red meat then sniffed it to make sure it hadn't gone bad. Sean was relieved when the man put the corner of the cut in his mouth and tore off a chunk, chewing it slowly, still unsure if he would like it.

An impressed expression lit up Firth's face. "You know, it isn't half bad," he commented before putting the rest of the meat in his mouth.

Adriana was busily checking one of her two handguns, making sure everything was clean and working properly. She slid a full magazine into the black grip and clicked it into place.

"You think we may need that?" Sean asked. He was also armed, but wanted to know what she thought.

"You never know. Do you?"

He shook his head. "Can't be too careful."

"In some things...you can." She left him with that thought and a sly smirk as she grabbed her bag and headed out into the cold air.

Outside, the snow had already been melting. A warm front had followed the storm, so any accumulation didn't last long. Sean imagined up in the mountains that would not be the case. He knew their vehicles could handle most types of weather, but slippery roads on high mountain passes didn't sound like something he wanted to test out any time soon. That was exactly what they were about to do.

"We should be alright, even with the snow in the mountains," Jabez read his thoughts. "The roads are not paved, so the dirt and rocks will help us. And the shoulders of the road angle up, so it will be difficult to slide over the edge."

Somehow, the man's confidence didn't resonate in Sean's mind. The whole thing seemed like a sketchy proposition, but they didn't have any choice. Time was running out.

He turned his phone on, remembering it had been off over the course of the night. Most of the battery had been used and he didn't want it to die before getting a chance to recharge it in the SUV. After a few seconds, the home screen came on and the device began searching for a satellite signal. As soon as the connection was made, his phone began to ding. He had six voicemails and eleven text messages.

"That's a tad above average," he commented silently.

"What is it?" Jabez stopped as he was carrying his backpack out the door.

"I have several messages from Dr. Solomon at the Centers for Disease Control in Atlanta. It looks like Mac and his wife were able to get a sample of whatever it is to her. She says it's bad." He scrolled further through the long text messages from his friend Joe. From the time they'd been introduced, Sean had always called Joe, *Mac*.

"How bad?" Adriana had overheard Sean's comments and joined the conversation.

He looked up at her. "She says that it will make the Spanish Flu epidemic look like the common cold. Worst case outcome, ninety percent of the world's population could be eradicated."

"How could she predict that?" Jabez had to ask.

"I don't know. But I know that Jenny knows more about that stuff than anyone I've ever met. She must have run some tests in her lab. It goes on to say that the World Health Organization has been alerted, but no one is going to take any action until the morning. They think she's overreacting."

Adriana was clearly concerned. "Someone has to stop that company from sending out any of those vaccinations."

"Yeah," Sean agreed. "She said Emily is sending a team down there to blockade the building. But the world authorities need to take over. And Axis can't just hold a building siege for long. Eventually, the authorities will be called in, and her team will have to stand down."

Firth's demeanor changed to one of being unnerved. "So, it's true about the virus?" His voice was filled with disbelief.

Sean turned his head and faced the professor. "Seems that way, doc. If it makes you feel better, I wish we hadn't been right about it."

"It sounds like we may not have much time," Jabez interjected. "We must hurry to the canyon. If we can get there in time, we can destroy the chamber permanently."

47

CARTERSVILLE

T he cold steel barrel continued to press hard into Helen's skull while the man get a firm grip on her throat. He was much stronger than her so, struggling was like trying to push a three-ton boulder up a hill.

"Don't make me say it again!" he yelled, painfully loud in her ear. "Drop your weapon and come out with your hands up. I know you're sitting there in the front of the house with your gun aimed at those trucks. If you don't come out right now with that vial and your hands in the air, I will execute your wife, and we will come in and kill you next."

Helen never feared much in life. She'd been raised in the country, and as a country girl she had faced all kinds of things that would have caused most people to wet themselves. But now, knowing that she was five inches away from a bullet that could end her life, a twinge of fear entered her mind.

She didn't want to die. But she wasn't about to beg, either. Whoever the man was holding her neck would not get that satisfaction.

"You may as well shoot me," she forced the words through clenched teeth. "He's not going to give up that vial." If the men believed the virus was in their possession, no reason to let them think otherwise. And she certainly wasn't going to tell them where it actually was.

"Don't worry, lady. We're killing both of you anyway." The gruff voice had a sinister sound to it.

The man was probably former military gone mercenary. Killing, for those types, was second nature. When the armies of the world no longer needed their services, those people still needed to get their fix. Their bloodlust would never be quenched, so it seemed. She'd met several in her line of work. While she spent most of her time in an office, there were occasions when Helen had bumped into people like that. She didn't understand how they could enjoy something as wretched as killing other human beings. She had done it out of necessity, but never enjoyed it. Not like the man holding the gun to her head probably did.

"You may kill us both," she said, "but there is no way my husband is coming out of that house and giving you that vial. You will have to pry it from his cold, dead hands."

Taking a cue from her statement, he yelled out again. "This is your last chance! Come out with your hands up or your wife dies!"

Helen could feel the man tense as the finger on the trigger tightened slightly. She didn't say a word. Instead, she closed her eyes. Memories of her life began to drift into her mind's eye. Events and people from her childhood swept by. Christmases, Thanksgivings, weddings, funerals, school, graduation, and her own wedding day all came to her in a rush.

The last caused her to think about Joe. He'd been a good husband. He was always loyal, always caring. She wished she could have told him more about her previous life. He may have found it intriguing. Helen doubted he would be mad at her for not previously revealing some things. That was another things she loved about him. He always seemed to understand. In the darkness, she imagined his smiling, bearded face. The vision brought a strange sense of peace.

For a second, she wondered if Joe would drop his gun and come out with hands in the air, like her captor had ordered. But Joe was no fool. He would know that the second he did that, the mercenaries would kill them both. If she were going to die, Joe McElroy would do whatever it took to avenge her death, even if it meant dying.

She opened her eyes again, flicking them toward the SUVs that still sat running near the end of the driveway. The people inside them were still awaiting the order to exit and push forward.

"I guess your husband doesn't care if you die or not, lady," the man grunted. "Personally, neither do I."

A solitary tear formed in the corner of her eye. She knew that wasn't true. Joe loved her very much. The tear rolled down her face and fell to the dry leaves below, making the subtlest of pats as it hit, just before a booming gunshot rang out through the woods.

48

ARMENIAN MOUNTAINS

The night had been uneventful except for the constant flapping of the wind against the inflatable tent. The room had stayed surprisingly warm, thanks to the heaters in the corners. Alexander Lindsey had known the devices were supposed to have eight hours of power, but usually claims like that were somewhat exaggerated.

The sun was beating down on the white surface of the tent, causing the room to be naturally illuminated. Lindsey sat over a hot cup of coffee, reading through Drake's diary, scanning it for anything that might prove helpful on the final leg of what had been a tumultuous journey.

Will entered the tent, followed closely by Kaba. "The snow didn't last long," he reported. There is a layer of it still on the ground, but down in the valleys it's already melting. Looks like it will be a clear day, so as soon as we refuel, we can begin the search again."

"Excellent," Lindsey nodded at the younger man.

"Would you like us to take the bird back and fill it up then return, or do you want to come along? The nearest airstrip is about twenty minutes away."

"Thank you for asking, Will. I believe I will stay here until you return. I am still weary from all this travel and I need to continue my research. When we find this place, it is essential we understand how to make it through the three tests."

Will could tell his benefactor was exhausted. The toll evidenced itself under the older man's eyes, and in the color of his skin. He didn't appear to be in good health. Will had never been a big believer in whatever it was Lindsey was looking for. But he did believe he owed the man his life, despite the quirks. More than that, Will hoped his benefactor would leave his vast fortune to him. With the incredible amount of money Lindsey had at his disposal, Will could finally leave a life of danger behind. He and Kaba could buy a small island somewhere and drop off the grid completely. It would be an amazing turnaround for a boy who had been given such a rough start by life.

That difficult period made him strong, though. And it made him ruthless. Will was willing to do whatever it took to get what he needed. When The Prophet had found him, he redirected that combination of resourcefulness and diligence into something greater.

Initially, when Will had met Lindsey, his first inclination had been to simply kill the old man and take whatever he could off him. But something inside the back of his mind thought better of it. It was a decision that could reap enormous benefits in the future. The Prophet had already been extremely generous. Will had no doubts that generosity would continue in the foreseeable future.

"Kaba," Will turned toward the black haired woman. "You and two of the men stay here while we go back and refuel. If you need anything you can reach me on our SAT phones."

She gave a quick nod and disappeared back out the entrance of the tent. Even in a heavy coat she was beautiful. Will watched her leave, letting his eyes linger for a few moments.

"You two are my only legacy," Lindsey spoke with a rattle in his voice.

Will's head snapped back to the old man. His tired eyes were looking up at him with a sense of pride.

"You have done much for us, Sir."

Lindsey looked down to the rocky ground then back up again,

deep in thought. His breaths were coming in labored efforts. "If we do not find the tree, my time here on this earth will be short."

"No," Will disagreed, shaking his head. Though, inside he knew the old man could very well be dying at that moment. "You will be around for a long time, Sir."

A twinge of guilt stuck through Will's chest. He'd been snippy with his benefactor during the escapade in Atlanta. Now that he could see the man was dying, Will realized how much he actually cared.

Lindsey coughed a few laughs. "I appreciate the sentiment, Will. But we both know I don't have much time. If we do not find the tree in time, I want you to keep looking for it. The only thing I ask of you is that you complete the mission. It is all that matters. It must be seen through. You must give me your word, that if I die, you will finish what we have started."

"You have my word, Sir," Will answered after a few seconds of thought.

"This world has become a desolate place. The cities are a shambles, and filled with corruption. Crime is rampant, and those who lack, steal from those who have. The world has gone too long in this degenerated state."

Lindsey reached into his coat pocket and withdrew a piece of paper. On it was a phone number, and another sequence of numbers. At the bottom was a name Will didn't recognize.

"What is this?"

"That," Lindsey explained, "Is the direct line to the man in charge of our Biosure facilities. He will carry out the order to ship the vaccinations. You will need to give him that number to verify the order."

Will stared at the paper for a few long moments. In his hand was the order to execute billions of people across the globe. The weight of that thought wore heavy in his mind. He'd killed more people than he could remember over the course of his life, but billions? That was a strange thing to think about.

Lindsey could sense the apprehension on his apprentice's face. "The world has needed a new beginning for far too long, Will. Soon, there won't be enough food for everyone. There won't be enough space for everyone. And when those things happen, chaos will ensue. It is better to send them all to their rest and start anew. We will bring about the New Jerusalem that Revelation speaks of. We will start over with a new Earth, free of crime and depravity." He decided to give the younger man one more incentive. "You and Kaba will be the King and Queen of this new world."

The last part certainly did appeal to Will's ego. He and Kaba could rule the world. They would gather in the few survivors and bring them under a common rule.

"But if we don't find the tree, we will not be able to survive the virus."

Lindsey smiled weakly. "You will find it. We are so close, now. I know you will."

"You will find it," Will corrected, though he didn't really believe it. "But, I have to ask. What if we cannot locate the last chamber? It's been hidden for several thousand years. What will happen if it remains undiscovered?"

The old man's eyes narrowed. "I have a backup plan for that contingency. The mission will go on as planned, whether we find the Garden of Eden or not."

"A backup plan?"

"In my mansion, I have built a bunker where we can wait out the epidemic as it sweeps across the world. There are enough supplies there to sustain us for several months. By then, the virus will have run its course."

Will appeared confused. "If you have that in place, why go through all the trouble to find the tree of life? You could just wait it out in the bunker."

Lindsey smiled feebly. "Because, Will, if I don't find the chamber and the tree of life, I will die. When you get older, you will understand what that means. If I find the tree, I can lead this world into a new age, free of chaos and crime. That bunker is meant for you and Kaba, in case I don't make it to the tree in time."

In a sick way, it was the greatest gift anyone had ever given Will.

His benefactor had provided him and Kaba a way to survive even if they didn't find the last chamber. It was a gesture that motivated him to see the task through to the end and find the lost Garden of Eden.

"Sir," Kaba rushed in through the entrance of the tent, interrupting the intense conversation. "You need to see this."

Lindsey got up out of his chair, energized by the young woman's enthusiasm. He knew she wouldn't burst in like that unless it was something significant he needed to see. Kaba was also not very excitable. Since he'd met her, Lindsey had never seen Kaba lose her cool over anything.

The three stepped outside into the chilly, mountain air. A thin layer of snow remained on the ground, but it was melting fast. The temperature had risen in the early parts of the morning, returning the region to its more typical climate. Above, the sky was clear, producing the brightest sun they'd seen in a while.

They all slipped on sunglasses to protect their eyes as Kaba led the small group to where some of the other men were standing near the edge of the ridge. DeGard was with the men, staring down into the valley at something.

"What is all this fuss about?" Lindsey demanded as he reached the drop off.

No one needed to answer the question. He saw what the ruckus was about. A thousand feet below, a narrow road wound its way through the mountains. On the road, two SUVs were making their way slowly through the mountain pass.

"Wyatt," Will realized out loud.

"Get everything ready," Lindsey ordered, still staring at the vehicles below. "They may lead us right to it."

49

CARTERSVILLE

The shot echoed through the woods behind the McElroy cabin. Helen stood stiffly in the darkness for a moment. The hand on her neck slid off, and the one holding the gun to her head dropped instantly as the man's body collapsed to the ground. She felt something warm and wet on the side of her face and neck, and reached up to touch it with her finger. Blood.

She looked down at her attacker, but quickly turned her eyes away. A large hole penetrated the man's forehead, and the back of his skull was completely obliterated. Before she could say or do anything, the men in the SUVs quickly exited and began opening fire on the cabin.

Joe had shot the man in the head. It was a gutsy thing to do, but it had saved her life. Now, though, he was in trouble. She grabbed her bow and hurried along the edge of the woods, back around the rear of the tool shed and farther up the property, closer to the driveway. In thirty seconds, she was behind the men firing from the protection of the SUVs.

"Sit tight, Joe," she whispered to herself and pulled her own AR-15 around to her shoulder. "Mama's got you."

Inside the cabin, Joe had taken a huge gamble. He knew he was a good shot with the assault rifle, but his target was only a few inches from his wife's head. Any slight movement and he would have shot her instead of the mercenary. Fortunately for both of them, he hadn't missed.

As soon as he'd seen Helen was okay, he dove back into the laundry room, knowing there would be repercussions from the action. Sure enough, bullets started zipping through the shredded remains of the house. Fortunately, the thick logs the walls were made from withstood the barrage. As long as Joe stayed down, he was okay. The problem was when the men decided to come into the house. He needed to get to the trap door again. If he could get outside, he could take up a position in the tool shed and flank the men as they approached the house. They would be sitting ducks. Getting over to the trap door was a dangerous proposition, though. Even with the walls stopping most of the projectiles, he didn't want to risk one getting through.

Suddenly, he heard the familiar sound of Helen's assault rifle outside. The men attacking their cabin all used sound suppressed weapons. Joe and Helens were all natural. The thunderous boom of the gun shook the remaining glass fragments from the windows, sending them clacking to the floor. He smiled from his hiding place. It sounded like his wife was pissed.

From the edge of the woods, Helen picked off three of the men who were closest to her. She crouched on one knee, taking down one, then another. The men were dead before they realized what was going on. There were still several left, though. And her line of sight was blocked by the one of the vehicles. The men's legs on the other side, however, were not.

Helen got down on her belly and lined up the first attacker. She let out a deep breath and squeezed the trigger, sending the round through the man's kneecap and dropping him to the ground. The next bullet ceased the man's sudden screaming permanently. By the time the mercenaries had realized what was happening, Helen had already picked off four of them.

The rest of the assault team redirected their fire to Helen's position. She rolled behind a broad oak just as bullets began to splash the leaves and dirt around her. The men's voices carried into the woods, barking out orders. She quickly loaded a fresh magazine into the base of her weapon and cocked it, ready to go on the attack again.

She stuck her head around the edge of the trunk when more rounds whizzed past her face, causing her to withdraw back to cover. More booming shots rang out from the front of the cabin, and she smiled. Joe was still alive.

When Joe heard Helen's gunfire, he knew the men in the SUVs would be immediately thrown off by the flank attack. That was the chance he needed to rush over to one of the windows and take up a position. He heard their return fire, but when no more rounds were zipping through his living room, it meant they were shooting at Helen.

Joe didn't wait another second. He popped up in the window and started spraying a hail of deadly rounds at the men in black outfits. Two had made the mistake of leaving the safety of their trucks while their other team members laid down covering fire. It would have been a good plan if Joe hadn't been in the window.

He cut the two men down easily, leaving the only remaining six members of the hit squad scrambling for the last SUV in the line of vehicles. The slide fire on Joe's assault rifle allowed him to fire rapid shots almost like an automatic weapon. By the time he was done, two of the three trucks had flat tires and most assuredly, severe engine damage. Now that he had gotten the men's attention again, he thought it best to make an exit through the escape tunnel and join his wife outside.

Helen watched the attackers take cover between the two outside cars, huddling around the one in the center. Three of the remaining six continued to fire rounds toward where she had taken refuge. What they didn't notice was that Helen had moved when Joe started firing on their position. When they were caught off guard, she sprinted from her hiding place and moved further up the driveway to get in a better position. Two of the men had started moving toward the front of the house. It seemed they had grown tired of being on the defensive. Being peppered from two sides had left them little choice but to move forward.

From where she was sitting, Helen had a clear angle on the two men in the rear. The two approaching the house would be slightly more difficult because of the distance, but she thought those targets were both within her range. If Joe was still in the house, she would need to take them out first, which would mean her position would be given away to the two men in the rear. She knew what she had to do.

Helen raised her weapon and trained it on the man who had taken up a position at the base of their porch next to the stairs. The other was directly across from him. If she did it right, both targets could be knocked out before the remaining four realized she had moved.

Something moved in the leaves behind her, and she spun around with the assault rifle held level.

"Don't shoot," a familiar voice begged from behind a thin tree.

Joe's body stuck out from both sides of the narrow pine, while he held both hands up. "It's me, Helen."

She lowered her weapon. "Joe, get over here," Helen hissed, dispensing with the pleasantries. She kept her emotions in check at seeing that her husband was okay.

He padded over to her spot and crouched down next to her. "What's the situation?" he asked.

"Two guys are getting ready to go in the front door. Two more are by the middle truck, and the last two are covering the rear. I was just about to take out the two next to the porch before you snuck up on me."

"Sorry."

"You should be," she sneered. "I almost blew your head off." She offered a grin that told him there were no hard feelings, but that her threat was real enough. "I'll take out the two at the porch. But as soon as I shoot the first one, those guys taking up the rear will know where we're shooting from."

Joe nodded, understanding the situation. "Looks like the best plan is for one of us to take out the guys in the front at the same time the other takes out the men in the back."

She liked the plan and approved it with a quick smile on one corner of her mouth. "I'll take the two near the house; you get the ones in the back."

"Why do you get the harder shot?" he asked as she got set up in her position again and took aim.

"Because I'm the better shooter."

He couldn't argue with that, not that it mattered anyway. Joe got down on his belly and took aim at the first man in the back. The guy was scanning the woods fifty feet to Joe and Helen's left near the woodshed. The man's weapon went back and forth as he searched for any threat.

"Ready?" she asked.

"When you are, dear."

"Fire."

The two targets were knocked over immediately. A moment later, the other two panicked men were dropped with nearly simultaneous shots.

"Good job," Helen said, almost in a surprised tone.

"Did you think I would miss?" he tried to sound wounded.

Helen glanced back at him. "You never know with men," she smirked again. "We have two left in the center."

The last two men she spoke of were scrambling to take cover anywhere they could. At present, the only place they found protection was underneath the center SUV. Both of them scurried under the carriage of the vehicle, lying on their stomachs. Their heads darted back and forth, wondering where the shots were coming from.

"You think you can hit the gas tank from here?" Helen asked, sure to keep her voice low.

Joe answered with a sarcastic nod and crouched back down, lining up the exposed underbelly of the vehicle's fuel tank. He squeezed the trigger and sent a round straight into the metal container. He frowned at the result. Gas had started leaking from the hole in the tank, splashing freely onto the ground and on one of the men.

"Why didn't it blow up?" he asked, perplexed.

"That only happens in the movies," she asked. "Fire off another one and see what happens."

He put his eye back to the scope and squeezed the trigger again. The second bullet had the same result, ripping another hole in the gas tank. This time, however, the shot got a reaction from one of the men under the vehicle. He started firing his weapon, spraying bullets into the darkness, completely forgetting the consequences for such an action.

The gas ignited instantly, setting both men on fire amid terrifying screams. The blaze shot up into the tank of the SUV and immediately turned the vehicle into a giant torch on wheels. Both men hurried out from under the carriage, their bodies completely engulfed in flames. They ran away from the burning truck and tried to douse themselves by rolling around on the ground, but the damage had been done. After a minute or so, both charred bodies had stopped moving as the deadly flames began to die down.

Joe turned away from the sight. "That's got to be a bad way to go."

Helen had a resolute look on her face. "They were going to kill us, Joe. These were really bad guys."

"I know," he nodded. "I'm glad you're okay."

"Me too," she exhaled. "That was a heck of a shot, by the way. I thought I was done for when that guy had a gun to my head."

"You ain't getting' off that easy," he chuckled. Then a worried expression washed over his face. "The dog is probably freaking out down in the bunker."

Helen smiled. "He's going to wonder what in the world happened to the house."

The two stood up and started walking down the driveway, weapons slung over their shoulders and in their hands. They had only taken ten steps toward the wreckage when they heard a strange thumping sound in the distance. It grew louder and louder, causing them to stop and turn around to see what it was. Joe had a feeling he already knew.

Sure enough, over the treetops beyond the clearing, a helicopter searchlight came into view. Through the trees, they could make out a few more headlights rolling down the long driveway.

"You gotta be kidding," Helen sounded exhausted.

"I guess this is it," Joe said, holding up the assault rifle and taking aim at the body of the helicopter.

She looked over at him for a second before copying his stance and pointing the barrel of her weapon at the oncoming machine.

"I love you, ya know?" he said.

"Me too, Joe."

As they were about to squeeze their triggers, a female voice boomed through the area from a speaker on the helicopter. "Put your weapons down! This is AXIS team three here to assist. Repeat. We are an AXIS support team here to secure the area."

Joe and Helen lowered their weapons apprehensively. They glanced at each other, both with a look of relief. Joe raised a hand and waived to the pilot as two SUVs rumbled up to where they were standing. Four men and women piled out of the vehicles and ran toward the cabin, checking the bodies and the hit squad's trucks for any threat.

The helicopter landed in the small field next to the driveway. A moment later one of the back doors opened up and a brunette woman wearing a black business suit, white blouse, and her hair pulled back tight exited the flying contraption.

She jogged over to where Joe and Helen were standing. Black smoke from the burning wreckage swirled around in the slowing helicopter rotors.

"Are you two okay?" Emily asked stopping short of the heavily armed couple.

Joe looked at his wife then back at the house. "We're fine. But our house is a mess. If we'd known you were coming over we would have cleaned up first." Emily stared at Joe for a second before she forced a few laughs. "I guess Lindsey sent his goons here to recover the vial we took from his Biosure facility. Unfortunately for him, Jenny Solomon has it now."

Emily nodded. "Yeah, we have another unit over at their building keeping an eye on things. We'll keep it locked down as long as we can until the WHO takes over." She looked around at the carnage, assessing the situation. Her face produced a suspicious grin. "Remind me to never come over to your place unannounced."

50

ARMENIAN MOUNTAINS

A driana eyed the map on her tablet. According to the GPS tracker, they were very close to the place she had pinpointed as the possible location of the ark.

"It shouldn't be far, now," she said to Jabez.

The Arab had driven them from the town of Ararat, leading the other vehicle up into the mountains along the precipitous road. The snow hadn't been as treacherous as they had anticipated, but just to be safe, both vehicles were locked in four-wheel drive.

They had been driving for over an hour, making slow progress toward the waypoint. Conversation in the vehicle had been almost nil. The only sounds were the occasional wind gusts and the crunching of rocks and dirt under the tires.

The mountain range was impressive yet unspectacular. It spanned hundreds of miles to the north, but the peaks' bland brownish color did nothing for eye appeal. The patches of melting snow helped improve the visual, but soon that would be gone. The rise and fall of the road had become monotonous, causing Firth to doze off a few times in the back seat next to Sean.

Up ahead, the road came to a sudden halt, ending in a drop off into a narrow canyon. He was relieved the second vehicle in the caravan didn't hit them from behind and drive them over the edge. Jabez turned off the engine and got out. A cold gust of air burst into the cabin of the truck, shocking Firth to a more alerted state.

Sean and Adriana got out as well, joining their Arab driver at the edge of the cliff. Over the edge, the rock wall shot straight down a hundred feet. The wall itself wrapped around a slight rise in the center of the canyon floor below. Sean got down on one knee and felt the smooth stone inside the canyon. The light brown stone of the ravine had been molded by erosion, but it seemed different than other canyons Sean had seen. It was enclosed in a much tighter space. But the thing that made this particular canyon strange was the fact that there weren't any other like it in the entire mountain range. Adriana had spent hours scanning the region via satellite images, and had not seen a single anomaly like the one resting before them.

He stood back up and stared at the strange shape of the canyon. "Is this it?" he asked in a semi-quiet tone.

Adriana glanced down at her tablet. "I think it might be," she answered reverently.

"The shape is unmistakable," Jabez commented. "Look at the outline of the canyon," he pointed out the top edge of the wall that wrapped around to where they were standing. "It is surely the final resting place of Noah's Ark."

Sean peered around the perimeter. "It would have been easy for anyone to look over this place and think it just an ordinary geological formation. No wonder no one discovered it yet."

"What is it?" Firth shouted from an open window in the vehicle. Apparently, the professor didn't want to leave the warmth of the car.

"You're going to want to see for yourself, Professor!" Sean yelled back.

The window rolled up slowly before the door opened and the older man carefully stepped out of the vehicle. As he neared the edge where the others were standing, he looked out across the span of the little canyon, his jaw dropping wide open.

"You believe in all this hocus pocus now, Doc?" Sean asked with a glint in his eye.

Firth quickly recovered to his dubious self. "I'm simply impressed by the view. But," he added, "if your theories are correct and this canyon wall was formed by the exterior hull of the ark, where is the entrance to the chamber?" He followed Sean's eyes down to the bottom of the ravine to get his answer.

"It's somewhere down there, Doc. You've come this far. You may as well come a little further."

The professor tried to suppress something. He clenched his face tightly, but he couldn't help but let a sliver of a smile escape. Sean figured it had probably been years since the old dog had done anything exciting in the world of archaeology. While he'd been a grumbling pain in the rear, Sean wondered if deep down inside Firth was enjoying himself.

"Very well, Mister Wyatt. Let's see if this wild goose chase produces a goose after all." Firth spun around and started to return to the SUV.

Adriana stopped him. "Professor. We will have to walk in from here."

"Oh," his smile disappeared. "Right."

Five minutes later, the group was trekking across the lip of the canyon toward the other end. The terrain was rocky and treacherous. Sean almost rolled his ankle on a loose stone that he'd not seen in his way. Fortunately, the walk wasn't a long one, and the group had reached their destination at the other end of the canyon within ten minutes.

The plateau they were standing on sloped down to the level of the canyon floor, leading to a narrow opening. Jabez looked at the members of the group and continued down the hill. The others followed close behind. Firth moved slower than the others, which Sean had foreseen as an issue. Fortunately, most of the snow had already melted away, so footing wasn't a huge problem.

They reached the bottom of the slope with relative ease and stood at the slim entrance to the canyon. The rock walls had come together, separated only by three feet of space. Standing at the bottom of it and looking up, the vision was imposing.

Again, Jabez took the lead and started through the narrow pass. The rest followed with Jabez's four men taking up the rear.

"I've never seen anything like this," Adriana said, staring up through the narrow space.

"We have something like this back home, in Tennessee. We call it fat man's squeeze. Though, it doesn't go this high." He pointed up to the top.

The ground at the base on which they were now walking was much smoother than up above. It was flat and even, filled in with a mixture of sand and dirt. Down in the ravine the wind had disappeared, and the air had become a little warmer.

As the group passed through the other side of the pass the canyon opened up again, sending a chill through their bones as they were reintroduced to open air.

"Which side should we check first?" Adriana wondered out loud. "Should we split up and examine both sides of the canyon?"

That plan would have made sense, but Sean remembered something he'd seen a long time ago as a child that made him think otherwise. "When I think about Noah's Ark, the pictures from my childhood always had the door to the ark on the left side."

"But how do we know which way it sailed in?" Jabez asked.

"It would have been coming from the same direction we came from."

"Why do you say that?" Firth entered the conversation.

Sean smiled. "Because the Bible speaks about the original location of the garden. It talks about where the Tigris and Euphrates rivers meet. That means originally it would have been to the southwest. If it sailed to the northeast and entered this valley from the same direction we came that would have put the door on that side over there?" he finished his rationale by pointing to the right side of the curved wall.

"You're assuming they put the door on the same side as the one on the ship," Firth remarked.

"If you want to go over and look on the other side, be my guest.

But if there is anything to find down here, my money is on the right side."

Sean started trudging across the canyon floor. Contrary to much of the surface they'd walked upon so far, there were still a few inches of snow left on the ground that crunched under his shoes as he walked. Adriana stayed right behind him.

"Fine," Firth said and fell in line with the others.

There was a smooth path that seemed to line the ground around the wall of the canyon. The center had formed a slight rise, making it impossible to see all the way to the ground level on the other den. The group marched along the narrow path, scanning the wall for any trace of evidence that they were in the right place.

Then, they saw it. Up ahead, cut into the smooth stone, was a narrow hole. It stood about eight feet tall, and three feet wide. The opening had not been cut smoothly, and the edges of it were jagged, making it appear as though it were a natural recession in the rock.

No one said anything for a few moments. Then, Jabez spoke up. "We are on very sacred ground," he said as he bent down to one knee.

His men did the same, all with heads bowed in silent prayer or meditation. Sean wasn't sure what to do so he simply bowed his head. After half a minute, the men all stood again. Jabez gave an approving nod toward Sean, which he took as meaning it was okay to go forward.

Sean removed a flashlight from a coat pocket and turned it on, proceeding into the darkness of the cave. Adriana and Jabez's men did the same, leaving Firth standing out in the cold.

"Are you sure it's safe to go in there?" he asked. The last of the brethren entered the cavity without responding. Finally, the old man produced a flashlight of his own from a coat pocket and followed the group in.

Inside, their flashlights cast a dim glow on the stone walls. They were in a narrow corridor, roughly hewn from the mountain stone. The group proceeded in single file, with Sean in the lead and Firth in the back, much to the latter's dislike. For someone so apprehensive to lead the way, he certainly didn't enjoy bringing up the rear.

As they moved deeper into the mountain, the air became thick, damp with moisture. The walls were wet to the touch, though the ground under their feet remained mostly dry. After winding their way through the tunnel for several minutes, the passage opened up into a larger space. As each person left the corridor and entered the giant room, more and more light was cast upon the walls, enabling the visitors to get a better look.

Flashlight beams danced along the grayish-brown walls that extended high to a domed ceiling fifty feet overhead. The rock had been carved out with laser precision. Unlike the jagged passageway through which they'd come, the sides of the enormous room were perfectly smooth.

Jabez's men set their duffle bags down and produced several battery-operated floodlights. As each lamp was turned on, the incredible sight before them began to piece itself together. Across from the corridor, a mural of astounding detail had been carved into the wall, spanning sixty feet across. The images engraved into the stone depicted a story in a seven stages. All of them featured an enormous boat. In one of the pictures, animals of every kind were lined up in twos, making their way to the ship. Other images displayed eight people in long, flowing robes performing some kind of examination on the animals. Another part of the mural portrayed a bearded man standing on a hill, speaking to a throng of people. The next scene showed the boat on ocean waters.

Below the mural of the flood story, three dark doorways were cut into the wall. But the thing that got everyone's attention wasn't the shadowy portals. Strewn across the floor, and the stone steps leading up to the doorways were dozens of bodies.

Firth jumped back at the sight, startled for a man who had surely seen his share of skeletons, given his field of expertise.

The decomposed corpses were decorated in a strange variety of clothing. Some appeared to be warriors from the Bronze Age. Their shields and short swords were still in remarkable condition. A few bodies bore the armor of Roman Legionnaires. Some of their large shields had massive dents in them.

Sean moved slowly across the floor toward the scene. He stopped near a skeleton of a man whose shield bore the Templar cross, his tattered white cloak had darkened with time, and become brittle.

Adriana had stepped away from the group and was checking out a body off to the side. "Sean, you should take a look at this."

He quickly took a few big steps over to where she was standing and immediately realized what had gotten her attention. At their feet were three corpses in a much lesser state of decay than the others. But it wasn't just the tissue and bone that had piqued their interest. The bodies were clothed in Russian Red Army uniforms.

"Professor?" Sean got the older man's attention. He was still standing near the entrance of the room. "How long ago did these men die?"

Firth shuffled over to where Sean and Adriana were standing, Jabez followed closely to see what was going on. The professor slipped straight into research mode as he knelt down with his flashlight in hand and examined one of the bodies.

"Based on the state of decay and the timeframe of when those uniforms were used, it appears they were here sometime in the late 1940s, perhaps early fifties." He made the statement as if it were irrefutable fact. "But what are they doing here?"

"Interesting you should ask that, Professor?" a new, gravelly voice interjected into the conversation.

Everyone spun around to see who else was in the room. Jabez's men started to withdraw their weapons, but they couldn't react fast enough. Five men and a woman in winter coats and black pants were standing in the doorway to the corridor with weapons aimed at the group. From behind them, an old man stepped crookedly through the mercenaries, followed by a taller, narrow figure.

Sean's face grew grim as he realized they'd just walked right into checkmate. "Lindsey."

51

ARMENIAN MOUNTAINS

T he air was almost sucked out of the room. Sean cursed himself under his breath for not being more careful. It was starting to become a bad habit. All those years of government work and training were apparently wearing off. The old man stepped toward him as Jabez's men were forced to lower their weapons slowly to the ground. Lindsey's men watched them all carefully, making sure no one made any sudden moves. Sean elected not to raise his hands like Firth, a few feet away, choosing instead to keep them at his side.

"How'd you find us?" Sean asked coolly.

"We followed you, of course. Seemingly, as we have been doing for the past few months." Lindsey's voice sounded harsh like he'd caught a cold. The cool, damp air of the cavern probably wasn't helping with that.

"Yeah, you're pretty good at that," Sean replied. "And I know a little something about following people."

Lindsey stopped a few feet short of Sean. The older man was a few inches shorter, and looked up as if assessing his nemesis. "Yes, Mr. Wyatt. I know all about your exploits with Axis. You were quite the little soldier, weren't you?"

"I was okay at my job."

Lindsey snorted a quick laugh, which began short fit of coughing. Sean noticed Will Hastings start to move toward the older man, but Lindsey held up a dismissive hand, keeping Will where he was near the door.

"I wonder, how you feel about all the lives you have taken, Sean? Do you have nightmares? Do you feel remorseful about the killing?"

Sean shook his head. "Every life I took was to save another. The people I killed were evil, pure and simple."

A sinister smile eased across Lindsey's wrinkled face. He took a step toward the steps leading up to the three doorways then turned around. "It seems you and I aren't so different after all."

Sean's eyebrows lowered, curious as to what the mad man meant.

"You see," Lindsey went on, "I too, believe that the wicked people of the world should die. It is the work of God to eliminate evil to give the world a chance at redemption, at salvation."

"Oh, I see," Sean took a slow step to the side. "You're talking about your little plan, the one where you send out that super virus all over the globe and kill off ninety percent of the world's population. That plan?"

Lindsey remained stoic. Sean wasn't sure if that fact he knew about the virus affected the guy or not.

He pressed the issue further. "Yeah, that plan...not so good, actually."

"And why is that? You think that I will be infected?" Lindsey shook his head. "I have a plan for that."

Sean laughed, causing Firth to jerk his head sideways to look at him. The Englishman's face showed he couldn't believe Wyatt was actually toying with the guy, despite having six guns trained on him. While the two continued talking, Adriana stood perfectly still. She noticed DeGard moving slowly, as if in a trance, up the steps toward the doorway in the middle.

"No," Sean answered. "Right now there is a team of Axis agents surrounding your Biosure facility in Atlanta. There's no way they are going to let that virus leave the building. So, you're little plan is shut down. It's over, Prophet. You can kill all of us, but the world will be okay."

For a moment, Lindsey's face trembled. Sean figured he'd finally gotten to him. An odd laugh began coming from the man's face, causing the loose neck skin to jiggle slightly.

"That's it? You set up a little blockade around my Atlanta facility?" The old man's tone became mocking, and he raised his hands to add insult. "You do realize that we have warehouses all over the world. I have already given the order for them to ship out the virus immediately. Within twelve hours, planes, trucks, and trains will be delivering those vaccinations all over the world. Atlanta only represented a small fraction of our supply. Sure, if we were able to use it, the virus would spread faster, but you have done nothing but bought a few extra days for a world that will be cleansed of all unrighteousness."

Sean fought to keep his poker face. He'd known about the other facilities, but assumed either Atlanta had the only supply of the virus, or that if they could shut that building down, the others would follow quickly. It seems the old man had thought of that. Out of the corner of his eye, he saw DeGard at the top of the steps, creeping toward the center door. He was staring at an inscription in the stone just over the top of the opening.

The thin man wasn't listening to the banter between Wyatt and Lindsey, instead mesmerized by the words in the rock.

"The treasures of the kingdom of God lie within," he mumbled, just loud enough for his voice to echo off the walls and reach everyone else's ears. He turned around and pointed at the top of the portal. "I can't believe it is true," his thick accent grew more pronounced. "I was wrong not to believe you. We have found the tree of life. This will be the greatest discovery in the history of the world." He continued moving, almost involuntarily as he spoke, stepping closer and closer to the darkness within the doorway.

"Are you sure?" Lindsey asked, distracted for a moment from the conversation with Wyatt.

"Oui," he answered and pointed at the strange engravings over the opening.

The marks were nothing but a series of indentions: vertical, horizontal, and diagonal. Sean knew what they were. He'd seen cuneiform before, though he couldn't read it. It was the oldest known form of writing in the world, and was extremely difficult to interpret. The fact that the Frenchman knew how was somewhat impressive.

DeGard neared the threshold of the door, only a step away from it now. He shone his flashlight into it, trying to get a better view inside.

"I see a path," he turned his head back toward the group again. "I think this is the way." He took another step, this one across the threshold of the doorway.

"DeGard, wait!" Lindsey shouted.

A grinding rumble filled the room for a second followed by a quick thud. The Frenchman's body flew thirty feet across the room. They all stepped out of the way quickly as the man rolled to a stop in the middle of the dusty floor. His face and torso had been caved in, making him an almost unrecognizable, bloody mess.

Lindsey moved away from Wyatt, inspecting the corpse from a few feet away. Something of incredible force had struck DeGard, killing him instantly. The shock on the old man's face washed away quickly.

"You just saved me a bullet, Monsieur. Thank you for your service," he mocked the dead man before turning his attention to the group of Jabez's men.

"Will," he called out. "Could you encourage one of these men to test another door?"

Will stepped over to Jabez's group, and pressed his gun to the head of the first man he came to. "Move," he ordered.

The young Arab looked to be in his upper twenties. But he showed no fear. His face was resolute as he slowly turned and began walking toward the steps. Will followed him closely, keeping the pistol aimed at the man's back. When they reached the steps, Will seemed reluctant to follow any further.

The man slowed his pace as he veered to the left, staring into the doorway on that side of the wall. His feet shuffled along the floor as he drew closer to the portal. Everyone in the cavernous room watched closely, holding their breath to see what would happen. Jabez's lips moved quickly, whispering a silent prayer for his young friend. His eyes were closed as he did, but there was no worry on his face. Sean knew those men had prepared themselves for just such a moment. But he had a sneaking suspicion the young Arab had no idea what he was doing.

The man stopped short of the portal's threshold and looked up at the Cuneiform inscription. He stared for a few seconds at the confusing engraving. Sean wasn't sure whether the guy was able to translate the symbols or not. Then, the man took another step forward, crossing a broad line of stone marking the edge of the door. Nothing happened, so he took another step, disappearing into the darkness beyond. Sean let out a relieved breath until a blood-curdling scream stopped it short. The young Arab's voice trailed off as if he were falling into a deep pit. After a few seconds, the voice was gone completely.

Sean, Adriana, and Dr. Firth all glanced over at Jabez. The man's eyes had opened wide at the terrifying sound of one of his own screaming. For a few moments, he stood waiting, as if the man would somehow appear back through the doorway. When it didn't happen, the Arab's head dropped for a second. His breath came in deep, slow heaves.

Will came back to the group and pointed his gun at another of Jabez's men. "You're next. Move!"

"Wait," Jabez begged.

His request halted Will and caused everyone in the room to look over at him.

"Take me."

Will hesitated for a moment and stole a quick glance over at Lindsey, asking for permission. When the old man nodded his approval, Will grabbed Jabez by the arm and shoved him toward the steps in the front of the room, sticking his gun out at arm's length.

Jabez stumbled for a second then caught himself. He looked back at his remaining men then over at Sean and the others. He didn't say anything, instead offering a slow nod of the head, as if to say goodbye.

Then, he turned toward the darkened doorway on the right and began walking toward it again.

As he reached the top step, he stopped for a moment, staring up at the inscription above the cavity. Sean couldn't hold back any longer. He'd been standing there, watching the man they had only just met, wondering if there was anything he could do to save Jabez.

"Stop," Sean shouted across the room.

Will turned back to see what the problem was. Lindsey's other men started for a second, quickly training their weapons on the person who had interrupted.

"Keep going," Lindsey turned and yelled out the order. Jabez had twisted around, now wearing a confused look on his face.

"No, wait!" Sean insisted. "I'll do it. I think I can get us through."

Lindsey's head swiveled around. He looked skeptical. But he was considering the idea. A silent moment of thought passed before he answered.

"Very well, Sean Wyatt. You may as well die now rather than later."

Sean raised one hand slowly, pointing at Firth. "I need the professor, just to help me read the inscription over the doorway."

A look of fear doused the professor's face. He clearly didn't want to be brought into this little ruse. He shook his head quickly, desperate not to be involved.

"Fine," Lindsey said gruffly. "Take him, too. We were going to have to kill him anyway."

"No," Firth begged, moving back a few steps toward the wall behind him. "This is your mess, Sean Wyatt. Don't try to drag me down with you."

Lindsey's head drooped to the side, tired of the theatrics. "Kaba, if you would?" he pointed a hand at the professor.

The mocha-skinned woman took a few long strides over to Firth then grabbed him by the arm and jabbed the gun into his back. He let out a short howl as he tripped forward.

Sean caught him before the professor could fall over. "It's going to be fine, Doc," he whispered in Firth's ear.

The archaeology professor was still leaning over from his near fall. He looked up into Sean's eyes, trying desperately to find any reason he should believe the younger man. What he saw was conviction to the point where he realized Sean didn't care whether he died or not. But he also saw belief.

"I just need you to interpret the Cuneiform for me. You're one of the few people on this planet that can do it. Just be sure to stand clear of the opening."

He looked back at Adriana. For the first time he saw a pained expression on her face, one that told him not to go. But he had to. Deep down he knew he had the best chance of getting through the ancient traps.

Firth straightened up. His expression had changed to one of resolve as he nodded slowly. "Alright, Sean."

52

ARMENIAN MOUNTAINS

S ean and the professor slowly made their way past where
Lindsey stood. The man scowled at them as they went by. He
was hunched over slightly. Sean figured years of some spinal
problem were likely taking their toll. The two men made their way up
the steps as Jabez descended them. The Arab didn't look ungrateful.
Rather, he seemed awed that Sean would make such a sacrifice for
someone he'd just met.

Sean had stared death in the face on more than one occasion.
One more wouldn't kill him. He snorted a short laugh at the thought.
That's exactly what it could do. When they reached the top of the
steps, they stopped in front of the door on the right.

"What does it say?" Sean asked as they stared up at the symbols
etched in stone.

Firth pushed his glasses a little further up his nose while
squinting to view the inscriptions. His lips moved silently as he translated the ancient language in his mind. After a minute, he turned to
Sean.

"The righteous stand for the right."

"That's what it says?" Sean was clearly hoping for more than
that.

The professor nodded. "Yes. It would seem there is some sort of riddle at play here. Do you have any idea what it means?"

Sean crossed his arms and lowered his head. The gears in his mind were running at a million miles a second. He thought about humility and what it meant. People who were humble were usually quiet, reserved types. They didn't get out of line much.

None of those facts seemed to help with his current situation.

"What are you waiting for?" Lindsey shouted. "Go." He turned back to Kaba and jerked a finger at Adriana. Kaba immediately snagged Adriana's arm and put her pistol's barrel to the back of Spaniard's head.

Will followed suit, taking a few threatening steps toward the stairs to make sure Sean saw his weapon was aimed right at the IAA agent. Will also flashed a menacing grin that begged Sean to make him pull the trigger.

"Either move or get down on your knees and let me put a bullet through the back of your skull," Will said through clenched teeth. "I want to do it. And I want her to kill your pretty, little girlfriend over there."

Sean's eyes drifted to the side of the corridor. They widened slightly. There was a black line of stone running along the edge of the wall on the right side. "The righteous stand on the right, not for the right," he whispered to himself. Sean hoped he was right. If he pressed against the wall, there might be just enough room to get by the huge pendulum.

Sean shoved the anger he was feeling deep into the back of his mind, and stepped quickly over in front of the doorway. At the threshold, he took a long, deep breath. He stared ahead into the darkness. His hand unconsciously put the flashlight back in his coat pocket as his eyes peered forward. A slight draft blew from the mysterious passageway, tossing a few loose blonde hairs around. He stepped over to the right corner of the passage and pressed his body against the stone wall. He scooted his left foot sideways and shuffled forward with the right.

His left foot crossed the dark, stone line marking the doorway, his right followed slowly. There was a sudden rumbling accompanied by a gust of wind. Sean pressed his chest harder into the wall, keeping it as flush as he could. Suddenly, the huge pendulum swung by, nearly scraping his back. The thing shook the floor and walls, whooshing past him at an incredible velocity. He forced himself to stay close to the wall as the object swung back through again in the other direction.

After what seemed like an eternity shuffling sideways, Sean found himself clear of the ancient pendulum's reach, and was able to stand in the clear on the other side. He pulled out his flashlight and shone it on the wall. A few feet away, a lever made from stone stuck out through a narrow slit in the wall. He reached over and tugged on the device as hard as he could. Slowly, the lever gave way and slowly descended to the bottom of the slit. A loud clicking resonated through the corridor, followed by a grinding noise. The pendulum began to slow until it finally reached a complete stop. It was designed in the shape of a double-sided war hammer, with conical points sticking out of the hammer's head.

He took a relieved breath, and looked back through the slim space between the wall and the hammer's side. "I'm through," he yelled.

In the atrium, Lindsey seemed surprised, while Will was clearly disappointed.

"He made it," Lindsey sounded astonished.

Beyond the enormous swinging hammer, Sean had turned his attention back to the passage in front of him. He took a cautious step forward and immediately realized there was a new problem. A black abyss opened up in the floor in front of his feet. The ceiling loomed high above the deep pit. On the other side of the gap, a long, narrow stone stood at the edge of where he needed to be. The plinth reached about twenty feet into the air. It was difficult for him to gauge the distance. He figured it to be about twelve to fifteen feet. With a running start, and just the right push, he might have been able to clear it. But there wasn't enough room to get up the momentum it would require. And therein was the problem with the riddle of the second trap.

He flashed his light on the wall to his left, but found nothing of value. When he shined it to the right, it was a different story altogether. More Cuneiform script had been engraved into the side of the passageway. He took a step closer and felt the cuts of the symbols cut into the smooth stone.

"Professor," he shouted back. "I'm going to need you to come through. There's another message you'll have to interpret."

In the first room, Firth looked back at Lindsey with a face full of apprehension. Will also seemed leery of the notion.

"Follow him through," Lindsey ordered his apprentice. "If they try anything, shoot them both." Will acknowledged the order with a nod, waving his gun at Firth in a motion to move forward.

The professor hesitated for a second until Will stepped closer and stuck the barrel into his chest. "After you, Professor."

Firth obeyed and moved toward the deactivated mechanism. He still looked at it with a certain degree of fear, as if it might somehow come to life again. Slowly, he wedged himself between the giant hammer and the wall and wormed his way along the floor. Will followed closely behind, mimicking Firth's movements and keeping the gun forward as he progressed.

"Will and your friend are coming through, Wyatt," Lindsey shouted, making sure Sean heard him. "If you try anything stupid, I will execute the girl and the rest of this rabble."

Sean heard the threat as the professor appeared on the other side. He stepped over and reached a hand out to help the older man through. The next thing he saw was Will's hand, the one holding a black pistol. Sean stepped back to make sure Will didn't perceive him as a threat, instead turning his attention to the inscription on the wall.

"What can you make of this, Doc?" he asked and shone his light on the message.

Firth stared at the strange language while Will pulled himself up off the ground and stayed at a safe distance on the other side of the corridor.

"Give me a moment," Firth requested. After a minute of running his finger along the lines he believed he had the translation. "This one says that only the strong shall pass through to taste of eternal life."

Sean frowned at the answer, and then looked back at the wide pit. He flashed his light down into the dark cavity; the bottom didn't appear.

"Only the strong?" he wanted to clarify. "That's it?"

"That's what it says."

Behind them, Will said nothing, keeping a wary eye on both men.

Sean eased back over to the lip of the drop and scanned the walls carefully. It didn't make sense. Sure, if he were a little stronger, maybe the jump would be possible. But he didn't think even the most powerful Olympic jumper could clear that without a running head start. In high school, he'd seen a few of the track stars jumping pretty far from a standing position. But this was too far.

He stared across at the other side. While the jump was long, the distance was short in relation to how far they'd come over the previous few months. He thought about how Tommy had discovered the clue in north Georgia that had led them to the first chamber of gold. They had unraveled a mystery as old as any in North America. And they'd gone beyond. Whether he died or not, Sean had to finish the journey.

His eyes drifted to the wall on the right, catching a glimpse of something he hadn't seen before. About waist high, a notch had been cut out of the wall, just large enough for someone to fit the tip of a shoe. He looked further up the rock face and saw another notch, and another. It reminded him of the rock climbing wall at his gym, except with less friendly hand holds, and potentially much worse implications if he fell.

Sean moved over to the rock face and tested out the notch, shoving the toe of his shoe into it. He put the small end of the flashlight into his mouth, holding it with his teeth, and reached up to the next notch.

"What are you doing?" Firth wondered.

"To get to the other side, I'm going to have to scale this wall," he said through teeth still gripping the light.

Will moved closer to make sure his prisoner didn't try anything.

Sean grabbed the slit above his head with his left hand and pulled up. He shot his right hand upward, feeling for another grip. His fingers found it, directly above his head. He pushed them into the groove as far as they would go and pulled hard with his right hand, simultaneously moving his left foot up to where the left hand had been. Sweat began to form on his fingers and palms. He was glad the rock was dry in that part of the cave, though he wished for his chalk bag he used to carry when he would go climbing on Saturdays in college. He was thankful for that experience as a rock climber, as he continued to replicate the movement, going higher and higher, moving out and over the deep abyss.

One of the things he'd always told himself was never to look down. Always look up. Never put the possibility of failing into the mind. Just look at the wall, and the next place to put your hand and foot.

He had nearly reached the top of the wall, halfway across the gap, when his left foot slipped in one of the edges. The movement caused his body to drop slightly, putting all his weight on the fingertips barely clinging to the highest cut in the wall. The jarring motion loosened his jaw's grip on the flashlight, and he dropped it, sending beam tumbling down the shaft, disappearing into the darkness below.

Firth was still shining his light on Sean's location when he slipped and nearly fell. The professor watched Sean's light drop into the cavity, forgetting for a moment that his own light drifted off of Sean's location.

"Doc?" Sean yelled in a strained voice. "I need that light up here."

"Sorry!" Firth sounded genuinely apologetic as he turned the beam back on Sean's position.

Sean struggled, but found the foothold again with his feet and was able to take the weight off his hands for a second.

Descending was another animal altogether. Going down could be tricky, possibly more difficult than climbing up. That was one reason they had always just repelled back to the bottom of a climb when he'd done it in college. At this point Sean would have gladly accepted the luxury of a rope with an easy descent.

He maneuvered his left foot over and jammed it back into a notch then cautiously lowered his left hand to the next grip. The going was precipitous. And at this stage, he had to look down to find the next place to put his feet and hands, bringing into view the terrifying drop below. Sean's only true fear in life had always been heights. Over the course of the last few months, he'd found himself hanging over a number of high places. He'd not gotten accustomed to it.

After several minutes of careful movement, Sean's feet landed safely on the other side of the gap. He squatted down for a moment, taking in rapid breaths. Staring down gunmen didn't seem to bother him. But the possibility of falling unnerved him. He knew it didn't make sense. He just figured it was his thing, and everybody had a thing.

"Well done, old boy," Firth shouted across the pit.

Sean eyeballed the narrow column in front of him. The piece of stone appeared as though it would stretch across to the other side and was wide enough to walk on. It was already leaning slightly toward where Will and the professor were standing, requiring only a little more energy to tip it over.

"Stand back," Sean shouted across the pit. "I think this thing is a bridge."

The other two moved back toward the huge hammer as Sean stepped around behind the stone column and leaned against it. He bent his knees and pushed his back into the stone, and was surprised to feel it give a little. The movement encouraged him, and he shoved harder, feeling the quads in his legs begin swell. He let out a grunt as the heavy object reached the tipping point and began to topple over.

A loud thud boomed through the corridor and out into the first room. Dust erupted all around Will and Firth, shooting a horizontal plume of debris out to where the rest of the group stood waiting. The entire room shuddered from the crashing stone.

It was the only moment Adriana had to break free. Kaba had flinched for a second, moving the weapon away from the Spaniard's head to see what had happened. Adriana whipped her left arm up, knocking away the hand that held the weapon. The second shot came from her right fist, going straight to Kaba's jaw. Metal clanking on stone echoed through the cavern as Kaba's gun fell to the floor hitting just before she did.

Lindsey's men spun quickly toward the commotion. Between the pervading darkness and the dust cloud hovering over the two women, it was nearly impossible for the mercenaries to see anything.

A muffled pop echoed from the dust, sending a bullet into the forehead of the mercenary nearest the entrance. Another shot struck another man in the throat. The remaining two men didn't know whether to fire or not. If they did, bullets would ricochet around the room, possibly hitting them in the process. Their indecisiveness gave Jabez and his men the opening they needed. The Arab and two of the brethren lunged at the remaining two henchmen, tackling them to the floor. The rough landing jarred the weapons from the men's hands. The brethren pounded the men's skulls against the stone to finish the job, rendering the mercenaries either dead or unconscious. They didn't bother checking to see which.

Jabez turned his attention to the spot where Lindsey had been standing. The man was gone, though. Dust was still settling in the eerie glow of the lights on the floor. Jabez moved quickly to where the man had been, but he had vanished.

He looked over toward the still pendulum and noticed the bottom of a shoe being pulled into the narrow gap in the corridor. Jabez ran quickly over to the steps but muffled pops echoed out of from between the wedge, sending bullets pinging off the rock nearby. The Arab jumped back and took cover off to the side where he would be out of range.

Inside the passage, Will pulled his dust-covered employer the rest of the way through to the other side. The old man appeared even older amid the thin layer of gray that had settled on him. Lindsey let out a few coughs before patting himself down to get rid of some of the dirt. In his right hand, he held a black 9mm Walther with a silencer on the end.

He looked dead at Firth then across the stone bridge at Sean. "After you, Professor." He wagged the gun as he spoke.

Firth had been surprised to see Lindsey drag himself under the pendulum, but now his surprised turned to dread as he realized he was the guinea pig for the newly dropped bridge.

"It's going to be okay, Doc," Sean shouted across the gap. "Just move slowly, and everything will be fine." He held out a hand toward the professor, beckoning him to come across.

The Englishman hesitated for a few seconds before moving to the edge of the pit and putting a foot lightly down on the top of the fallen stone. The walkway was easily a foot or two thick, but the stability of the thing wasn't Firth's issue. Falling off of it was.

He placed his second foot on the plank and began slowly shuffling his way across gap, keeping his arms up on both sides to help maintain his balance. After what should have taken much less time, Firth reached the other side and grabbed onto Sean's arm, hopping down gratefully onto the ground.

Will was already on the bridge with his gun in front of him, aimed straight at Sean.

"You know, I always thought there was something fishy about you, Will," Sean said as his counterpart easily arrived on the other side. "You were so eager, and acted way to green to be a cop, even for a rookie."

Will jumped down from the bridge and motioned for his employer to come across before turning his attention to Sean.

"Well, it worked. Didn't it? So, I don't really care about your opinion. All I care about is finding this thing, killing you, and going someplace where there is a beach and a margarita waiting on me."

"Lofty goals you have there," Sean jabbed.

His adversary took in a deep breath through his nostrils before responding. "You know what? You're right. I should aspire to something more. I think when I'm done killing you and your little professor friend here, I may have a little fun with Adriana. I bet she'll be a ton of fun."

Something inside of Sean wanted to snap. He wanted to reach over, grab Will by the neck, and choke the last breath of life out of him. But Will had the gun, and any move at this point would provoke him to shoot.

Lindsey was shuffled across the bridge the same way Firth had done. When he reached the other three, he turned around and fired two more warning shots through the opening at beneath the stone hammer. He spun around with devious intention on his face.

"Move."

53

Emily paced through the tattered remains of the McElroy cabin. She had been on the phone for the last hour with a number of different authorities, including some very highly positioned people from the World Health Organization. No one was budging, though. Everyone she had spoken to had given her the same bureaucratic bull as the previous.

They splashed around terms concerning protocol and due diligence, but the truth was they wanted to do it during working hours. The underlying part was that they likely didn't want to believe something so large scale could have slipped past their notice.

She had a team of her own agents standing by at the Atlanta Biosure facility, making sure none of the shipments actually left the building. But something had been troubling her since the moment she'd made the first call. She knew that Alexander Lindsey had more than one facility in the umbrella of Biosure. There were several buildings under that name across the country, not to mention any subsidiaries there might be. If he had decided not to put all his eggs in one basket, all it would take would be one phone call to put the wheels in motion. The virus could ship out to any number of undisclosed locations. There would be no stopping it. And if it were as bad as Jenny Solomon believed, the results would be cataclysmic.

Emily had one more play she could make. It would be risky. And if she were wrong, it would cost her reputation, career, and everything she'd worked so hard for through the years.

"Any luck?" Helen asked as she sifted through the wreckage that used to be their home.

"No," Emily shook her head and ended the call. "They want to know too many details, and for this time of day, we just can't expedite that information fast enough.

"So, what can we do?" Joe seemed bewildered.

Emily let out a deep sigh. "There is another option, but it's a last resort. If we are wrong about any of this, it'll cost me everything."

"Jenny isn't wrong, Em," Joe reassured. "This thing is the real deal."

She nodded at his comment. "The director of the CIA owes me a huge favor. I saved a few of his agents a couple of years back when none of the other agencies would touch the situation. He can help us secure the other Biosure facilities before it's too late. If it isn't too late already."

Joe appeared skeptical. "You're talking about a huge operation, spanning across several major cities in the United States. You think they could pull that off?"

"Believe me, they have the resources in place. All it will take is a phone call from him, and the assets will be put in position. And after what we did for him, I have the feeling he won't question my request."

"You sure he's going to honor that obligation?" Helen asked. "Those high up agency guys have a pretty short memory when it comes to that sort of thing."

"He'll remember," Emily began dialing the phone. She put it to her ear as it started ringing. "One of the agents we saved was his son."

54

ARMENIAN MOUNTAINS

The four men trudged forward, going deeper into the underground passage. The ceiling had dropped significantly, and was only seven or eight feet. It had narrowed, too, getting to only a few feet wide. Three flashlight beams barely illuminated the tunnel as they continued ahead.

No one said anything, though the special agent inside Sean's head was constantly watching for a moment where he could turn the tables. So far, Will hadn't made any mistakes.

Will Hastings made sure to stay close behind Wyatt, but far enough away that if his prisoner decided to try anything, he would be at a safe distance. Keeping Lindsey in the back of the group was the safest thing to do. While the old man had proven himself a little more spry than Will had thought, Sean Wyatt could probably find a weakness and exploit it.

It had only been five minutes since the group had left the bridge when they began to notice the air becoming warmer. The temperature increase wasn't insignificant, becoming warmer by several degrees as they continued deeper into the mountain.

"Are there any underground volcanoes around here?" Firth asked, not really expecting an answer.

He unbuttoned his heavy coat as he walked ahead. Sean started to unzip his coat, but Will stopped him.

"Keep yours just the way it is," he ordered. Sean obeyed, and kept marching forward.

Strange sounds began to seep into the corridor. The noise was faint at first, but the farther the men walked, the louder it became. What was more disconcerting was the faint glow that shone off the walls of the tunnel.

"It sounds like water flowing," Firth stated as he rounded a curve in the passage. "And there's a light up ahead."

"Impossible?" Sean said, despite seeing the glow resonating from up ahead. "We can't be on the other side of the mountain. Cold air would be blowing in. It's way too warm."

"Keep going," Will ordered.

The professor moved ahead until he finally reached the end of the tunnel. The passage opened up into an enormous room. Every mouth gaped wide at the sight. The chamber was at least hundred and fifty feet wide and a hundred feet high.

The walls were covered in brilliant, sparkling gold that stretched all the way up to a dramatic, domed ceiling. Images of people and animals adorned the shiny yellow surface as far as their eyes could see. On the ground, a pathway made from solid gold wound its way across the stone floor to where a small creek flowed through the room. Various gems and precious stones littered the floor all over the place.

Lindsey's eyes remained glued to the center of the room, fixated by what he saw. A gigantic tree soared high into the air, nearly brushing the ceiling. The plant was like nothing they had ever seen before, growing from two trunks, one on either side of the little river. The leaves were vibrant green, like shimmering emeralds. And the fruit dangling from the branches looked like something from an alien planet.

It was shaped much like a pear, but each piece had radiated a pale, glowing light. The men realized that was where the light had been coming from.

"Go on," Lindsey ordered with a wag of his pistol.

The four moved slowly along the golden path until they reached the base of the tree. Standing close to it, they could see into the water. The liquid was as clear as glass, and they could see to the bottom where diamonds, gold, and precious gems lined the riverbed. It was like a scene out of a weird dream.

"This is it," Lindsey stated. He motioned for the two captives to move aside, virtually pushing Firth out of the way. Will slid to the side, keeping his gun trained on Wyatt, but watching as his employer stepped over to a branch hanging just low enough to reach.

Lindsey extended his hand up and grasped one of the glowing orbs. "The wise will reach to the heavens, and find the path to immortality." He plucked the fruit from the tree and brought it down to eye level, inspecting its strange beauty.

"What was that?" Sean decided to interrupt the man's moment of triumph.

"It's from the diary of Sir Francis Drake," he said in a trance. "Many will wander in darkness, but the wise will reach to the heavens, and find the path to immortality," he repeated the last part.

"Sir Francis Drake?"

"Yes. I happened upon a lost diary of his several years ago. It's what led me to seek out the tree." He waved around his hand in dramatic fashion. "This beautiful tree of life. With it, I will live forever. I will destroy mankind the way God did during the flood, and build a new, righteous kingdom on Earth."

Sean's eyebrows rose slightly. "So, you're playing God now?"

"Sometimes," Lindsey said, still clutching the fruit in front of his lips. "God waits too long."

He looked back at the fruit again then sunk his teeth deep into it, taking a big bite. He pulled the orb away from his mouth, savoring the taste. A little dribble of juice rolled off the corner of his lips. His eyes closed as he chewed the piece.

"It's so warm," he said. "To the touch. On the tongue. It radiates warmth. And it's like nothing I've ever tasted before. It's so sweet and juicy."

Will watched apprehensively as his employer took another bite of the glowing fruit. "I can feel the power already coursing through my body."

Sean's curious expression turned to one of concern as Lindsey took another bite of the fruit. The man's eyes were beginning to glow like the fruit. Even Will took a step back.

Lindsey kept eating, not realizing the change in his appearance. "I am thinking so clearly now. I can feel my brain expanding. It is like seeing into the mind of God himself."

Suddenly, his body froze stiff. The remainder of the fruit dangled in his hand for a moment before dropping to the ground. The gun in his other hand clacked onto the ground, temptingly close to where Sean was standing. A look of sheer horror filled the old man's face. He glanced down at his hands. They were glowing like the fruit.

"What's happening to me?" he looked over at Will. "It feels like my skin is on fire." Desperation filled his voice as he began to stagger slightly, his body wavering as if he were about to lose his balance.

Will took another step back, unsure of what was going on.

"Help me, Will," the old man begged, dropping down to his knees. His hand outstretched to the young apprenticed whose life he'd once saved. "Please."

"What is this, Wyatt?" Will asked, glancing over at Sean. "What's happening to him?"

Sean kept his voice even, and his face steady, though his tone carried a heavy dose of malice. "If I remember my Bible correctly, I seem to recall there being two trees in the garden."

"Two trees?"

Firth took a step backwards.

"The tree of life was only one. The second was the tree of knowledge of good and evil. It was the one God told the garden's inhabitants not to eat, and if they did, they would die."

Lindsey interrupted with a piercing howl. "Help me!" he begged again.

"Where is the other tree?" Will asked frantically. "We have to find it to save him."

Sean shook his head slowly, staring through his adversary. "There is no other tree, Will. Your prophet is as good as dead."

"No," Will shook his head.

Lindsey fell over on his side, his body convulsing violently. Blood trickled out of the side of his mouth. He rolled over on his back and took in a deep, gurgled breath. "Complete...the mission." His head went limp, thumping against the ground. Wide eyes stared lifelessly up at the ceiling; the odd glow had already begun to fade.

"Prophet?" Will bent down to check the man who had taught him everything. It was the window Sean had been waiting for.

He launched at Will with his right foot, driving the top of his boot into Will's hand, knocking the gun loose. It splashed into the river nearby, sinking to the bottom. Sean didn't hesitate to strike again, sending a jab right into Will's jaw.

The younger man stumbled backwards for a second. Sean was on him instantly, taking another swing with his right hand. The split second Will had fallen back had given him time to regain his wits. He caught Wyatt off guard by blocking the punch to the side and bringing his own counter straight into Sean's stomach.

Sean doubled over right into an uppercut that sent him reeling back for a second before he rolled to the ground. Will quickly broke for the gun lying on the ground near Lindsey's body. On the second step, Sean twisted around, swinging his leg across Will's shin and tripping to the ground. Both men popped up simultaneously, facing each other again.

Will's eyes were orbs of hatred, piercing through Sean. "I should have killed you a long time ago, Wyatt. I told the old man to let me. But he was convinced we needed you alive a little longer."

"He should have listened to you," Sean sneered and launched another assault.

His hands blurred in the furious attack. Will was equal to the task, dodging and blocking nearly all of the punches. Sean overextended on one strike, allowing Will to counter with a kick to the abdomen.

Sean crumpled over, dropping to one knee for a second. Will

brought his knee squarely into Sean's face, sending him flying a few feet to the side and tumbling to a stop near the river.

Firth stood off to the side, paralyzed with fear as Will walked over to the tree and plucked another piece of the glowing fruit from a low branch. Sean groaned, blood oozing from his bottom lip as he rolled over onto his back.

The room swirled in his vision as he tried to regain balance. His head and jaw were pounding. He squinted his eyes closed for a second, and tried to reopen them to focus. When he did, Will was standing over him with a piece of the deadly fruit.

"Open wide, Wyatt," Will grabbed the back of Sean's head and forced it toward the fruit.

Sean resisted, trying to twist his head back and forth, keeping his mouth closed as he did, but he was so dizzy. Will's grip on the back of his hair was firm, making it difficult to move at all. Sean could feel the warmth of the fruit as it touched his lips. He kept his mouth shut, but Will was pushing so hard that some of the juice began to squirt out onto his face. It was all he could do to keep any of the liquid from squeezing in.

"Come on, Wyatt," Will jeered. "Just relax and take a bite. It will all be over soon."

More of the glowing juice spurted onto Sean's face. He was having trouble breathing through his nose, a product of it being nicked during the fight. Not enough air was getting through the one clear nostril.

He grunted as he struggled, but there was no getting free. His lungs screamed for air. Just as he was about to open his mouth to inhale, a gunshot rang out through the room.

Will dropped the fruit onto the ground and turned toward the entrance to the chamber. Adriana stood just inside the room, a black pistol stretched out in front of her. He looked down at his side where a blackish hole was beginning to leak thick, red. He touched it for a moment and stared nostalgically at the blood before turning to face her. Will took one step toward her, but that was as far as he made it.

Adriana unleashed a flurry of rounds, emptying the entire

contents of her magazine, each one sinking deep into Will's chest. He staggered backwards and fell over next to Lindsey's body, his face staring lifelessly up at the domed ceiling.

Sean fell over forward, bracing his fall with his hands. Adriana ran from the edge of the passageway, followed closely by Jabez. She reached Sean quickly, and bent down to see if he was okay while Jabez checked the two bodies.

"Are you okay?" she asked, putting a hand on Sean's back.

He nodded, as he spit out a little blood onto the floor. "Yeah. I'll be fine. Just not as quick as I used to be, I guess."

Sean pushed himself up off the ground with a little help from the Spaniard. Jabez was digging in one of Lindsey's pockets for a moment before pulling out a leather bound book.

"What is this?" he wondered, examining the front and back of the object.

Sean winced, still trying to regain his balance. "It's probably a diary. He mentioned something about a diary that belonged to Sir Francis Drake."

Adriana's face twitched sideways at him. "The privateer?"

"I don't know of another," he shrugged.

Jabez handed Adriana the book and fished around in another pocket of the old man's coat. "What happened to Lindsey," the Arab asked as he removed a small, stone disc from the body.

"That isn't the tree he was looking for," Sean pointed at the gargantuan oddity. Their faces seemed confused. "Our friend, The Prophet here, forgot that there were two trees in the Garden of Eden. This one isn't the tree of life. In fact, it's quite the opposite."

Sean reached out his hand to take the disc from Jabez, who was looking absently at the thing. "Do you mind?"

Firth had been standing silent for the last few minutes, his fears slowly subsiding. "If that isn't the tree of life then where is it?"

"Thanks for your help by the way," Sean said sarcastically. "That guy almost killed me." Firth hung his head ashamed for a moment. "I'm just kidding, Doc. It's okay. My guardian angel had it under control." He smiled at Adriana.

His grin forced a small one onto her face. "That's twice I've saved you." She drew close to him as she spoke.

He could hear the voice in the back of his head telling him to jump. Despite having a bloody lip, he wanted so badly to kiss her.

Jabez's voice interrupted the moment, though. "Yes, where is the tree if this is not it?"

Sean pulled away from her and looked down at the stone in his hand. "Lindsey said that in the diary, Drake mentioned that the wise will reach to the heavens to find the path to immortality."

"What does that mean?" Firth questioned, coming near as he cleaned his glasses.

Sean ignored him and walked slowly past the tree, toward the far wall where the river disappeared under the golden façade. Among the myriad of images engraved into the yellowish surface, one stood out above the others. It was unmistakable, as if someone had recently created the image. Eight planets revolving around the sun, all in their designated orbits, were carved into the golden wall. Where the sun was located, a shallow recession had been cut from the surface. It was almost the exact size of the stone disc in Sean's hand.

"Reach to the heavens," he whispered quietly as the other three gathered around.

He lifted the disc up and pushed it into the hole. A deep rumble began from the depths of the mountain. The ground shook violently, causing the four companions to widen their feet so as not to fall over. A seam opened in the center of the golden wall, splitting it in half. The space continued to widen as the two giant pieces of wall opened up like two double doors.

A minute later, the grinding rumble had ceased and the huge panels had stopped moving. Beyond, they had revealed another chamber, smaller than the one with the tree, but no less impressive. Cold air wafted out of the new room, sending a cloud of chilly mist billowing over the astonished faces of the visitors.

Inside, the walls were carved from the rock of the mountain, unlike the gilded walls of the first chamber. Animals of every kind were represented in strange drawings along the surface. What caught everyone off guard however, weren't the drawings. Shiny metal cabinets lined the walls, reaching up to five feet high, and wrapping around the entire room.

"Those containers appear as if they're made from chrome?" Sean observed as he stepped into the chilly room.

"They look like something you would see in a laboratory," Firth added.

"Or a morgue."

The four cautiously moved forward, none knowing what exactly they were looking at. The little river from the first room meandered through the second, leading to a pool in the middle of the floor. The pool emanated an eerie, white light that was reflected from the ceiling, casting the dim illumination all throughout the chamber. Placed near each corner of the room were four massive, stone tables. The heavy pieces almost looked like altars.

"What is this place?" Jabez whispered.

Sean stopped for a moment, scanning the room meticulously. He turned to the left and stepped over to the nearest metal cabinet. It looked much like a filing cabinet with four drawers. He reached out and grabbed the frigid metal handle. The drawer opened easily, sliding out from the cabinet on chrome rails. On the rack were sheets of glass, each about an eighth of an inch thick, and each with an image etched into the top.

He warily pulled up one of the panes and examined it. The glass was perfectly clear, with a yellowish piece in the center. Sean recognized it immediately. Amber. But he couldn't make out what the two blots were inside of it.

"This is amber," he stated. "But I'm not sure what this stuff is."

The others huddled around, gazing at the artifact. Sean looked back up at the top. The image was an odd looking animal. He placed the glass back in its space, and pulled out another one. It was exactly like the last pane, except that at the top a different animal's image had been engraved into the surface. Again, there was amber in the middle with two distinct blobs locked within the hardened residue.

"Is that what I think it is?" Firth spoke up.

The other three turned to him with questioning faces. "It can't be. They didn't have the technology or the knowledge to do that back then. How would they have known?"

"Doc," Sean cut into the one-person conversation Firth was having with himself. "What are you saying?"

The professor moved closer to the opened drawer and withdrew a plate. He put it back and repeated with the next one in the line, and again.

He turned back to the other three. "This is it," he said, astonished. "I can't believe it."

"Professor," Sean pleaded. "What is it?"

Firth's eyes were staring off beyond his three companions for a moment before coming back to the present.

"Don't you see? This is a genetic storage facility." He took a few steps over to another drawer and pulled on the shiny metal handle. The cabinet's contents were similar to the first's. "They must have taken a sample from every animal on the planet and stored it here."

"Why would they do that?" Adriana wondered.

"They made a backup," Sean realized. "Just like backing up a hard drive. To ensure the survival of every species, they must have taken these specimens and stored them here."

"It is magnificent," Jabez said as he stared in wonder at the ancient facility. "But how is it powered? And how did they have the technology to do something like this?"

Sean smiled. "I don't know. I'll leave that up to the scientists."

Despite reveling in what would surely be the greatest archaeological discovery in history, Firth still found a way to appear disappointed.

Sean noticed his demeanor. "What's the matter, Doc? You should be thrilled right now. You've just helped make the discovery of a lifetime."

"I guess the tree of life isn't here," he said solemnly.

Sean put a hand on his shoulder. "It's probably just as well, Doc. I don't know anyone on this planet that should live forever." As soon as the words passed his lips, he remembered that Biosure was still in possession of the super virus.

"We need to get back to the surface," he said urgently.

55

ARMENIAN MOUNTAINS

"The situation has been neutralized," Emily said through the speaker on Sean's satellite phone. "I called in a favor with the director of the CIA, explained to him what Jenny had discovered, and he called in the cavalry. Every Biosure facility in the country is locked down, and research teams are going in to extract samples."

"Nice," Sean was impressed.

"Well, the guy owed me one for saving his boy when no one else would."

"Yeah. I'm starting to think I owe you a few myself."

There was a momentary pause before Emily spoke up again. "Well, you could erase that debt by coming back to work for Axis."

She was so predictable. He knew that request was coming.

"I don't know, Em. I kinda got the crap beat out of me earlier. I think I'm losing a step or two."

She laughed. "Nothing a little re-training couldn't fix."

He refocused the conversation. Both of them knew he wasn't going back to work for the government.

"Are Joe and Helen okay?"

Another laugh came through the line. "Oh, those two are fine. In fact, if you won't come back to work for me, I may just have to persuade the two of them to sign up." He didn't know what exactly she meant by that, but he had a feeling he would be hearing all about it when they arrived back in Atlanta.

"Thanks again, Em. You realize you saved the world today?"

She let out a deep sigh on the other end of the line. "It's why we're here, buddy. I'll catch you when you come back stateside."

"See you then."

He ended the call turned around, surprised to find Adriana standing right behind him. She gazed up into his gray eyes with her chocolate brown ones. The sky was perfectly clear, a warm sun beating down on them from high above. She drew closer, putting her hands on his arms.

"Are you sure there is nothing going on with you and your friend, Emily?" she asked playfully. A sly grin swept across her full lips.

"Positive," he replied, putting his hands on her shoulders.

Inside his head, he heard the voice again. He'd been ignoring it for too long. He remembered the pool in high school, and every other chance he'd never taken in life. As he leaned forward and pressed his lips into hers, he could still hear Tommy yelling at him.

"Jump."

56

ATLANTA

S ean had been packing up things in his office for the last hour. He tried not to be sentimental about it, but the years working for IAA had given him a lot of great memories. He picked up a picture of him and Tommy on a boat off the coast of Italy. They'd been there a few years prior, investigating a sunken ship speculated to date back to the time of the Trojan War. He smiled as he gazed at the image.

"You sure you want to leave, buddy," a familiar voice asked through the doorway.

Sean turned around and found Tommy standing there. His arm was in a sling, and he had several little bandages on his face.

"I'm sure, pal. I've seen too much action for five lifetimes."

Tommy stepped into the room and helped himself to a seat. "Well, now I know how Emily feels," he joked. Both of them shared a quick laugh at the comment. "But I understand."

Sean placed the picture frame in one of the boxes and leaned against his desk, crossing his arms as he did.

"So, you're off to Destin, huh?" Tommy asked.

"For now," Sean nodded. "I plan on spending a little time there first while my cabin is being built over in Blue Ridge. Don't get all sentimental on me. I'll be back plenty. And I expect you to come visit me at the beach. We can do a little ocean kayaking together."

Tommy smiled, letting out a deep sigh. "Sounds good, brother." He paused for a few seconds before speaking up again. "Sean, I just wanted to say thank you...for everything. You've been just like a brother to me...ever since mom and dad died. And if you ever need anything—"

"I told you not to get sentimental," Sean stopped him. "But thanks. I will call you if the need arises." He waited for a few seconds before speaking again. "I thought you were going to die."

Tommy nodded and stood up. "I know. I would have thought the same thing. But we're okay, buddy. And I can't thank you enough for watching out for me. If you hadn't been there, I might have died." The two stepped toward each other and embraced for a few seconds in firm hug. When they let go, both had watery eyes.

"You be good to that Spanish girl," Tommy ordered as he headed out of the room. "She's definitely a keeper."

Sean snorted a laugh. "Yeah, I know. And I will."

57

DESTIN, FLORIDA

The clear blue waves splashed gently up onto the perfect white sand. During the winter months, there weren't many tourists in the panhandle region of Florida, so the beaches were almost completely empty.

Sean stared into the blue sky at a few streaks of white clouds hovering overhead from behind his trademark pair of black Oakleys. The constant sea breeze blew his dirty blonde hair around like cattails in a summer storm.

He turned his head to the left, taking in the vision of the Spanish woman next to him. Her dark hair cascaded down to her shoulders where the black strings of her bikini top met her neckline. She was reading through the same book she had been reading a few weeks before in Armenia.

"Still investigating that Greek mechanism?" he asked with a smile.

They'd spent the last few days setting up Sean's new bungalow on the beach, moving furniture and other belongings. It was the first day they had taken some time to relax since arriving in the sunshine state.

She returned the smile and nodded. "Yes," she answered in her seductive accent. "There is just something I cannot figure out about this device."

"Oh?"

"It seems the Greeks had several of them. And while the accepted theory is that they were used for navigating the seas, something just doesn't add up."

He scooted his beach chair closer to hear what she had to say.

"While the devices seem to account for celestial bodies, this book says they served another purpose."

"And what would that be?"

He was close to her now. The wind picked up and blew a strand of her hair across his face. She unconsciously set the book down in her beach bag, pulling closer to him.

"It can wait."

THANK YOU

I just wanted to say thank you for reading this story. You probably hadn't heard of me before you read the first book and made it into this one, and I truly appreciate you taking a chance on an author you didn't know. Your time is the most valuable resource you have and I want to make sure I give you the best entertainment I can.

So, thank you again for reading this story. I hope you will continue the Sean Wyatt saga with book four, The Grecian Manifesto.

Happy reading,

Ernest

OTHER BOOKS BY ERNEST DEMPSEY

FACT VS FICTION

We come to the end of this three part story with questions about what is real and what is not. This is always one of my favorite parts of a book where we get to learn the truth. I won't take up too much of your time, but I think it's important to understand a few key items within the story.

First, the events of this story and the present-day characters involved are all fictional. That's easy enough.

However, nearly every single location in these three stories is real.

Even here, in book three, the location where the imprint of Noah's Ark was discovered is a very real canyon in the mountains of Armenia. It took days of searching via satellite images before I found the one anomaly that fit, and I have to tell you, it gave me chills.

It absolutely looks like the description of the ark, as well as the size.

The science behind that conclusion is one that I've never heard of before and was of my own invention and discovery. It hit me, one day, as I was on the beach in Florida and I let the water wash over my foot. After a minute, I withdrew my foot and saw the imprint. That's what gave me the idea. After speaking with some geologists and earth science professors, they agreed that the idea was indeed plausible.

Khor Virap is a very real place and the sanctuary there is one of the most unique and interesting locations in the world. It also has incredible sweeping views of the entire region from its perch atop the hill. Not to mention the fabled Mount Ararat is just across the plains, jutting up majestically into the sky.

The people from history are also real, including Father Carlos Crespi from book two and the Russian fighter pilot from book three. That entire sequence regarding the Russian airplane photos is also real, though I added my own imaginings to what happened to the pilot. I have a bad feeling it could have been spot on.

The Order of Rosecrucians is also real, though their current standing in society—if there is one—could be vastly different than I infer.

Lastly, and the most interesting piece to the story, is the discovery of the chamber where the Tree of Knowledge of Good and Evil is located along with the genetic storage facility.

In Genesis, it says that God said, "We must remove them from the garden so that they won't eat of the Tree of Life and live forever in sin."

I grew up reading that story, but it wasn't until adulthood that I reread it under a different light. Now, I see that as a suggestion that the Creator designed something that granted humanity eternal life, a very real fountain of youth, so to speak.

Once removed from that, death began to take hold. I was fascinated by this and had to wrap a story around it.

As to the genetic storage facility, that isn't my original idea. I've read it in multiple scientific and historical journals as a valid explanation to how Noah could have saved the species of every living animal on the planet without having to have two of every kind actually on the boat with him.

If you think about it, even as large as the ark was, it would have been impossible to keep two of every kind of creature on that ship. There are simply too many animals all over the world. However, with 120 years to build the boat and with advanced genetic understanding in the antediluvian world, constructing a genetic storage facility from which they could re-create the animals of the world seems like a viable solution. After all, he was being guided by the most powerful mind in the universe.

Who knows? Maybe that's what really happened. I know that I look forward to finding out someday.

ABOUT THE AUTHOR

ERNEST DEMPSEY is the author of high octane action/adventure thrillers and edgy science fiction adventure stories that have entertained tens of thousands of readers all over the world. His novels reveal to the world historical secrets, scientific mysteries, and new theories, all at a pace that keeps readers turning pages faster than they ever thought possible.

ACKNOWLEDGMENTS

A big thank you to Lɪ Graphics in Athens, Greece for the great cover designs they do for my books. Also, to my editors Jason Whited and Anne Storer, thank you so much for your hard work in making these stories shine. I appreciate you both.

First Edition

ISBN: 978-1-944647-00-1

71482784R00215